FINDING JEENA

FINDING JEENA

A Novel

Miralee Ferrell

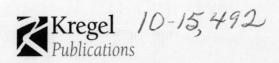

Kregel
Publications

Finding Jeena: A Novel

© 2010 by Miralee Ferrell

Published by Kregel Publications, a division of Kregel, Inc., P.O. Box 2607, Grand Rapids, MI 49501.

Scripture taken from the HOLY BIBLE, NEW INTERNATIONAL VERSION®. NIV®. Copyright © 1973, 1978, 1984 by International Bible Society. Used by permission of Zondervan. All rights reserved.

The persons and events portrayed in this work are the creations of the author, and any resemblance to persons living or dead is purely coincidental.

Cover photo by Miralee Ferrell.

Library of Congress Cataloging-in-Publication Data
Ferrell, Miralee
    Finding Jeena: a novel / Miralee Ferrell.
    p. cm.
    I. Title.
PS3606.E753F56   2010   813'.6—dc22   2009035532

ISBN 978-0-8254-2645-2

Printed in the United States of America

10 11 12 13 14 / 5 4 3 2 1

To Grammie,

who believed in me always

and loved me every day that I lived.

I miss you.

ACKNOWLEDGMENTS

So many people blessed and supported me while I wrote this book. First, my husband, Allen, who patiently listened to my brainstorming, my rejoicing, my complaining when nothing seemed to be coming together, and my thoughts about my writing in general. You're a saint! The rest of my extended family cheered me on through each book and enthusiastically waited for news on the next one, as have so many of my friends and church family. Thanks, gang!

Special thanks go to Maureen Harris, who lived and then eventually worked at a women's shelter and advised me on various aspects of shelter life; Sue (Kendrick) Bridie, a registered nurse and personal friend, for her help with the medical scenes; and Eric Nisley, Wasco County District Attorney for his help with the legal aspects of the court case.

I especially want to thank Ellena Wimp, a good friend and my model for the book's front cover. She also happens to be the mother of Kayla, the girl I used as the model for the front cover of *The Other Daughter*. I am blessed that Kregel chose to use my photos for both of my covers, and that I had such awesome models who perfectly depicted the characters.

I so appreciated the comments given by my editor, Becky Fish. Thanks also to Steve Barclift for championing the book at committee. Becky, Steve, and the rest of the Kregel staff are such a blessing to work with. Thank you all for making this book as strong and rich as it is . . . each of you brings a unique gifting to the publishing process.

Tamela, my agent, deserves a special word for her work on my behalf. I so appreciate you and all that you do—both professionally, and for your prayer support and friendship. Bless you, my friend!

My dear "Grammie" went to heaven before this book went to press. The character Grammie was patterned just a little after her. I'll be forever thankful that she got to read the rough manuscript— she was a staunch supporter of my work and everything I ever attempted. She almost achieved her hundredth birthday, and she blessed me every day of my life.

And of course, all praise, honor, and glory goes to Jesus for any good report that comes as a result of this story being written. I write for Him, and pray that somewhere along the way at least one life will be touched as a result.

CHAPTER 1

J eena Gregory chewed on her lip as she stared at the red silk dress hanging in the closet. Would it be enough? She wiped her sweaty palms down the legs of her jeans, trying to vanquish the knot in her stomach. The same feeling she'd experienced as a ten-year-old hit her. She'd walked into her new school and tried to ignore the snickers as some of the students eyed her worn-out sneakers and hand-me-down clothes.

She refused to let fear or insecurity take control. Fear couldn't hurt her—only men could do that. And Sean loved her.

No way would she believe the rumor she had heard from Connie, the biggest gossip in her small group of friends. Sean couldn't be seeing someone else. He was close to proposing; she'd sensed it more than once. Jeena shook her head, trying to dislodge the disquieting thoughts. He'd have a good explanation.

Her confidence level soared after applying makeup and slipping into the dress. It had cost her two days' salary, but it was worth every cent. Hugging her in all the right places, the dark red silk accented her long, black hair and green eyes. Working out at the club kept her figure where she wanted it.

Sean's car flashed past Jeena's window and halted in front of her small condo. Jeena ran a hand over her trim hips. She'd be thirty later this year, and her body still looked like that of a twenty-year-old—she'd maintain it if she had to work out every day.

The doorbell chimed, but this time Jeena didn't rush to answer. Sean Matthews needn't think her life revolved around his arrival, even if it did. Playing a little hard to get might work in her favor.

The bell chimed a second time, and Jeena imagined its tone changed to one of impatience. Better not overdo it. She opened the door and stepped back into the glow of the entry light to give him the full effect.

A small frown turned down the corners of Sean's mouth, giving a serious aspect to his rugged face. His tapping toe stilled, but his lowered brows didn't lift until he stepped across the threshold.

The smile Jeena expected didn't appear. Apprehension flickered through her mind. "Something wrong, Sean?" She touched his arm.

He ran his fingers through his dark blond hair, giving a slightly rumpled look to a man who prided himself on his appearance. "Our reservation is in fifteen minutes. We're going to be late."

He hadn't seemed to notice the gown or the accentuated curves. "I had a bit of a struggle zipping up this dress."

"You might need a jacket. That looks a little skimpy for a chilly evening."

The small wisp of fear grew, fanned by the coolness of his impatience.

"Skimpy? That's it?" She stepped back, folding her arms.

He shot a quick, cool look at the dress. "You look great. Is it new?"

She pursed her lips. Something was up. "Yes, it's new." She swung toward the closet. "Fine. I'll get a jacket." She yanked open the door and pulled a black cape off the rack. *Great start to our evening.*

He helped her into his silver Lexus, then slipped into his seat and turned the key. "You really do look stunning." Sean paused. "It's been a crazy day, and I've had a lot on my mind." He gave her a soft smile before turning his attention back to the road.

They pulled out into the street and headed through the residential area toward the edge of town. Silhouetted against the skyline, tall fir trees flanked the elegant homes along the way. Kids still played in front yards, and a couple of eager homeowners mowed their yards. Jeena sighed. She missed having a yard and flowerbeds. The new townhouse she'd put a deposit on boasted a small backyard and window boxes in the front, so she could indulge her gardening hobby on her days off.

She sank deeper in the seat and released a small breath. Peaceful silence enveloped her as the quiet car snaked around the curves and the sun glinted off the nearby Columbia River. Sean loved her. Losing sight of that was foolish. Sure, he'd neglected to kiss her when he'd arrived, but she understood the stress generated by work. His job as a financial consultant to a large corporation in Portland often kept him distracted.

Connie was being catty and nothing more.

Jeena gave a low laugh. "You had me worried. I thought aliens had taken over your body when you didn't react to this dress."

He pulled away from a stop sign and glanced in his mirror, then reached over and took her hand. "Never fear. If aliens attempt a takeover, I'll shoot 'em dead." His quick smile flashed. "Hungry?"

"Very." She'd been foolish to listen to Connie. An hour earlier, she couldn't have eaten a thing, but now she was ravenous.

⚜

Sean had chosen a small, rather exclusive restaurant, a rarity in River City, Oregon. They could have driven an hour up I-84 to Portland, but the recent growth of tourism in the Columbia River Gorge had birthed new hot spots, popular with locals and tourists alike.

They were seated by a window that afforded a breathtaking view of the river, and Jeena could see the colorful sails of windsurfers kiting along in the evening breeze, the soft glow of the late April sunset bronzing the multicolored sails. Candles glowed against the damask tablecloth, giving off a subtle air of luxury. Strains of low music added to the ambiance, creating a soothing background for the trickle of diners still drifting in.

Sean had requested a quiet spot in the corner, giving a sense of privacy that still allowed a good view. While he ordered, Jeena glanced around the room, wondering if any of their friends might be here tonight. No familiar faces appeared within her line of sight. Good. She wanted this evening to be theirs alone.

Maybe they could sort out the nasty rumor starting to circulate and kill it before it morphed into something worse.

Sean leaned back in his seat and sighed, stretching his legs out from under the heavy brocade cloth.

"Long day?" Jeena reached across to stroke the side of his face. He didn't pull away, but he didn't wrap his long fingers around hers as she'd expected. A tiny alarm went off in the back of her mind.

He gave a small shake of his head, dislodging her hand. "Not really. It feels good to sit across the table from a beautiful woman, instead of looking at bored businessmen all day."

She sat back in her chair and relaxed. "Something going on at work that's bothering you?"

"Very little. How about you? When does your lease start on the new townhouse?"

"In ten days, so I'm boxing everything up now. I've got my final interview a week from Monday with Browning and Thayer."

"It's too bad it's only a temporary job, but with your expertise in design, they can't go wrong contracting you." He straightened in his chair and leaned toward her, an affectionate smile flickering across his lips.

She flashed him a grateful look. "Thanks. I hope they feel the same. But being a private contractor has its advantages, and the project is big—it should last at least a year."

The waiter arrived, placing steaming plates of fragrant pasta in front of them and gathering the empty salad dishes. A few minutes passed in comfortable silence, and Jeena's misgivings evaporated in the relaxed intimacy.

Candlelight cast a warm light across Sean's face, accentuating his masculine good looks. Jeena smiled and settled deeper into her chair. "So tell me about your family. Last time we talked, you were concerned about your mom living alone, now that your dad's gone. How's she doing?"

"Great, from what I gather when I have time to call." He wound the last strand of pasta onto his fork and took a bite, then wiped his mouth with a napkin. "I'm sorry—I see a client I need to speak to.

I'll only be a minute. Do you mind?" He nodded across the room to a silver-haired man sitting with an elegantly dressed woman.

"Not at all." She smiled, then watched him make his way through the tables.

She'd first spotted him at a party a little over a year ago. Tall, mid-thirties, dressed in an Italian three-piece suit, and built like a model, he stood out in the crowd of older businessmen. An air of sophistication clung to him, enhanced by vivid blue eyes set in a deeply tanned face. A striking blonde who'd had too much to drink was hanging on his arm. He looked slightly disgusted and appeared to be searching for an escape.

Setting aside her drink, Jeena strolled across the room, knowing she'd captured his attention even before she approached.

She extended her hand and smiled when he held it longer than necessary. "I don't think we've been introduced. I'm Jeena Gregory, a friend of our hostess."

"Sean Matthews. This is . . . I'm sorry, what's your name again?" His bored gaze turned to the blonde.

The woman released her grip on his arm and glared at Jeena. "Angie."

Sean cocked his head toward the woman. "Right. Sorry. This is Angie."

Angie's lips turned down in a pout. "I'm getting something to drink. I'll find someone more interesting to take me home." Angie flounced across the room without looking back.

Sean's blue eyes shone with something more than amusement. "I didn't bring her, but she's had too much to drink and must have forgotten. She latched onto me when I arrived. Thanks for the rescue."

Jeena spent the rest of the evening in his company—and many evenings after that. Within a few weeks, she knew she wanted to spend the rest of her life with this man. Intelligent, witty, generous, and advancing up the corporate ladder at a fast pace, he possessed much that she found attractive.

Sean, however, remained an enigma. While engaging and attentive, he had yet to commit to a permanent relationship. Jeena sensed his frustration at her adamant refusal to move in together. She enjoyed the party life and didn't judge others for their lifestyle choices, but she drew the line at moving in with a man before marriage. She deserved more. Besides, too many of her crowd had gone that direction, and she'd seen disaster strike more than once.

"Jeena? I'm sorry I took so long. I hope you weren't bored." Sean's deep voice woke her from the memories.

She brushed the hair from her eyes. "Not at all. Just remembering our first meeting."

"Ah, yes. The party."

Jeena tried to suppress a smile but failed. "And poor Angie."

Sean laughed outright. "Poor Angie, nothing. That woman clung like a leech with no encouragement from me. You came along just in time."

She leaned toward him and stroked the back of his hand. "Did I?"

He slowly pulled back, and the smile disappeared.

"What's wrong?" Her heart rate accelerated.

He cleared his throat and picked up a napkin. "There's something I want to tell you."

Tell. Not ask. Jeena leaned back and crossed her arms. "Yes?"

"I've been offered a new job. It means a huge increase in pay and could lead to a partnership."

"That sounds wonderful. I didn't realize you were looking."

"I didn't mention it until I knew something would come of it. I didn't want to worry you."

"Why would I care?" Her palms grew clammy, but she refused to panic.

His lips set in a firm line; then he took a deep breath and plunged forward. "It's taking me out of the States. A large construction conglomerate wants me in the Middle East."

A small shiver of fear traveled up her back. "But that's dangerous. Tell me you're not going to take it."

"I've said yes. I'll be living in Kuwait and going across the border occasionally, and then only to areas that are deemed safe. I leave in two weeks."

"Two weeks," she whispered. "What about us?"

He shifted slightly and looked at his hands, then raised his eyes. "I'm sorry, Jeena."

"What do you mean, you're sorry? You're not asking me to come with you or wait? How long will you be gone?" She tried to keep the pain out of her voice, but her words rose in tone and volume.

An irritated look flashed across his face. The small, secluded spot he'd chosen closed in around her. No longer did the flickering candles on the table give off an aura of romance—instead, they gleamed with an ominous light.

"I'll be gone at least a year, maybe two. You didn't want to live with me here in the States, so I didn't think you'd be willing to move to Kuwait." Sean leaned back in his chair, holding her gaze.

She'd probably keep him if she gave in, but something inside protested. Her parents' marriage had been lousy, no doubt about that. But her mother had saved herself for the man she married and had often urged Jeena to do the same. Besides, Grammie would be horrified if Jeena made that decision. A deep love for both her mother and grandmother had prompted Jeena to walk the same path.

"But if we were married . . ." She could have bitten off her tongue for letting the words slip.

Sean's lips twisted in a wry smile. "I have no desire to get married."

"So all of this has been what . . . a game? You aren't in love with me? Never have been?"

He shrugged. "I think a lot of you. But marriage isn't part of my plan. I thought we'd have a good time. Frankly, I hung around hoping you'd change your mind."

"You knew how I felt about living together. It's not something I'm comfortable with."

Sean smirked. "You told me your dad was a religious Jekyll and Hyde and you had no use for God. I never expected you'd stick with your decision and be such a prude."

His words brought the chaos in her mind to a halt. An icy calm washed over her. "Prude. I see. So, who is she?"

His face flamed red, then faded to a dirty white. "Who?"

She rose quickly, her chair sliding into the waiter who was walking behind her. Pride stiffened her spine and held her head high. "I nailed that one. Never mind. I'm sure you'll be very happy together, and my prudish life will be better off without *you*."

She slipped around the table and started to walk past him, but he reached out and grasped her wrist. "Jeena. Don't be that way. I'll drive you home. I'm sorry."

Shaking off his hand, she stepped out of his reach and lowered her voice, conscious of the curious looks from the tables nearby. "I'll get a taxi. Have a great life, Sean."

Somehow she managed to exit the restaurant without calling more attention to herself. Humiliation at making a scene while leaving the table forced her to increase her pace and not look back. The poor waiter—she'd nearly bowled him over while rushing from the table. But no way could she allow Sean to see her cry. She needed to get home and face this. The tears would come later, and no telling when they'd stop.

Men. Anger bubbled inside, momentarily pushing aside the sting of tears. Her father had proven men couldn't be trusted— he hadn't loved her, either. Why had she forgotten? Never again would a man suck her in with promises and lies. From now on, her career would come first. She'd show them all. The only person in the world who mattered was her grandmother. She'd neglected her recently, but tomorrow was a new day. Grammie would be happy to see her, and Sean was no longer important.

CHAPTER 2

Jeena spent the evening in a wash of tears, unable to shut off the flow once it started. Nightmares plagued the early hours after sleep claimed her, causing her to awaken with a pounding heart. She felt like she'd been run over by a train, and she hadn't even been drinking. *Good thing it's Saturday and I don't have to work.*

How would she go on without Sean? She'd been so sure he would propose, so sure this man was the right one. How had she missed the truth all these months—that he was willing to live with her but not willing to marry her? Because she loved him, and love truly *was* blind. At least, it had blinded her to Sean's personal agenda.

"I hate him." The words spoken aloud made her wince, but it might be the only way she would get through this. Love must turn to hate if her sanity was to survive.

She needed an aspirin. Fumbling out from under the blankets and slipping into her robe, she belted it and stumbled to the bathroom.

She stared at her reflection in the mirror. Red-rimmed, puffy eyes stared out of a pale face surrounded by disheveled, dark hair. Coffee might help. She popped two aspirin, washed them down with water, and headed for her kitchen.

One day at a time. Right now, toast and coffee would create a small, bright spot in her morning. She pushed a button on the stereo, and the room filled with soothing music. Her mouth watered at the fragrance of the coffee beans as they ran through the grinder.

How could Sean dump her? Maybe she needed to rethink her decision. Jeena reached for the coffeepot. No way. She loved him, yes. But sacrificing her principles wasn't an option, even if she had a guarantee it would work. Besides, he was seeing someone else. The pain of his betrayal shot through her heart like a dagger in the grip of an assassin.

She released a loud breath and shook herself—she'd been standing in the middle of the kitchen clutching the coffeepot. Time to knock it off. Depression couldn't be allowed to sink its claws into her life.

Maybe having someone to talk to would help. She reached for her cell phone and sank onto her couch, its softness and depth welcoming her aching body. Tammy didn't homeschool on Saturday, so this might be a good time to call.

The phone on the other end rang six times, and Jeena almost hung up. But a soft, breathless voice answered, "Hello?"

"Hey, Tammy, it's Jeena." She paused a moment. Maybe this wasn't such a great idea. Tammy had her own problems to deal with. "So . . . how's your day going?"

Tammy laughed, the sound chiming over the phone like a musical note. "It's fine. What's up? You don't sound like your normal, cheerful self."

Jeena leaned against the back of the couch and played with a strand of her hair. "Uh . . . yeah." She took a deep breath. "Sean just dumped me." She slipped her fingers over her mouth, horrified at the words she'd blurted out.

"Oh, hon, I'm sorry. What happened?"

"He's moving to Kuwait on a job, and from all appearances, he has a new girlfriend." She spent the next few minutes catching Tammy up on the facts of her evening, while her friend listened with an occasional sympathetic, well-placed word.

"The jerk! All I can say is he didn't deserve you in the first place." Tammy's words sliced through the air and sent a small shaft of comfort into Jeena's heart. "But how are you doing? I mean, really doing? Want me to come over?"

Jeena gave a shake of her head, then realized Tammy couldn't see her. She plucked a tissue out of a nearby box. "To be honest, not so great. I feel like I stepped on a land mine and the blast took out my heart. The rest of my body is still walking around, but my heart is lying on the ground in little pieces."

"Ouch—I'm sorry, sweetie. You need a hug."

"I just needed someone to listen. But if Matt doesn't mind watching the kids, maybe we can take in a movie later? I hate spending Saturday night alone. At least this first one."

"You bet. And when I get there, I'm giving you a gigantic hug."

"Thanks . . . and thank you for listening."

Jeena flipped shut her phone. She was grateful she had Tammy in her life. Maybe she'd call Susanne as well. She glanced at her watch, a precious gift from her grandmother on her twenty-first birthday. No. Susanne's birthday celebration with her husband was tonight, and she'd mentioned that she had a list of things to get done before they went out. Besides, there was no need to put a damper on her friend's special day.

Jeena snuggled farther down into the leather softness of the couch and glanced at the calendar hanging on the wall near her desk. Work. That would be her salvation and help fill her time. The new contract with Browning and Thayer suddenly surged in importance. With Sean gone, there remained little else to care about but work, her two best friends, and Grammie. She'd throw her energy into the new job and prove she was more than a trophy to be displayed at the whim of a man.

✺

Sunday morning, Jeena spun toward her kitchen sink and banged her shin on the corner of an open drawer. Blast it! She loved cooking, but this miniscule kitchen set her teeth on edge whenever she tried to use it. Her move into the new townhouse couldn't come fast enough.

She set the coffee going and placed the bread in the toaster, then froze at the sound of the phone. Sean? Had he changed his mind? She needed to stay calm . . . no way could she act anxious. She'd already showed her feelings too much last night.

But he typically called her cell. Not many people called the landline she'd gotten as a backup for her grandmother's calls, in case the cell tower ever went down. On the fifth ring, she dashed to the handset and picked up. "Hello."

"Jeena, honey. I almost hung up." Her seventy-eight-year-old grandmother's quavering voice shot disappointment through her. Why hadn't she checked the caller ID? She'd set herself up and worried Grammie.

"Hi, Grammie. I'm sorry. I was making breakfast." Jeena slumped down in the straight-backed, wrought-iron chair and pushed her toast aside.

"That's all right, dear. I wanted to see if you were coming to visit today."

Jeena stifled a sigh. Two weeks since she'd visited. She needed to make more time for Grammie.

"Sure, I'll be over after a bit. Is there anything you'd like?" She always asked, although she'd bet money she knew the answer.

"Surprise me." A sweet chuckle gurgled over the line, and Jeena's lips tipped up in a smile.

"Give me a couple of hours; then I'll stay and have lunch with you."

"That sounds lovely, dear. I'll see you soon. 'Bye."

The line went dead, and Jeena put down the phone. After her mother's death, Jeena had been invited by Grammie to live with her. She'd graduated from high school by then, but having a home away from college meant the world to her. The peace she'd felt those weekends at Grammie's stood in stark contrast to the turbulent years growing up under her father's roof. Grammie was the dearest person in the world, and she depended on Jeena's income to keep her in a decent facility.

Keeping Grammie in comfort was one of the most important things in Jeena's life. Landing this new job was critical. She grinned. Besides, having a nicer car and a larger home wouldn't hurt her feelings, either.

⚘

Jeena walked across the living room in her grandmother's small apartment and leaned over to kiss her weathered cheek. "Hi, Grammie. They treating you okay?" She settled into one of the two comfortable easy chairs and drew it close.

The wrinkled hand reached over and squeezed Jeena's. Faded green eyes twinkled. "Well, nobody's proposed this week, if that's what you're asking."

A smile played at the edge of Jeena's lips, but she flinched inside, the thought of a proposal hitting a little too close to her sore heart. "How many have you had since you moved in here?"

Grammie leaned back in her chair, the sparkle in her eyes replaced by a thoughtful look. "Let's see . . . I think I hit three after your last visit. Men just can't tolerate being alone, can they, dear?"

A small jolt ran through Jeena, and her smile faded. Sean had certainly proven that true. He'd found a replacement before she was history. "It must keep life interesting, all those good-looking charmers squabbling over you. Do they ever get jealous?"

A sly smile tipped the corners of the woman's mouth. "Oh my, they can't get jealous over what they don't know. That would spoil the fun!"

This time, Jeena let the laugh she'd been holding spill into the room, creating a sense of joy for the first time all weekend. "Shame on you! Those poor men. I feel sorry for them. Aren't you a little old to be stringing them along?"

A shameless snort flew from the older woman's lips. "I may be nearing eighty, but I'm not dead yet! Besides, two of those old codgers have been flirting behind my back and think I don't notice. Now . . . what did you bring me today?" She crossed her arms over her tiny form and raised a penciled eyebrow.

Jeena reached for the bag by her side. Why had she waited so long to come? She'd do better. No more allowing other obligations to stand in the way. Maybe when she moved into her townhouse, Grammie could stay with her. If she'd agree to leave her suitors, that is.

"Almond Roca, and chocolate with gooey caramel inside." Jeena pulled out the box and presented it with a grin.

"Ohh . . ." A smile tugged at Grammie's lips. "You have a piece first, dear. You always bring the best gifts, and you certainly know where my weakness lies."

She eased out of her chair and walked to a handsome wood bureau on the far side of the room. She slid open a drawer and pulled out a package, then tucked it behind her back and returned to stand beside her chair. "I've got something for you. It's more your style then mine, and I hope you'll like it."

Jeena sat up straight. "I'd love anything you give me, Grammie, but it's not necessary."

"I know, but I want to." Grammie slipped a small, ornate silver box from behind her back and held it out. "Your grandfather gave this to me years ago. I only wore it on special occasions, as the stone looked too large on my hand. But it'll be stunning on you." She settled back into her chair with an expectant air.

Jeena gazed at the box for a moment, then carefully opened the hinged lid and gasped. "It's beautiful!" The purple stone in the center of a gold ring sparkled and glinted in the sunlight coming through the nearby window. "Why, the amethyst alone must be over three carats, and the diamonds on each side are close to a carat apiece. This is an expensive ring—are you sure you want me to have it?" She glanced up at Grammie and caught her wiping moisture from the corner of her eye.

"I'm sure. Your grandfather was precious to me, and so are you. I'd rather you enjoyed it while I'm alive than wait till I'm dead." She gave a wry chuckle. "Although that may be sooner rather than later. One never knows at my age."

Jeena pushed to her feet, alarm bells sounding in her chest. "Are you okay? Is there something going on I don't know about?"

"Oh my, no. I didn't mean to scare you. Sit down, sit down." She nodded at the chair. "I've been having a little more trouble with my breathing, but nothing out of the ordinary." She reached over and patted Jeena's hand. "Now, how about we play a game of Scrabble? Your mind is sharp, unlike some of those doddery old wolves who don't know how to spell to save their lives."

Jeena sank back in her chair, only partly reassured by her grandmother's protest. "Promise to call the nurse if you start feeling worse."

Grammie waved a dismissive hand. "Nothing to worry about, I tell you."

A quiet knock on the door quelled Jeena's response.

A diminutive woman stood at the slightly open door. "Oh dear, I've come at a bad time."

Grammie stayed seated, but a sweet smile lit her face. "Not at all, Irene. You know my granddaughter, Jeena. We were going to play Scrabble, and a third person will make it more interesting. Come in, come in!"

Irene stood on the threshold, her gaze wavering between the two women, her eyebrows raised. "Are you sure?"

Jeena rose and took three strides over to the white-haired woman, giving her a brief hug. "Of course we're sure. Grammie's right. We'd love to have you."

"All right, then." Irene walked with steady steps to the chair Grammie indicated, then paused. "Are those chocolate-covered caramels?"

Jeena reached for the box and slid them over to the table next to Irene's chair. "Yes, they are, and yes, you may." She chuckled. "One of Grammie's favorites."

Jeena couldn't imagine Grammie being willing to live any-where but here, surrounded by the men who doted on her and by the old friends who shared her interests. Having her stay at Jeena's home had been a good thought, but it wasn't practical at present—although, who knew what the future might hold?

CHAPTER 3

J eena set her phone down and raised her arms in the air, twirling around the room. "Yes!" Life was good. Her new job started on Monday.

She'd long coveted this position with Browning and Thayer, a high-powered construction firm that was building a multimillion-dollar townhouse complex in Portland.

The final interview had come the week after her breakup with Sean, which had helped ease her pain. During the day, she worked hard to stifle the memories, but thoughts of Sean continued to haunt her nights.

She'd arrived at the final interview wearing her new, dove gray designer suit, her confidence level high. A stab of disappointment momentarily marred her joy when she discovered neither of the two owners had chosen to conduct the interview. But the man the firm sent seemed impressed by her credentials and, before the interview concluded, had offered her a contract for the duration of the job.

He pulled a small stack of papers from his briefcase. "Now you understand because you're an independent contractor we won't be paying into unemployment or offering other benefits. But we're prepared to give you a handsome salary, and we're giving you an advance, since we don't have a firm start-up date. We don't want to chance losing you to another firm."

"Thank you." She'd waited too long for this opportunity to look anywhere else, but she certainly had no intention of letting her new bosses know that.

She didn't doubt her skills or her ability to do the job. But the size of the advance she received made her wonder just what their expectations were. It wasn't often a company paid more than a minimal retainer, and she hoped she'd made the right decision when she accepted their offer.

Time to quit dreaming about her career and get back to work. Jeena stood in the middle of her townhouse and gazed at the furniture delivered just an hour ago. This set of couches had been calling her name for a long time, begging to find a place in her home. Wrought-iron-and-glass tables were the perfect accent to the couch's rich black leather.

"Lady, you happy with where things are now? We'd like to get paid and move to our next job." The disgruntled voice of the deliveryman spun Jeena around.

"I'll take a look at the bedroom first."

If his frown was an indication, he wasn't too happy. But if she wanted them to move the furniture a dozen times, they shouldn't complain. She was certainly paying them enough.

The padded leather headboard looked perfect centered between the two windows looking out over the Columbia River, offering a magnificent view of the river traffic during the day and the lights of the town at night. Nightstands and a matching, mirrored dresser completed the look, needing only pictures, bedspread, and pillows to brighten the room. "It's fine, thanks." She reached for her purse and pulled out her checkbook, dashing off the amount on the invoice.

Maybe this job would help keep the boredom and loneliness at bay. Time had dragged the last few days, and knowing Sean had flown out to his overseas job last week hadn't improved her mood. Visions of a faceless but beautiful woman hanging on his arm and boarding the jet plagued her.

Jeena's thoughts turned back to her grandmother—she'd spent more time than normal visiting there lately, but sitting at the assisted-living center was hard. Grammie doted on her, yet the constant reminder of old age and impending death pulled Jeena's spirits down.

She'd love to move Grammie to this larger townhouse. The older woman's increasing fragility, however, wouldn't allow it. Grammie's health needed to come first.

She sank down onto the bed and stretched out, letting her muscles relax. Having Grammie here would eliminate the discomfort Jeena occasionally experienced when she visited the complex. Most of the area was given to small apartments and suites to encourage independence, with one wing reserved for the frail residents in need of more intense medical care. She walked briskly past that area on her way to see Grammie, but an elderly man had wandered from his room and followed her down the hall. "Sheryl? Wait for me, Sheryl. I want to go home. Why won't you take me home?"

She'd turned, hoping a member of the staff might be near, and watched with a sinking heart as he drew closer.

He reached out shaking fingers and plucked at her sleeve. "Take me home, Sheryl. I don't like it here."

She patted his shoulder. "I think you should go back to your room. Wait here, and I'll find someone to take you."

"But I don't want to go back. Why won't you take me home?" He reached for her arm again. "Please?" His smile revealed dentures losing their grip.

Jeena beckoned to a blue-clad figure hurrying down the hall toward them. "Excuse me? I think this man needs help."

The woman slowed her pace and stopped in front of the elderly man. "Mr. Thompson, what are you doing in the hallway? Come on, I'll show you where your room is." She patted his arm. "Thank you," the nurse mouthed over her shoulder before turning away.

Jeena had felt sorry for the man, but being around people like that raised a terrible dread. What if Grammie's mind started to go, or her health failed and she died? Losing her mother had wounded Jeena, but not having Grammie in her life would devastate her. The older woman was all she had left.

Jeena's love for her grandmother overrode her feelings of unease, and she intended to find ways to include Grammie in her life as often as possible. Spending money was a high for Jeena but nothing compared to the feeling of joy at the light in Grammie's eyes when Jeena entered her room.

Using her creative skills to transform someone's home from a dive into a castle had its merits, as well. Of course, not many of Jeena's clients started out with a dive. Most of them were wealthy, but not all had the taste to match.

This commercial building job would be the biggest of her career. The advance they'd paid comprised only a fraction of what her income would be over the next few months. It might be wise to wait on her spending spree, but her credit cards wouldn't be maxed out for long.

Jeena walked across the bedroom and flung open the doors to the walk-in closet. *This is almost as big as my bedroom in my old condo.* Why not donate a box or two? The local women's shelter could surely use some good quality clothing. She needed to dress the part of the successful career woman, and many of her outfits were outdated.

Her wardrobe differed from the run-down clothing her mother had always worn. Mom would've been proud of her, had she lived. She'd worked hard, taken good care of her daughter, and done the best she could. Jeena didn't hold any ill will against her mother. At least one parent had loved her.

Jeena shook her head, dislodging the troubled thoughts. Her father was dead and couldn't judge or hurt her anymore. She'd moved on, put the old life behind her. None of this doom-and-gloom nonsense.

Her energy level running high, she pulled out dresses, blouses, and pantsuits, piling them onto her bed. She'd seen a story about the shelter on TV. The founder, a local woman who had faced hard times earlier in her life, had always remembered the stress of living on the streets in a town that didn't have any services for the homeless. Certainly Jeena's castoffs could help some poor woman make a better impression at a job interview.

Yes. First thing tomorrow, she'd take these to the shelter. A fairy godmother bestowing a wonderful gift on a peasant girl had nothing on how she felt now.

CHAPTER 4

Jeena's purr of generosity almost matched that of her high-powered BMW as she headed to the women's shelter the next morning to drop off the boxes of clothes.

The glow faded as she parked across the street from the shelter. This was the first time she'd been to this run-down part of town. Littered streets, graffiti-covered walls, buildings that screamed their need for new paint, and an assortment of shabbily dressed people hung around dirty doorways. Few thriving businesses remained in this area, having apparently fled years ago to the safer side of town.

Jeena opened her window halfway and spent several minutes staring at the scene, trying to get up the nerve to step a foot on the curb. She wasn't sure this was a safe place for a lone woman to walk, even in the daylight. Her hands began to tremble. She'd heard about gangs roaming the streets in the bigger cities, looking for trouble, and although River City wasn't that large, this looked like a rough neighborhood.

A man who appeared to be in his thirties leaned against a wall almost halfway down the block, a smoldering cigarette dangling from his lips. Standing close beside him, a young man dressed all in black peered to the side and behind him, then dug into his jeans pocket and pulled something out, pressing it into the other man's hand. He shoved himself away from the wall, pocketed the item, and passed a small packet to the young man, then turned and sauntered away. A drug deal?

What was she doing here? Jeena sank deeper into the leather of her new Beemer and studied the building across the street with the Haven of Hope sign blazoned across the front.

The shelter was located in a three-story brick, probably about fifty years old. The small space around the building was spotless. On either side of the door, geraniums poked their colorful heads out of wooden boxes sitting against a wall surprisingly free of graffiti. Windows lined the front of the building, glinting in the morning sun like dancing prisms casting beams of light over the scene.

She felt a bit perplexed. She'd expected dirty windows and a littered street, not the neat and tidy setting before her; this building emerged as though a proud parent had dressed it for a special occasion.

The sound of something metal hitting the sidewalk rang out, making Jeena jump. She turned to see a man dragging a large garbage can. He stopped, grabbed the handles, then placed it close to her car. The strong odor of rotting garbage wafted on the warm breeze. She closed her window, anxious to shut it out.

A shiver of fear ran across Jeena's skin as she looked from one poorly dressed piece of humanity to another. Close to the shelter's front door, a group of women stood out on the curb under the city bus sign. Were they all trying to escape from the place or just bored and hoping to pass the time?

Jeena sucked in a small breath. A child. What was a child doing out on the street near the shelter? She couldn't be more than four or five. She peeked out from behind a woman's long skirt and stared right at Jeena. The little girl's large eyes were set in a beautiful oval face. A tattered blue ribbon captured her flaxen hair in a ponytail.

The woman she hid behind seemed different from the rest—her face shone as though recently scrubbed, and her flowered skirt and white blouse appeared neat and clean. A shout sounded from down the street, and the child ducked back behind the skirt, her small arms wrapped around the woman's legs.

On closer inspection, the rest of the women didn't look dirty. Only a couple of people looked unkempt, and Jeena couldn't be sure they were part of the small cluster standing on the curb. Time to end this. Maybe she could dump the stuff outside the door and beat it back to her car without having to speak.

She slid out of the car, and moving around to the back, she removed two of the smallest boxes from the trunk, then slammed it shut. Balancing one box on top of the other, she headed toward the building, keeping her gaze trained straight ahead. Hopefully, they'd send someone for the rest, as she didn't relish walking through the knot of women a second time.

A thickset woman lurched away from her leaning post against the side of the front door as Jeena drew near. "Hey, what-cha doing?" Her voice was tinged with a hint of menace. "Bringing some castoffs for us homeless losers?" She turned her leering grin on Jeena and stepped into her path.

"What?" Jeena jerked her attention away from the door of the shelter and to the face of the woman blocking her way. Her appearance would have been comical, except for the fierce expression that made Jeena take a step back. A tight, polka-dot blouse squeezed out more curves than it hid. Large, worn sneakers housed her feet. Pink plaid pants and a long, red scarf thrown over her shoulder finished the crazy ensemble. The woman grasped the ends of the wispy scarf and wiped the beads of sweat glistening on her forehead. Jeena couldn't tell her age—maybe in her late thirties, possibly older. "Were you talking to me?"

"You heard me. Women like you think you're too good for us. Drivin' your fancy car down here. I'm surprised ya didn't just send yer maid with the stuff." She crossed her arms over her ample chest and scowled at Jeena, her wild hair making her look like an over-endowed scarecrow.

"Excuse me. I'm in a hurry." Jeena pushed on past, her philanthropic feelings waning.

A tiny musical voice piped from behind the woman in the long, flowered skirt, and the child edged toward Jeena. "Mama, what's the pretty lady doin'?"

"Bringing things to the shelter, honey. Come on. Let's don't get in the way." The mother gripped her daughter's tiny hand and drew the little girl aside.

The child's clothing appeared worn, but the air of poverty and neglect from living on the street didn't hover around these two.

"Do you think there's a dolly for me, Mama?"

The longing in the child's voice smote Jeena's heart, leaving her with a feeling of emptiness. The little girl would be disappointed and probably not for the first time.

The woman flashed a brief, apologetic smile at Jeena and pulled her daughter back. "Shhh. It's not our business, Kirsten."

As Jeena struggled to grasp the doorknob, an older woman reached out a wrinkled hand and grasped the handle, swinging open the heavy wood door. She appeared to be at least sixty, and a grin that sported a broken tooth stretched her round and wrinkled face.

"Don't mind Sarah, miss," the raspy voice whispered. "She's new here and ain't learned how to act. Besides, she's kinda down on her luck right now. It ain't personal, you know?"

The heavyset Sarah snorted and cast a glum look at the small woman. "Aw, Mary, I'm not, either. I just get tired of these ritzy women thinking they're so much better than us. That's all."

Jeena peered over the top of one of the boxes, grateful for the helping hand and sweet voice that seemed such a contrast to the grating speech of Sarah. "Oh, uh, thank you," Jeena stammered toward the gentle-faced Mary, then rushed through the door.

She dropped the boxes with a loud thump on the floor beside the dinged-up metal desk in the entry, obviously kept more for its functionality than its beauty. The young woman sitting behind it didn't jump, just raised her eyes calmly and smiled.

"Hello. Can I help you?" She laid aside her stack of papers and leaned forward, her brilliant blue eyes reminding Jeena of a calm pool of inviting tropical water.

Some of Jeena's irritation stirred by the angry woman outside subsided at the sound of the placid greeting. "Yes. There are a couple more boxes in the car I'd like to donate. Could someone bring them in?" She glanced around the empty room, wondering where all the help might be hiding.

"I'll be happy to, but I need to call someone to watch the front. Is that your car across the street?" She stood and looked out the large, plate-glass window next to the door.

"Yes. Maybe I shouldn't have driven it down here."

"Don't worry. None of the women will bother it. They might look rough, but they appreciate what we do for them here."

"I'm sorry. I didn't mean to imply they'd damage it." Jeena kicked herself for her thoughtless comment. "What are they doing?"

"Waiting for the bus." The younger woman headed around the corner of the desk, then stopped. "I'm sorry. I'm Rachel Stevens." She extended her hand.

Jeena shook it, then crossed her arms. This place disturbed her in a way she hadn't expected. A memory from the past rose to the surface, but she pushed it down. "I'm Jeena Gregory. I don't know if these clothes are suitable. Maybe I should take them somewhere else."

She looked at the threadbare couch in the corner and the faded linoleum on the floor of the entry. Two more chairs stood off to the side, both serviceable but plain, giving the impression of a recent upholstery job. A simple, wood coffee table sat unobtrusively between the two, and neatly stacked magazines lined one edge. Only the essentials were here—nothing luxurious graced this area. She wouldn't be surprised if the furnishings were castoffs from someone's home. The room smacked of common sense, poverty, and hard work and made Jeena withdraw in discomfort. She pushed the memories it raised back down into the dark hole where they'd been buried so long ago.

Rachel shook her head, her auburn curls bouncing lightly with the motion. "We're grateful for anything you bring. We have a thrift store near here. If the women at the shelter can't use the donations, we'll sell them. The money helps keep this place open."

"Oh. I see." Jeena didn't care to get into a conversation with this young woman, no matter how kind she might seem. The quicker she got the boxes out of her car, the happier she'd be.

"Wait here? I'll just be a minute." Rachel crossed the foyer to the hall, and the sound of her low heels echoed off the worn linoleum.

Jeena was tempted to bolt; although it was rare that anything shook her nerve, this place came close. It even smelled old. Not dirty, exactly, just old. Nothing about this place looked dirty, but it still gave her the creeps. How could anyone live here? She was amazed this area still existed. She'd gotten used to the nicer downtown areas of River City and nearby Portland. It had been years since she'd ventured into this older section of town.

Rachel stepped back into view with a mousy-looking woman in tow and nodded at Jeena. "If you'll come with me, I'll get your other boxes."

"If you're sure." Jeena looked askance at the young woman, wondering that an apparently intelligent person would choose to work in this place.

The older, gray-haired woman settled behind the desk, nodding and smiling shyly at Jeena as Rachel opened the front door. Jeena led the way through the knot of silent women and across the street to her car.

"Why are they waiting for the bus?"

Rachel smiled. "A couple of them are checking in with their parole officers, one is keeping a doctor's appointment, and we often have women visiting their children in foster care."

"Parole officers? You let women come here who've been in jail?" Jeena knew Rachel could see the horror on her face, but she couldn't hide it. "Don't you worry about your safety?"

"We have to be careful, but no, I'm not worried. While we serve one meal a day to anyone who cares to come through our doors, we only allow women to stay who show a desire to change. We have troublemakers occasionally, but we screen them before we take them long term."

"Why do you do it?" Jeena asked, her curiosity overcoming her desire to escape.

Rachel's eyebrows rose, and her head tipped to the side. "Do what?"

Jeena unlocked the trunk and raised it. "Work at a place like this."

Rachel leaned her hip against the side of the car, her face thoughtful. "I've been down the career route, and it didn't bring much satisfaction. This job can be difficult at times—I won't deny that—but it's my true love. There's nothing that can bring as much joy as seeing God change one of these women's lives."

Jeena's curiosity changed to surprise. "God? What does God have to do with it? This is just a women's shelter, right?"

"Not entirely. It's also an outreach for women who need a fresh start. Some are victims of abuse, as well as addicts. We help women who need a hot meal or clean clothes, but our goal is to make a difference for women who desire true change. Only God is able to bring about that kind of transformation."

"Does a church run this place? I assumed it was government run, not somewhere you preached at people."

"It isn't run by any particular church, but it's sponsored by individuals and churches and set up to help hurting women. We believe that God can make a difference in women's lives, but they have to be open." She took a step away and trained a questioning look on Jeena.

Jeena pursed her lips and reached into the trunk, pulling the two remaining boxes to the front. She'd had religion forced down her throat all her life and didn't care to get hit with a sermon today.

Rachel fixed a warm gaze on Jeena. "Thank you. We appreciate the donation, but if you're uncomfortable with this being a Christian shelter and you'd rather take them elsewhere, I understand."

"It's not my business. I don't particularly care for Christianity, but if you're helping women, who am I to judge?" Jeena set the boxes on the sidewalk and shut the trunk. "Besides, it looks like the women could use them." She straightened and smiled, hoping to erase the worried expression from the kind young woman. "Look, I need to run. Thanks for helping me out." She walked around the car and opened the door.

Rachel reached into her pocket and withdrew a small white card. "If you ever need anything, don't hesitate to call, okay?" She stepped forward and placed it in Jeena's hand.

Jeena slid the card into a pocket of her purse. "Thanks. And hey—I'm sorry. I guess I've got a lot on my mind, but I didn't mean to snap."

"No worries. We all have days like that." She stepped back and gave a small wave.

Jeena stepped into her car and started it, then returned the wave and pulled away from the curb. A brief glimpse in her rear-view mirror showed the cluster of women still standing in front of the building, and Jeena saw a small hand wave from behind the flowered skirt. Her heart contracted as she remembered the pixie face of the girl with the blonde curls. Something about that little one tugged at her heart. She tapped her long fingernails against the steering wheel. "God, if You care about people like Grammie believes You do, please take care of that little girl."

CHAPTER 5

The picture of the child stuck in Jeena's mind, refusing to be dislodged. A lifetime ago, she'd experienced all the typical feelings of a romantic young girl who longed to be a wife and a mother. Visions of a curly headed toddler had tickled her thoughts, and Kirsten's cherubic face and sweet smile sparked a renewal of the daydreams she'd thought dead. She loved being a career woman and had boasted to her friends that succeeding at her profession mattered more than anything, but meeting Sean had awakened Jeena's long-dormant hopes for a family of her own.

She shook off the thought of Sean, determined not to allow paralyzing pain to engulf her again. She gave a quick look toward the intersection as she brought her car to a stop at the light. The neighborhood seemed unfamiliar. How had she gotten so far off course? That's what happened when she let her mind wander in territory better left forgotten.

The surrounding area appeared shabby and unkempt, like an old man who'd lost interest in living and let himself go. Lawns left uncut and trash lining the streets brought back sharp memories of where she'd grown up. The neighborhood appeared heavily riddled with rundown manufactured homes, no longer called trailers as they were when she lived in one as a child. The windows on many were drab, some empty, looking like lost souls gazing hopelessly on an uncaring world.

She'd hated being poor and the teasing it entailed. Trailer trash, the other kids called her. Always dressed in hand-me-downs and made to feel like someone's leftover garbage. An image of the shelter returned, and a long-submerged memory surfaced.

"The kids make fun of me. Why can't I have new clothes like everybody else?" She'd swiped angrily at the tears she didn't want her father to see. Even at eleven years old, she'd hated showing her emotions, especially to him.

His voice grew harsh. "Quit whining. Do you want to become a materialistic hussy when you grow up?"

She wanted to scream that dressing in style didn't make you a hussy. But she knew where that would get her. A single tear rolled down her cheek, stirring a deep loathing in the pit of her stomach. She hated him when he made her cry, almost as much as she hated him when he made her mother cry. Sometimes she wished he'd die so they could be free.

Her thoughts returned to the present, and Jeena tried to shake off the ghosts of her past. Her hands trembled on the steering wheel, and tears threatened to spill over onto her cheeks. She detested reliving those memories. They always made her stomach clench and her heart hurt. Staying in this neighborhood wasn't an option. She needed to get out, but she wasn't sure where she was.

She whipped her car around, not caring that she'd made an illegal U-turn. If a cop stopped her, she'd claim she was afraid of being mugged, which wasn't far from the truth.

�֍

Jeena parked her car in front of Tammy's modest, one-story house and looked at the clock on the dash—five minutes early. She slid out of the car and shut the door, then headed up the flower-lined sidewalk to the house. Tammy wasn't part of her faster crowd of friends, and they didn't see each other often, but Tammy had been under a lot of stress recently. Jeena knew she'd enjoy setting her problems aside for the afternoon.

She rang the bell and a few seconds later heard light footsteps approach the door. The door swung open, and Tammy's freckle-faced, tow-headed, ten-year-old son gazed solemnly up at her from his four-foot height.

"Hi, Jeena! Mom's almost ready." He continued to stand unmoving with the door cracked open.

Jeena smiled and shifted her purse on her shoulder. "Hi, Ron. Should I wait in the car?"

He backed away from the door, swinging it wide. "Gee, sorry. Mom said manners don't stick to me very well. Come in and sit down." He shut the door after her. "You can come to the kitchen if you want. I'm baking cookies."

"Your mom's pretty lucky to have a son who likes to cook."

"Naw, I don't like to cook. I just make cookies. It's the only way I get to eat the cookie dough." He grinned and shuffled across the worn rug toward the kitchen. "Come on. You can try one."

The fragrance of warm cookies made Jeena's mouth water. She hadn't eaten a fresh, homemade, chocolate chip cookie in ages. Her careful calorie counting didn't allow for excess sugar, but the look of eager anticipation on Ron's face clinched it. "Thank you. They look awesome and smell even better." She took a bite and couldn't hide her smile. "Hmm . . . and they taste fantastic!"

Ron's face glowed, and he hung his head for a brief moment, then raised it and grinned. "Aw, they're not *that* good." But he set the plate down and popped one into his own mouth.

Rapid footsteps coming down the hall alerted Jeena to Tammy's approach just before she popped around the corner into the kitchen. "Hey there. I see Ron's making you at home." Her wide smile and warm brown eyes leant a soft radiance to the room.

Ron turned a huge grin on his mother. "Can I send some with Jeena?"

"Sure. Toss some in a ziplock bag." Tammy reached for a sweater that lay across the back of a chair and slipped her arms into the sleeves.

"Thanks, sport." Jeena ruffled Ron's hair, then reached for the bag. "I'll have to come more often, now that I know what a great cook you are."

The two women headed for the door. Jeena held it open for Tammy, then pulled it closed behind her. "Lunch is my treat today, and no argument."

"You bought last time. It's my turn."

Jeena hit the button on her car remote and unlocked both doors, then slid inside and fastened her seat belt before replying. "Nope. This was my idea. I got a very nice advance from the company, and I want to celebrate." She held up a hand when Tammy started to protest. "Not another word. Besides, I'm eating your cookies, so I'm treating."

Tammy laughed and leaned back in the seat. "All right, I give. I'll admit, we don't have a lot of extra money for eating out these days, so this *is* a treat. Thank you."

Jeena started the car and turned to look over her shoulder. Not much traffic in this quiet neighborhood of small, older homes. "Matt still hasn't found a job?" She eased the car onto the road, then turned her gaze back to Tammy.

"Not yet. But I know God's got something good planned."

Jeena tried not to wince, reminded of why she didn't get together more often with Tammy. Her friend was sweet but not averse to sharing her faith with others. It didn't bother Jeena too much coming from Tammy, but Tammy's husband, Matt, was another matter. When he spouted anything about God, Jeena's hackles shot up. Part of her knew it wasn't fair to get irritated with Matt—he just didn't know when to stop. Maybe he'd made her his own personal witnessing project, but she cringed whenever he approached her with his newest "answer to prayer."

She tapped her nails on the steering wheel and turned a quizzical look toward Tammy. "But he's got his unemployment benefits, and you're still babysitting, right?"

"Yeah. It's been a struggle lately, but Matt's sent out a lot of résumés. Something will break soon."

Jeena had her doubts, but she kept them to herself. If Matt was as open about his faith at work as he was with his wife's friends, she couldn't imagine most employers wanting him around. "I'm sure." She reached out and squeezed Tammy's arm. "I didn't tell you—and I hope you won't mind—but we have a hair appointment at the mall. I'm getting mine cut and styled, and you can do whatever you want."

Tammy tossed her long brunette curls across her shoulders. "I can't let you do that. Lunch is more than enough."

"Nope. I made the appointments already. The beautician is a manicurist as well, so you can have your nails done if you'd rather. Pampering is more fun if you can share it with a friend."

Tammy sighed. "I'm not sure what to do with you, Jeena Gregory! Pampering sounds nice, but just because you got a big advance doesn't mean you need to spend it on me."

"Hey, I like spending money on my friends. Sure, I need to buy some new clothes, but it's cool doing things together. You don't want to ruin my day, do you?" She grinned at Tammy and cocked her head to the side.

Tammy giggled and settled deeper into the leather seat. "Nope. Can't have that. Guess I'd better have fun with you, so you won't feel neglected."

"That's my girl." Jeena hit the freeway and headed down the Columbia Gorge toward Portland.

The rest of the day passed in a blur while they drove from one mall to the next, ending up in the exclusive downtown area. Jeena finished maxing out two credit cards and came close on a third, but she didn't care. The results of this shopping trip would fill her closet with some of the most up-to-date clothing available, not to mention the shoes and makeup needed to complete her look.

They'd had a wonderful lunch, and then Tammy had opted for having her hair layered and styled. By late afternoon, their feet were starting to hurt, and they agreed to head home.

Tammy snapped her seat belt in place. "You look great! I wasn't so sure about cutting six inches off your gorgeous hair, but the beautician was right—it's very flattering and professional."

Jeena glanced across the car and smiled. "You look pretty hot, yourself. Better watch out. Matt's going to go nuts when he sees his new wife."

Tammy blushed and fingered her hair. "He's always telling me to splurge on myself, but I can't bring myself to do it when we're short on money. With the three boys crammed in one room, we need a bigger house, but with the job situation the way it is . . ." She shrugged. "I'm sorry. I've had a wonderful day, and I'm not going to ruin it by complaining."

"You're not complaining, sweetie. You're stating facts. You guys *do* need a bigger house, and you are in a bind right now with Matt out of work."

"I know, but I also need to keep my focus on the Lord, not our problems. Dwelling on the problems only pulls me down, and I need to stay up for my family."

"You're doing a great job—you're the most positive person I've ever met. It kind of bugs me, though. It doesn't seem like God is doing a lot for you guys." Jeena tried not to scowl. Images of her mother praying for things to change and the harsh visage of her father flashed through her mind, but she shook them off. No time for bad memories now.

Tammy turned, settled her shoulder against the door, and faced Jeena. "No one said being a Christian was easy. I don't expect God to play Santa and grant all our wishes, but He promised to give us peace when we hit hard times."

"I'm sure you're right." She tossed Tammy a smile, then checked her rearview mirror.

They'd been friends since high school, but Tammy's decision to trust God during college still rankled. If it hadn't been for her own religious upbringing—Jeena pushed away the thought, not willing to deal with the wide range of negative emotions she knew would surface. Right now, she needed to concentrate on keeping up the professional image she'd worked so hard to build—the image that would hopefully help along her career, as well as keep the childhood memories at bay.

*

Jeena kicked off the blanket and tried to wake from the nightmare, but sank into its grip as soon as she drifted back to sleep. "No! Please stop! Leave me alone!" the dark-haired little girl screamed, then turned and fled down a long, black hallway, nearly falling in her haste to escape. An open door beckoned, and she dashed in. Where should she hide? Under the bed? No . . . he'd find her there.

"You get back here. I've told you never to run from me." The voice thundered behind her, and the girl dove for the closet, wrenching the knob and jerking open the door.

"No, you don't." He reached out and grabbed her arm, yanking her back toward the dim hallway.

"Don't hit me. Please don't hit me!"

The sound of the keening wail tore through the night, and Jeena woke with a start, her legs entwined in the sheet and sweat pouring from her body. The images in her nightmare were too real. She'd lived through them countless times before, both at night and in the flesh.

She climbed from her bed, anxious to leave the confines of her tangled bedclothes. Light—she needed light. She reached for the lamp, and stared at the lighted dial of her clock. Four in the morning. No way would she return to sleep now. A cup of coffee might help chase away the demons and put her world back to rights.

Minutes later, she slumped into a kitchen chair and switched on her stereo, comforted by the music and the sound of the perking coffee. Silence wasn't an option right now, and neither were her memories. Nightmares hadn't plagued her for months— why now?

She searched back, wondering what had set it off, then remembered. Ah, yes. The trip to the shelter, the talk about the thrift store, the sight of the little girl's big eyes—and to top it all off, getting lost in the seedy neighborhood that smacked of her old home. Any one of those events might have triggered the memories, but all four? A perfect combination for trouble. Had she known the consequences, she'd never have donated the clothes. Burning them or throwing them in a Dumpster would've been preferable.

CHAPTER 6

The first Monday in May arrived and with it a sense of excitement that caused Jeena's heart to soar. The day would be perfect. Mr. Thayer himself had called her first thing to confirm her presence in their downtown suite of offices later that day. Much of the work needed completion ahead of the construction phase, and her expertise on the look and layout of the grounds was crucial to the interior design of the homes.

She pulled into her reserved spot in the parking garage of the twenty-story office building in downtown Portland. *Now this was living.* If only her father could see her. All his preaching about fancy clothes and money sending her to hell. He couldn't have been more wrong. If this job were any indication, heaven had already arrived.

She was running a little ahead of schedule and took a minute to enjoy the luxury surrounding her. A fairy princess just awakened by her long-lost prince couldn't feel happier. She swung her legs out of the car, noting the new leather pumps with gratification.

Reaching the sidewalk in front of the building, Jeena hesitated. A homeless man sat against the wall with a set of crutches and an empty pant leg, his hat in his hand. He turned flat black eyes up to her and drew his lips in an attempted smile, but it came off more like a grimace. "Money for a veteran, lady? Got a dollar to spare for some food?"

Jeena smiled at the man, then snapped open her purse and pulled out a twenty-dollar bill. "I think there's a shelter for men in Portland. I'm sure they'd be willing to help."

"Bless you, lady." He took the bill she'd dropped in his hat and tucked it into his shirt pocket.

She nodded and hurried through the door toward the elevator. She'd always assumed that most people asking for handouts were phony, but she felt sorry for this man who seemed genuinely disabled. Portland must have something for men similar to the women's shelter in River City. She pushed at the sense of sadness that almost choked her.

The elevator doors slid open, and she stepped inside. Gratitude flooded her heart for this new job and her cozy home. She couldn't imagine being crippled, alone, and living on the street.

The elevator moved up through the stately building on silent wings, leaving Jeena feeling like a child about to step onto the stage for her first production. If she excelled at this job, the industry would recognize her as a premier designer. She'd be able to choose the jobs she wanted and turn down the rest.

On the twentieth floor, the elevator halted, and the doors opened onto a waiting area that looked more like the foyer of an elegant home. *Nice. Very nice.* Browning and Thayer Inc. reserved the entire floor. Money didn't seem to be an issue here, and Jeena drew a deep breath of contentment as she moved into the room.

"Ms. Gregory?" A receptionist across the room spoke, startling Jeena from her observations. "Won't you take a seat? Mr. Browning and Mr. Thayer are in conference." The woman nodded toward one of the plush, overstuffed chairs situated beside a large window overlooking the city.

Jeena sank into the comfort of the soft leather, barely containing the small sigh of satisfaction that almost slipped past her parted lips. Now that she had a few minutes, she hoped to look around without seeming to gawk.

The sage-green walls complemented the wide ivory trim encasing each window and running along the crown of the ceiling. Elegant, yet restful. What a difference from the women's shelter. She suppressed a shiver at the contrast. *This is definitely more my style!*

She had to admit that whoever had designed this room knew what they were doing. Luxurious rugs graced the area between her chair and the receptionist's desk, accentuating the richness of the bamboo floor. That flooring alone would cost a small fortune; the finish was exquisite.

Each wall presented a single piece of high-priced artwork. Custom-framed, but tasteful, not ostentatious.

Jeena's face remained still, but inside she rubbed her hands together and jumped up and down in glee. *Home at last.* She'd worked toward this for years. There was nothing lacking, nothing left to chance. With her skills, long-term success was all but assured.

"Ms. Gregory, they'll see you now." The receptionist's voice snapped Jeena back to her reason for being in the office. She rose to her feet, her steps brisk as she crossed to the imposing wood door on her right.

Pausing for a moment, she took a deep breath, rapped, then pushed open the door leading to the private domain of her new boss. An understated, silver plate announced the name of the occupant: Charles Browning. Mr. Thayer's door must be on the far side of the room and hidden from view by one of the large potted plants. Two men sat inside the room, one behind an imposing cherry-wood desk and the other slightly to the side. Shelves lined one wall, built from the same rich cherry as the desk. Rather than stepping onto a hardwood floor, her feet sank into a carpet so plush she felt like she trod on the deep, mossy floor of an ancient forest. Leather chairs sat off to the side, and a couch lined one wall, flanked on either end by glass-and-cherry tables.

"Good morning, Ms. Gregory. We're sorry to keep you waiting." Mark Thayer's deep voice broke the stillness of the room.

Jeena once again felt a tiny shock at the man's voice. She'd only met him in person one time and had been disconcerted at his appearance, having built an image in her mind after discussions on the phone. She'd expected a large man, rugged in appearance and handsome. Instead, she'd met a man slight in stature, slender almost to the point of skinny, with a hawklike nose and oversized glasses. He stood and extended his hand, offering a firm grip.

The man sitting behind the desk drew her attention. This must be Charles Browning, the senior partner and driving force behind the much-touted construction empire. Scuttlebutt around town said he'd not earned all of his money in a way to make his mother proud. But no one dared say it to his face.

This man was everything his partner was not. He stood up slowly, reminding Jeena of a jungle cat stretching after a nap, looking for its next meal. She suppressed a small shiver. It must be his powerful personality, nothing more. Too many years of listening to her father's tirades about sin had warped her perception.

"We're happy you're joining our project, Ms. Gregory." The smooth voice of the man ran over her skin like warm oil, calming her nerves. Strikingly handsome, the man exuded an aura of power.

"I'm pleased you decided to use me." Something about this man commanded that she either bow or snap to attention in his presence. Instead, she extended her hand. She sensed he would tolerate nothing less than subservience from those around him. One glance at his partner confirmed her guess. Mark Thayer leaned forward, his hands locked around his knee, eagerness in the eyes pinned on the arrogant face beside him.

Charles reached across his desk and took her hand. "Your reputation is only surpassed by your beauty, my dear." He released her hand slowly and sat, his penetrating blue eyes never leaving her face.

"Thank you, Mr. Browning."

"We know you're going to be an asset to our project." He turned to the silent man sitting beside him. "Mark, why don't you show Ms. Gregory to the office we've reserved for her when she's not out in the field?"

"Yes. Certainly, Charles." Mark Thayer jumped from his chair as though wired with high-voltage electricity and almost stumbled in his eagerness to comply.

"We have more to discuss," Mr. Browning said to Jeena, "but it will wait. I'll see you before the day is over. I have an important client waiting in the conference room, and I must excuse myself."

He bestowed a charming smile on Jeena that didn't quite reach his eyes and left her feeling chilled. Confidence radiated from the man, a quality she found desirable, so what was wrong? Nothing that she could see; nothing she could put her finger on. It must be her upbringing rearing its head again. Her father wouldn't have trusted this man.

"Certainly, Mr. Browning." She turned to follow Mark from the room.

"Charles."

"Excuse me?" She almost stammered in her confusion.

"Call me Charles. And would you mind if I call you Jeena?"

"That would be fine. I mean . . . I'd like that." She struggled to regain her composure, mesmerized by the man's stare. What was going on? This man had the reputation of business being his highest priority, almost his god. There were no women in his life, if the local gossip was true.

"Good. I'll stop by your office later, Jeena." He smiled, then strode around her and disappeared out the door.

"Right this way, Ms. Gregory." The deep timber of Mr. Thayer's voice jarred Jeena out of the spell Charles had woven.

She noted that Mr. Thayer hadn't asked her to call *him* by his first name and no mysterious energy floated around this man. She followed him across the reception area, hiding her elation at the welcome she'd been given by the senior partner.

CHAPTER 7

Jeena picked up her pace, hating the thought of disappointing her grandmother by showing up late for dinner. At least she'd make it in time for dessert, and she could visit with Grammie and her friends. She breezed through the open doorway into the large, cheerful dining area. Residents could eat in their own apartments, but many chose the more active social time afforded by gathering together for meals.

Grammie rose from her seat at one of the small, round tables and waved. "Jeena. Over here!" She smiled when Jeena stopped and planted a soft kiss on her weathered cheek. "I'm so glad you made it, dear."

Jeena slipped into the green upholstered seat and grimaced. "I'm sorry I'm late. I worked longer than usual." She took a bite of the pie her grandmother offered. Coconut cream. One of her favorites.

A man with snowy white hair and a sweet smile leaned over to pat her hand. "Your grandmother told us about your new job. Congratulations! I imagine you're pleased."

Jeena nodded and swallowed her bite of pie before answering. "I've been there almost four weeks, and I'm loving it! I've waited a long time to find a job this challenging. Of course, the salary doesn't hurt too much, either." She chuckled along with the others, who settled into silence as they enjoyed their dessert.

Grammie sat next to her best friend, Irene, a tiny sparrow of a woman who didn't stand much over five-feet tall in her bare feet. The older woman gave her a wink and a smile. "You need to come back and play Scrabble again, my dear. I must say, it does help keep this old brain sharp, having to come up with words good enough to beat your grandmother."

Jeena nodded. "Don't I know it. I can count on one hand the number of times I've been able to beat her in the past ten years. Maybe we can play a game today."

Irene clapped her hands. "That would be lovely."

The gentleman with snowy white hair who'd congratulated Jeena sat on her left. A wizened man burdened by an oxygen tank and a walker slumped in the chair just beyond.

Grammie patted Jeena's arm and nodded to the man with the walker. "This is Henry Stellar, and this"—she smiled at the white-haired man between them—"is Cable Hornby."

Cable's firm grip surprised Jeena, and the man's genial smile delighted her. His charm and grace were that of a southern gentleman. "A pleasure, miss." He bowed over her hand and raised twinkling eyes. "Your beauty almost rivals that of your grandmother."

Grammie's laugh blended with the rest, but Jeena saw a soft flush stain her cheeks. If her guess was right, this was one of Grammie's suitors.

A rasping voice drew her attention to Henry. "Pleased to meet you, too. I'm afraid I'm not as smooth as Cable, here, but my sight isn't failing me even if my lungs don't work like they used to. You're a looker, all righty." He winked. A coughing spasm halted his words, and he covered his mouth with a handkerchief.

The coughing grew steadily worse, and Jeena wrinkled her brows in alarm. "Is there anything I can do? Would you like a glass of water, or should I call someone?"

He shook his head, keeping the handkerchief over his lips. "No," he choked, then drew a shallow breath. "It'll pass. But I may need to lie down for a bit."

Jeena slid back her chair and rose. "I'll walk you to your room."

"I'm all right, really. I can manage." He tried to wave her away but got caught in another bout of wheezing coughs.

"I insist." Jeena slid a hand under Henry's elbow and drew him to his feet. She smiled at a bustling, uniformed attendant who arrived at her side. "If you want to take his other arm, I'll help Mr. Stellar to his room."

"Thank you, miss," Henry rasped. "And I'm sorry to break up your party when you've just arrived."

"Nonsense. I'll come back down and visit after we get you settled." She smiled at the quiet faces ringing the table. "You'll wait for me, won't you?"

"Yes, dear." Grammie nodded, a gentle pride shining on her face. "On second thought, I think I'll be in my room. I seem to have a bit of indigestion after that big meal."

Jeena frowned and hesitated, pulled between a desire to help the old man at her side and concern for her grandmother's health.

Grammie waved her away. "It's nothing. I just should have stopped a bit sooner and not had that pie. Go on now." She leaned over and patted Henry's shoulder. "You get some rest. Irene and I will stop and check on you later. And see that you mind my granddaughter."

A little color returned to Henry's pallid face, and he managed a smile. "She's prettier than my regular nurse." He managed a wink at Jeena, then turned to the attendant on his other side and shook off his arm. "Give me my walker. I'm not dead yet."

✣

Jeena sat at the desk in her office the following afternoon, only half aware of her elegant surroundings. The past few weeks at her new job had been great. No, that was too tame a word. It had been an amazing experience working for this company. It seemed to run in such a way that nothing ever slipped out of place. *Well oiled* didn't do it justice. Charles was the driving force behind the business, and Mark implemented the senior partner's plans almost as fast as they hatched in Charles's mind.

Even so, something bothered her. As a rule, she didn't pay attention to the business end of the companies she worked for. But recently, a couple of comments made by the secretary had Jeena wondering if something unusual might be occurring in the finances of Browning and Thayer. Normally, she was out in the field and spent only limited time in the office for the pre-design stage. That wasn't the case here on this gargantuan project, which would require weeks in the office working on the layout of the grounds before she moved on to the job site.

"Pat?" Charles Browning's disembodied voice floated over the office intercom. "I need to speak to you. Step in here immediately."

Jeena moved to get up and shut her office door, needing to concentrate.

"Yes, sir. Certainly." The scrape of Pat's chair on the expensive wood floor and the tap of her heels crossing the room signaled her retreat, closely followed by the click of a door in the distance.

Jeena sank back in her seat, glad for the quiet, and reached for a folder on the corner of her desk. Her work had progressed smoothly, but she didn't intend to get behind. The promised bonus at the end of this project was a major incentive, but she also found satisfaction in doing a thorough job.

"I have a rather sensitive matter I need you to take care of personally."

The unexpected voice in the next room made Jeena jump. Hadn't Pat shut off the intercom? She'd be mortified and Charles would be livid if they realized they'd been overheard. Better take care of it. Jeena rose from her chair and walked purposefully across her office.

"We're getting a large deposit on the townhouses from the shareholders. I want you to follow the directions on these papers to the letter, then destroy them."

Jeena paused. She stepped over the threshold. It was none of her business.

Pat's voice drifted across the room. "You want the money shifted to your offshore account—"

"Don't *ever* mention that again." Charles's voice ripped across Pat's words and covered the short distance to Jeena, making her jump. "Just follow these directions and make sure there's no paper trail. Don't worry. You'll be taken care of."

"Yes, sir. Thank you, Mr. Browning," Pat said.

"That'll be all." The brusque voice broke off, and footsteps sounded across the inner office.

Jeena flew toward Pat's desk and punched the intercom button, then raced on silent feet toward her office. She pulled the door behind her and slipped into her chair, trying to stifle her rapid breathing. What had she overheard? She thought Pat had said something about an offshore account, but that couldn't be right. A large percentage of the funds for this project were contributed by a Mr. Hanover, a major shareholder in the corporation, from what she'd gathered. Surely Charles wouldn't tamper with the investor's funds?

"Jeena?" Charles's voice caused her to jump. He'd crossed the outer room without making a sound and stood in her partly open doorway.

"Yes?" She controlled her voice, willing it to be sweet. Surely nothing inappropriate had transpired. Her overactive mind had made more of this than existed.

"I'd like you to bring your designs into my office." The words were no sooner out of his mouth than he'd disappeared.

Wonderful. Had he realized the intercom was on and decided to grill her? It was possible—the man was uncanny. She needed to be careful about leaving her door shut from now on. On the other hand, maybe she should leave it open more often. Jeena shook her head, annoyed. Better get to Charles's office before he appeared at her side again.

She tapped on his door before stepping into the room.

Charles held out an authoritative hand. "Let me see how you're progressing on the designs." He began to scan them almost before she released them into his grip.

She sank into a chair near the desk. "I've gotten farther than I expected. I think you'll be pleased."

His face seemed carefully neutral as he shuffled the pages. A frown pulled down the corners of his normally handsome mouth as he scanned the last one. Eyes that looked like twin daggers raised to Jeena's.

"This won't do." The words were clipped.

"Excuse me?" Jeena leaned back into the chair, glad for its support. She felt like a mouse caught in the gaze of a lion.

"I think it would be a wise idea if you slowed your pace. We wouldn't want to rush too fast and make any mistakes, would we?" A smile crossed his face, but his eyes remained hooded, looking like half-closed blinds that allowed only a small amount of light to penetrate a room.

"You want me to slow down?" This didn't make sense. She assumed she'd been hired for her skill and ability to get the job done.

His tone softened. "Please don't misunderstand. You're doing fine work. But with a job this size, we must make sure every detail is checked and re-checked before we present it to the board and shareholders. You see the wisdom in that, don't you?" He leaned forward, hands clasped around his knee, but his eyes still bored into hers, leaving no doubt of his tension.

She didn't see at all. Her work had never been questioned, but she knew better than to dispute this man. "Yes, of course. If you want me to slow down, I will."

"Thank you, Jeena. I appreciate your willingness to work with me. I knew I could count on you." His voice was silky. He stroked the arm of the chair where he sat, pulling Jeena's gaze to the long, powerful fingers.

She gave him what she hoped was a charming smile. "Of course you can, Charles." She watched his lips turn up the slightest bit.

"That will be all for now." He stood and turned toward the door, his movements abrupt.

"I'll get back to work then." She pushed herself out of the depths of the chair. Had she said something wrong?

"Why don't you wrap things up and take the rest of the afternoon off? You've worked hard since you arrived, and I wouldn't want to see you burn yourself out." He swiveled toward her again, his smile almost genuine.

"If that's what you want." She smiled, and then walked from the room.

✤

Jeena sat at her desk, finishing the last bit of work on her computer and mulling over Charles's strange request. It seemed innocent enough, only it didn't make sense. How would it benefit him or his company for her to slow down? She thought back to Pat's brief slip of the tongue. Could there be more simmering under the surface than she'd realized?

Her unseeing gaze fixed on the wall as she tapped her long nails against the polished surface of the cherry-wood desk, trying to work her way through the quandary.

Charles remained a puzzle. One moment he seemed relaxed and happy, and the next, he rushed her out of the room.

The perplexing thing was that no mistakes existed in her plans. She excelled at her work. The designs for this job were exceptional, but for some reason Charles couldn't see it. Or didn't want to. But that didn't make sense, either. The faster she finished, the sooner the company could move on.

Time was money, right? Or was it?

She clicked her mouse on the screen, exited out of her program, and commanded the computer to shut down. No need to give herself a headache. She didn't own this company. Let Charles or Mark worry about the profit-and-loss side of things.

"See you tomorrow, Pat." Jeena waved her fingers at Pat, and the rich purple hues of the amethyst ring flashed in the light reflecting from the desk lamp.

"You're leaving early?" Pat's head jerked up, small wrinkles appearing around her lips as she made no effort to suppress a frown.

"Charles insisted I take the rest of the day off. I'm ahead of the game and he doesn't want me to do any more today." She hoped the woman didn't know about the request to slow down. Pat irritated her with her know-it-all attitude. Let her think Charles was rewarding Jeena for a job well done.

An odd look flitted across Pat's face, but a broad smile quickly replaced it. "Oh, if Mr. Browning said so, then have a wonderful day."

"I intend to." Jeena didn't return the smile. Something was off in this place, but there was no way she was going to force the issue. Jobs like this didn't come along every day. Whatever was going on was none of her business, and she meant to keep it that way.

CHAPTER 8

Jeena drove aimlessly around the streets of River City after the forty-minute drive back from Portland. Leaving work early wasn't something she normally did, and going home to an empty apartment didn't sound inviting. Shopping was always an option, but caution reared its head after her big splurge. Charles had informed her it would be another two weeks before the next pay draw, so she'd better curtail her spending.

Something looked familiar about this neighborhood, but she didn't think she'd been here before. She tried to avoid places like this and never took a job in this section of town. The residential area ended, and she drove through the edges of a more commercial section. A mixture of neglected homes, deteriorating vintage apartment buildings, and vacant shops lined the street. That building. Hadn't she seen it before? The women's shelter. No wonder the area looked familiar.

She rounded the corner of the block where the shelter sat, more determined than ever to put it behind her. A dirty-looking man lounged against a nearby wall, leering at her car as she passed.

A movement caught her eye as she pulled away from the stop sign. It looked like the little girl from the shelter. The cute little blonde who wanted a new doll. What was she doing near the street? Where in the world was her mother?

A blaring horn woke her to the girl's danger. This was an unsavory neighborhood and a busy street with both pedestrian traffic and cars. The smell of diesel from the exhaust pipes of delivery trucks colored the air, laying a foul-smelling blanket over the area.

Jeena hit the brakes and made an illegal turn. She wanted to get home, but her conscience wouldn't let her drive off

without making sure the child was safe. What was her name
. . . Kirsten?

She opened the passenger window and coasted to a stop near
the curb, shutting off the motor and poking her head out the
window. "Kirsten? I'm the lady who brought the clothes to the
shelter. Do you remember me?"

The little girl stood on the corner, the middle two fingers of
her left hand stuck in her mouth and tears streaming down her
cheeks. A bedraggled-looking teddy dangled from her fingers,
his ears touching the sidewalk. Wide eyes swung toward Jeena,
and recognition sprang into them. She took a step toward the
car. "Help me find Mommy?"

Jeena didn't need to hear more. She shoved open the door
and all but jumped from the car. Mustn't scare the child. She'd
better slow down. "Kirsten, where is your mommy?"

"Don't know. The big door shutted, and I can't get back in. I
want my mommy." Tears flowed, and Jeena heard sobs mixed
with hiccups.

She stepped gingerly toward Kirsten, not sure how to pro-
ceed. The movement must have given the little one hope. She
flew at Jeena's legs, wrapping her arms around them and holding
on as though Jeena were a superhero flying to her rescue. She
scooped up the girl and cradled her close, crooning and stroking
the baby-fine hair.

A door slammed against the building with a clang of metal.
"What are you doing with that girl, woman?" The booming voice
sent shivers up Jeena's back—Sarah, the one who'd badgered her
when she brought the clothes. The large woman in gaudy clothing trotted across the gravel lot, her bulk bearing down quickly
on Jeena.

"Kirsten! Are you all right?" Another woman Jeena recognized as Kirsten's mother came flying across to the curb where
they stood, then loosened Kirsten's grip around Jeena's neck and
pulled her into her arms.

Sarah plowed to a halt beside Jeena, gasping for breath. "She
all right, Joy?"

Joy nodded, and the panting Sarah turned back to Jeena. "I asked what you're doing with Kirsten, and you'd better answer before I call the cops." Hot breath blew into Jeena's face, and she grabbed Jeena's arm.

In less than a second, the shock wore off and Jeena took command. "Get your hands off me!" She yanked away and glared at Sarah.

"You better explain yourself." Sarah pressed her imposing size to its full advantage. She crowded Jeena back against a light pole, before she swung away from Jeena and stepped over to Kirsten, held close in her mother's arms. "Did the lady bother you, honey?" The rough voice had softened to a tone Jeena wouldn't have imagined possible. And then Sarah tucked a loose strand of hair behind the little girl's ear.

Kirsten wrinkled her little brow. "No. She hugged me—she saved me and Teddy." Kirsten patted Teddy on the back with one small hand and wiped away a stray tear with the other.

Joy drew her daughter against her shoulder and threw a smile at Jeena. "Thank you. I'm not sure how you happened to be here, but if Kirsten says you helped her, then I'm very grateful."

Jeena squared her shoulders and tossed a frown toward Sarah before turning to Kirsten's mother. "How in the world did she get out here, and why wasn't anyone watching her?"

Sarah grunted and turned back toward the building. "I'll see you inside, Joy. I've had enough of this."

"Thanks, Sarah." The young mother reached up to stroke Kirsten's head, where it rested against her neck. "I'm not sure. I went to get a snack for Kirsten while she was napping, and when I got back to our room, she was gone. I guess I stayed in the kitchen too long, and she must have come looking for me."

"I sorry, Mommy." Kirsten reached up to wipe the tears off her mother's wet cheeks. "I sorry you crying again." She puckered her mouth and stifled a sob. "I want to go home."

Jeena frowned. "Kirsten was dangerously close to the street. She could've been hurt."

Fresh tears welled up, and the woman buried her face in Kirsten's hair. "I know."

Jeena regretted her hasty words, seeing the impact they had on Joy. Why were these two here? They certainly didn't seem to fit with someone like Sarah or most of the other women she'd seen at the shelter.

"I need to get Kirsten inside. Please accept my thanks again, Miss . . . ?"

"Jeena Gregory, but Jeena is fine. I'm glad I came along." Maybe the woman needed an awakening. After all, the girl could've been snatched, let alone been hit by a car.

Joy put a shaking hand to her mouth. "God must have sent you here to protect her. At least, that's what Rachel would say. My name is Joy. If there is anything I can ever do for you . . ." She shook her head, a small smile breaking through the tears like a sliver of sunlight piercing the clouds. "That's stupid. I live in a shelter, and you drive a BMW and leave expensive clothes here, and I offer to help you."

"It's okay. I appreciate it. Really." For once Jeena felt at a loss for words.

"Tell the nice lady thank you, Kirsten," Joy said.

"Thank you." The child's muffled voice came from her mother's shoulder, as sparkling wet eyes peeked at Jeena.

"You're welcome, Kirsten. Stay with your mommy from now on." Jeena stepped toward her car, opening the door and waving at the little girl before climbing inside. Her emotions were warring, leaving her feeling like she'd competed in a grueling marathon and lost. This place and everything it stood for made her uncomfortable. She shuddered thinking about Kirsten straying so close to the busy street. Someone needed to keep an eye on the mother, too.

Jeena drew the door shut and started the motor. She pulled away from the curb and heaved a sigh. Time to go home. Nothing else sounded as good right now.

She longed for something to push down the trickle of depression trying to seep in. She'd told herself she wouldn't keep drinking. She wasn't an alcoholic. Why, it'd been weeks since she'd had more than a few glasses of wine. Well, maybe only days, but she didn't make it a habit. She'd seen people who abused it and what it did to their lives and, almost as bad, to their bank accounts. No way she'd let anything control her life or drain her finances. Maybe just this one time. Maybe she'd stop and pick up a bottle of something a little harder on the way home and treat herself. After all she'd been through, she deserved a boost.

CHAPTER 9

Jeena padded around the kitchen in her slippers and pj's, humming while she buttered toast and created an omelet. She glanced at the clock and reached for her phone. Time for a quick call before settling down to savor her Saturday morning breakfast.

The phone rang five times before her grandmother picked up, creating a nagging worry that Jeena might have woken her.

"Hello?" Grammie sounded slightly out of breath.

"Grammie, it's Jeena. Is everything okay?" She turned the burner to warm. Breakfast could wait.

"Fine, dear. My blood pressure's been up a bit, but it's nothing to worry about."

Guilt struck Jeena's heart, and she sank down in the chair, breakfast forgotten. Work had consumed her lately, and she hadn't visited Grammie nearly as often as she'd planned.

"How would you like to go for a drive and maybe have lunch out? Better yet, let me take you shopping. I can tell you about my job, and you can tell me how many new proposals you've gotten."

The hesitation on the other end was brief, but Jeena didn't miss it. "That would be lovely, but I think just lunch. I'm not quite up to shopping today. Do you mind?"

"Of course not. Would you rather stay there?" A trickle of fear ran through Jeena's mind.

"No, no, going out would be nice. I could use a change of scenery. Give me a couple of hours, will you, dear?" Her voice trembled, then grew stronger. "I'm not as spry as I used to be, and baths take a little longer to get in and out of."

"Sure, Grammie, that's fine. Love you!" Jeena hung up the phone and stared at the instrument, then picked it up and punched in another set of numbers.

"This is Jeena Gregory. I'd like to speak to the nurse on duty, please. It's about my grandmother."

Minutes ticked by, and Jeena's toe tapped the floor, keeping rhythm with her mounting irritation. If there wasn't anyone around who cared enough to come to the phone, then they probably didn't put much effort into their residents, either.

"Hello, Ms. Gregory, this is Pamela. How can I help you?" The brisk voice on the end of the line stilled Jeena's foot.

She pushed herself out of the chair and leaned her hip against the edge of the counter. "I just spoke with my grandmother, and she complained of being tired. Has she been ill?"

"She had a small episode a couple of days ago when she complained of mild stomach pain, and her blood pressure was elevated, but the doctor brought it back down."

"My grandmother is the youngest seventy-eight-year-old I've ever met. If it wasn't for her medical problems, she'd be living in her own home and caring for herself, instead of relying on assisted living. Sometimes she has more energy than I do. I'd appreciate you speaking to the doctor about it again, as I'm sure she won't bring it up herself."

"I agree. Mrs. Thomas isn't one to complain, and if she admitted she's not feeling well, then we'll speak to her about another checkup."

"Thanks. Please don't tell her I suggested it, or I'll get a good scolding."

The nurse chuckled. "I've gotten a couple of those from your grandmother in the past. Don't worry. I'll be sure the doctor is advised."

Jeena hung up, determined to keep an eye on Grammie. If better care required more money, she'd provide it. Her grandmother was precious to her and deserved the best. Nothing must ever happen to Grammie.

Jeena settled into a corner booth at Los Reyes, her favorite Mexican restaurant in the small town of Bingen, Washington, across the Columbia River and a bit east from River City. Tammy's request to meet for lunch was a welcome respite from her busy schedule, and the eagerness in her friend's voice pricked her conscience. She'd neglected to call Tammy since their shopping trip and had no idea if Matt had been able to find a job.

The owner, Miguel, stopped by her table, his face lit in a smile. "Jeena, I haven't seen you in a while. Are you here alone?"

"No, Tammy's meeting me. How's business?"

He set down a glass of water and a menu. "Excellent, as always. Of course, it doesn't hurt that the tourists are coming in now. Pepsi or iced tea today?"

"Hmm . . . raspberry iced tea, thanks."

"Right, and do you know what Tammy will want?"

Jeena took a sip of the water and smiled. "Pepsi, if I know her."

Miguel grinned and moved away. Jeena looked around the colorful, open area, impressed with the changes he'd made in the décor. He'd improved the menu as well since purchasing the establishment a couple of years before, and the atmosphere was peaceful and friendly to all who entered. She settled into her booth and sighed, glad to be resting and not having to think about work. Not that she felt like complaining. The fast pace at her new job had kept her mind off Sean. Knowing that he'd dumped her for someone else made the loss easier to bear in some ways—no man who'd do that deserved to be mourned for long—but spouting facts to oneself didn't always heal a heartache.

Miguel set two glasses on the table in front of her, then beckoned toward the door. "Your friend has arrived."

Jeena spotted Tammy standing in the open doorway, and she raised herself up off the bench and waved. Tammy's face lit with pleasure, and she walked briskly to the table. Miguel stepped aside, and Tammy stooped to give Jeena a quick hug.

Jeena returned the hug—she'd missed Tammy more than she'd realized. "Hey there, girlfriend. It's great to see you."

A sweet smile brightened Tammy's face. "You, too. Sorry I'm late."

Jeena waved her hand, then took her seat across from Tammy. "No worries, I've been chatting with Miguel."

Miguel set down the chips and salsa. "Sorry for taking so long. I'm shorthanded today."

Tammy took a sip of her Pepsi and sighed. "Perfect, thanks." She turned to Miguel. "Your salsa is definitely worth waiting for."

He smiled and bowed his head. "Thank you. You need a few minutes?"

Jeena glanced at Tammy. "I'm ready." She raised her eyebrows. "How about you?"

"Absolutely. Shrimp salad with ranch dressing."

"Make that two." Jeena slid her menu to the edge of the table and took a warm chip from the basket. "So catch me up on what's been going on with you." She leaned forward and took a sip of tea, her gaze locked on Tammy's face.

Tammy shrugged. "Just the same old thing, I guess. Kids, homeschool, housework, the usual."

Jeena hesitated, almost hating to ask, but plunged ahead. "How about the job situation? Has Matt found anything?"

Tammy brushed a strand of hair from her eyes. "Not yet. Thank the Lord he still has unemployment, or I'm not sure what we'd do." She took a deep breath and paused, then continued in a rush. "I'm going to try to find a job. I thought I'd check with Miguel today and see if he needs anyone."

Jeena tried not to let the shock she felt register in her expression. "But you homeschool your kids. Has it gotten that serious?"

Tammy nibbled a chip and nodded. "Yeah. We're getting worried we could lose the house, but please don't let Matt know I said that. I haven't told anyone, not even my folks."

"Could they help?"

She shook her head. "No. Dad's health isn't good, and they're on a fixed income. That's why I don't want them to know. They'd try to help and put themselves in a bind."

Jeena glanced down at her hand clutching her drink and

winced. Her grandmother's ring sparkled in the sun streaming through the large, plate-glass windows, seeming to mock her friend's need. She met Tammy's eyes. "Would you let me loan you some money till you get on your feet?"

Tammy smiled. "Thanks. I appreciate it, but Matt would never agree, and I wouldn't feel good about it, either. Borrowing from friends is a fast way to hurt a friendship—especially if something happened and we couldn't pay it back."

"Then it doesn't have to be a loan. It could be a gift." Jeena reached across the table and grasped Tammy's hand. "I know Matt's trying to find a job, but what if it takes a while? My job pays more than I need, and I'd love to help."

Tammy squeezed her fingers, then sat back. "I can't. Really. But thank you." She took a sip of her drink and mustered a smile. "God's not going to let us down, and it won't kill me to work for a while. Matt can take over the homeschooling, and drive the kids to sports functions. It's not forever. Now, tell me about your new job. I want to hear everything. The last time I saw you was just before you started."

Jeena drew a deep breath and released it slowly, knowing her friend well enough to recognize the firm set to her mouth. She didn't mind pushing some of her friends, even insisting when she believed she was right. But she'd never felt comfortable doing that with Tammy. Maybe it had something to do with her quiet but firm faith and the deep-seated belief that God was in charge.

Jeena had her doubts about God taking care of anyone, based on the hardships her parents had endured during her growing-up years. But somehow, Tammy's relationship with God seemed different than her father's—more like Grammie's. That must be it.

Jeena had never really pinpointed the problem before. Most of the women she knew who'd found religion seemed to cling to it with their hearts, while her father's relationship with God was based on an outward show of piousness and a large dose of pride. Over the years, she'd met other men who seemed cut from the same mold as her father and had decided that Christian men were best avoided when possible—and rarely trusted. Multiple hurts and rejections over the years had dug their talons in deep and never let go.

"Jeena?" Tammy cocked her head and smiled.

Jeena blinked and focused on her friend. "Sorry. You asked about my job. It's been a dream come true, and the work is satisfying and challenging. I'm doing the design for the grounds and landscaping right now, and you know that's an area I love. It's been amazing to watch the plan come together. I'll be resuming the interior design for the townhouses soon, but the grounds layout has been a breath of fresh air."

A server stopped beside their table and set two heaping plates of crisp salad topped with large shrimp in front of them. After he left, Tammy bowed her head and said a silent prayer. Jeena winced but waited till her friend finished. How did Tammy do it? Keep trusting and believing when life seemed to be spiraling downhill. It didn't make sense. Nothing she'd seen while growing up coincided with the strength and peace expressed on Tammy's face.

Jeena shrugged and picked up her fork, determined not to let the situation get to her. She was happy for Tammy that her faith seemed to help her, but her own life was good. She didn't need the crutch that older people like Grammie and families like Tammy's seemed to need when life became difficult. No, other than the breakup with Sean, Jeena didn't see any need for God in her life, and she doubted greatly that He thought too much about her, either.

CHAPTER 10

Two weeks later, Jeena paced the floor of her office, her door firmly closed. Her enthusiasm for this job had started to wane, and her anxiety level had increased. The last pay period had come and gone, with little of monetary value to show for her work. Pat had handed her a small check with a half-hearted excuse. Both Mark and Charles were out of town, and Pat wasn't authorized to write large checks.

Something wasn't right. Jeena had been trying to ignore it, but her instincts were screaming. Pat seemed closed as a frozen clamshell, and there was no thawing her out. Oh, she was polite enough and certainly put on a great act if clients came by. But Jeena had tried prying information from her and gotten nowhere, fast.

Jeena usually ignored conversations Pat had on the phone—but this time the name of the man funding their project, a Mr. Hanover, caught her ear. Little snippets of conversation had floated through Jeena's door more than once, sending off small rockets of warning. This one seemed different—nothing concrete, but enough to make her worry.

"No, Mr. Hanover. Neither Mr. Browning nor Mr. Thayer are available right now. They should return within the week."

Jeena heard Pat's foot tapping under her desk, a clear indication of her agitation and not typical for the normally unflappable secretary.

"I'm sorry. I'm not at liberty to say. Mr. Browning handles the accounting. I have nothing to do with the deposits or withdrawals."

Silence. Mr. Hanover must be unhappy. Jeena strained to hear.

"I'll be sure to tell them. You have my word . . . Yes, I realize you're concerned. I'm sure everything is in order. The job is moving along well . . . Yes, they just had some business to attend to. There's nothing to worry about, Mr. Hanover."

The sound of the phone hitting its cradle announced the sudden end of the conversation. Whether brought about by Pat or by an irate Mr. Hanover, Jeena couldn't be sure.

She'd like to know more but doubted she'd get information from the close-mouthed Pat. Hopefully when her bosses came back, things would straighten themselves out.

Jeena sank back in her chair, staring at the computer screen. Three o'clock. She liked to work a full eight hours, but she'd make an exception this time. Her work had advanced at a crawl after the warning Charles gave her to slow down a few weeks ago, and there was little more she could do.

She pushed back her chair and reached for the new briefcase she'd purchased to impress her boss. She stalled in the act of shoving a sheaf of papers into the open case. What was the point of taking them home? Charles didn't want her working overtime. No, she had a better idea.

She snapped the case shut and slid it to the back of the desk. Her purse took its place. She strode to the door, pulling it open and shutting it behind her with a click.

Pat's head snapped up. "Leaving so soon?" A frown clouded her sour face as she glared at the purse slung over Jeena's arm.

Jeena paused near the door. "I'm getting some exercise. I'm stiff from sitting, and there's not much I can do till Charles or Mark returns."

"Humph. It's not like you work very hard." Pat's narrowed eyes peered over the top of her glasses.

"Well, thankfully it's not your problem, is it?" Jeena snapped.

"Good-bye, Ms. Gregory." Pat's frown deepened before turning back to the papers stacked on her desk.

Jeena didn't look back.

❧

The soft leather of her car seat cradled Jeena's body and welcomed her into its embrace. She hadn't realized how much she'd wanted to escape from the depressing atmosphere generated by the gloomy secretary. A small grimace twisted her lips. What she needed was a workout at the club, followed by a soak in the Jacuzzi.

The drive from Portland back to River City flew by as she reflected on the one-sided conversation she'd overheard, but a screech of brakes when she hit the edge of town snapped her attention back to the upcoming intersection. Some idiot had run the stop sign, nearly getting broadsided. Probably another tourist. They were coming in droves, and the increased traffic made life difficult.

Windsurfing in the Columbia River Gorge drew people from all over the world. Many of the visitors had decided to stay, building new homes and buying up the old ones, and the once sleepy town of River City had grown to hold twelve thousand year-round residents, as well as thousands of tourists. The almost century-old streets hadn't been designed for this much traffic, and parking in the summer months became a competition, occasionally causing tempers to flare. The once-quiet streets teemed with pedestrians, and getting from one end of town to the other took three times as long as it did a few years before.

Well, to be fair, maybe not everything was more difficult. The huge influx of tourists brought about the building boom and had helped pay her bills. New building firms had sprung up around town, and for a long time, nearly everyone connected with the construction industry had prospered. Things were slowing now, and housing had dipped, making her even more thankful for her secure job in Portland.

"Finally." Jeena parked her car in the reserved parking area for club members and took a moment to collect herself.

What a difference this was from the shelter. The image of the little girl standing on the curb in front of the building flitted through her mind. Run-down buildings and bums standing on the corners. Certainly no place for a child.

Kirsten had touched her in a way no one but Grammie had been able to do in a long time. A picture of Sean filled her imagination.

Home. Family. Jeena shook off the longing, determined to drive the vision of Sean from her heart.

She didn't have the time or energy to get close to anyone other than the people already in her life. Trusting people only succeeded in getting her burned. Hopefully Kirsten's mother could take care of the little girl.

Besides, this was her world, with its upscale neighborhoods and condos. Money made a difference in one's life, but it was more than that. In her estimation, only people without any vision landed in a shelter. No one had to end up in a place like that. What those people needed was some initiative; then they'd make something of their lives.

Her thoughts stilled, and she sucked in a breath. Tammy. She and Matt both had a desire to succeed, but life had dealt them a number of blows lately. Maybe she'd been too quick to judge the women at the shelter. She cringed inwardly at the thought of Tammy's family in the same situation as little Kirsten and her mother. No way would she allow that to happen. Tammy's resolve not to accept help was fine for now, but if the family's home were jeopardized, Jeena would step in and see that they didn't lose it. Her thoughts flashed back in time to the comfortable home they'd lived in as a child before her father decided to move them to California. He'd lost his job, found another, lost that one, and eventually landed one that barely paid the bills.

Pushing the old memories aside, she reached for her door handle. Her roots were far, far behind, and her future looked bright. Her little side trip the other night with the bottle of scotch might've been a mistake. She'd need to watch herself for a while. It had been a wonderful high for the time that it lasted, even if the crash afterward brought on a mild depression. But a couple of glasses of wine helped soften the effects and drove away the demons of memory that plagued her.

"Time to get going. Enough thinking." She spoke briskly and swung her legs out of the car, then reached for her bag and shut the door, activating the alarm on the car.

Ten minutes later, Jeena headed for the weight room, clad in the new outfit she'd purchased last week. She stopped at the front desk to pick up a bottle of water and glanced toward the glass walls of the racquetball court.

"Wow! Who's that?" She turned to the desk clerk, a young woman sporting a deep tan and obviously bleached hair.

"Huh?"

"I said, who is that in the racquetball court? The hot guy with dark hair."

"Oh, him." The girl snapped her gum before blowing a bubble and popping it. "That's the preacher."

"A preacher? That guy? No way! Besides, he has a wild-looking tattoo on his arm. Preachers don't have tattoos, do they?" Jeena stared at the young woman before turning to watch the man dive across the floor in pursuit of the ball.

The girl shrugged. "Beats me. Maybe he was in the military or something. I don't suppose he's been a preacher *all* his life."

Jeena shook her head. "No. I've seen military tattoos."

"He may be good looking, but I think he's boring. I've tried flirting with him, and all he does is talk about God." She wrinkled her nose. "So, did ya want water, or what?" The gum popped again.

"Oh. Yeah, I guess." Jeena tried to take in the fact that a preacher could be athletic. *And what's with the tattoo?* It almost looked like it could be gang related, from what she remembered in high school. Strange. She dug out her money and reached for the water bottle, twisting off the cap and taking a long pull.

She couldn't help herself; she had to take one more peek. Slowing at the glass, she watched for a moment. *Huh. Tall, nice build . . . probably married. Isn't every preacher?* The last thing she needed was someone who spouted God all the time.

Time to stretch and work out, then take a soak in the Jacuzzi. She strolled past the glass-enclosed court and tossed a look his way, but he didn't appear to notice. *Oh well, there's always another day.*

After an hour-long workout, Jeena sat in the large Jacuzzi, relaxing her stressed muscles. She'd stopped by the desk on the way to ask if the preacher was still in the building.

Gum-popper-girl blew another bubble before answering. "Nope. He left. Said, 'God bless you—have a nice day,' and flew out of here before I could so much as bat my eyes at him."

Jeena sniffed in disgust. It was amazing the girl could hold a job—all she thought about was men. Not too bright, either, and no manners—popping her gum and blowing bubbles in clients' faces.

"Oh, this feels good." She sank under the froth kicked up by the high-pressure jets, letting herself float as she leaned her head on the edge of the small pool.

Other than the concern about her job, life was good. The job would straighten itself out soon enough, and she wouldn't start worrying now. A grandmother who loved her, a new car, job, and townhouse—what more could a girl ask for?

Sean. "Ha." She startled herself with the loud remark. What a jerk! Why hadn't she seen what he'd really wanted all those months? No, she did *not* need him, and she refused to let her mind go there. She'd spent enough hours crying over him; it was time to move on. Maybe she'd call one of her friends. Susanne or Tammy might want to get coffee or take in a movie.

Her cell phone's familiar tune jarred her from her thoughts. She reached for her towel near the edge of the Jacuzzi and quickly dried her hands, then pulled her phone out of her bag. Susanne! Perfect timing. "Hi, Susanne, how's it going?"

"Hi, Jeena. Did I catch you at a bad time?" Her voice was hesitant, unsure.

Jeena hadn't heard from her friend in a while, and the sound of her voice brought a smile. "No, I'm sitting here alone in the Jacuzzi at the club. I was just thinking about you. Want to go to a movie or something?" Their last conversation a few weeks ago hadn't gone well. Susanne had forgiven her husband, David, when he'd neglected to tell her the truth about a past indiscretion. Then she'd refused Jeena's offer of a place to stay. Maybe a night on the town would help restore their friendship.

"Uh . . . no. I'm afraid I can't tonight . . . and I just have a second to chat."

Jeena was quiet for a moment. "What's up?"

"I didn't want to just disappear from your life and never call again. I . . . I . . ." Susanne stumbled. "I didn't think that would be fair."

Jeena sat up straight and frowned. "Disappear from my life? What are you talking about?"

"David and I have been talking, and well . . . it might be a good idea if I don't see you for now. My last evening out with you caused some problems. I shouldn't have stayed out so late, and drinking only compounded things. I'm not saying it was your fault, but I need time to work things out, if you know what I mean."

"No, I don't. Or maybe I do. David has you under his thumb, and you refuse to think for yourself."

"Jeena, just because I didn't take your advice about leaving him doesn't mean I'm letting him walk on me."

"Like I told you before, David's claim to be a Christian is phony. Look at him—allowing a strange girl who claims to be his daughter to move into your house. And if she really is his daughter, that makes it even worse—lying to you all these years."

"He's not a phony. I understand more now than I did when I saw you. I'm sorry you don't like him, but that's part of the problem. I can't hang out with someone who's so set against my husband. I'm sorry."

"I think you're making a huge mistake trusting him."

"No, I'm not. That attitude is the reason I need to call it quits. I care about you, but this isn't going to work."

"Fine. If the time comes that you need my help, I'll be there for you. But please don't say I didn't warn you. If you change your mind, call me." Jeena snapped shut her cell and tossed it onto the towel beside her bag. Susanne's husband was poisoning her against their friendship, and Susanne had allowed it. Why couldn't she be stronger? Their marriage would end in disaster; Jeena knew it.

She sighed and closed her eyes. The feel of the water beating against the small of her back loosened the tension lodged there like a knotted fist. After Sean left, she thought she could count on Susanne, but she'd been wrong. Again.

Losing friends stank. If she were honest with herself, it hurt. Was something wrong with her that she couldn't seem to keep friends? Jeena felt dismay at the thought. She'd believed she had a real friend, but Susanne proved that wrong. All she'd tried to do was help, and how did Susanne repay her? She'd cut her out of her life without a second thought.

Beneath the hurt and anger, Jeena knew Susanne believed she was making the right decision, and that's what scared her. The girl who had showed up at their door might be David's real daughter, but Jeena didn't buy for a minute that David was different than any other man who'd fathered a child and not stayed around to help. *Men.* She shook her head. Maybe all of them weren't bad—she'd met a few who were decent. But if her father and David were any indication of what men claiming to be Christians were like, she'd prefer to keep her distance.

"Well, hello there," a voice drawled in a distinct southern accent. Jeena's eyes flew open, and she sat up straight. Disappointment set in when, instead of the preacher, she saw a plump man with fuzzy, blond hair and oversized glasses step into the pulsing water. A dark tan ended on his arms just below his shoulders, and pasty white skin covered the rest of his torso and legs. His roving gaze sliding down to the water made her submerge a little deeper and sent a shudder over Jeena. His smirk told her he thought more of himself than she cared to know. It was definitely time to leave.

"No. Good-bye," she replied shortly. Just when she was starting to unwind, some stuck-on-himself man disrupted her day. She stepped from the water, grabbed her towel and wrapped it around her turquoise-clad hips, and headed for the women's locker room. *Time to go home. Alone.* She shook off the thought. She still had Grammie and Tammy. Maybe she'd give one of them a call and set up a visit. Grammie would love it if she dropped by, and Tammy might be willing to go with her. She'd need to tread carefully with Tammy. The last thing she'd want to do was lose her friendship the way she had Susanne's.

CHAPTER 11

Mid-July arrived on a wave of heat, taking the breath from Jeena's lungs when she stepped outside. The town lay under a hush, with not even a light breeze breaking the warmth of the day. The early morning hours were tolerable, but Jeena was thankful for the air-conditioning installed in her townhouse. Without it, sleeping would be nearly impossible.

The drive into work didn't hold its usual joy, and Jeena's eyes weren't drawn to the high-rise apartments near the heart of the city. Her mind, normally filled with speculation about the people living in that much-coveted area, dwelt on other matters today.

Charles hadn't returned to the office, and Pat wasn't giving any details about his reasons for staying away. Mark Thayer had taken up the slack and seemed to wear a frown more often than not. She'd gotten another draw against her salary upon his return, but still not the full amount and certainly not enough to maintain her bills.

She'd take a stand today. Mark had the authority to pay her in full, and it was time he did. No grim-faced Pat would keep her from getting what she'd earned. If they wouldn't honor their agreement, Jeena would find another job. She didn't believe it would come to that; there must be an explanation for the continued spate of delays.

Her sports car slipped noiselessly into her reserved spot in the underground parking garage. She loved everything about this car. She patted the steering wheel—she felt like a mother commending an accomplishment of her favorite child.

Time to go beard the lion in his den, or take the castle by storm, whatever the saying was. She had to smile thinking of Mark

Thayer as a lion. A very intelligent hamster might be more like it. Fierce he was not.

Now if only Charles were here—her thoughts stalled as she thought back over the change in his attitude toward her the past few weeks. At first, she'd been sure he was interested, but that impression had died a quiet death. No hint of a flirtation had occurred since he'd called her into his office and demanded she slow the progress on her designs.

Now she wondered if everything had been a sham, including this job. Requests to slow down her work, late paychecks, the strange conversation she'd overheard between Pat and Charles, unexplained absences when the boss should have been on the job: they all raised a deep sense of unease, questions that hadn't been answered—and the assurance that Charles's so-called interest didn't exist. She'd already used most of the funds she'd been stashing in savings the past two years and would have to dip into her CD soon if things didn't change.

The elevator opened into the suite, and Jeena scanned the area looking for Pat. The ever-present secretary wasn't in her usual place. Jeena stepped into the foyer, alert for movement from the offices nearby. A rush of air hit her face as Mr. Thayer's door whipped open. Pat stormed out, slamming the door behind her.

"You need to go home," she snapped.

Jeena took a step back. "Why? I just got here." She planted her hands on her hips, and her chin went up in the air. "And by the way, don't take that tone with me. I'm not your employee."

"If you know what's good for you, you'll leave. Now." Pat folded her arms and glared. Jeena saw sullen fear simmering in her eyes.

"I'm not going anywhere without the rest of my pay. If I have to find another job then so be it, but I intend to get paid. I don't know what's going on around this place, but I'm about fed up with whatever it is."

"You stay around much longer, and you'll be more than fed up. I don't have time to explain, but you'd better get out of here." Pat hurried to her desk and frantically opened drawers and pawed through them. "There's an attorney for Mr. Hanover, one of our investors, in the other room and . . ." Her words faltered for just a moment as she looked over her shoulder toward the door of Mark Thayer's office.

"We're starting a full-scale investigation into this company, Mr. Thayer." The voice boomed from Thayer's office just before someone flung open the door.

Jeena watched, stunned, as a tall, austere man wearing a dark gray suit and carrying a briefcase strode from the room. On his heels faltered a pale Mark Thayer, wringing his hands. He didn't seem to notice Jeena standing off to the side, and she decided it might be wise to keep it that way. Her paycheck could wait while she figured out what was happening here.

"We'll be looking into your books, your employees, and all of your past accounts. Charles Browning had better return soon and be able to answer for the large discrepancies in my client's investment with your company. My firm is considering alerting the IRS that something is amiss here." Mark Thayer stopped wringing his hands and straightened his small frame. "Charles will return soon, and he'll answer all your questions. Our firm is reputable, and there's no need for threats."

A bark of laughter spewed from the attorney's lips. "Reputable? Ha. You have one week to return my client's money, or we'll subpoena your records and contact the district attorney. If I have to, I'll request a grand jury investigation and drag your firm through the mud. Good day, Mr. Thayer."

The man didn't so much as glance in Jeena's direction, but she felt the force of his anger slam into her chest when he stalked by and headed out the door.

Mark Thayer swiveled on his heel and glared at Pat. "Do you know what's going on here? Why isn't Charles back yet, and why are there large discrepancies in the funds for the townhouse development?"

Pat banged the desk drawer shut. "I have no idea, Mr. Thayer." The nervous darting of her eyes away from his face belied the firm tone of her voice.

"You take care of all the accounting and banking. I've completely trusted Charles with that area. I tried reaching him this morning, but his cell phone seems to be turned off. You've been in touch with him more recently than I. When is he coming back?"

"I'm sure in the next day or so. Mr. Hanover's attorney is probably worried over nothing." She wiped her palms down the sides of her jacket.

"He'd better be." Mr. Thayer seemed to notice Jeena for the first time since entering the room. "Ms. Gregory, what do you know about this?"

"Nothing. I just walked in when Mr. Hanover's attorney was leaving. I'd like to talk to you about getting caught up on my pay." Her hopes sank at the frown that spread from his eyes to his mouth.

"That will have to wait until Charles can sort this out. I apologize, but I don't know what's happening here and hesitate to take any action until I do." He turned abruptly on his heel and strode toward his open office door. "Pat?"

"Yes?"

He swung around. "Get our attorney on the phone and put him through to my office. Then the two of you go home."

Pat opened her mouth to reply, but the door shut, cutting off whatever she planned to say. She turned to Jeena, her face drawn and her hands shaking. "You should've listened when I told you to leave."

"What's going on here, Pat? You know more than you're telling Mark. Where is Charles, and what's this about missing money?" Jeena stepped closer to the secretary's desk and glared at Pat.

The woman shrank back. "You heard Mr. Thayer. Just go home."

"Yes, and I heard Charles tell you a few weeks ago to shift money from this project into another account. I didn't think much about it at the time, but I'm wondering about it now."

The woman's face paled to a dirty shade of gray. "Keep your questions to yourself and your mouth shut. You didn't hear anything, and you don't know anything. You'd do well to remember that." She spat out the words and leaned over her desk, hands braced against the surface. "Now get out."

Jeena backed up a step, confused and taken aback by the hate gleaming in the woman's eyes. "I'm leaving, but I won't be working here anymore, and I expect to be paid."

"Ha! You'll be lucky if you get another dime and luckier still if you aren't dragged into this." Pat's mouth snapped shut as though she seemed to regret her warning.

Jeena stared at the woman for a full minute, then turned and headed for the exit. Someone was going to pay, and she didn't want it to be her.

CHAPTER 12

Later that night, the shrill ringing of the phone by her bed jolted Jeena awake. Who would be calling at two o'clock in the morning? Her mind scrambled to think, and she shot upright. Grammie. Her shaking hand fumbled with the handset, nearly knocking it off the nightstand before getting it firmly in her grip.

"Hello?" She held her breath, afraid of the response. No good news ever came in the middle of the night.

"Is this Jeena Gregory?" a brisk voice inquired.

"Yes. Who's calling?" She slid her feet out from under the sheet and onto the floor, groping for her slippers with her toes and reaching to switch on the lamp.

"This is Sue, your grandmother's nurse. I'm calling to let you know that Mrs. Thomas was taken to the hospital with back and abdominal pain."

"Abdominal pain? But I saw her a few days ago, and she was fine." She needed to get off the phone. "Which hospital?"

"Memorial General. Apparently she's had some pain recently but didn't want to bother anyone. It got more severe tonight, and we felt she needed to be seen."

Jeena groaned. Grammie must have ignored the nurse's suggestion to see the doctor again. "Please let them know I'll be there as fast as I can." She hung up and raced around the room, panic clawing at her throat and making her clumsy. "God, You need to take care of Grammie. I couldn't bear it if anything happens to her."

The ten-minute drive to the hospital felt like an hour. The cars on the road drove at a crawl, and every light seemed to be red. Jeena pounded the steering wheel. "Get out of the way!"

Grammie would be okay. It was probably something simple like achy muscles and a sour stomach, and with the medical technology they had today, they'd figure it out and have her home in no time. Before long, she and Grammie would be joking about her newest suitor.

Her car flew around a corner and pulled into the parking area close to the emergency room doors, narrowly missing another vehicle. She threw the Beemer in park and bolted from the car, hitting the remote security lock as she jogged to the front of the large, brick building.

She tore through the emergency room entrance and skidded to a halt at the reception desk, planting her hands on its edge. "Where can I find Naomi Thomas?"

A middle-aged lady with graying hair and a name badge identifying her as Joyce peered at Jeena over the edge of her bifocals. "Are you a relative or a friend?"

"I'm her granddaughter. I got a call that she'd been brought here. Is she in the ER?"

Joyce typed the name into her computer and turned back to Jeena with a smile. "It looks like she's already been admitted. Room 327. Down the hall, turn right, take the elevator to the third floor, and she'll be up the hallway on your left."

"Thanks." Jeena hurried through the corridor to the elevator and waited impatiently for the doors to open. They slid shut behind her and opened seconds later on a quiet hallway with a nurses' desk.

She stepped out and waited, taking a deep breath. No sense in rushing into Grammie's room and scaring her. She'd better get a grip on her emotions and calm down. With measured strides, Jeena followed the sign directing her to room 327.

She stood outside the open door for a moment, wondering what she might find. A nurse stepped around the curtain separating the two beds and headed her way. "Are you Mrs. Thomas's granddaughter?"

"Yes. How is she?" Jeena whispered.

Warmth filled the nurse's face and dispelled the solemn look she'd had a moment before. "She's sleeping, but you can sit with her for as long as you'd like. She asked for you earlier."

"Is she going to be all right?"

"We did an abdominal X-ray and ruled out air in the abdominal cavity. There's nothing punctured or restricted from what we can tell. It may be something as simple as muscle strain in her back that's causing the discomfort. The doctor wanted to keep her overnight for observation and run more tests in the morning."

Jeena released a long breath and nodded. "Have you given her something for the pain? She rarely complains, and I'm amazed she told anyone about it. If she mentioned it to the staff, it must have been pretty bad."

The nurse peered at her clipboard and back at Jeena. "Yes, she's been given pain medication, and she's on a saline IV drip. We'll increase the medication if necessary, but she seems to be resting more comfortably. If you need anything, just step across the hall to the nurses' desk or push the call button on the rail of her bed, and one of us will come."

"Thanks." Jeena managed a smile and stepped around the curtain, almost afraid of what she'd find on the other side.

CHAPTER 13

Jeena sat beside the hospital bed, holding her grandmother's fragile hand and trying not to worry. They'd elevated her bed a little, and the tightly tucked blue blanket revealed a tiny form. She looked so small and helpless lying there. The nurse didn't appear to believe the cause of the back and abdominal pain was anything more than a strained muscle, but one never knew. Once Grammie was back in her own home, Jeena would breathe easier.

Grammie's eyelids struggled to open. Her normally bright eyes seemed hazy and clouded and didn't light in eagerness when they spotted Jeena.

"Gram? How're you feeling?"

"Jeena? I'm so glad you came, dear." The feeble voice sounded raspy, hoarse. "Could you give me a sip of water?"

"I'd better ask the nurse if it's okay." Jeena stepped out in the hall and over to the desk.

A nurse who appeared to be in her forties looked up and smiled. She peered over the edge of dark-rimmed glasses. "Is there something I can help you with?"

"Grammie is asking for water, but I didn't see a glass by her bed. May I take some to her?"

"I'm afraid not." The nurse rose to her feet and stepped around the desk. "I'll get you some ice chips for her to suck on, but until we know for sure what's causing the abdominal pain, we can't allow her to drink fluids. I know that sounds hard, but it's for her own good."

"I understand, and I'll take the ice to her and explain." She watched the nurse disappear into a nearby room and return a minute later carrying a cup and a spoon.

"Here you go. Just a couple at a time." She gave them to Jeena and nodded. "Someone will be in to check on her soon."

"Thank you." Jeena hurried back to the room, hoping to find her grandmother still awake. "Grammie?"

The frail fingers lying on the sheet moved, and Grammie's eyelids fluttered, then opened. "I'm awake."

Jeena stepped near the bed and leaned over. "The nurse said you can't have fluids yet, but she gave me some ice chips." Jeena elevated the head of the bed as gently as possible. "Here you go." She spooned a couple small ice chips between Grammie's parted lips.

"Thank you, dear. Have you been here long?"

"An hour or so. Are you in much pain?" She eyed the IV bag suspended above the bed, its tube running down to the blue-veined arm.

"Not so much, now. Whatever they gave me seemed to ease it some."

"How long has this been going on? Why didn't you tell me you were hurting?" Jeena settled into the padded chair near the bed and pulled it close, then gently cradled Grammie's hand.

Grammie tried to raise her free hand, then let it fall against the covers. "I didn't want to worry you, and it didn't seem important. I've had far worse pain in my life, especially when I gave birth to your mother. This is nothing."

Jeena tried to smile. The last thing she wanted to do was cause stress or worry. "No more secrets, okay? If something like this ever happens again, you have to promise to tell me."

"Humph." Gram gave a weak snort. "If I do, you have to promise not to tell the old codgers at home. They'd be afraid to marry me if they thought I'd die on them."

"Grammie!" Jeena's shocked tone brought a little smile to the older woman's face.

Grammie's hand gave a small squeeze, and Jeena renewed her grip. "You know I can't live forever, dear. And I'm ready to go home. I've been tired lately. Not so much physically tired . . . I guess I'm just tired of this old world and all its troubles. If it weren't for leaving you behind, I'd love to move on and see your mother again. And Jesus. I long to see Him."

"Don't talk that way, please? You're not close to dying, and I don't want to hear you even joke about that. You're all I have left, and I want you to stick around till you're at least a hundred. You hear?" Jeena tried to sound stern, but some of the fear she felt trickled into her voice.

"I wish you knew Him, honey. I know your dad turned you against God, but someday, I pray you'll understand that your heavenly Father and your dad aren't alike." Her voice broke, and tears gathered at the edges of her eyes.

Jeena gently placed her fingertips over Grammie's lips. "Shhh . . . I don't want you upset. I promise I'll think about what you've said. You need to rest for a while. I'm going to get coffee, and I'll be back in a couple of minutes."

"I love you, Jeena. You'll always remember that, won't you?"

Jeena reached over and kissed Grammie's pale cheek. "Of course I will, and I love you, more than you know. But you'll have years and years yet to tell me. You'll see." She straightened, then turned toward the door. "I'll be right back. Rest now, okay?"

"All right. I'll try."

Jeena hurried out of the room and back down the elevator, hunting for a vending machine. Something gnawed at her mind and urged her to hurry. She shoved quarters in the machine and waited impatiently for the paper cup to fill. No time for the cafeteria where she'd probably find a better pot of coffee. She needed to get back.

As the elevator slowed at the third floor, she balanced her cup to keep it from spilling. She'd made good time. Chances were Grammie hadn't fallen asleep again and she could sit and visit or read to her till she got tired. The nurses' station might have a supply of magazines. She stepped out the door and headed in that direction, intent on her errand.

"Code Blue 327! Code Blue 327! Code Blue 327!" The words slashed through the air, and people began to sprint down the hall. Nurses erupted from their stations, and a stairwell door at the end of the hall slammed open, ejecting an out-of-breath doctor who raced past Jeena, with another man close on his heels.

Jeena picked up her pace. "Nurse?" A sense of urgency hung in the air. "What's happening? Is my grandmother all right?" She spotted a trash receptacle and tossed her coffee, her desire evaporated.

The nurse spun on her heel and took Jeena's arm. "You're Mrs. Thomas's granddaughter?"

"Yes. What's wrong?"

The nurse drew Jeena to the side of the hall. "Your grandmother just stopped breathing, and they've called a code blue."

"Out of the way. Crash cart coming through." Another nurse propelled the cart down the hall and through the open door of the room.

"I want to see her!" Jeena pulled away and started to move, but the nurse grasped her wrist and tugged.

"Wait. You mustn't get in the way. I'll stay with you as long as you don't go past the open doorway. You can stand close in case you're needed, but you can't go to her yet. Do you understand?"

"Yes." Jeena rushed to stand by the open doorway of her grandmother's room, unsure of what she'd find.

Orderly chaos reigned in the room. Precision and speed were the driving forces, with constant motion and staccato phrases filling Jeena's sight and hearing. She stepped aside as nurses shoved excess furniture out of the room, including the bed that contained the neighboring patient.

A nurse positioned the crash cart beside the bed, while another placed a bag over the unconscious woman's mouth. A second nurse attached electrodes to the frail chest and called out rapid-fire stats.

"What are they doing? What's going on?" Jeena's voice smote her ears, the shrill note so uncharacteristic of her normal calm.

"They've started CPR and have intubated her air passageway. They're getting ready to shock in hopes of restarting her heart." The nurse's voice was steady, unshaken. How many of these crises had she experienced before today?

A doctor studied the monitor. "She's in V-fib. Stop CPR, and get ready to shock."

A nurse readied the patient, placing the pads on her chest and back. "Ready."

In the surreal scene playing out before Jeena, three successive jolts shot through Grammie's body.

A doctor's voice barked, "Nothing. Resume CPR and let's give an amp of Epi."

A nurse bustled by.

A pair of hands flurried around a beeping machine. Then a female voice. "She's flatlined. We're losing her."

Jeena gasped and clutched the woman's arm. "Do something. God, You have to do something. Please!"

She couldn't drag her eyes from Grammie's still form. God could save her; Jeena knew that. Even if she didn't personally believe in Him, she knew He was real. Grammie claimed to know Him and said that He loved her. It was time that He proved it.

"Let's try an amp of Atropine."

Bodies kept flitting through her line of vision. CPR was continued. Was that movement? They were bringing her back!

Jeena would stay by Grammie's bedside and nurse her back to health. And after Grammie was well enough to go back to the home, she wouldn't allow a day to pass without visiting. She would definitely—

"Nothing. No pulse. No heartbeat." The voice filled the room.

The doctor stood beside the bed with the still body lying exposed on the sheet. "I'm going to call it. Stop CPR." All motion ceased. "Time of death, 4:07 AM. You guys did a great job; there was nothing more you could've done. Thank you, everyone."

A gentle arm slipped around Jeena's shoulders and drew her a step away from the door. Someone covered Grammie with a sheet, and all life seemed to drain from the room.

"Nooo . . ." Jeena heard a wail fill the room seconds before she felt it rip from her throat. "I saw her move. They gave up too soon. I saw her move!"

"No, honey, you didn't. She flatlined some time before they

called it. There was no pulse, no breathing, no heart rate, nothing. You saw it. They did everything they could to save her."

"I want to see her." Jeena jerked from the nurse's embrace and flew back to the door.

The nurse followed and stood by her side. "No, dear. Let everyone do their job. Your grandmother is gone, and there's nothing more you can do."

"But she was fine a few minutes ago. She talked to me. How could she be gone? She only had a stomach and backache. That can't kill someone. What happened to her?" Her voice rose, and panic washed over her mind. Grammie couldn't be gone. She was the only lifeline left in Jeena's world.

She watched in a daze as nurses began to clean up the disorder. They picked up the crash cart readouts and placed them on a tray under the cart. IVs, discarded pads, electrodes, and other medical gear were assembled and taken from the room.

"What happens now?" She turned tear-drenched eyes back to the nurse, who drew her away to a seat near the desk.

"I'm so sorry. We have a counselor here, if you'd like to talk to someone, or I'll be happy to call your family." She squeezed Jeena's hand.

"No." Jeena swiped at her eyes. "There's no one to call. She *was* my family."

The nurse didn't remove her hand. "Is there anything I can do?"

Jeena took a deep breath and tried to steady her voice, but the sympathy set off the tears again. "Just tell me what happened. Why did she die?"

"There will be an autopsy at the coroner's office. He'll notify you as soon as the report comes in."

A shudder ran through Jeena, and the tears flowed in earnest. She reached for the box of tissues sitting on a nearby table and pulled one from the box, pressing it against her eyes. "I'm sorry. I can't seem to stop crying." She hiccupped and blew her nose. "I can't believe she's gone."

The nurse patted her shoulder. "There's nothing to apologize for. You've lost someone you love, and you'll need time to grieve. Why don't you go on home and try to get some rest? You'll have a lot to take care of the next few days. And you've got to take care of yourself, too."

Jeena nodded, but she couldn't seem to make her body move from the chair. Home. It would feel like an empty shell, now. This couldn't be happening. Grammie was gone. Nothing much mattered anymore. Now, no one cared whether she succeeded or not. And as far as she was concerned, God had failed her one more time.

CHAPTER 14

A couple days later, Jeena lay on the couch, listening to the phone ring once again. Let the voice mail get it. Chances were it wasn't good news. She looked at the caller ID. The coroner's office! She snatched up the phone and began to pace. "Hello?"

"Ms. Gregory? This is Dr. Jensen, down at the county coroner's office."

"Yes, Doctor. Do you have the autopsy results?" She settled into a kitchen chair and shoved her coffee cup aside. It had only been three days, but it felt like forever.

"We do. I'll keep the explanation as simple as possible. Your grandmother died from a dissecting abdominal aortic aneurysm."

"You mentioned simple, Doctor? I know what an aneurysm is, but you lost me on the rest of it."

A tired sigh came through the line. "Sorry. The main blood vessel leaving the top of the heart travels down through the abdominal cavity, then splits and goes down each leg. A weak spot developed in the aortic vessel within the abdomen. It built up pressure during the days prior to your grandmother's death, which caused her back and abdominal pain. The wall of the vessel grew weaker, and when too much pressure built up, it ruptured. She lost a tremendous amount of blood in a very short amount of time."

Jeena winced. She almost wished she didn't need to know. "Why couldn't the doctors at the hospital find it and correct it?"

"They might've found it with a CAT scan or MRI, which I believe they had scheduled for the morning after she was admitted. But surgery probably wouldn't have been recommended at your grandmother's age, regardless."

She tried to take in the implication. Her grandmother would've been allowed to die? "So you're saying they wouldn't have tried to save her?"

His voice hesitated, then became brisk. "No, I'm not saying they wouldn't have tried, but it would have been a long shot. It's doubtful she'd have survived the surgery, even if they'd been able to find the aneurysm before it ruptured."

"How long did she have this condition? Why wasn't it found during one of her normal checkups?"

"The onset of the back and abdominal pain is the only indication a doctor would have of a potential problem. The aneurysm probably wasn't present at her last checkup, and without symptoms, her doctor wouldn't suspect one. It's a sudden-onset problem, oftentimes with very little warning."

Jeena frowned. "But why couldn't they do surgery as soon as it ruptured and tie it off or something? How could she have died so quickly?"

"When someone slices the artery in their wrist, they can bleed to death in a short amount of time. Multiply that by five on the amount of blood that's being pumped from the heart and into the abdominal cavity. When that main artery blows, a person can literally die in seconds. There was no time for surgery. The doctors couldn't have saved her, no matter what they'd done."

"I see. Thank you, Doctor."

"You'll need to start making arrangements for your grandmother's body. We'll be releasing her soon, and you'll have to decide what you'd like done."

Jeena bit her lip and tried to stop its trembling. She'd cried enough the past few days to last a lifetime. Time to make plans, no matter how hard it might be to face her loss. "Grammie wanted to be cremated, and didn't want a big fuss. I think she'd like a simple service in the chapel where she lived. Maybe the chaplain there would take care of the details."

"We can see that she's sent to the mortuary, if you'd like, or do you want to handle that?"

"Please, if you don't mind? I'd appreciate it."

"I'll mail the report to you. And please accept my condolences for your loss." His voice was weary, and the words almost sounded rote. How many times had he offered the same sympathetic phrase?

"Thank you." Jeena hung up the phone and leaned back in her chair, trying to shake off the feeling of weariness that threatened to overwhelm her. The picture of Grammie helpless and dying horrified her. She needed something to drink.

✴

Jeena's throat closed with fresh tears at the sight of so many people attending Grammie's memorial service at her assisted-living home. The small chapel seemed ready to burst. It looked like everyone who could walk or be wheeled had turned out.

Tammy had wanted to come, but her youngest son was home with a bad case of the flu. After her last chat with Susanne, Jeena had decided against calling her. Right now, she'd almost be thankful to see Connie, town gossip or not.

The eulogy was brief, and for thirty minutes, everyone who knew Grammie best came to the front and shared fond memories. Jeena clutched a soaked tissue, unsure if she could take much more. All she wanted to do was bolt—run home, curl up in bed, and never come out. The reality of her loss slammed into her heart with each person who spoke. Each shared a tender moment or sweet story centered around her grandmother, and each brought a new rush of tears.

An older gentleman walked to the front—his erect, almost military bearing and brisk stride belying his years. His steady hand took the microphone, and keen blue eyes faced the quiet crowd.

"Naomi blessed every life she touched, and mine was no exception." He paused, then cleared his throat and continued, his voice husky with emotion. "When I came to this place, I'd just endured a tragedy that I believed would destroy me. Bitterness and anger were eating me up, and I'd shut out everyone around me, determined to die." He reached in a pocket and pulled out a snowy linen hanky, then wiped his nose.

"Naomi noticed me right from the start, and for some reason, she made me her own special project. That woman didn't pull any punches." He waited a moment as gentle laughter rippled across the room. "She told me straight out that she wouldn't tolerate any pity-party nonsense from me and she intended to stick to my side until I decided to live. I snapped at her, growled at her, and generally made her life miserable for weeks, but she didn't let go—instead she sunk her teeth into me like a pit bull and held on."

He paused, taking the time to look into several faces. "I'll make this short. Naomi saved my life. She brought joy back to me when she taught me what God's love and forgiveness are about. I'm standing here before you today, a whole man, because Naomi didn't give up on me." He blew his nose one last time, pocketed the handkerchief, and strode to his seat near the back as a hush settled over the room.

The chaplain stepped to the front. "Thank you all for coming. For any of you who haven't met her before, Naomi's granddaughter, Jeena, is here, and she'll be staying for a while. We'll close in prayer; then you can move to the dining area for refreshments and a time of fellowship." He bowed his head and led in a simple prayer, then dismissed the group.

Jeena sat a moment as chairs creaked and wheels moved, transporting people toward the exit. She'd had no idea Grammie's life had had such an impact on those around her. She'd always been special to Jeena, but she was just . . . well, Grammie. Seeing her grandmother through others' eyes amazed Jeena.

She shifted in her seat and glanced around for some of Grammie's friends she'd met, knowing they'd be here. A sense of pride and awe had threatened to overwhelm her when the last man spoke. How many of the people who Grammie befriended would say the same? Most, she was sure.

Had Grammie's faith made such a difference in her life that others could see it? Of course it had. She'd never preached, but

Jeena had often heard her grandmother mention the Lord. Many were the times she'd take meals to shut-ins when she'd still had the strength and energy to do so. She'd told Jeena that her hands were Christ's extended to others and even the smallest need deserved a prayer. Her faith hadn't taken root in Jeena, but not because Grammie failed to try. It looked like she'd had more fertile ground in her final home.

Time to go. Jeena pushed to her feet and headed for the dining room, not sure what to expect next.

"Jeena?" A slim hand rested on her shoulder, feeling more like the whisper of a blessing than bone and flesh.

She turned to look into Irene's faded brown eyes. A sweet smile graced the woman's countenance, one that caused her entire face to glow.

"Irene, how are you, sweetie?" Jeena gathered the still-smiling woman into her arms, bending over and resting her cheek against the soft, gray hair.

"Ah, that's what I'd like to know about you, my dear. I know how much you loved your Grammie. She was my dear friend, but I can't be hurting like you are." Irene patted Jeena's back; then pulled away and stood on her tiptoes to kiss Jeena's cheek.

Jeena sank into a chair at a nearby dining table. "I'd love to say I'm fine, but I think you'd see through that, wouldn't you?"

Irene settled down beside her and squeezed Jeena's hand. "I think I would, my dear. Naomi loved you so very much and was proud of having you as a granddaughter—I hope you know that. But she's all you had left, wasn't she?"

Jeena nodded and swiped at the trickling tears that managed to escape. "Yeah. My mom and dad are both dead, and I don't have any other close relatives. Grammie was supposed to live forever, know what I mean?"

Irene's soft chuckle brought a weak smile back to Jeena's lips. "Yes, I think I do. At your age, you don't plan on ever dying, and I suppose it's a shock when someone close to you does. But you know she's in heaven, don't you dear? You'll see her again."

Jeena twisted her lips, unsure what to say. Heaven had only

figured vaguely in her future plans. It was fine for people Irene and Grammie's age to believe in heaven because it probably brought them comfort, but she had no real interest in anything but the present. "Thanks, Irene, I appreciate that," was all she could manage.

She stood and leaned over Irene's chair, giving her a long hug before releasing her. "I guess I'd better make the rounds and speak to some of Grammie's suitors. She wouldn't be too happy with me if I neglected them."

Irene smiled and sank deeper into her chair. "You go ahead. I'll just sit here for a while and wait for one of those gentlemen to offer me something to eat." She gave a sly wink and waved Jeena away. "Someone has to take care of the old dears in Naomi's place."

Jeena laughed and moved away. It felt good to laugh again and know there were people who'd loved Grammie. Somehow, it helped her feel connected and not quite so lost. Maybe she'd come back and visit here again, if time allowed—Grammie would be happy about that, she was sure of it.

CHAPTER 15

Stress was piling up. Jeena sat at her new glass-and-metal kitchen table, running her fingers through her hair, staring at the pile of bills. Since losing her job, she'd fallen behind on her car payment. All of her credit cards and high-interest accounts with department stores were well past due—and no one had compassion for hard-luck stories. She knew; she'd called each one. A mutual fund and a small CD were both tied up for another month or so, but she'd decided to cash in the CD and take the loss.

The pain surrounding Sean had grown less intense, but the loss of her grandmother was fresh. She desperately needed the numbness that a drink would bring, and she'd allowed herself to slip into heavier drinking the last couple of weeks. Besides, it helped her forget. She struggled to make it through the week without some type of help, and life barely seemed worth living with Grammie gone. If the financial stress would let up, it would help.

The sound of her cell phone jerked her from the feeling of despair that threatened to swamp her, and she flipped it open. "Hello, Jeena speaking."

"Jeena, it's Tammy. Can I pop over for a few minutes?"

Jeena hesitated. She'd love to see Tammy, but she probably wouldn't make the best conversationalist. Her hesitation only lasted a second. A hug sounded good right now, and a friendly face even better. "Sure. I'd love that. I'll put the teapot on."

Five minutes later, the doorbell chimed, and Jeena hurried to the door. No way could Tammy get here this quickly. She lived on the other side of town. She swung open the door and gaped.

Tammy stood with an embarrassed grin, her hands locked behind her back. "To answer your question, no—I didn't fly, and

I didn't break any speed laws getting here. I was a half mile away and called from my cell."

Jeena took one step forward and pulled Tammy into a hug. "Thank you for coming," she whispered. "I didn't realize how much I needed to see a friend."

Tammy returned the hug and patted Jeena's back before pulling away. "I've been neglecting you since Grammie died. I'm sorry. And even sorrier that I wasn't able to attend her memorial service."

"It's okay." Jeena drew Tammy inside and shut the door. "Really. I know Matt just started his new job, and it's not like you can leave a sick child with a babysitter."

They headed for the kitchen, and Tammy sank onto a stool at the breakfast bar. Jeena pulled two mugs from a cupboard and poured hot water, then offered Tammy her choice of exotic teas.

Tammy dunked her tea bag in the hot water and bounced it around, then looked up. "So how are you doing? Really doing, I mean?"

"I guess it depends on the day. Sometimes I'm okay, and other days . . ." Jeena drew a shallow breath, then placed her fingers over her lips. "I'm sorry. I don't mean to be a baby." She sank onto a nearby stool.

Tammy leaned over and squeezed Jeena's shoulder. "You're not being a baby at all. I know how much you loved your grandmother and what a hard adjustment it must be. Did you take some time off work?"

Jeena hesitated. She'd forgotten Tammy didn't know what had happened at work. "Yeah, but not exactly because I chose to."

"You mean your boss decided that you needed some time off after the memorial service?"

"No." Jeena took a sip of tea. She hated dumping her problems on Tammy's shoulders, but the thought of confiding in someone else sent a surge of relief pulsing through her body. "I kind of got laid off."

"Laid off? Wasn't this a multimillion-dollar project that was going to last up to a year?"

"Yeah, that was the plan." Jeena mustered a feeble laugh, but it came out more like a sputter. "It seems the boss decided to embezzle money from at least one big investor and got caught. The IRS is investigating for tax evasion as well, and the investor is threatening to sue. I'm not sure what's going to happen at this point, but the job is on hold."

"That's awful! Do you have anything else lined up?"

"Not yet, but I'm sure it won't take long. It was too hard right after Grammie's death. I've put in a few applications, and I'm sure I'll land something soon."

"You can count on me to pray. Hey, how about you come to church with me Sunday? We're having a special speaker—an older man who's spent a lot of time in Korea over the years. I remember your grammie had an interest in an orphanage there, didn't she?"

Jeena thought for a moment, then nodded. "Yes, I guess she did." She paused, not wanting to hurt Tammy. She'd love to honor Grammie's memory by hearing the speaker from the orphanage, but if she remembered correctly, Tammy attended the same church that Susanne's family did. No way did she want to bump into her or David. "I'll think about it, but I kind of doubt I'll make it." She took another sip of tea, then set the cup down and met Tammy's gaze. "I'll be honest. I had a falling out with a friend who goes to your church, and well, I guess I'd rather not see her right now."

A small frown tugged at Tammy's lips, then she relaxed and smiled. "Sure. I understand. If you ever change your mind, we'd love to have you. I know you don't believe the same as I do, but God really does care about you." She reached over and tugged a strand of Jeena's hair. "You're special to Him, and to me."

Jeena smiled but didn't reply. Tammy meant well and her tender comments went a long way to soothing Jeena's sore heart. But if God cared, He sure had a funny way of showing it. First losing Sean, then her new job, and now Grammie. She hoped His caring would slow down. She didn't think she could handle the stress of many more losses.

✺

After three sleepless nights, Jeena hit the streets of Portland, looking for work. She spent her first day calling firms she'd worked for in the past; then over the next few days, she called in favors from other contractors.

She trooped from one business to the next, starting with the familiar ones. Something would break soon. It didn't matter that she'd failed to land a job her first day—it wouldn't be long before someone saw her value and snatched her up.

Then she remembered. Travis. He'd flirted with her in the past and emphasized how much he'd love to hire her. She'd never been willing to consider it before. His business didn't pay much, but a job with him would help cover the bills until something better turned up.

There was no need to call ahead for an appointment. She'd heard he had a new project starting and doubted he'd lined up anyone for the decorating phase. Confidence poured through her as she pushed open the door of his office and strode into the small anteroom that housed his secretary.

"Hi. Could you let Travis know Jeena would like to see him?"

The girl at the desk leaned back and nailed her with a bored look. "Jeena who?"

"Gregory. We're old friends."

"Take a seat. I'll let him know."

The girl walked across the tiny space to the door marked "Private," and gave a brief rap, then entered and shut the door behind her. Jeena expected to see Travis pop around the door, a big grin splitting his homely face, but several minutes passed with no movement from his inner sanctum.

Maybe he was on the phone. That had to be it. She'd never been attracted to Travis, but he'd never made any pretense of how he felt about her.

The secretary came out smirking, before nodding toward the door. "He said you could come in, but he needs to leave soon and can only give you a minute or two."

"I doubt that. Travis and I are old friends." She raised her eyebrows at the woman and got a disdainful look in return.

Jeena walked across the room. When she reached the door, she pushed it open and slipped in, then closed it behind her and gave the man behind the desk a bright smile. "Travis! It's been too long. I've been meaning to stop by, but I've been so busy lately."

"Jeena. What brings you here?" His face seemed remote, and his voice didn't hold the warmth Jeena expected.

"I've just finished a big job here in Portland. I don't have anything starting right away. I thought you might like me to put together a design plan for your new project." She moved lazily across the room and placed her palms on the corner of his desk.

"Yes, I heard about the job you finished."

She forced a laugh. "Oh, that. You know how rumors get started. The job ended a bit abruptly, but it's no big deal."

"I'm afraid I have someone lined up. Too bad I didn't know you were available sooner." His tight smile didn't quite reach his eyes.

Jeena felt her confidence slip a notch as he sat stoically behind his desk. He should be falling over himself to accept her offer.

She perched on the edge of a chair. "You can come up with an excuse to let her go, Travis. How often do you get a chance to hire someone with my credentials?"

"Sorry, Jeena. No can do. It was great of you to stop by, though. I hate to rush, but I need to leave for an appointment." He pushed his chair back and stood, then came around his desk and reached for the door. "Stop by again sometime, once you're settled in your next job."

"Your loss, Travis." Jeena slid off the chair and threw him a cold look, hoping it would freeze him in the same way she was feeling right now.

"Nothing personal."

"Sure. I know exactly what you mean."

"Uh . . . maybe we could do lunch sometime?"

"Right. And maybe I'll wake up as a man tomorrow, but I doubt it." She pushed past him and headed across his small outer office.

✳

Fear set in. Over the next five days, Jeena forced herself to face the remaining acquaintances who might hire her. The faces of one-time employers and friends were carefully neutral as they gave lame excuses about lack of work or positions filled.

She was finally reduced to cold calling, going to smaller firms and presenting her résumé, hoping she'd find someone willing to give her a chance. The response was always the same, polite but firm: *Thank you for checking, but you aren't needed.* Travis's refusal of work had seemed strange, but she'd shaken it off. Now she wondered. Could rumors of the court case be traveling through the building industry and affecting her job prospects?

Today, she'd given in to temptation before heading out the door. She needed the boost a couple of drinks would give her. While she'd prefer a stiff martini, two glasses of wine had to suffice. No sense pushing her limits and not staying sharp. Constant rejection was getting her down, and she struggled to keep her mind focused on the job at hand. After the pleasant jolt hit her system, she felt more relaxed and ready to conquer the world.

The boost didn't last long, and depression followed close on its heels. *Not needed* was getting under her skin. *Not wanted* was more like it. The idea stung, coming too close to penetrating the thin veneer covering the hurts from her past.

She stepped into the women's powder room in a mid-sized firm on her fourth day out, sinking onto a small chaise lounge in a corner tucked out of the way. Ah, peace and privacy. She leaned against the wall and rested her feet on the end of the padded bench, wanting another minute or two before tackling the head of the firm.

The door of the outer area whooshed open, and two sets of footsteps entered the restroom. "Did you hear about the scandal with Browning and Thayer?" The voice around the corner dripped with eagerness.

"Just that Charles Browning is under investigation and some type of lawsuit might be imminent. What've you heard?" The second voice dropped, making Jeena strain to hear the reply.

"Talk is he skimmed most of his investors' money into an off-shore account. It looks like it's been going on for quite a while, and his secretary has been in on it, too." A stall door bounced shut and water gushed in the sink. Jeena leaned forward desperate to hear the rest of the conversation.

"How much did he take?"

"Millions. I overheard my boss, and he said the IRS is involved."

"How about the designer working for him? Is she in on it, too? What's her name?"

"Jeena Gregory. She's one of the best in the business, if you believe the talk around town."

Jeena's breath caught in her throat. *Vindication!*

"They say she had to be in on it from the beginning, the same as Mark Thayer." Jeena sat frozen on the bench, her decision to spring to her own defense dying a sudden death. The women's voices drifted away, and the outer door closed behind them.

The impact of the gossip pushed her up from the bench and forced her legs into motion, propelling her out to the hallway and toward the front of the building. She walked briskly across the foyer. The receptionist chatting on the phone didn't look up, seeming unaware of her presence. It was just as well. No need to stir up more speculation. Just get out of the building and go home.

⁂

Jeena grabbed her cell phone on the second ring. She'd left her résumé at enough businesses. This just might be the one that came through. "Hello?"

"Jeena, darling! How are you?" Connie's purr resonated across the line.

"Never better, Connie. How about you?" The eagerness in Jeena's voice amazed her. Had she fallen so low that a call from the town gossip made her day?

"I'm doing fine. I'm a little surprised you sound so . . . good, if you know what I mean." Vinegar coated in honey oozed from her tone.

Jeena perched her hip on a wide window ledge and frowned. "Meaning?"

"Oh, nothing at all. I guess I thought you'd be depressed, considering . . ."

"Out with it. Considering what? I'm sure there's something you're dying to tell me." She didn't care that her words sounded short and clipped. This cat-and-mouse game was getting old.

"Just that you seem to be having a hard time finding work. I'm sure it's only a nasty rumor, though." A smirk colored the words.

One that you're helping along and loving every minute of, Jeena fumed inwardly. "Not at all. I've got résumés out around Portland, and I expect a call any time."

"I wouldn't count on it, darling. Talk around town says you're being blackballed."

Jeena shot up from her seat and gripped the phone. "Blackballed? What are you talking about?"

Connie's chuckle barely disguised the sneer. "No one believes you could work for Charles Browning and not know he's dirty. They all think you must've known about the money disappearing, even if you weren't part of it."

"Are you implying I had something to do with the stolen funds?"

"Oh, of course not," Connie cooed. "You and I are old friends. I just wanted to make sure you were doing all right. But if you say you're fine . . ."

"I'm perfect," Jeena snapped. "And I appreciate how much you care. I need to go."

"Don't let me keep you. I'm sure you've got so much going on in your life. 'Bye, darling."

Jeena glared at the phone. So much for friends. No wonder she hadn't heard from anyone else she hung out with. Surely it wouldn't last long. Possibly the rumor mill hadn't started to grind in River City yet. She might be able to land a temporary job there till this whole thing blew over. People in her own town wouldn't be worried about the gossip from Portland.

CHAPTER 16

J eena shook open the morning paper and reached for her cup of coffee, thankful for the restful sleep she'd just woken from. She was flipping pages, headed for the business classifieds, when a headline caught her eye. A small gasp slipped out as she read the words blazoned across the page: Browning and Thayer Under Investigation.

She scanned the two-column article, praying she wouldn't see her name. The two words seemed to explode from the page—Jeena Gregory—along with the names of the rest of the employees in the firm to be called in for questioning. She pushed her coffee aside, fear twisting her stomach and driving all thought of food from her mind.

The ringing of the phone cut across Jeena's nerves and sent them screaming for cover. Nothing good seemed to come from the phone these days, but the prospect of a job opening pushed her to answer.

"Jeena Gregory, can I help you?" Hope fluttered in the slim breeze of possibility, and her professional voice kicked in.

"Yes, Ms. Gregory. This is Mark Strong at the district attorney's office in Hood River County, and we need to ask you a few questions." The strong male voice spoke in a clipped, no-nonsense tone.

"Questions? About what?" She sat upright on the edge of the sofa and frowned.

"Your involvement with the firm of Browning and Thayer."

Jeena bolted to her feet. "I worked there less than three months. I don't know anything."

"We'd like to be the judge of that, Ms. Gregory. Would you care to drive yourself in later today, or should we send a patrol car to pick you up?"

"A patrol car? What, am I under arrest?" She paced the length of the room, unable to sit.

"Not at this time. If you'd like to drive yourself in, we could see you in, say . . . two hours. Would that work for you?" The firm voice didn't leave much room for escape.

She stopped in the middle of the living room and gripped the phone, feeling her long nails digging into the palm of her hand. "I suppose I can make it." She glanced at the clock. "How long will this take?"

"I'm sorry. I don't know."

"Do I need an attorney?" She willed her voice not to shake.

"We're not charging you with anything, but that's your decision. Either way, please come to the courthouse. We're in suite 202 on the second floor. We'll see you in two hours." The phone clicked, and a blank silence followed.

Jeena spent the next two hours alternating between pulling herself together and scanning the yellow pages for attorneys. Would it make her look like she had something to hide if she retained one? Probably—and that was the last thing she wanted. She hadn't been involved in Charles's theft of Mr. Hanover's money and knew next to nothing about it. Better play it innocent, stay low-key, and let it blow over.

⚜

The drive to the courthouse passed with little thought of her surroundings. Jeena stepped out of the car and made her way up the short flight of concrete steps to the brick building set back from the street. For nearly sixty years, it had housed the justice system for this county, but Jeena had yet to visit its interior. Hopefully, today would be the first, and last, time.

She pulled open the heavy double door and stepped inside. The small foyer had signs directing visitors to three different floors. As she'd been told, the second floor housed the district attorney's office. She took the steps at a rapid pace, determined to get this behind her.

A woman looked up when she entered, peering at her through the glass-enclosed cubbyhole facing the door. "May I help you?" She spoke through a small metal disk set into the glass.

"Yes." Jeena stepped closer and leaned down. "My name is Jeena Gregory. Mr. Strong asked me to come in."

The receptionist nodded and waved toward the four chairs lining the short wall near the door. "Have a seat. I'll let him know you're here." She picked up her phone and spoke in a tone too low for Jeena to hear, then returned to the pile of papers on her desk.

Ten minutes later, the phone on her desk rang. "Yes. All right. I'll show her in." She stepped over to open the door beside the glass enclosure and beckoned Jeena inside. "Mr. Armon will see you now."

"I thought I was seeing Mr. Strong." Jeena stopped just inside the open door and faced the receptionist.

"Mr. Strong is the district attorney, and he's been called away. Mr. Armon, the assistant district attorney, will see you." She ushered Jeena toward a closed door on the other side of the short hall and opened it, then waited for her to step inside and pulled the door shut behind her.

A man who appeared to be in his late thirties sat behind a black lacquered desk. His strong chin sported a small goatee, and his neatly clipped dark hair barely touched the top of his ears. His office shouted an almost military obsession with neatness and organization, with nothing out of place. All bespoke an orderly overseer with a strong sense of justice thrown in.

He glanced up at Jeena and smiled, then rose. "Ms. Gregory?" He waved her toward a seat and settled his slim figure into his chair. "I'm Ryan Armon, the assistant DA." He beckoned toward a pot on the nearby counter. "Before we get started, would you care for a cup of coffee?"

Jeena unclenched her hands and began to breathe more easily. "No, thank you. Mr. Strong said you had questions for me."

He picked up a pen and tapped the end on the oversized calendar on his desk. "Yes. I'll get right to the point. We've called you in to discuss your relationship with Charles Browning."

"I didn't have a relationship with him. I simply worked for him."

The pen continued to tap. "In what capacity?"

"As an independent consultant hired to design the interior and the grounds of his new townhouse complex in Portland." She gripped the handle of her purse that she'd kept in her lap.

"But you worked in the office and saw both Mr. Browning and Mr. Thayer?"

"Yes. They had offices on the same floor where I worked."

"And Pat Semonds, their secretary, did you have occasion to work with her also?" The pen ceased tapping and poised over a blank notepad.

"Yes, when I worked in the office, but not on the days I spent at the job site."

"Were you asked to make deposits for the company or take care of any of the bookkeeping?" His pen scratched across the surface of the paper, jarring Jeena's nerves.

"No. I had nothing to do with the company finances."

He sat back in his chair and laid the pen on the pad. "I'll level with you, Ms. Gregory. Everyone in that office is suspect, and that includes you. Browning has been skimming money for years. The federal government is considering a case against him for transferring money out of the country illegally. We've got investigators looking into his finances, and it doesn't look good. If you're willing to turn state's evidence against him, we might be willing to give you a certain degree of immunity."

Jeena shot from her chair, aghast at what she'd heard. "I haven't done anything wrong to need immunity! I only worked there for three months, and I had no idea what the man was doing."

His dark eyes bored into hers, and his cool voice tightened. "That may be true, and it may not be. We're not prepared to agree yet. Now sit down." He waited till she sank back into her chair. "We've subpoenaed your bank records, and we'll be looking for any unusual deposits over the past few months. You may have been put on the books three months ago but working behind the scenes prior to that."

"I'm telling you, I don't know anything." She felt the blood leave her face in a rush. No way could she mention what she'd overheard and not put herself in jeopardy with Charles. Her hands grew clammy as she remembered the large initial advance she'd deposited and spent.

"The DA is questioning Mr. Browning. You can do yourself a favor by agreeing to testify to anything you may remember when his preliminary hearing convenes." He picked up the pen and resumed tapping.

Jeena gritted her teeth to keep from screaming. Losing her job was bad enough, but being suspected of involvement in something illegal? If this got out, she'd never find work in this city again, much less this state. "I'd be happy to cooperate. Just let me know what you need."

"You'll hear from us. In the meantime, be thinking about anything you may have forgotten." He tossed the pen to the desk and stood, his tall frame seeming to fill the room. "You're free to go for now, Ms. Gregory." He stepped around the corner of the desk and reached past her to open the door.

Jeena walked through the open door and headed toward the front of the courthouse, feeling like a woman trapped in an ongoing nightmare. She exited the small outer office and continued down the hallway heading to the stairs, when a man rushed up and shoved a microphone in her face.

"Are you Jeena Gregory who once worked for Browning and Thayer? Are you being questioned by the DA? Can you tell us if you're under indictment, too?"

Jeena put her arm in front of her face and kept moving. "No, I'm not."

"But you worked for him? Will you be testifying at his hearing?" The questions shot from his lips faster than a young boy firing a new BB gun.

"No comment. Now please excuse me." She ran for the stairwell, shock coursing through her mind and bringing her thoughts to a standstill. The reporter pursued her down the steps and almost to the outer door, only to rush back when the assistant district attorney appeared on the staircase. The aftermath of the interrogation left Jeena reeling, and she didn't speak a word, just walked woodenly out the exit, trying to sort through what had happened.

She wiped the sweat trickling down her forehead before it hit her eyes. What an unusually hot August day, even for the Northwest. She shivered, suddenly feeling as though she'd stepped from a sauna into an icy cold pool. *What's wrong with me?* The intense heat almost suffocated her, and now she couldn't stop shivering.

Jeena stood outside the courthouse, staring at the short flight of concrete stairs leading down to the busy street below. She shook her head, hoping to clear it, but only succeeded in causing it to pound harder.

She covered her face and sank down on a stone bench not far from the entrance, groaning in frustration. Tears flooded her vision. She would get home, take a long hot bath, and have a drink. When she got up tomorrow morning, things would return to normal.

Jeena pushed to her feet and began jogging down the stairs to the parking area, nearly colliding with a woman. "I'm sorry! I didn't see you."

"Jeena? What are you doing here?"

"Susanne?" Her turncoat friend stood before her.

"You've been crying. What's wrong?"

"Nothing. Look, I have to go." Jeena started down the steps, but Susanne reached out, grabbing her wrist. "I just had some legal business to take care of." She tried to step back, but Susanne didn't let go.

"Please, Jeena, I'd like to tell you something."

Jeena pulled her arm away.

Susanne drew a step closer. "I want to apologize. I wasn't very kind to you, but that's going to change. I've given my heart to the Lord."

"I'm sorry, but I need to get home."

"I'd like to talk to you about it."

"That's okay. I've had enough religion crammed down my throat."

Susanne's eyes widened. "You don't mean that!"

"When you called me a few weeks ago, you were right. I don't see the point in continuing our friendship." Jeena nodded toward Susanne's family standing silently by and turned to go, then whirled to face David, a twist to her mouth. "Sounds like you finally got your way, David."

She marched down the steps, propelled by the sadness engulfing her. The loss of Susanne's friendship cut, but Jeena controlled the urge to quicken her pace. No way would she reveal the depth of sorrow that swamped her emotions.

Determination drove her as she walked away, head held high. Susanne had been a real friend, one of the only people who'd seemed to care. *Keep it in perspective, Jeena.* One more person turning their back couldn't compare to the mess her life was in right now.

She slid behind the wheel and inserted the key, then rested back against the seat. She was under investigation, along with the rest of the company. Her recent job search had made it clear that, in the eyes of the business community, she'd been tarred with the same brush as Browning and Thayer. All hope of finding a job seemed dead, at least for now.

It probably hadn't been a good idea, signing a twelve-month lease on that expensive townhouse. Maybe she needed to consider moving out of the area. She could sell her car if it didn't get repossessed first and see about downsizing.

Home. She needed to get home and away from here. Everyone passing her car stared at her. Had word already spread about the events inside, or was she getting paranoid? Surely the court case wouldn't hit TV till tonight. What if Tammy and Matt saw the broadcast? Of course, they could have read about the indictment in the paper already. She rested her face against her steering wheel and groaned. She started her car and threw it in gear, punching the accelerator and squealing out into the street. *Slow down.* The last thing she needed was a ticket.

She pulled into her garage with an immense sense of gratitude. Maybe things weren't so bad after all. The district attorney hadn't brought any formal charges against her—just told her to be available if he had more questions. She'd grab the mail out of her box and go put her feet up. A few glasses of wine would block it all out of her mind.

The door shut behind her with a sharp click, like the distinct snap of a casket lid. The sound that she'd heard at the close of her father's funeral service still had the power to give her the chills. She felt disgusted—she was getting morbid, and all over some stupid questions. Worse things had happened to her, and she'd made it through fine.

I've got to think, figure out what to do next. There must be a way out of this mess. The mail could wait. Maybe a short nap would help sort things out. If nothing else, she'd escape for a bit, and sleeping through the early evening news might not be so bad.

CHAPTER 17

Two hours later, Jeena padded around her kitchen in her slippers and pj's, disgusted that she'd been unable to sleep. Her mind swam with images of the district attorney wading through her finances and finding something incriminating, although her common sense assured her there was nothing to find.

She had one area of joy that had kept her going. Her mutual funds matured tomorrow, and she'd catch up on her bills. It wouldn't pay all that she owed on the back car payments, but it should satisfy the bank and keep the manager of the townhouse off her back until she found a good job. Her credit rating was already shot, so the department store and credit cards wouldn't take priority. Food, housing, and transportation were at the top of her list.

The teakettle whistled, and she decided on her favorite tea, orange mango, then settled into the comfort of her couch and picked up her mail. She'd neglected to look at it the past couple of days, as nothing came anymore except bills. The longer she could ignore those, the better.

What in the world? Her hand stilled over the stack of envelopes, then gingerly plucked one out. Why would the IRS be contacting her? She'd filed her taxes on time, and there was nothing that would have flagged her for an audit. At least she hoped not. She thought over the last return. A sense of dread washed over her, making her feel light-headed. Maybe she needed the wine instead of the tea, after all.

Snap out of it, Jeena. Slitting open the envelope, she pulled out the sheaf of papers, thumbing through them quickly.

What did this mean? All accounts are frozen. What accounts? She felt a sense of panic as she raced through the document.

A few minutes later, she laid the papers on the table, her tea forgotten. She had to call somebody. But who? She reached for her cell but only managed to knock over the cup of tea. "Blast!" She jumped to her feet, anger and fear vying for top place in her mind.

She wished she could call Susanne. *No way.* She blocked out the kindness she'd seen in her friend's face. David didn't approve, and he had Susanne under his thumb—especially now that Susanne was a Christian.

Maybe Tammy would help. But help how? She didn't have legal expertise, and they were barely getting back on their feet financially. The last thing Jeena needed was to burden her friend with this mess. A lawyer, that's what. She grabbed her purse, remembering a business card given to her by an attorney who'd been hitting on her, wanting a date. The man was married, and that was a line she never crossed. Maybe he'd be willing to give her some free advice.

She flipped open her cell with fingers that shook and tried to focus on the small print on the card. *Good grief, get a grip! The IRS can't just freeze someone's bank account.* She waited impatiently as the phone rang on the other end and briskly gave Daniel her name when he picked up.

"What can I help you with, Ms. Gregory?" Daniel asked in his most professional voice. *Ha! His wife must be home.* She decided to let it go, although on a better day, she would have reamed him for it. "Could I ask your advice on a legal issue?"

"Go ahead, but I need to keep it brief."

"I got a letter from the IRS. They've frozen all my accounts, and I can't touch any of my funds. Can they do that?"

"Do they give a reason?" The voice on the other end turned brisk as Daniel moved from sneaky husband into smooth attorney.

"The document says it's because I worked for Browning and Thayer. Mr. Hanover made good his threat and turned them in to the IRS. Everyone in the firm is under investigation."

"So they've named you as a person of interest?"

"Yes. But I only worked there three months and had nothing

to do with the bookkeeping or taxes. If I call them and explain, will they release my accounts?"

"They can do pretty much anything they want to. I doubt calling them will help. The freeze won't be permanent, but they have the right to keep it in effect until they're satisfied you aren't liable for the company's taxes and had no part in the tax evasion.

"If they found you culpable in any way, they would drain your accounts and probably throw you in jail. Be thankful you didn't have anything to do with the bookkeeping."

"How long could this drag on? I need my money." She tried to keep the panic out of her voice.

"No telling. I've seen cases like this drag on for months, even years. It all depends on how far it goes back and how deep they need to dig."

Jeena jumped to her feet. "Years! I can't go years! I can't even go months. I need to eat, buy gas, pay my bills. There has to be something I can do."

"Sorry, I can't help you. Retain a good tax attorney, but they don't come cheap. In the long run, he'd probably take your money and tell you what I have. Tough it out till they clear you."

"This can't be happening! You've got to help me, Daniel." She stormed across the room and careened around the corner of an end table, narrowly missing the lamp sitting near the edge.

"I have to go. My wife's coming. Sorry I can't help more."

She heard the click of the phone before she was able to say good-bye. Great. But it wasn't as if he cared. He was so worried about his wife finding out what a jerk he was that he hadn't even registered her fear.

God, why are You doing this to me? Are You paying me back for hating my dad? Is that it? Jeena sank onto her sofa, all hope draining from her like water draining out of a kettle shot full of holes, and tried to still her shaking hands. It was time for that bottle of wine.

CHAPTER 18

Jeena lay in bed Saturday morning and stared at the ceiling, her thoughts in turmoil. Late August, and she'd been out of work for well over a month. She'd exhausted the top-quality job openings in River City. Prospective employers insisted they weren't accepting résumés. Jobs that would've seemed beneath her a year ago now seemed worth having, but even those didn't materialize.

She swung her feet over the edge of the bed and slid her feet into her plush, tan slippers. Sulking in bed would be easy, but that wasn't her style. Meet the world head-on and come out swinging. *Don't let them know I'm hurting*: that was her motto.

A good, stiff drink often dulled her pain, but she'd pushed the limits the last couple of times and needed to back off. Waking up in the wee hours of the morning draped over the couch left her neck sore and her heart unsatisfied. There had to be other ways of dealing with stress; she just needed to figure out what they were.

She reached for her robe. It wasn't over yet. She still had a couple of places she hadn't tried. The housing industry had leveled off, and no one needed her services right now. Of course, the rumors could have spread their tentacles to River City, since many of the residents took the Portland paper.

Her slippered feet sank into the luxury of the new carpet. The thought of leaving her home and downsizing to a smaller place wasn't a pleasant one, but money was tight, and she'd barely managed to pay her landlord rent two months ago. Where the money would come from to pay her car and credit card, she didn't know. At least she'd saved a bit by disconnecting her land line, and hopefully some of her creditors didn't have her cell number.

She headed to the kitchen but stopped at the sound of the musical chime, signaling someone at her front door. Drat, she didn't have any makeup on, and her hair was a mess. Who would stop by at nine o'clock on a Saturday morning?

Muttering under her breath, she yanked open the door. It had better not be someone wanting money.

She stared at a short, rather heavyset man dressed in slacks and a white shirt. "Yes? What do you—"

"Are you Jeena Gregory?"

"Yes."

He held out an envelope. "You've been served."

Jeena gasped. "Great. Just what I need."

The man turned on his heel, striding down the sidewalk and back to the dark sedan parked in front of her townhouse.

She continued to stand at the open door, gazing down at the envelope. She stepped back into the house and closed the door, then walked slowly to the couch and sank down before opening the envelope.

She scanned the document, and then read it once again. They'd called her in for questioning in the investigation of Browning and Thayer—a preliminary hearing to see if an indictment might be leveled. Mr. Hanover, the primary investor who'd filed the charges, lived in Hood River County and had chosen to pursue the matter there. A sense of foreboding shook her, leaving her feeling like a doll in the hands of a petulant child.

She grabbed the papers again and quickly flipped through them, then leaned against the couch, the feeling of relief so strong it left her weak. No mention that *she* was under indictment, just that they wanted her to respond to questions about her employment.

What was the date of the court case? She looked at the papers again. Monday. Why hadn't she been given more warning? It didn't matter; they couldn't pin anything on her. Get it over with, then move on with her life. Surely the worst would be behind her when Monday had come and gone.

She glanced at her watch—midmorning. Maybe she'd give Tammy a call and see if she'd like to take in a matinee or go for a cup of coffee. Anything to take her mind off her problems for a couple of hours.

⚜

"All rise. The Honorable Judge Glenn Oldham presiding in first district court in the matter of *The State v. Charles Browning*." The clerk's booming voice sent a dark shaft of fear shooting through Jeena on Monday morning. "Be seated. Court is now in session."

Jeena sat just outside the courtroom, and the words spoken into the microphone at the front easily penetrated the thin double doors. She'd peeked inside for a moment and quailed at the sight of Charles Browning's imposing figure sitting at the defendant's table near the front of the room.

Tammy reached out and drew Jeena's hand into her own. "I'm going to stay out here while you testify. I can concentrate on praying that way."

Jeena tried to speak, but her throat was clogged. She cleared it and tried again. "Thank you. I'm so glad you came. I'm not sure I could get through this on my own."

"I'm just sorry you didn't call me sooner. How we managed to miss all of this is beyond me. I've been busy preparing lessons for school next month and don't pay much attention to what's going on around me."

Jeena shrugged and tried to smile. "I didn't want to drag you into it. You have enough on your plate without worrying about me."

The voices continued to drift out and kept her on the edge of her seat. "This is a preliminary hearing, where testimony will determine if sufficient grounds exist to prosecute Mr. Browning. The state will also look into allegations against Mark Thayer and any other parties who might be involved. Mr. Strong, call your first witness, please."

Hopefully she'd be called soon, and they could go home. The doors swung open and a court officer stepped toward her and beckoned her inside.

Jeena turned back toward Tammy, who held up her hands in a gesture of prayer. A wash of gratitude flooded Jeena's heart. She didn't expect the prayers to do much. They never had—not when she hid from her dad in the closet or when she begged God to let her have a friend at school. But the honest caring in Tammy's eyes warmed her in a way she hadn't felt since before Grammie's death.

She followed the officer up the aisle and walked to the front, her shaking legs almost too weak to hold her weight. She took the seat he indicated on a bench near the front of the gallery. It didn't seem possible that three short months of employment could involve her to any degree, but the sooner she gave a statement and cleared her name, the better she'd like it.

A motion at the front caught her attention. District Attorney Mark Strong rose to his feet, an imposing figure who looked to be well over six feet, with his suit doing little to hide the large bones and massive build beneath. A frown creased his face as he glanced at her; then he faced the judge and turned his back to the gallery. "Thank you, Your Honor. I'd like to ask Jeena Gregory to step forward."

The black-robed judge settled behind the dark-hued desk and adjusted his glasses, then nodded. Jeena was called to the stand and sworn in.

Jeena took her seat, determined to get through this with as much speed and grace as possible. But why were all these people here? She focused on a woman sitting off to the side, and a small groan almost escaped her lips. A reporter from Portland TV News.

She'd thought it couldn't get much worse, but she'd been wrong. It just had. Her back straightened, and she nodded at the reporter. No way would she convey an air of guilt.

"Ms. Gregory?" The deep, rumbling voice of the DA jerked her attention back to the present problem.

She forced a smile. "Yes?"

"Please tell us what your position was with Browning and Thayer." He stepped away from the small table in front of the gallery and walked toward her, brows drawn together.

"I'm a subcontractor and worked as a design consultant on their townhouse project in Portland."

"How long did you work in their employ?"

Her lips pursed together as she took a moment to think. "A little over eleven weeks."

Mr. Strong leaned toward her but didn't step closer. "And during that time, did you have occasion to work with Mr. Thayer or Mr. Browning?"

"Yes, on a number of occasions."

"At any time, were you privy to the financial records or involved in any discussions regarding the finances of the company?"

Jeena drew a deep breath, thankful for the way he'd phrased the question. She settled back in her chair, relaxing her grip on the hard armrests, and smiled. "No, sir. I had no involvement at all with any of the finances."

People in the gallery shifted in their seats, and a couple near the back whispered to one another. The female TV reporter appeared almost bored with the proceedings. So far, so good. Maybe Jeena would make it through without bringing too much attention to herself.

Mark Strong stepped closer to where she sat on the elevated seat, his tall form placing his face just above hers. "What do you know about the missing money? I doubt you could've worked there without *some* knowledge of what was happening."

Jeena drew back in her seat and blinked at the sudden attack. "No. As I stated, I wasn't involved in the finances. I spent most of my time in my office working on the layout of the grounds and the interior design of the buildings. Nothing more."

"At any time, did you see or hear anything that would cause you to think funds might be disappearing from the investors' accounts?"

Jeena felt her face blanch, and she worked to smooth out her features. "I beg your pardon?"

The district attorney leaned his hands on the wooden rail that enclosed Jeena's chair and brought his face close. "I think you heard me, Ms. Gregory, but I'll repeat the question. Did you ever hear or see anything that would indicate there might be a potential problem within the company finances?"

"Nooo . . . not really." She tightened her grip on the armrests and worked to maintain control of her voice, then chanced a look at Charles. The normally bland face had darkened, and the intensity of his stare seemed to penetrate to Jeena's marrow. A small prick of fear tingled the surface of her skin, and she tore her gaze away from the smoldering warning. The last thing she wanted was to turn against Charles. Not that he'd done her any favors, but she'd seen his anger and the way both Pat and Mark scurried to do his bidding. Charles was a powerful man; there was no doubt in her mind about that. But the thought of committing perjury wasn't pleasant, either.

The DA seemed to sense her hesitation. "Remember, Ms. Gregory, you're under oath. Now I'll ask you again. Did you overhear anything, or see anything, that might make you suspicious?"

"Yes. But I didn't hear much."

Strong straightened his large frame and crossed his arms. "Tell the court exactly what you did hear, and please don't leave anything out."

Jeena blew out a frustrated breath. "I was sitting at my desk, and my door was ajar. Charles Browning called Pat Semonds over the intercom to step into his office. She must have left the intercom on, as I heard them speaking a few minutes later. He told her to shift forty percent of the funds from the townhouse account to his other account."

"Did he indicate what account that might be?"

"No."

"How did his secretary respond to his suggestion?"

"She asked, 'Do you mean the offshore account.' Then Mr. Browning cut in and stopped her. He told her she was never to mention that again, and she apologized. That was all."

"But you heard her state the words 'offshore account' right after he'd asked her to shift money to his account?" The DA leaned toward her, his face intent on her answer.

"Uh . . . I think so."

"Speak up, Ms. Gregory. And remember, you're under oath."

She squirmed in her seat, then straightened and answered clearly. "Yes, sir, I did."

"Nothing else?"

"No, nothing." There, she'd told the truth, and now her neck would be in a noose with Charles.

The questioning continued, but a haze covered the rest. She testified that Charles had ordered her to slow down on her work and she reiterated that she wasn't involved in handling the money. At last, she was dismissed and allowed to leave.

She dreaded looking at Charles, certain of his reaction. One quick glance at his angry face was enough—she fled the court-room, feeling as though demons chased her down the aisle.

CHAPTER 19

The next three weeks dragged by, and Jeena no longer bounced out of bed in the morning. She slept later than she had since high school summer vacations. Why rush and try to look perfect? There was no job to go to and no one to appreciate how she looked, so she might as well sleep in.

It was eleven o'clock on Friday morning, and she'd only been up for an hour. She lounged in her summer pajamas, enjoying her second cup of coffee. When the phone rang for the third time, she ignored it. No job offers were going to jump out of the brush unexpectedly, and the demands for money never ceased. Even Connie had stopped calling.

Jeena had pretended to be gone last week when the manager of the townhouse had stopped by. Her rental payments were seriously past due, and he'd left an eviction notice. If she didn't catch up on the past-due amount as well as next month's rent, she'd be escorted out of here in two weeks.

Her car payments were behind, and they didn't care that her accounts were frozen—her problems weren't their concern.

The quiet neighborhood grated on her nerves. Kids were back in school, and most adults were at work. Her mouth twisted in a bitter smile. Work. Now there was a foreign word.

A loud vehicle eased to a stop outside her door. The rumbling motor and the beeping of a truck backing up jarred her from her thoughts. It wasn't garbage day.

She pushed her chair back from the table, the legs screeching in protest on the wood floor. The doorbell pealed, stopping her in her tracks. What now?

She covered the area to the door and yanked it open without

taking time to look out the peephole, not caring she still sported her pajamas.

"What?" She stared at the man standing on her step; it couldn't be anything good.

He handed her a folded piece of paper, his face grim. "I've come for your car, miss."

"My car! Who're you?"

"I've been hired by your bank. They've sent me to pick it up."

"You can't take my car!"

"It's all on that paper. They've tried notifying you, but you haven't replied, so they're taking it. Sorry, miss, but you need to open the garage door."

"No way. I want you off my property. Now." She planted her hands on her hips and leaned toward him, but he seemed unimpressed.

"If you don't open the garage door, I'll bring the sheriff, and he can open it. I'll have to hook it up to my tow bar if that happens. That'll cause a scene. I doubt you want your neighbors knowing your business. Or you can open the door, and my partner can drive it off, nice and quiet." He gestured toward the truck, and a man on the passenger side rolled down the window and nodded.

Jeena drew in a small, sharp breath. Were the neighbors already peeking out their windows, wondering at this newest development? She didn't want a scene, not after the paper mentioned her name in connection with the court case. Maybe she'd better let them take it, then see if she could get it back.

"Fine. Take it. The garage is unlocked." She stepped back inside, slamming the door with a hard thrust of her foot. She leaned against it, breathing hard and trying not to cry. What next? No job and now no car. She kept almost a thousand dollars of mad money on hand, but that was dwindling fast and wouldn't last forever. She didn't dare use it to pay bills, or she wouldn't have any food. She kicked herself now for not trading the Beemer in for a less-expensive car, but she owed too much on it, anyway.

A sharp rap at the door stopped her midstride on her way back to the living room. "What?" She all but yelled at the grim man still standing on her step.

"I need your keys. Be sure you take any others off your ring." His eyes looked weary and kind, but Jeena ignored the sympathy.

"You mean you don't just hot-wire the cars and drive them off? You have to have keys? Ha! Not too great at your job, are you?" She didn't wait for an answer, but grabbed the keys off a nearby hook. She stepped into the garage and used the remote to unlock the front door, then whipped open her car door. She snagged her designer sunglasses and leather jacket, slammed the door, then spun on her heel and slapped the keys into his open hand. "I hope you sleep well tonight."

She plunged through the doorway into her kitchen and shut the door, leaning her back against it. "I guess I won't have to worry about paying for gas or insurance anymore." A sharp snort of laughter broke from her mouth, and she covered her lips. It wasn't funny, but she had to keep her sense of humor or start screaming.

⚜

It was over. Two weeks later, Jeena leaned against a blank wall in her stripped townhouse, looking at the bare floors and empty shelves. An overwhelming sense of sadness hedged in exhaustion once again brought her close to tears. But tears were for weaklings; she'd learned that early in life. Never let anyone see you cry, or they'd zoom in like a hawk on the trail of a rabbit and snatch you up in their claws.

She'd come close, though. Once on the phone with her landlord, when he called to remind her of the looming deadline. Then at her bank while trying to convince the teller to release her funds from the IRS hold. Nothing had worked. Not begging, screaming, pouting, crying, pleading, or demanding. She knew. She'd tried them all.

A couple of weeks ago, she'd made an appointment with the manager who'd been the mainstay of the local bank for years. Knowing his reputation as a conservative Christian, she'd worn her most modest outfit. She settled into a chair in his comfortable, well-ordered office and attempted a flattering smile.

"Cecil, you've been my banker for several years, and I need your help." She leaned forward and placed her palms on the corner of his desk, making sure her ring was visible. It couldn't hurt to let him think she had other resources beyond what he held.

"How can I help, Jeena?" He leaned back and laced his plump hands over his ample belly.

"You're aware of the difficulty I've been having with the court case and the IRS?"

"Unfortunately, yes."

"You're the bank manager. Surely you can give me access to my checking or savings account?"

"I wish I could. There's nothing I can do when the IRS gets involved. If I disregard their instructions, they'll come after me."

"But how about my CDs? They're maturing in a couple of weeks. Can you release those?"

He shook his head. "No. I have to roll them over for another three-month minimum. The good thing is they'll keep accruing interest." He tried to smile, but a shadow flitted across his face.

"But I haven't done anything illegal. They're holding me hostage with no justification."

"Unfortunately, they don't need proof—just reason to investigate. I'll notify you personally as soon as I'm allowed to release any money. It's too bad your grandmother didn't leave an estate, as it wouldn't have been touched by this."

Jeena shrugged. "She didn't have much—that's why I paid for the assisted-living program. I wish I'd seen this coming. I would have emptied my savings account and stashed it somewhere."

Cecil stood and patted her shoulder, his kind face twisted with concern. "I'm sorry, my dear. I wish I could help."

It wasn't his fault, but that didn't stop her intense frustration and anger. It was her money, after all. The IRS had no right to freeze it. Her biggest mistake had been trusting Charles. She should have listened to her intuition rather than her greed, but the job had been nearly impossible to resist.

She released a deep sigh and shoved away from the living-room wall where she'd been leaning. Time to finish up and get out of here.

The manager of the townhouses would arrive soon for the keys, and she didn't intend to hang around to see him take over her home.

Her biggest regret was her furniture. With no time to sell at top prices and no money to put them in long-term storage, she'd let most of the pieces go dirt cheap. She'd acquired the smallest storage unit possible for some of her clothing and personal belongings but knew she couldn't keep paying the rent more than a month or two.

She'd finally killed her pride and called Tammy. She'd kept the impending loss of her home from her friend up to the last. The thought of enduring anyone's pity made her stomach churn, but going through this alone created a black wave of depression she'd found hard to fight off. Tammy came to the rescue as Jeena half feared she might—offering a room at their home when she didn't have room to spare. Jeena refused to move the boys out of their space and agreed to sleep on the couch for a night or two, until she got on her feet. No longer than that, she promised herself. Something would turn up soon, and she wouldn't impose on Tammy's kindness beyond a couple of days.

With one last look over her shoulder, she hoisted her duffle bag onto her shoulder and picked up the suitcases. Time to get on with life, whatever that meant. *Maybe something will turn up. It has to, or I'll be out on the streets.* Her mouth twisted in a grim smile. Funny. Just a couple of months ago she'd thought that nobody lived in a shelter or on the streets unless they chose to. A part of her still believed that, but a tiny corner of her mind whispered she might be next. *No. Something will change.* She wasn't like those people and never would be.

She hooked her toe around the corner of the door and gave it a tug. Time to close this chapter of her life and move on. After all, this was as low as she could go, and it had to get better from here. It had to.

✄

The reprieve with Tammy had extended from Jeena's intended two days to a total of six. Tammy begged her to stay, but the time had come for Jeena to move on. It wasn't fair tying up their living room or imposing on their family time. Besides, the extra money for another person at their table simply added more stress to a budget that was already stretched beyond its limit.

Jeena hated to lie and worked hard to convince herself that the end justified the means. She evaded Tammy's queries about where she'd go next by stating she had a safe place to live for a while. Jeena's cell phone had been cut off a week earlier, so she'd used Tammy's phone when no one was home, checking to find the cheapest hotel in River City. She'd made a reservation for a couple of nights, with the option of staying longer if something didn't change. The job hunt still continued, but she'd hit a wall. She'd have to follow Tammy's example and hope to find a waitress job soon, but Jeena wanted to try a little longer in her chosen field, the only place she could make the type of money necessary to put her back on her feet.

She stood on the porch of Tammy's small house, reveling in the warmth of her friend's long hug. The house couldn't compare to the size and luxury of the townhouse she'd lost, but in the week she'd stayed, it had felt more like a home than anything she'd experienced in years.

Tammy gave her one final squeeze, then stepped back and brushed a tear from her cheek. "You keep in touch with me, you hear? Don't you go getting all proud on me and disappear."

Jeena's heart contracted at the words—how well her friend knew her. If a job materialized she'd stay in touch. If not, well, it might be a while before Tammy heard from her. "Not to worry. I'm sure I'll find a job soon."

"But if you don't, I want you to promise you'll come back here and stay."

Jeena smiled and stooped to pick up her bags. She couldn't afford the taxi that had pulled up in front of the house, but didn't want Tammy to follow her down the street to her destination or offer to give her a ride. She'd already used the excuse that Mikey was taking a nap and shouldn't be disturbed—and besides, a taxi wasn't a big deal. Tammy had reluctantly agreed.

"I'll keep in touch. Now I'd better run before that taxi driver starts honking." She started down the stairs, then paused and turned back for one last look. "Thank you. You'll never know how much your friendship means." Tears blurred her vision as she hurried to the waiting taxi.

She'd love to disappear, but a little privacy and time to think would have to do instead. Curling up in a cheap motel bed for the rest of the day wasn't her first choice, but it was her only option at the moment.

CHAPTER 20

A gritty haze seemed to blanket Jeena's next few days. Sleeping, looking for work, forcing herself to eat . . . they all blended into one excruciating challenge. She'd lost weight, and she couldn't afford to; already her clothes hung on her. *No one wants to hire someone who looks like they have an eating disorder,* she reminded herself.

Would anything ever change? The IRS was unyielding. She'd gone as high up the rank of command as possible, to the supervisor of collections. Nothing. They didn't care. She was simply another statistic in the huge government machine that ground on, regardless of how many lives it reduced to powder.

Today, she'd treat herself to a meal out. No more soup on a hot plate in her cheap motel room. She wasn't going to be extravagant, but she'd go crazy if she ate another meal from a can. There was a nice little café at the end of the next block. Heavenly odors wafted out on the breeze every time she walked past, making her mouth water and her stomach grumble in protest.

She stood in front of her miniscule closet, sorting through the small selection of clothing she'd kept out of storage. *What to wear? Did it really matter? Yes.* Her ego needed a boost. No telling who might be on the street or in the café.

She decided on a royal blue, sleeveless designer dress with a small white collar and large buttons down the front. Simple, but classy, and it made a statement. No one would guess she was broke.

A last glance in the mirror showed her hair and makeup were flawless. If only this were a dream she'd wake up from soon. No such luck. It appeared to be a never-ending nightmare instead. It would be so much easier if she hadn't lost her car and cell phone. Trying to find public phones and walking to every potential job to drop off applications made it doubly hard to find decent work.

She shut the door and reached back to make sure it locked. *Not that there's much to steal.* But old habits died hard. Besides, having lost both her home and car, she wanted to protect the few things she could still call her own.

A wolf whistle sounded from across the street, and her head turned, only to drop in disappointment. A dust-covered city maintenance worker. *Just what I need in my life.*

The door of the café passed in a blur as she kept on walking. Four more blocks went by before Jeena realized she was in the nicer part of town. She released a large sigh and stopped to get her bearings. A small but classy restaurant sat just across the street. Did she dare? *Maybe this one time.* She couldn't make it a habit, but what was one meal?

Her mind made up, she quickened her pace and reached the door, stopping to sniff appreciatively before stepping inside. The fragrance of broiled chicken and the tang of something exotic floated on the air. She mustered a smile as she slipped through the entrance.

The hostess gave her an approving glance and seated her at a small table by the window. "Will anyone be joining you, miss?"

"No, not this time. I wonder if you could get me a glass of red wine before I order?"

"Certainly." She moved quietly away from the table and came back with a smile. "Take your time, miss. It's a little early yet for our dinner clientele." She nodded toward the nearly empty room and bent over Jeena's glass to pour the burgundy into the crystal goblet in front of her.

"Thank you." Jeena took a sip, then opened her menu as the woman walked away. "Oh my," she whispered. She'd had no idea it would be this expensive. One glass of wine was half of what she'd planned to spend on her meal. Frantically she searched the menu, hoping to find something she could afford. Leaving was not an option, but neither was ordering anything more.

"Jeena, honey! I'm so surprised to see you *here*." The familiar

voice seemed drenched in honey, with the edge of a knife glit-
tering through.

"Connie." Jeena stood quickly and reached for the woman
standing next to her table, giving the obligatory small hug
expected in her circle. Good etiquette dictated she ask Connie to
join her, but the thought turned her stomach.

"Darling, I thought you moved away from the area."

Jeena tilted her chin up. "I'm sure I don't know what you
mean."

"Why, that terrible business a few weeks ago. You know,
Charles Browning and the IRS, and all those dreadful accusa-
tions." Connie raised a perfectly manicured hand and patted her
mouth, covering the delicate yawn she allowed to escape.

Like you care. Jeena's mouth turned up in a smile, and she
chose her words carefully. "It was simply a misunderstanding."
She needn't give Connie more ammunition than she already
seemed to have.

Connie's eyes narrowed. "Misunderstanding? I heard Charles
Browning jumped bail and can't be found. A friend of mine who's
close to the DA says he left the country and is hiding out down
south."

Jeena shrugged and mustered a smile, but her stomach roiled,
and she fought a wave of nausea. "I gave my statement, and I'm
clear." She forced a laugh, hoping it sounded natural. "I wouldn't
be here, would I, if they were seriously interested in me?"

"Hmm. You certainly look well enough." The grudging tone
and sharp eyes seemed to probe for dirt.

"Did you want to join me?" It was the last thing she wanted,
but Jeena counted on the woman being here to meet friends.

Connie glanced at her cell phone. "Sorry, no can do. Jerry is
meeting me at the back table, in the corner." She giggled, obviously expecting a reply.

"Oh? How nice for you." She wouldn't give Connie the satisfaction of asking who Jerry was or why she'd chosen the back
table.

"If I can ever do anything for you, darling, just give me a call.

That's last year's dress, isn't it? It must be so hard for you, not having a job and no family money to fall back on." She smirked, all the while fiddling with the two-carat diamond on her right hand.

Jeena tossed the most condescending smile she could muster, then glanced at her watch. "Oh my, I didn't realize the time, I must run. Have a nice lunch." Jeena signaled to the waiter hovering nearby. "Check, please."

Connie huffed and moved away, casting a scathing look over her shoulder. *Why do I bother?* The gossip couldn't get much worse than it already was.

She paid her bill and walked out the door. Her stomach growled, reminding her she'd left without eating. Maybe she could find a fast-food place nearby. She wasn't in the mood to tackle another restaurant.

Charles Browning had jumped bail and fled the country. The revelation sat on her chest like an overgrown monkey, screeching in glee and pounding the news into her heart. At least Charles was out of the country, and maybe he'd be so concerned about his own skin that he'd forget about her. How could Connie sound so smug when she imparted her gossipy bombshell? Worse yet, how could she have ever believed that cat was her friend?

Dare she go back that way with the city worker still there? It wouldn't hurt to swing around the block in the other direction. The longer walk would give her time to cool down after Connie's rude comments. *Some people don't have any respect for others' feelings, that's for sure.*

CHAPTER 21

Jeena's money was gone, and nothing had materialized. The rumors might've died down, but the consensus still seemed to remain. Her name linked with Browning and Thayer had cast her in a poor light, and no one wanted to hire her. She'd even put in applications at a couple of restaurants, with no results. Something needed to break, or she'd be out on the streets.

She walked through the cheap motel lobby on the way back to her room, hoping the desk clerk wouldn't notice.

"Lady, I need the money for your room." Footsteps sounded behind her, and Jeena quickened her pace. "Lady! You're only paid up through last night. You need to pay if you plan on staying any longer."

She took a deep breath and released it slowly, then turned and gave the freckle-faced young man her sweetest smile. "I'm sorry. I planned to go to the bank before they closed, and I didn't make it. I'll have cash for you in the morning. Would that be all right?"

He hesitated. "I suppose we can let it go one night."

"Oh, thank you! I'll be down to see you after the bank opens, and we'll get it all squared away."

✼

The night seemed to drag, and Jeena woke in the morning, knowing she didn't look her best. Her stomach growled as she applied her makeup a little heavier than normal. What she wouldn't give for a tall, caramel, double-shot espresso. Too bad this hotel didn't serve a full continental breakfast, but the coffee and bagel they offered would have to get her by—possibly for the day.

She slipped down to grab something to eat, then sped out the side door. A few hours away might keep anyone from nailing her about payment. Hopefully, the same clerk was on duty later today.

She slipped back to her room just after twelve and waited until three o'clock to saunter into the cramped lobby. No one at the desk. She frowned. What was his name? Oh well, it didn't matter. Might as well get it over with. He'd just come up to her room after her, otherwise. Better take the offensive and keep him off balance.

No one appeared, so she reached over and tapped the bell.

"Yes?"

Oh, no. A woman. Where was Pete or whatever his name was? She whirled on her heel and headed back for the hall.

"May I help you? Oh . . . it's you. I was just coming to your room to collect."

Jeena turned toward the woman and glanced at her name tag. "I'm sorry, Maggie. I honestly planned on paying you, but my cash is gone. Could you let me stay another day or two?"

The large woman crossed her arms over her ample bosom and frowned. "Your cash is gone? You mean somebody robbed you?"

Jeena thought fast. It would be so easy to claim the maid took her money from her room and demand they allow her to stay. But had she really sunk that low? Could she lie and put someone else's job in jeopardy? No. She still had to live with her-self, and the thought of what Grammie would say struck at her heart. "No." She sighed. "Nobody robbed me. I'm just broke and need a place to stay."

Maggie drew herself up and took a step forward, leaning into Jeena's face. "I don't do charity cases, or I'd be broke, too." The hard lines in her face seemed to soften a little. "It's too late for a maid to clean your room tonight, and we're not full, so you can stay till morning. You've already had one free night. Don't know why I'm not kicking you out now."

Jeena nodded and took a step back. "Thank you. I'll be out in the morning, no problem."

Maggie shrugged. "Just be out before eleven." She walked

into the back room, leaving Jeena standing in the middle of the empty foyer.

⚘

A knock at the door pulled Jeena out of her doze. She groaned and rolled over, groping for her watch on the bedside table. *What time is it?* She forced her eyes to focus. *Ten thirty?* She bolted out of bed. *It couldn't be!* Why, it seemed like just minutes ago, she'd been awake and tossing in her bed, and it had been pitch black outside. The lighted dial on her watch had said four in the morning, and she hadn't been to sleep yet. It couldn't be ten thirty!

"Maid service." A strongly accented voice sounded outside the door.

"I'm not dressed." Jeena slid deeper under the covers.

"I need to clean your room. The boss, she send me up."

"I have until eleven o'clock, and it's only ten thirty." She could hear muttering in a foreign tongue fading away outside the door.

Jeena slipped out of bed. *Better get moving, or she'll probably call the cops.* Maybe that wouldn't be so bad. At least she might get a free room in jail. She stifled a sob and began throwing clothes in her suitcases, unmindful of the mess.

Jeena was glad she hadn't tried to claim the maid had stolen her money. All of her life, she'd taken pride in her truthfulness. At least she hadn't fallen flat in that area. Fear slowed her movements—where could she go from here?

She could sell her ring, although she hated the thought of parting with her last memento from Grammie. She held it up to the window, sun casting tiny violet prisms of dancing fairy light on the dingy white wall. If only there were other options, but nothing seemed to be working in her life. This ring might be the only thing standing between herself and living on the street.

Thirty minutes later, suitcases and duffel bag in tow, she headed across the lobby, aimed at the door. In her peripheral vision, she could see Pete and Maggie silently watching her trek. She felt a slow flush creep up her neck and flood her cheeks, but she kept her head high. What she wouldn't give for a decent job and some regained self-respect in the process.

She pushed through the door and peered up the block. Hadn't she seen a jewelry store nearby? It wasn't exclusive, but at this point, she couldn't be too picky. She headed that way, dragging her wheeled suitcases behind her, and stopped at the shop window. Typical department-store jewelry with a smattering of nicer pieces sprinkled in, but nothing very expensive. Better get it over with. She pushed open the door, letting the breath she'd been holding out with a whoosh.

"May I help you?" A matronly lady with iron gray hair stood behind the glass display case.

"Yes. I'd like you to look at my ring."

"Is there a problem with it?" The woman put on her thick glasses and stared over the top of them at Jeena.

Jeena slipped the ring off her finger and took a step forward, holding it out to the woman. "See what you think of it."

The clerk dropped her gaze to the ring. "Very nice." She turned it in her hand, adjusting her glasses and peering a little closer at the center stone.

"Would you consider buying it?"

The woman's head snapped up, and her eyes narrowed. "Is it stolen?"

Jeena raised her chin. "No, it's not stolen! My grandmother gave it to me." She waited for the woman to drop it in her open palm. "Do I look like a thief? Now will you buy it, or not?"

A sniff sounded from the stony-faced woman. "We can't."

"What do you mean? You just said it's nice, and I'm telling you I own it, so what's the problem?"

"I said it's nice, but I didn't say I'd buy it. It's used. We don't sell used jewelry. You'll have to go to a pawn shop for that."

"A pawn shop! They won't give me ten cents on the dollar! It's worth over three thousand dollars. It's eighteen karat gold, and these are high quality diamonds. It's not some piece of junk jewelry." Jeena ground out the words through clenched teeth, trying to keep a rein on her temper.

"I'm sorry, miss. There's a pawn shop just a couple of blocks down. That's the best I can do." She grabbed a rag and a bottle of cleaner and began to scrub the glass countertop.

"Right." Jeena picked up her bags, wishing she had her hands free to slam the door, but knowing it wouldn't improve the situation.

No way would she take it to a pawn shop. The ring stayed in her possession. The idea of finding some alcohol flitted through her mind—she'd be able to soar above her problems for a while. But the memory of Grammie handing her the ring pulled her away from temptation. Selling the ring in exchange for a place to stay and a few decent meals seemed acceptable, but she hadn't fallen low enough yet to do more.

CHAPTER 22

The pain in Jeena's feet sent little daggers shooting up to her knees, and her arms felt like rubber bands stretched to the snapping point. She had to find a place to sit down. She felt like she'd been lugging these suitcases for hours, but it was only early afternoon. She'd heard a bell in a nearby clock tower strike noon not two hours ago.

Where was she? She'd never made a point of hanging out in the seedier areas of town. The sound of children's voices floated on the air. Was she near a school? No. A park—just up ahead. Jeena quickened her steps, anxious to sit for a while.

An empty bench close to the playground equipment drew her, and she sank onto its hard surface with a sigh of relief. *Ahhh, that's better.* Shoes off and bags on the ground, with cool grass under her feet. September in the Columbia Gorge was a warm month, bringing Indian summer close on August's heels. Another couple of weeks, and the nighttime temperatures would drop, bringing the first frost of the season. She shivered just thinking about it. She needed to find shelter, and soon.

She'd love to call Tammy. She kicked a pinecone. No, she wouldn't impose on her friend again. Tammy would insist on Jeena moving in until she found a job, and that wasn't an option. A couple of nights outside wouldn't hurt while the temperatures were mild. Parents brought their children here during the day, so it might not be too bad of a place, just for one night. She had a jacket and could use her duffel bag for a pillow.

It looked safe enough. Not many fathers playing with their kids, but that wasn't unusual, and the mothers looked normal. One raised her voice in irritation at her little boy, who kept pestering children smaller than himself. Repeated scolding did little to deter him, making him scream in frustration and rage.

What a perfect reminder of why she didn't enjoy most children. In her experience, many were either spoiled, troublemakers, or whiners. Tammy's boys were a rare exception from what she'd seen. The more distance she could put between herself and this child, however, the better.

An empty bench fifty feet away beckoned her. The canopy of an ancient oak draped its gnarled branches protectively over the spot. It seemed a little more isolated, but safety didn't seem to be an issue here.

"No! You can't make me!" The shrill voice of the boy sent shivers up Jeena's back. Yes, definitely time to move. She gathered up her belongings and stuffed her swollen feet back in her shoes, then glared at the harried mother trying to pacify her obnoxious son.

Jeena carted the heavy suitcases and duffel bag to the clearing under the tree and sat down on the bench with a sense of relief. The screams of the boy were muted, and a feeling of peace gently enfolded her.

The soles of her feet burned, and the narrow pumps pinched her toes. *These shoes have to go.* Her toes tugged at the heel of her shoe, and she watched with a sense of detachment as it flipped into the air before landing a few feet away. Blue jeans and tennis shoes would have made more sense, but Jeena's spirit had rebelled at the thought. Her remaining remnants of pride wouldn't allow her to leave the hotel looking less than her best.

It was hard enough letting that manager know she was down to her last dollar. She'd given her neighbors at home plenty to gossip about as they watched the owners of resale shops carting her belongings out to their trucks. She might as well have taken her belongings to the dump, for all she got.

What is that smell? It was tangy, but acrid, stirring a faint memory. She pivoted on the seat of her small sanctuary, hoping to spot the source. Her mouth watered at the thought of food as her stomach began to clamor.

The light tinkling of a bell heralded the approach of the cart. Hot dogs and sauerkraut. That had to be it. Her nose wrinkled in aversion.

"Hot dogs! Get your fresh, spicy hot dogs here. Just two dollars for the best hot dog of your life, folks. Smother it in sauerkraut for two dollars more!"

Jeena dug in her purse, praying she had enough for just the hot dog.

The singsong voice of the colorful vendor carried across the park. Balloons festooned the top of his cart, obviously placed to entice children and their mothers into his sphere. He continued his chant as he pushed the brightly painted, two-wheeled cart across the grass, seeming intent on reaching the area where Jeena sat.

Her stomach rumbled, reminding her she hadn't eaten today. But the memory of her last experience with sauerkraut caused bile to rise in her throat. Oh, how she hated that white, rotten cabbage.

"You will eat it, Jeena." The distant voice of her father pursued her, and the tinkle of the vendor's bell seemed to fade.

"I'm going to throw up." She'd eaten three bites of the nasty-tasting dish and pushed her plate aside.

"No whining. You'd better not make yourself throw up, young lady." His chair legs screeched as he pushed away from the table. He leaned toward her and reached for her fork, determination smeared across his heavy face.

"I can do it." She picked up her fork and poked at the sour-smelling concoction.

"Then do so."

Her hand shook as she clutched the fork, but the small bite found its way to her mouth. *Don't chew, swallow.* The result was disastrous. She bolted from the table and didn't reach the bathroom in time. The pleading sound of her mother's voice made its way to the spot where Jeena crouched.

"No." Heavy footfalls sounded behind Jeena, stiffening her shoulders. "Rinse your mouth out, then get a bucket and clean this mess up. When you're finished, I want you back at the table."

Somehow, she managed to clean up the mess and choke down the last bite of the cold food on her plate. Jeena guessed her mother had slid most of it into the pot while her father was away from the table. Her desire for the hot dog faded, as the memory of that meal enveloped her. She didn't have the energy to drag her bags to another location. All she could do was hope the vendor would leave.

※

The hours drifted past, and dusk began to fall. Jeena continued to sit, her hunger and depression growing. She stared down at her ring. The emerging streetlights cast a soft glow on the amethyst, creating deep purple shadows as she turned it from side to side. Why hadn't she gone to a pawn shop? Any money would've been better than nothing. What good would an expensive ring do—even if it was a family heirloom—if she starved to death?

She heaved herself up off the hard bench, fear and exhaustion driving her. Maybe she'd find someone on the street willing to buy it. It might bring a better price that way. Her gaze fell on the two suitcases—just looking at them made her arms ache. They had assumed the proportions of gargantuan weights. Would it be safe to leave them here as long as she stayed within sight? The park was empty, and her arms were weak from lack of nourishment. She'd only go as far as the sidewalk and keep her eyes on the bags.

The walk to the street was short, but she kept turning to check on her bags, lit by the glow from a nearby pole lamp. Almost everything she owned was in those three cases. If no one came along soon, she'd go back.

The headlights of a car glinted around the corner, then caught her full in their glare. The car slowed, then drifted to a stop beside her, and the window came down.

"Hey, doll. Need a lift?" A husky voice sounded from the darkened car.

She drew back, uncertainty almost turning her around. But desperation drove her forward. Food and a bed were necessary, and she'd never sell the ring if she didn't at least try. "Uh, no. But I have something to sell if you're interested."

"Oh, I'll bet you do." The voice deepened, and the man laughed suggestively. "Why don't you get in the car and show me what you've got?" He reached across the car and shoved open the door, turning the overhead light on and revealing a cruel mouth set in a cadaverous, lewd face. His hooded eyes leered from under dark, bushy brows.

Jeena recoiled from the car and took a step back. "I'm not that kind of woman. I just have a ring I want to sell."

"I'll buy your ring, if that's what it takes, baby. I haven't seen the likes of you on the street in a long time. You're quality. I could set you up real good." A large diamond set in heavy silver glinted on one of his long fingers braced against the door. He licked his puffy lips and gave what passed for a smile, exposing crooked teeth. "Come on. Slip in here, and I'll take you to my place."

Jeena drew back and stiffened. "No way." She pivoted on her heel and headed back to her bags, thankful they were still there.

The man let loose a string of curses. The door opened and slammed shut behind him. "No one strings me along. I'll teach you not to play games with me."

She lengthened her stride and started to run. The panting breaths of the man grew louder. Her stockinged foot landed on a small pinecone, and she let out a yelp and stumbled.

The man behind her laughed and drew so close she could smell his heavy aftershave. "Got you now, little girl." His hand snaked out, and he grasped Jeena's wrist and yanked her toward him.

Jeena screamed and struck him. Impervious, he dragged her toward his car. What had she gotten herself into? She'd heard stories about women being sold into slavery but never believed they could be true. Now she wasn't so sure—the very essence of this man screamed evil, and her imagination kicked into overdrive as she struggled to release herself from his hold.

Another set of headlights rounded the corner of the block and flashed across the dark grass ahead. A surge of adrenalin shot through Jeena and she yanked back hard. The man slowed, then cursed, turning his gaze toward the passing vehicle. He dropped her wrist and pivoted, taking long strides toward his car.

The rush of adrenaline that had surged through her at the man's attack left as quickly as it had come, and she almost collapsed on the ground. No way would she wait for that monster to come back. She jogged back toward her bags, slowing long enough to glance over her shoulder. The retreating man reached his car and yanked open the door. The door slammed and the engine started, then the car pulled away from the curb and disappeared down the block. What had deterred him? She looked toward the oncoming lights. *A police car! Thank God! Well, maybe not God, exactly, but thank somebody, that's for sure.*

Exhausted emotionally and physically, Jeena sank down on the grass beside her bags, shivering from the aftereffects of her encounter with the man in the car. How stupid could she be? It never occurred to her someone might mistake her for a prostitute.

She pulled her jacket out of her smallest suitcase and slipped her arms into it, trying to still her shivering body. Tired, so tired, but she doubted she'd sleep. A row of carefully tended homes sat across from the park. Would anyone allow her to stay for a night? Maybe she could call the assisted-living home where Grammie had stayed and sleep in their lobby.

She looked down at herself. If she were more presentable, she might have a chance of a neighbor taking her in. Right now, she looked like a homeless person and doubted anyone would open their door at night. No. The light didn't penetrate as much under the dense shade of this tree, and it felt safer than being within view of the street.

But what if that horrid man returned? She'd stay awake all night, just rest and guard her belongings. She spread another sweater on the ground and knelt down, positioning her shoulders on the sweater. She stretched out on the grass and pulled a wool skirt over her legs. Drawing her duffel bag under her head, she tucked her feet and legs under the bench. Somehow, tomorrow would be better . . . if only she could get something to eat.

What felt like hours passed, and the cool night air pushed her deeper under her makeshift covers. Sleep pulled at her eyelids, but time and again she forced them back open. Finally, her need to rest her eyes, if even for a few minutes, overrode her fear, and she allowed them to close. Only for a moment, no longer.

Wraiths and shadows of the past haunted her sleep. Her enemies came to taunt and torment her, and her friends stood shaking their heads in dismay. Several times she awoke, certain someone stood above her, ready to strike. Each time, she struggled to stay awake, afraid to drift back into sleep. But exhaustion wrapped its arms around her until in the wee hours of the morning she fell into a deep, dreamless slumber.

CHAPTER 23

The sun shone softly on Jeena's face. Disoriented and confused, she sat up, looked around, and tried to get her bearings. Why was she lying on the cold ground and not in her bed at home? Her memory returned, along with the events of the night before. Revulsion and fear made her scramble to her feet and reach for her bags.

Where was her biggest suitcase? Her duffel bag had served as a pillow, and the smaller suitcase had been tucked under the bench out of anyone's reach. But she couldn't cram the big one beside it, so she'd left it at the end of the bench, near at hand. She stepped behind the bench and walked around the nearby trash container. Nothing. It was too big to misplace.

A wine bottle lay nearby. Oh, no . . . a wino must have lifted her bag. Maybe she could still spot him. She grabbed her duffel, slipped into her shoes, grasped the one remaining bag and limped across the dewy grass toward the street.

"Ohhh, I'm stiff!" Every muscle in her body felt wrenched in the wrong direction. She stopped on the sidewalk and peered both ways, desperate to find her bag and the bum who'd stolen it.

Her hopes sagged when an hour went by with no results. Not that she didn't see unsavory-looking characters lurking on the street and alleys, but none of them were toting an oversized bag. *Now what?*

She remembered a police station up the block, a one-story concrete building with small windows and petunias in pots placed on each side of the door. She'd file a stolen-property report, and maybe they'd find her bag. A burst of energy propelled her to the station, and she pushed through the heavy glass door.

She hurried up to the desk. A female officer raised a weary, cheerless face. "Yes?"

Jeena dropped her small suitcase. "I need to report a theft."

The woman looked her up and down, glancing pointedly at Jeena's soiled clothing. "What's been stolen?"

Jeena drew back, surprised at the woman's cool attitude. "My suitcase. Some wino stole it from me in the park during the night." She hadn't thought through her explanation, and it suddenly occurred to her that sleeping in the park might not put her in the best light.

The officer waved dismissively toward some straight-backed chairs that lined the wall. "Take a seat. Someone will be with you when they have time."

Jeena placed her palms on the front edge of the desk and leaned forward. "I need to see someone now. The longer you wait, the better the chance he has of getting away."

"Lady, you aren't our highest priority. We have a mugging, a break-in at a convenience store, and a domestic dispute that all need attention. An officer will get to you when there's time. Take a seat." Her phone rang, and she snatched it, leaving Jeena standing in front of the desk, ignored and put in her place by a public servant. Weren't they supposed to work for the public? Wasn't *she* the public?

Jeena stared at the woman for a full minute with no effect. People walked by her as if she didn't exist, and phones rang all over the crowded area. A uniformed police officer stalked across the room, while two others conversed at a desk nearby. Sitting might not be such a bad idea. She remembered her little joke two nights ago about landing in jail and getting meals and a bed. Little had she realized she'd be standing here wondering where her next meal would come from.

The smell of coffee smote her senses. A large, uniformed officer brought in a heavily laden tray of doughnuts and placed it on a table near the female officer's desk, while another man set a fragrant pot of coffee alongside. Jeena's mouth watered, and her stomach growled so loudly she wondered if everyone in the room would stop to listen.

Jeena stared at the doughnuts. "Uh, miss?" She pushed herself

from her chair and took a step toward the cold, unfeeling crea-
ture still on the phone. "Officer?"

The woman raised her brows while continuing to talk. Jeena
gestured toward the coffee and doughnuts.

"Yeah," she mouthed, before going back to her conversation.

It was all Jeena could do not to leap onto the food. If an officer promised to find her bag this minute on the condition she
abandon the doughnuts and fill out a report, she'd turn him
down flat.

Fifteen minutes and three doughnuts later, Jeena sat replete,
drinking her coffee loaded with cream. She had a sugar headache, but in spite of that, she felt satisfied and thankful. How
wonderful not to be hungry. She'd never appreciated food like she
did now. Never again would she take a comfortable bed or any
type of food for granted.

A while back, she'd believed nothing could be worse than having her car repossessed. Funny. She'd settle for a motor scooter, a
clean bed, and three meals a day. Her BMW and fancy townhouse
seemed like things from another life.

"Ms. Gregory?" The female officer's voice broke through her
daydream and jarred her back to the present.

"Yes?" Jeena passed her hand over her tousled hair, aware
that her appearance wasn't all it should be. Better get it over with
and hope for the best. She needed her suitcase—and after all,
she'd been a homeowner and taxpaying citizen for a number of
years. That should count for something.

"An officer will see you now. Come this way, please." The
woman turned smartly and wove her way through the cluster of
desks and file cabinets toward the back of the room.

Jeena tried to ignore the curious glances as people took in
the duffel bag and suitcase. They must see a lot worse characters
in here every day, so why were they staring? She felt tempted to
frown, but it mightn't be prudent to make enemies of the very people who held it in their power to help her. Instead, she remained
focused on the back of the uniformed officer, who halted at a cluttered desk.

"Stan, this is Ms. Gregory. She wants to file a complaint." With a brief nod at Jeena, the woman turned to go, her duty apparently done.

The broad-shouldered officer looked to be in his early thirties. He rose and waved her to a seat. "I'm Stan Evans. If there's stuff on the chair, toss it on the floor. I'm not a tidy person." He ran a hand over the top of his head, making the short, almost military haircut stand smartly at attention.

It was on the tip of Jeena's tongue to comment that he'd stated the obvious, but she kept silent and took the chair offered. His lack of uniform, loosened tie, and untucked shirt didn't strike her as being either tidy or competent. *Great. Just my luck. Get landed with a messy cop who doesn't care.* But his piercing blue eyes and square jaw somehow countered that first impression.

"What can I help you with?" He leaned back in his chair and crossed his arms over a muscular chest.

"I need to report a theft. Someone stole my suitcase last night." Better keep it brief.

"Where exactly?" He magically fished out a notebook from the middle of the pile, and a pen seemed to materialize in the same way.

"Uh . . . at the city park."

"Uh-huh." He scribbled a note and looked up again. "What time? Did you get a look at the guy who grabbed it?" The questions shot from his lips, and the deep blue eyes that had seemed uncaring just minutes earlier were unexpectedly sharp and probing. "Were you on your way from the bus with your bags?"

"No . . . I was just walking and decided to rest in the park on my way to where I'm going," she hedged. "I didn't see anyone."

"He ran up behind you in the dark, grabbed it, and took off? That why you didn't get a look at him?" One bushy eyebrow raised while the other plummeted.

"Not exactly."

"Let's start from the beginning, shall we? Your name?"

"Jeena Gregory."

"Address and phone?" He waited, pencil poised, while the silence stretched over several seconds. "Address and phone?"

"I'm kind of between places right now." She fidgeted in her chair.

"You don't have an address or a phone?" His voice sharpened.

"Not at the moment."

"What time did this happen?"

"I'm not sure. I was asleep."

"So the bag was stolen from your hotel, not the park?"

She'd no idea a man this large and untidy could talk so fast. "No."

"No, what? Listen lady, you need to level with me. Where were you when this happened? I'm guessing that maybe you slept in the park. You've got twigs and leaves in your hair, dirty clothes. You homeless?" A glimmer of sympathy shone from the man's eyes, and the strong line of his jaw softened.

"Of course not. I told you I'm between places right now." Her back stiffened. "I fell asleep in the park while resting, and when I woke up this morning, my bag was gone and an empty wine bottle was lying nearby. I had some important things in that bag and really need to get it back. Are you going to help me or not?"

"A wino, huh? That doesn't sound too hopeful. Good chance he sold everything within the hour. Could have traded some of the stuff for booze or maybe food, although that isn't their top priority. I doubt we'll find more than an empty case tossed in a nearby alley, if you want the truth."

"Aren't you going to try? You can't just assume everything's gone without trying." She willed her voice not to rise, when all she wanted to do was scream at this man, demand he leave the building this minute and retrieve her case.

He looked at the other bags on the floor, then raised eyes shadowed with kindness. "We'll take a look in the area around the park. Where do you want us to notify you if we find anything?"

"I . . . I'm not sure." She stammered to a halt.

"You don't have a place to go, do you, Ms. Gregory? Are you the Jeena Gregory who had trouble at the courthouse? I saw the article about the company closing and you being questioned."

"I don't need your sympathy. I just need my bag back." She dropped her voice. "Please."

"Right. Tell you what. Give me a few hours, then call this number. I'll let you know if we've found anything." He scribbled something on the back of a business card. "You have money for a phone call?"

"Of course." She took the card and stuffed it into her pocket without looking at it. "Thank you. I'll go now. I've taken enough of your time."

"Here. Take this card, too. You never know when you might need it. Not saying you do right now, but the time might come." He fished in the front drawer of his desk and pulled out another card, placing it in her outstretched hand.

"What is it?"

"Haven of Hope. It's a place where they help people who are, uh . . . between places. There's a lot of nice people there."

She shoved her hand forward, holding the card as though it might bite. "I don't need this. I'm familiar with that place, and I can't see myself going to a shelter."

"Look, just keep it, okay?" He pushed his chair back from his desk and stood to his feet, his massive figure towering over Jeena. "I'll be honest. Most guys in here wouldn't give you the time of day if they thought you were homeless. Sure, they'd take your report, but when you left, they'd toss it in the round file. I can tell you've had a hard time, and I'd appreciate it if you'd keep the card. Let's say it'll make my conscience rest easier."

"Why in the world would you care? You don't owe me anything."

"Yeah, I know. I catch a lot of flack from the guys, but I'm a Christian, and I try to live the way Christ would. If He were sitting here, I think He'd help you out of a tough spot. Just wish I could do more." His face creased in a sheepish smile.

Jeena stood and reached for her bags, then stopped and shoved the second card into her duffel. "I appreciate your help. I won't need the card, but I'll take it."

"Have you eaten?"

What was with this man? No one really cared about strangers like this, did they? "I had some doughnuts when I came in, and coffee."

He glanced around the room, then fished in his pocket and again held out his hand. "Here. Take this. Please."

She looked suspiciously at his tightly closed fist. "Another card?"

He shook his head, a slightly guilty look crossing his face. "No. Just something to help you through the day. Here." He pressed a bill into her outstretched hand.

"Isn't that against your rules?" This was beyond her understanding, and bravado and bluff were about all she could manage.

"Nah. The captain lets us do pretty much what we want to, in that department."

"You mean dealing with charity cases?" She couldn't help it. Her surprise at the offer had evaporated, and pride kicked in. "I can't take this." She held out the twenty-dollar bill lying crumpled on her palm.

He folded his arms across his chest. "Nope. A gift given can't be taken back. I never said you were a charity case. Anyone can tell you're a classy lady who's fallen on a spot of hard luck. Call it a loan. When you get on your feet, you can pay me back."

She shrugged her shoulders and tucked the bill into her pocket. "As long as it's a loan. Look, I'd better go. I'm not exactly used to hanging out in a police station. I'd hate to have anyone get the wrong idea." She tried to smile but grimaced instead. "I'll call you later."

"I'm not making any promises, but I will look into it." He walked around the corner of the desk and led the way to the front of the room, stopping where the female officer sat. "Nancy. This young lady will be calling me later today. I want you to put her straight through to my desk. No taking a message or passing her off to someone else, you hear?"

Nancy snapped to attention. "Yes, Lieutenant. I'll see to it."

Jeena gawked at the woman, then turned to the man who'd managed to amaze her yet again. "Lieutenant? But I thought . . ."

"Yeah, I know. My messy desk and all that. One of these days, I'll get on top of that so I can make a better impression." He chuckled and winked, then reached for the door. "You take care of yourself. And don't forget that card. You never know when it might come in handy."

"Thank you, Lieutenant. I'm grateful for all you've done for me. I really am."

"You're welcome. I have a feeling saying that doesn't come easy for you, so it's doubly appreciated. Don't forget to call." He swung open the glass door and held it as she walked through, making Jeena feel like a lady for the first time in days.

CHAPTER 24

Jeena lingered over her coffee in the small, run-down café just two blocks from the police station. An hour had passed while she'd consumed a bowl of soup, a large wheat roll, and numerous cups of coffee, and tried to figure out what to do next.

A glum-faced, skinny waitress refilled Jeena's coffee and mumbled under her breath, "Highfalutin' customers, always takin' advantage."

The woman's complaints ran off Jeena's conscience like rainwater off a new umbrella.

An hour later, the waitress stopped at the table. "You going to sit here all day drinking coffee or you going to order something more?" The surly waitress waited a few seconds, then tapped Jeena on the shoulder. "I said—"

"I heard what you said." Jeena jerked away. "It's not like your fine establishment is bursting with people waiting for a table. But if it'll make you happy, I'll have a piece of pie."

"Fine. What kind ya want? Apple, cherry, banana cream, or chocolate?" The woman crossed her arms across her flat chest and pulled her long, thin lips down till they looked as though they'd reach her chin.

"Cherry, all right?" Jeena watched the grumbling waitress stomp across the empty room to the pie case, then returned to pondering her dilemma. The hunger pangs she'd been living with the past twenty-four hours had ceased, but the problem of where to spend the night still loomed.

If she were careful, the twenty dollars the lieutenant had loaned her would last through tomorrow. The purchase of the pie was a mistake, but a worthwhile one if it bought her another hour to sit. This might be a dive, but the soft booth seat and air-conditioning felt wonderful. The sun still warmed the pavement for several hours in the afternoon, making standing around out-doors for any length of time uncomfortable.

A hotel was out of the question, and the thought of spending another night in the park made Jeena shudder. She desperately needed a shower and shampoo. She'd seen public showers at a marina near the river, but they were only free for people dock-ing their boats. Besides, the thought of taking a shower in such a public place made her skin crawl. No telling how many germs the floor contained. Maybe she'd sit here till they kicked her out or the place closed and see what turned up.

She needed a job. No way would the dour waitress consider hiring her. Tomorrow, she'd hit some of the local businesses and see if she could stir anything up. But without a phone or address, she'd found it increasingly difficult to fill out an application. Where would a prospective employer find her, should he care to extend an interview? And without a shower and fresh clothes, she could imagine what type of impression she conveyed.

Two hours and three cups of coffee later, the waitress clomped over to her table. "Time's up. It's four o'clock, and we're closing. We're not a late-night diner."

"What?" Jeena grinned. "You mean I don't get to spend the night?"

"Humph." The waitress's long legs propelled her scrawny body across the floor to the door. Her thin hand yanked open the door, and she flipped the sign. Closed. The word struck an icy note in Jeena's mind.

"Fine. I'm going. There's no need to be rude." Jeena grabbed her two remaining bags from under the table. She held little hope that her rescuer from the police station had found her stolen one, but she'd call before his shift ended.

Gratitude flowed through her when she spotted a phone booth outside the café. At least she didn't have to drag these cases down the street, hunting for one. Too bad they'd cut off her cell when she'd gone two months without paying her bill.

"This is Jeena Gregory. I'd like to speak to Stan . . . uh . . .

Lieutenant Stan . . ." She glanced at his card. "Evans. He's been looking into a stolen-property report."

"Just a moment, please." The impersonal voice put her on hold before Jeena had a chance to remind the woman that Stan was expecting her call.

She stood in the phone booth, trying to ignore the leers of an unsavory man passing by. One middle-aged man with a scruffy beard and greasy hair peered in through the glass and gave the semblance of a smile. Jeena turned her back, hoping he'd move on. At least it wasn't dark yet. Why didn't that diner stay open for more than breakfast and lunch? She tapped her nails on the metal tray in the corner, wondering if the woman who'd answered the phone had forgotten her existence.

"Miss Gregory?" A male voice vibrated across the wire, causing Jeena to slump with relief.

"Yes. Is that you, Lieutenant?"

"It is. I'm sorry I don't have good news."

"You didn't find it."

"No. I went to the area you mentioned and questioned a number of transients who hang out in that neighborhood. No one will admit to seeing anything."

"I see." She leaned her forehead against the glass, allowing a small sigh to escape.

"Have you found a place to stay?" His voice changed from that of an officer to a person who cared.

"I'm fine. I had a good meal, and I've got things under control, thanks." No way would she let this man do more. In her experience, men who started out with kindness usually had an ulterior motive. It wouldn't be long before he'd have expectations. After all, look at Sean. She'd cared about him, and he'd made it clear he'd only wanted one thing.

"All right, glad to hear it." His voice sounded skeptical, but he didn't push. "Let me know if you need anything, and feel free to check back in a week, in case anything changes."

As she hung up the phone, a feeling close to desolation flooded her heart. Her contact with Lieutenant Stan encompassed the only kindness she'd encountered recently. Too bad she didn't dare trust him.

Her skin crawled, and her stomach felt sick at the thought of leaving the safety of the booth. She'd been thrown out of her house, kicked out of a two-bit hotel, practically mugged, robbed of her last belongings, and reduced to taking charity from a cop. What next? And where in the world could she sleep tonight? How about her old friend Susanne? No. Her husband, David, wouldn't be happy if Jeena showed up at their door. Besides, Susanne had made it clear that their friendship had ended.

A thought struggled to take a foothold in her mind, but she plucked it out before it had time to take root. "No! I will not call that shelter. I'm not sinking that low." She spoke louder than she'd realized, causing a woman headed toward the booth to veer out and around the glass enclosure.

She slammed open the door of the booth, grabbed her bags, and strode down the street, feeling like a woman pursued by ghosts tugging at her coattails. Anything but the shelter. Only completely down-and-out people stayed there. She couldn't accept that her life had come to this. Fear shivered across her skin at the thought of another night in the park. There had to be an alternative.

⚜

Three hours later, dusk crept up, and Jeena's resolve weakened. She sat on a bench near the street. Maybe she could hop a bus, ride it as far as it would take her, and hope for the best. She scowled, disgusted at herself. She was an intelligent woman, but no one could tell it these past few days. Hunger and fatigue did strange things to a person's mind. Working at a fast-food joint sounded good right now—at least they might offer meals with the job.

Could she really handle spending another night outside? What if the man who'd stolen her suitcase hadn't been a wino? What if Charles had sent him, hoping to get even with her for testifying against him? Maybe the bum had been sent to hurt her but lost his nerve and taken the bag instead. She shivered and rubbed her arms, chilled at the thought. Charles was capable of that, but could exhaustion be driving her imagination? She wasn't certain what was real anymore.

She unzipped her bag, pulled out a heavy woolen sweater, and slipped it over her head. Another night in the park might be free, but the danger and isolation of last night didn't increase its appeal. She had to get out of here and find a safe place to sleep, if only for one night. She didn't have to make a commitment. If the shelter let her stay tonight, she'd get her bearings and start over tomorrow. One good thing about the shelter: Charles wouldn't think of looking there.

The phone booth she'd used earlier seemed miles away. She jogged the entire way, hefting her bags and struggling to balance her load. By the time she reached it, her breath came in ragged gasps. *Relax. Don't panic.* She threw her suitcase and duffel bag inside, slamming the door behind. She peered back the way she'd come and drew a ragged breath. No one appeared to be following.

Another thought slammed into her tired brain, right after she dropped her money into the slot. Tammy. Maybe just one more night? She started to dial, then hung up the phone, hearing the jingle of the quarters fall into the coin return. Her friend would be horrified at how far she'd fallen. She didn't want anyone she knew to see her. At the shelter, she'd be anonymous. Maybe she'd get lucky, and that woman who had helped her when she donated the clothes would answer the phone. What was her name? Rachel, that was it. Funny how that had stuck in her mind.

She fished out the change and squinted at the number on the card in the dim overhead light of the booth. The tight enclosure stank. Someone must have gotten sick in it recently. Disgusting. She shivered to think what the bottoms of her bags looked and smelled like.

Ringing sounded in the receiver pressed against her ear, and she felt a moment of fear. What in the world would she say? She almost hung up. Almost, but not quite. One more peek into the darkness firmed her resolve.

A woman's voice floated over the line, and fingers of peace stroked Jeena's spirit. "Haven of Hope, may I help you?"

"Would Rachel be working this evening?" Jeena stood bolt upright, doing her best not to touch the sides of the offensive cubicle.

"This is Rachel. Who's calling?"

"Jeena Gregory. You won't remember me. I dropped off a couple of boxes there, and you gave me your card." She stopped, unsure where to take the conversation.

"Jeena. Of course I remember you." Rachel's voice shimmered with warmth.

"Oh. Well . . ."

"What can I do for you?"

"I need a place to stay." Her heart thudded loudly in her chest, horrified at the words she'd blurted.

Rachel didn't hesitate. "That shouldn't be a problem."

"I–I was hoping I might be able to stay at your house for one night . . . or maybe you could loan me the money for a hotel, just for a couple of days?"

"I'm sorry, I can't. Policy at the shelter is firm on both counts. We're not to offer our house to anyone or provide cash. That might sound harsh, but over the years, the administration found it better for everyone involved if a person in need was directed to the shelter."

"Oh." She swallowed past the lump in her throat. Jeena hadn't expected much more, but the thought of a night at the shelter stung. She didn't fit with those kinds of people. Most of them lived their lives on the street and had never held a job. But better that for a night than the park. "So are you allowed to offer me a room at the shelter?"

"Absolutely. That's not a problem. Where are you? Can you get here, or do you need a ride?"

"I'm at Sixth and Benson, and no, I don't have a ride. I'm at a pay phone right now, outside Terry's Café." The words spilled out, unchecked.

"I'm getting off work in five minutes. Stay there. I'll come pick you up." The phone clicked off, and Jeena stood staring at the quiet instrument.

"Amazing. I'm spending the night at a women's shelter, and I'm actually relieved. That would be funny if it weren't so pathetic." She nudged the door open with her toe, positive a hideous disease would attach itself if her skin touched the glass. A wooden bench sat beneath an advertisement for a taxi service, but it looked relatively clean and offered a place to wait.

Just one night. Maybe that's all I'll have to endure. Surely one of the job applications I've submitted will come through soon. She scowled and shook her head. They couldn't track her down with her cell service disconnected. Checking in with the more promising ones might be a good idea.

CHAPTER 25

J eena glanced at her watch. A long, dreary half hour had dragged by with no sign of Rachel. Yet another person had broken their word. She shouldn't be surprised. People weren't dependable, and nobody really cared. The lieutenant had almost succeeded in lighting a candle of hope in her heart, but his kind was rare. Definitely the exception rather than the rule. Rachel had impressed her as different from the average person, but she'd proved Jeena wrong.

As Jeena leaned over and pulled her bag out from under the hard wooden bench, her back screamed in protest. The strap settling on her shoulder felt like a baby elephant had taken up residence in her duffel. Time to move on, wherever "on" happened to be.

"Jeena?" The soft voice sounded a car length away but still caused Jeena to start. How in the world had a car pulled to the curb and she had missed it? She must be more tired than she'd realized.

"Rachel?" She peered at the car in the semi-darkness, unsure of what to expect. What appeared in the glow of the street lamp pushed her back a step.

Sitting beside the curb was an older station wagon. Not one of the newer, all-wheel-drive models, but an ancient wagon, wood side panels and all. The back end looked long enough to hold an entire baseball team of Little Leaguers, and what she could see of the paint job looked as though a sanding wheel had run across it, handled by a drunk. A large dent mashed the fender in until it almost touched the tire.

"Is this your car?" Jeena sat back on the bench and hooked her toes around its legs. No way could that car be safe.

Rachel shoved open her door and Jeena winced at the screeching noise that tore from the hinges. Rachel stepped out and walked to where she sat. "I'm sorry I'm late. My car had a flat. Someone donated this car to the shelter a few days ago. A mechanic said it's safe to drive. It's not the classiest ride in town, but it'll get us to the shelter okay."

"I . . . maybe I should call a friend." Jeena reached for the bag at her feet and fiddled with the handle.

"It's pretty late to call anyone. But I can wait till you get in touch with them if you want."

Jeena sat frozen, feeling trapped between two impossible choices. Bother Tammy, who'd already done too much—or climb into the death trap sitting on the curb and take her chances at the shelter. Neither looked promising, but the idea of spending another night on the grass with winos and lecherous men haunting her sleep made up her mind.

She plunged into the treacherous waters. "You're right. It's late, and you made the trip out here to get me. I'll come." She tried, but it wasn't as gracious as it could have been.

"Let me help." Rachel slung the duffel bag over her shoulder and grabbed the handle of the suitcase before Jeena had a chance to blink. "You're probably exhausted. Let's get you home."

Home. What a funny thought. Did anyone really call a shelter home? Jeena climbed into the car and searched for a seat belt.

"Sorry. We need to have your side fixed. Looks like somebody got mad and took a knife to it," Rachel said. "Don't worry. I won't wreck on the way. You can slip into the back if you'd feel better."

"I'm not worried about it. It doesn't look like this car will break any speed records, and I doubt it would make any difference to the car if you did wreck." Jeena tried to smile.

Rachel chuckled and patted the steering wheel. "You're probably right. Poor old Rita would never know the difference."

"Rita?" What kind of crazy world was she heading for, anyway?

"Sorry. A silly habit I have of naming cars when they're old and have lots of character."

"Oh, is that what you call it. Character." Jeena sniffed, then mustered a half smile.

Rachel glanced at her passenger without answering.

"But I'm guessing I'm not looking much better," Jeena said. *Great. She'll kick me out before we even get there.* "I really do appreciate you picking me up."

"Can you tell me a little about what's going on?"

The abrupt change in topic jerked Jeena around. "Going on?"

Rachel kept her eyes on the road. "Yeah. Needing a place to stay and all?"

"Oh, that. Well, I'm kind of short on cash right now . . ." Jeena let her words drift off, unsure of how much to reveal.

"How about your house? And the new job you were starting?"

Jeena stifled a groan. She'd completely forgotten their conversation about her job. "Uh . . . that kind of fell through. You don't read the papers?"

"Not much. I'm pretty busy, and quite frankly, I don't enjoy all the negative garbage."

"I'm sure you'll hear about it sooner or later." Jeena paused and stared out the window at the silent businesses they passed by. "The owner of the place where I worked embezzled money from an investor and transferred it into an overseas account. I guess he's been doing it for months—possibly years—and finally got caught. He's under investigation by the IRS and the county DA. I lost my job as a result."

"That's terrible!"

"That's not the half of it." The sympathy in Rachel's tone pulled Jeena forward. "I had nothing to do with it, but the IRS froze my accounts. I couldn't pay my bills, and no one in town would give me a job. Then to top it off, the bank repo'd my car and I got evicted from my house. How's that for luck?" She was out of breath by the time she finished and amazed at what had spilled from her lips. No way had she intended to disclose so much. What was it about this woman that made her feel safe?

"I'm sorry you've been hit with so much trouble, but I doubt luck had anything to do with it. We make our own choices, and our lives are often a reflection of those choices. God may be trying to speak to you." Rachel spoke quietly, and she glanced at Jeena.

"He sure has a warped sense of humor in how He's going about it. I don't want anything to do with Him, and I'm sure He feels the same. Besides, if there really is a loving God, I don't think He'd be letting so much garbage happen."

"What kind of garbage?"

"Besides what's happened to me. You know. Murders, child abuse, wars . . . all the miserable things people do to each other. Especially the cruelty to little kids. That's the worst." Her voice sounded harsh even in her own ears, but Jeena didn't care. God didn't worry about kids; she knew that from experience. And those memories dug their talons deep into her mind. She didn't give a rip right now if she made Rachel angry.

"You're wrong, you know." Rachel's calm voice spoke again, seemingly unruffled by Jeena's anger.

"About what?"

"That God doesn't care. He cared so much He died for you. I'd say that's a pretty dramatic way of showing His love."

"Even if that were true, it wasn't for me. I'm as good as anyone else, and better than a lot of people I know. Besides, anything He did was for the people who lived at that time." Jeena stared straight ahead. How much longer till they got to this place? Was Rachel driving in circles trying to prolong the time she'd be trapped in this car?

"The Bible says He knew you while you were still in your mother's womb. He's numbered every hair on your head and loves you with an everlasting love. I'd say that's pretty personal, wouldn't you?" Rachel shot a look across the car, the light from passing headlights illuminating the small smile on her face.

"Yeah, *if* you buy all that stuff in the Bible, but I don't. Besides, you didn't answer the question about why God lets evil happen to innocent people. If He's so all powerful, He could make everyone stop killing each other."

"Yes, I'm sure it looks that way."

"So you think you have an answer?"

"I'm not claiming I have all the answers, but I'll tell you what I think based on what I've read in the Bible."

"Sure. Go ahead. Guess I don't have anything else to do."

"I'm sorry about the car. I'm driving a little slower since I'm not familiar with it, but we'll be there soon."

Jeena shrugged. "No big deal."

The progress of the car slowed as Rachel braked for a red light. They were headed into the older district of town. Streetlights sent their glow over the blank windows of old buildings staring like glowering gnomes into the night. Nothing about this part of town reassured Jeena she'd made the right choice. She shivered and pulled her jacket closer around her shoulders, suddenly wishing she'd called Tammy instead. Maybe when she arrived at the shelter, she'd use the phone. The illuminated dial on her watch showed nine o'clock. Too late to bother Tammy now.

Rachel smiled, then eased the accelerator down and moved the car forward again. "I think you're confusing people with God."

Jeena frowned and shook her head, then realized Rachel couldn't see the motion inside the dark car. "I don't get it."

"You seem to think God causes bad things to happen. He doesn't. People do. You can't blame Him for man's choices."

"But if He's all powerful like you Christians claim, He could stop it." She leaned back and crossed her arms over her chest.

The car navigated a hard right turn and straightened out on the road before Rachel answered. "He gave people free will. He didn't want robots. He created us able to choose—so if we decide to love and follow Him, we do it because we want to, not because He forces us."

"Yeah? But that doesn't answer the question about kids getting hurt and people doing horrible things all the time."

"Just like He doesn't force us to love Him, He won't force us to obey His laws, either. He loves us and wants us to love Him in return. Evil is real and has its own ruler who is constantly working to force his will on others, unlike God who wants us to come to Him out of our own free will. We can choose to obey one or the other. There is no in-between."

Jeena clamped her mouth shut, not wanting to reply. The entire conversation made her uncomfortable. Right now, all she cared about was a hot bath, then crawling into a warm bed and being left alone.

The brakes squealed, and the engine coughed, giving one final sputter before dying. Rachel switched off the lights and turned toward Jeena. "We're here. I'll take you in and get you settled. I don't have all the answers, but I'm willing to talk any time you have questions." She opened the door, and the dim overhead light feebly lit up the interior of the car, revealing a warm smile on the pretty face.

"Thanks. I appreciate what you've done already. I don't think I'll have any more questions, but I am a little hungry. Do you think I could get a sandwich or something before going to bed?"

"Sure. We'll take your suitcases in, then grab you something to eat. Before we do that, though, we need to make a quick stop at the nurse's station."

Jeena stopped midair on the way to grabbing her duffel. "Why? I'm feeling fine."

"I'm sure it won't be an issue, but we have a no drug, no alcohol policy. Everyone who comes in, even for just one night, has to take a Breathalyzer and a drug test."

Jeena felt her face redden. "I don't do drugs, and although I do enjoy a glass of wine occasionally, I haven't been drinking."

"I understand, but we often have mothers with children here, and we can't take any chances. I'm sorry if you're uncomfortable, but it won't take long."

Jeena tried to hide her dismay. Fear sent small prickles down her spine. How long since her last drink of hard alcohol? Would it show up on a test? Surely not. "You're right, it makes me uncomfortable. I'm not a street person. I owned my home and had a very respectable job. Can you make an exception this once?" She kept the anxiety from her voice and gave what she hoped was her most winning smile.

Rachel shook her head, true regret showing on her face. "I'm sorry, no. Doing so is cause for dismissal. But since you don't use drugs, there won't be a problem." She swung open her door and grasped the back-door handle, drawing Jeena's duffel bag out onto the sidewalk.

Jeena had no choice but to follow. This was humiliating, to say the least. If only she had somewhere else to stay. She opened her mouth, then realized what she intended and snapped it shut.

"Right. There won't be a problem. Let's get this over with." She swung her legs across the doorframe and reached back to grab her suitcase. "I just need a shower and some sleep. May I go to bed after the tests?"

"Sure. It won't take long."

Jeena hesitated a moment longer, watching Rachel walk toward the front door of the very building she'd vowed never to come back to again. She didn't belong in this world.

CHAPTER 26

The distasteful drug test was finished, and Jeena sat in Rachel's small office, nursing a tired headache. It felt as though she'd answered a hundred questions, when all she wanted was privacy and a comfortable bed.

"Mrs. Williams?" A man stepped around the doorframe and into the room. "Oh, I'm sorry. I thought I'd find Mrs. Williams here."

Rachel raised her eyes from the form she'd been filling in. "Hi, Pastor Paul. Mrs. Williams headed to Annie's room. She told me you'd be stopping by and asked that I point you in the right direction."

He smiled. "I'm sorry if I made you wait. I know you're usually off by now."

"I'm just getting some paperwork filled out for Jeena, so it's not a problem." She waved toward Jeena. "Jeena, this is Pastor Paul Grant. He volunteers here part-time as our pastor and counselor."

Paul smiled and nodded briefly. "Happy to meet you. It's always nice to see more help coming in."

Jeena felt a slow burn work its way up to her face, and she looked away. "I'm not working here."

"Oh. I'm sorry. Well, I'm glad to meet you anyway. I'd better get up to Annie's room." He backed out the door, then stopped. "Uh . . . which way would that be?"

Rachel rose from behind the desk and stepped into the hall. "Up the stairs one flight, turn right and the second door down. Room number two."

"Thanks." Paul dropped his voice. "Sorry about that." He jerked his head toward the open doorway, then lifted a hand and turned away.

Jeena sat across from Rachel, frozen with horror at the scene that had just played out in the small office. She wanted to bolt and run. Where she would run, she had no idea. This pastor and the one she'd seen weeks ago at the club were one and the same. She was sure of it. He thought she was here to help, only to learn she was an inmate instead. *Inmate* . . . that was exactly what she felt like, as though bars were closing in, trapping her in a place where she had no choice but to remain. What would Grammie think if she saw her now? She'd fallen so far from the goals she'd hoped to attain.

Maybe she should apply for welfare for a short amount of time and get her own place. She shivered. No. Standing in a line for welfare wouldn't feel much better than sitting in Rachel's office, and she'd already come this far.

"I think that'll do for now. I'm sorry it's taken so long. Let's get you a sandwich and settled in your room so you can rest." Rachel's voice jerked Jeena from her thoughts. "And please don't feel badly about what just happened. It's not shameful to spend a night in a shelter when you've been hit with loss."

"That pastor. Does he live here?" She reached for the handle of her suitcase lying nearby.

Rachel scrunched her forehead a moment, then her face cleared. "No. Pastor Grant leads a church on the edge of town and has his own home. He volunteers here on weekday mornings for chapel and on Sunday evening for a short service."

Jeena let out her breath and relaxed. Maybe it wasn't as bad as she'd imagined. "Why is he here tonight?"

"One of our women is sick and asked that he pray with her." Rachel stood and headed toward the door. "One more question. Are you on any medication?"

"Excuse me?" Jeena wasn't sure she'd heard properly. "Why?"

Rachel paused at the door and leaned against the jamb. "We don't allow anyone to self medicate. All drugs, even prescriptions and over-the-counter drugs, must be turned in and dispensed by the director or a nurse each morning."

"No, I'm not on anything. But why would you have to dispense it if I was?"

"Possible overdose, other women taking your drugs, that type of thing. We can't be too careful. Many of these women have a history of drug addiction." She tilted her head toward the door. "Ready?"

Jeena got to her feet, debating the wisdom of bolting back into the street. A bed sounded good, but the rules here were insane, and she wasn't crazy about chancing another encounter with the good-looking pastor. "I suppose. Yes . . . let's get to my room. I don't think I'm hungry, after all." A sudden thought propelled her through the door. If she hurried, she might get to her room before he finished praying.

They traveled down a well-lit hallway and up a flight of steps. Jeena took stock of the surroundings that would be her home for the next day or so. Her heart sank. She'd expected cheap linoleum to cover the floor, but painted concrete in the hall? This didn't bode well for what she'd find in her room. On the other hand, it had to be better than a park bench, and at least she'd have some privacy. Just being alone would be a blessing, and sleeping in tomorrow would be heavenly.

They arrived at a plain wooden door marred with small gouges and scars. The number five hung near the top as its only adornment. Rachel tapped twice, then turned the knob and swung open the door.

Light streamed from the doorway, and the sound of women's voices stilled as Rachel stepped across the threshold. "Ladies, I'd like you to meet Jeena. She's staying with us for the night."

Jeena froze in the open doorway, unable to comprehend the meaning of the scene. "I . . . I . . . thought I'd be getting my own room. I'm sharing?" She stared at Rachel, avoiding the gaze of the two women sitting on beds against the far wall.

Rachel gave a rueful smile. "I'm afraid private rooms are reserved for mothers with small children and occasionally for women who've made a commitment to our long-term program. If you're only staying a few nights, you have to bunk in a common sleeping room. I'm sorry. I should've explained before we came up."

She pointed to the empty bed near the door. "You can sleep here, and there's a locker at the foot for your belongings. You can store your empty suitcase and duffel in the closet."

Realization hit Jeena full force, and she gaped at Rachel. "Do you have a lot of theft? Am I going to be safe sleeping with these people?" She suppressed a shudder as she looked at the two silent women staring back at her, a sullen expression on one face.

Rachel stepped across the room and held out her open hand toward them. "Absolutely safe. Mary and Carla have been with us over two months now. You have nothing to fear from them, just as they have nothing to fear from you."

Jeena blushed and turned away. "I'm sorry. I didn't mean to imply . . ."

A step sounded beside her, and the older woman called Mary patted her arm. "No offense taken." She smiled up at Jeena. "I saw you some time back when you brought those boxes to Miss Rachel. You was driving a fancy car and in a hurry to skedaddle out of here. Hit on some hard times, did you?"

Jeena looked into the kind face of the woman who'd opened the door the day the obnoxious Sarah had blocked Jeena's path into the shelter. Mary's clean, damp hair clustered in small ringlets around her temples, and the smiling mouth in the round, wrinkled face gave her a cherubic look.

"I'm only here for the night." Jeena drew herself up, determined her declaration would prove true. "I've got some places I'll be checking where I might find a job."

"Well, I'm Mary." She pointed a pudgy finger at the silent woman sitting on the bed against the wall. "This here's Carla. You can turn in whenever you want to. We're not night owls, and we'll keep quiet, if you want to sleep." She pivoted away from Jeena and smiled at Rachel. "We'll see ya in the morning at breakfast, Miss Rachel. We'll take good care of our visitor. Never you fear."

Rachel patted the shorter woman on the shoulder and gave a brief nod to Jeena. "You ask Mary if you have any questions. She'll show you where the bathroom is and help you with anything else you need. Come down with her and Carla to breakfast in the morning. Seven fifteen sharp." She pulled the door closed behind her, shutting it with a decisive click.

"Seven fifteen?" Jeena gasped. "I can't sleep in?"

Mary sank back down on her bunk and tucked her sock-clad feet under her legs. "Why no, dearie. And if you need any meds dispensed, you have to be in line at the infirmary at six thirty. Breakfast is at seven fifteen, chores at eight, then a thirty-minute chapel. The rest of the day, we go to jobs on the outside or classes here at the shelter. Those are the rules if you stay."

Panic welled up in Jeena's mind. What had she gotten herself into? Chapel? She'd forgotten this place was run like a mission and hadn't realized she'd be required to attend anything religious.

She turned toward her assigned area to hide her trembling lips and blinked rapidly to discourage any tears. Life had dealt her some hard knocks, but she'd never have believed she'd be trapped in a women's shelter with nowhere else to go.

If only she had the strength and drive to hit the streets again, surely she'd find a job. At this point, any job would do. A sense of overwhelming lethargy pulled her down to the edge of her narrow bed. Sleep—she needed to sleep. Trying to find the energy for a shower tonight didn't seem possible. Crawling in bed and hoping her problems would go away sounded much easier.

CHAPTER 27

J eena woke in the morning with her brain feeling like overcooked oatmeal and her body aching in places she hadn't known existed. Still, it beat the park bench by a mile, and she felt grateful for the bed, however hard it might be.

"So you're awake, huh? I jest decided I'd have ta shake you awake if you didn't do it on your own pretty quick." The grinning woman called Mary sat on her bunk across the room, buttoning the bottom of her blouse.

A shudder passed through Jeena, and she sat up in bed, thankful she'd avoided the shaking, however gentle it might be. "Doesn't she ever talk?" She nodded toward the silent Carla shutting the bedroom door behind her as she exited the room.

Mary shrugged and stood up, making the bed creak. "Not much. She's kinda shy. Her husband beat her, and she ended up on the streets. Guess she don't trust a lot of people. You better hurry if you're going to make breakfast on time. The director don't like it when we show up late."

Jeena swung her legs over the side of the narrow bed and reached for her bathrobe before she realized it wasn't there. Of course not. Her suitcase didn't have room for her big, fluffy bathrobe, and she'd put it in storage. She stared around the small room. Where in the world was she supposed to dress with any sense of privacy?

Mary must have noticed her discomfort. "Jest take your things to the bathroom, dearie. First door on the right. We share it with another room, but there's more than one stall in there, and you'll have some privacy. You can wash yer face and get ready to go. Better hurry up, though."

"Thank you. I will." Jeena grabbed her duffel bag that she'd placed in the locker and headed for the door.

"Want me to wait for you? I can walk down to breakfast with you if you don't want to go alone." The smile appeared once again.

Jeena had no idea where the dining room might be and the thought of arriving alone terrified her. "That would be nice, thank you. I'll try to hurry."

"I'll jest sit and wait, then." Mary sank back onto her bed and leaned against the pillow.

Jeena rushed through getting dressed—she set a personal record for speed, she was sure of it. She slipped into her designer jeans and lightweight jersey shirt. Makeup didn't seem quite as important here, but appearances counted, and she couldn't let herself slide. A quick brush of her hair and a light application of powder, blush, and mascara made her feel more alive and ready to tackle this strange new world she'd stepped into. A good meal sounded heavenly. First, she'd satisfy her hunger. She'd deal with the balance of her problems later.

She followed Mary down the stairs and around a corner toward what she assumed was the dining area. The sound of voices and the clink of silverware increased the closer they moved to the open doorway. Jeena slowed her step, suddenly nervous of what she might find. Would the women all stare at her or poke fun like the one had done when she'd dropped off the boxes? Weariness settled over her spirit, and she found it difficult to move forward. The thought of trying to be strong and standing up against these women seemed almost impossible.

"Come on, dearie. It'll be fine. Jest follow my lead, and don't worry." Mary beckoned with a bony finger and sported a genuine smile that reached deep into Jeena's sore heart.

Jeena forced her feet to move. She could do this. Mary seemed to accept her, and the offer of help appeared real. Rather than cease, the noise level increased as she stepped over the threshold. A couple of curious glances were shot her way, but the interest soon died and women returned to the business of eating. Maybe this wouldn't be so bad, after all. Surely they had new people coming and going on a regular basis.

The meal was surprisingly good, and Jeena couldn't remember being so satisfied and content in some time. The eggs, hash browns, and ham had accomplished their task, and she felt ready to face the day. What had Mary said came next? Chores? A finger tapped her shoulder, and she started, then turned. Rachel stood behind her. "If you're finished eating, would you mind coming with me?"

Jeena pushed back her chair and stood, then glanced at Mary's upraised face. "Thank you, Mary. I'm not sure what else to say, except, thank you."

Mary reached out and patted Jeena's hand. "Yer welcome, dearie. Glad I could help. You come to me any time you need anything, ya hear?"

Jeena nodded, suddenly fighting the urge to cry. What was wrong with her? Before Sean broke up with her, she'd rarely cried. Since then, she couldn't seem to stop. She cleared her throat and pulled her eyes away from the kind ones gazing into hers.

Rachel led the way out of the room and back to the office where Jeena had sat last night. "Make yourself comfortable, Jeena. We need to talk about your plans." She waved toward the chair opposite the desk and settled into one across from it.

"Oh. Right." Jeena sank into the chair and scrambled to think what might be coming. A shaft of sun shot through the window and landed on her amethyst ring. She absently rubbed the stone, almost surprised it still retained its place on her hand. Would Rachel ask her to leave, now that she'd had one free night? Wasn't that what she wanted to do, get out of this place and find something better? A part of her mind screamed yes, she needed to get out as fast as she could. But the memory of Mary's kindness stilled that urge. Maybe this wouldn't be such a bad place to hang out for a few days, until she found a job and got on her feet.

"Did you sleep well?" Rachel's voice brought her back to the office and the looming question.

"Yes, thanks. The bed was a little hard, but I'm not complaining. At least it's a bed and not the grass under a park bench."

Rachel's eyebrows rose, and Jeena winced. She hadn't meant to let that slip. Looking like a perpetual charity case in Rachel's eyes didn't appeal to Jeena. The situation she'd found herself in might've been forced on her, but wallowing in self-pity wasn't her style.

"You're welcome to stay here for a couple of days or even a few weeks. I'm not sure how you feel about staying more than a night, but our doors are open to any woman in need."

Jeena's fingers ceased toying with her ring, and she stared at Rachel. "I didn't expect . . . I mean, you'd let me stay a few weeks?"

"If that's what you'd like to do, yes." Rachel leaned back in her chair and rested her soft gaze on Jeena's face. "There are still rules and conditions, but if you're willing to work within our boundaries, you're welcome to stay."

Jeena released her breath and silently commanded her tense shoulders to relax. "Rules. Yes, of course. I'm afraid I didn't take in much last night, and you may need to tell me again. But I might not need to stay long. I could get a call any day from one of the job applications I've submitted." She grimaced, suddenly remembering her lack of a phone. The thought of contacting the places where she'd applied and giving them the shelter's number shot a shaft of dread into her heart. She couldn't imagine an employer willingly hiring someone from a homeless shelter if he had another choice.

"You're not making a commitment or signing anything that forces you to remain. You're free to leave at any time. Our mission is to help you get on your feet, and if you're able to do that soon, we'll be thrilled for you." Rachel reached for a stack of papers and slid one across the desk. "Take a look, and tell me if you have any questions."

"Sure." Jeena picked up the paper and settled back in her chair. A list of house rules covered the sheet, and she scanned down the page, taking in each item in turn. "Mary mentioned chores. What would I do?"

"Everyone is responsible for their own room, and each room rotates weekly on cleaning the bathroom assigned to you. Besides that, you'll be asked to serve or clean up at one meal per day. I'd like you to help serve lunch day after tomorrow, and I'll assign one of the women to work alongside you until you're familiar with the job."

Jeena listened closely, but didn't comment, only nodded as Rachel continued.

"Each day, you'll be helping clean the floor you live on. That might mean vacuuming, dusting, washing windows, or whatever the person in charge of that floor needs done on that day. Chore time lasts for thirty minutes, and with everyone working, we're able to get quite a lot accomplished."

Jeena winced as memories of her childhood drifted into her mind. When she'd escaped her father's house and set out on her own, she'd sworn to never again put herself under the rules and dictates of another person. Maybe this wasn't such a good idea, after all. But then again, nothing ever came free; everything had a price, including this shelter.

The fumes of a diesel truck roaring past the open window drifted in, assaulting her senses. A vision of her racing through the darkened park with the ranting man on her heels loomed in her mind, and the feel of the hard ground under the bench made her rub her bruised ribs. Did she want to tackle life on her own? Would the rules and restrictions of this place be worse than what waited out there?

She laid the paper back on the desk and raised her eyes to Rachel's tranquil ones. "I think I can handle chores. What else? This list mentions attending classes, but I don't need further education. May I continue looking for a job?"

"Yes. But if you aren't attending classes that are job related, we'd expect you to attend personal-growth classes or work part-time."

"I'd love to be working part-time, and I plan on looking, so I'm not sure what you're asking."

"For the shelter. You can take classes, or work part-time at our thrift store, or both. You'd only be paid minimum wage at the store. There are normally spots available here as well, but right now the thrift store is the only thing open."

Jeena tried to suppress a shudder and barely succeeded. A thrift store. Long-buried feelings of shame and anger bubbled to the surface. The musty smell of the clothing and shoes, the stares of pity from the people who worked there, the snickers of the other kids when she showed up at school the next day in secondhand clothing, all came flooding back. She'd made a vow the last time her mother took her that she'd never, ever return. It might be the "in" thing for kids to find grunge clothes at a thrift store now, but it was a huge slam to her pride growing up.

She leaned back in her chair and rubbed the bridge of her nose. It felt like the wicked tentacles of a headache trying to wrap themselves around her brain. "What kind of classes are available? Anything that might further my career?"

Rachel shook her head. "I'm afraid not. We offer education classes for women who need their GED, as well as basic computer skills, preparing a résumé . . . that type of thing. Nothing that would benefit someone with your skills and training."

Jeena struggled to keep dismay from blanketing her face. "You mentioned personal-growth classes? How about those?"

Rachel's soft voice seemed tinged with sympathy, but she didn't hesitate. "We have a number of Bible studies that pertain to women's issues, a couple of parenting classes, a life and logic class that teaches women to handle personal issues, and classes that deal with addictions."

This was nuts! How could Rachel act as though she were presenting an acceptable menu of possibilities? The urge to run from this room and demand a job, any type of job, in her own vocation, almost pushed Jeena to her feet. A tiny voice of caution whispered to slow down . . . take it easy. How many choices would she be given if she turned this one away? She leaned forward, her hands tightly clasped in her lap.

"I see." She drew in a deep breath and released it. "So. I need to work part-time, do assigned chores, and be at breakfast at seven fifteen. Anything else?"

"You probably won't want to hear this, but we don't allow cell phones to be used in the rooms, only in the common area. And we have three tiers, or levels, for the women who stay here, earned by length of stay and trust earned. As a new resident, you're in tier one. Tier one and two residents must be back in the building by eight o'clock and in their rooms by nine thirty."

Jeena shot up from her chair and sputtered. "We have a curfew? But I'm an adult!"

Rachel pushed her chair back and stood. "Please, Jeena. Sit down, okay? It'll make sense when I explain. It sounds harsh, but every rule has a sound reason behind it." She beckoned to the chair Jeena had vacated and smiled. "Please?"

"Fine." Jeena plunked down on the seat and crossed her arms. She felt as though she'd been dealt an emotional sucker punch and couldn't crawl up off the ground.

Rachel moved back to her chair and sank into it, leaning forward with her elbows propped on the desk and her chin resting on her knuckles. "Many of these women come from backgrounds steeped in addiction. Some will try to call their drug dealer or their boyfriend, hoping to get drugs smuggled in. We've had women struggling to get free of prostitution who've called their pimps, and abusive spouses who've tracked down their wives and convinced them to return. We do it for their protection and to keep them accountable."

Jeena uncrossed her arms and let her hands fall into her lap. "Fine. I can understand that. But a curfew? What's with that?"

"Again, accountability. We don't want women trying to shake free from their past to be out on the streets at night. Many of them have never had a curfew, even as young children. They were allowed to run without constraints, and no one cared where they were or how late they came home, if at all. The rules are here to help them change their lifestyle. Plus, it helps them feel safer in ways you might not understand."

Jeena listened, taking in the implications of Rachel's words. Safety and accountability, rules and someone who cared enough to impose and enforce them. How long had it been since she'd experienced those things in her life? She tried to remember. Not for a very long time. Her dad had plenty of rules but no love or support to soften them. Her mother loved her, but her fear of Dad didn't allow for the support or nurture a normal mother might have given. Grammie. She was the only person Jeena could point to who unconditionally loved *and* supported her and gently tried to convey the need for accountability and structure in her granddaughter's life. And now she was gone.

"Jeena? Did you have a question? You were shaking your head." Rachel's question drew Jeena back to the present.

"No . . . sorry. I guess my mind wandered. I'd like to stay for a while. I'll need to make a couple of calls, if you don't mind. My banker and prospective employers will need a number to reach me." She attempted a smile. "I understand what you're explaining, and I see why you need the rules you've set up. I wish they didn't have to pertain to me, but I realize you can't make exceptions without causing problems."

Rachel nodded and smiled. "I appreciate that, and you're right. There's a rare time when a woman doesn't need as much structure, but we can't bend. Now, we'd better get going if we don't want to be late for chapel." She rose, and Jeena followed her lead.

Chapel. Great. How could she have forgotten?

CHAPTER 28

Jeena followed Rachel along the brightly lit hallway and wondered at the silence. Forty minutes ago, chattering women filled this area. They all must be in chapel. Just what she needed: more attention from walking in late. She felt her stomach lurch at the prospect. She'd like to disappear—maybe curl up in bed and pretend none of this had happened, but that didn't seem likely. The sound of singing drifted out through the double, swinging doors just ahead.

Her dad's voice slammed into her mind and added weights to her already dragging feet. *Jeena! Stop dawdling. God doesn't like little girls that pout. He'll punish you, if you don't change your attitude. Now walk sharp, or you'll feel my strap when we get home.*

The memory of the cutting words sent a shiver over her skin, and she paused at the door. The prospect of hearing anything from a "man of God" didn't appeal to her in the least.

"Jeena? You coming?" Rachel's soft whisper penetrated the fog.

"Yes." She took several deep breaths and pushed the memories back into the black hole where she'd kept them submerged for so many years. Her father couldn't hurt her now, and the words and sticks he'd beat her with so many times had no more power to wound her. She'd keep chanting that mantra until she believed it, whatever it took. If she ever allowed the memories to surface in force, she wasn't sure she'd survive the pain.

⚜

The buzz of voices and shifting of bodies as the women rose to leave roused Jeena from the blankness that had enveloped her the past thirty minutes. She'd blocked out the sound of the handsome pastor's voice as soon as he stepped behind the small podium at the front of the chapel. An empty cross hung at the front—behind and above him—with artificial flowers and greenery adorning both sides of the pulpit. Each pew had a hymnbook slipped into a rack at intervals along the bench, and Jeena realized with a start that the bench was padded, rather than the hard surface of the unyielding wood she remembered from her childhood.

"Well, who do we have here?" The slight sneer that edged the words jerked Jeena around. Sarah of the gaudy clothing and meaty body who'd tormented her when she'd helped rescue Kirsten outside the building stood nearby. "What's a rich snob like you doing hanging around the likes of us?"

Jeena stood, and a sharp retort trembled on the edge of her tongue.

Rachel stepped alongside Jeena. "Sarah! Jeena is a guest, and you need to remember your manners." Rachel's warning tone veered from its normally sweet note.

The large woman crossed her arms over her ample bosom and glowered. "What do you mean, guest? She's here to bring more of her castoffs, right?"

"I mean she's staying with us. I'm surprised you didn't see her at breakfast this morning with Mary." Rachel's matter-of-fact voice seemed to have the intended effect, and Sarah clamped her lips.

"Mommy! There's the nice lady who brought the clothes. She finded me when I got lost outside. Remember? You got a new pink blouse. But I didn't get my dolly." The piping voice changed the glower on Sarah's face to a beaming smile.

"Kirsten, honey! Come give Sarah a hug."

Jeena watched in amazement as Sarah's arms opened wide and blonde-haired Kirsten danced across the remaining space and launched herself at the glowing woman. How could a child change someone so dramatically?

"I love you, Sarah." Kirsten pressed her lips against Sarah's pocked cheek and gave her a decisive smack. She laid her head on the woman's shoulder and smiled, then popped the middle two fingers of her left hand into her mouth.

Sarah rubbed the tiny back and stroked the golden hair. "I love you too, precious."

"Kirsten, we need to go to our room so you can take a nap." The musical voice of the girl's mother drew Jeena's attention. Joy stepped alongside Sarah and reached for her daughter, who slid her arms around her mother's neck and burrowed her face in her shoulder. A minute later, the shining blue eyes peeked out of their hiding place and sparkled their way into Jeena's heart.

Rachel broke the spell. "Joy, Jeena is staying with us for a while till she gets back on her feet, and she's rooming with Mary and Carla. She'll have lunch duty with you day after tomorrow—do you think you could show her the ropes?"

Joy smiled, a gesture that reached from her mouth to the deep, aqua blue eyes that matched her daughter's. "Sure. I'll get one of the aunties to watch Kirsten while she takes her nap, and I'll come get you a few minutes early." She nodded to Jeena and smiled at Sarah and Rachel, then hurried away.

"Aunties?" Jeena asked. "Does she have relatives living here, besides her daughter?"

Sarah snickered, but covered her mouth when she caught Rachel's frown.

"No," Rachel said. "An aunty is a woman in the long-term program who's been interviewed and approved for child care. A number of women come through our program with their children, and they have to be with an aunty or their mother at all times. No one who isn't pre-approved by the director or pastor is allowed to care for the children."

Jeena frowned. "Isn't that dangerous?"

Sarah harrumphed beside her, and Rachel shook her head. "No. The safety of the child is paramount. We screen the women carefully before allowing them to be an aunty, and it's considered an honor and a privilege."

Jeena felt heat crawl up her face. She'd made an idiot of

herself again. "You're right, of course. I guess I'm not used to being around women like these, and I didn't think . . ."

Sarah pushed herself forward, every hair on her body seeming to bristle. "You got that right! What do you think we are, animals? You think we're all out to molest little kids or somethin'? Well, let me tell you. There's a lot of the women at this place what would die for that little one without blinkin' an eye. So you better watch your mouth, lady, or somebody around here might just shut it for you."

"That's enough, Sarah. You need to apologize." Rachel stepped between the two women and stared up at the furious Sarah.

"You're taking her side because she's rich. Well, it don't cut no weight with me, you got that? And I ain't apologizin', neither." She spun on her heel and stormed from the room. The double, swinging doors felt the force of Sarah's fists as she slammed them open and they flapped shut behind her.

Rachel turned toward Jeena, her face a study in sorrow and sympathy. "I'm sorry. Some of these women come from violent backgrounds. Sarah has a soft heart, but she can be unpredictable at times. She's grown and changed a lot since arriving, or we wouldn't allow her to stay."

Jeena sank into the empty pew beside her. Remorse draped itself over her heart. "No." The whispered word was almost too quiet to hear. She cleared her throat and tried again, louder this time. "No. I shouldn't have said that. I didn't think. Sarah was right. It's been years since I've been around someone as honest as she is."

Rachel sat beside Jeena. "I realize it's not going to be easy for you to fit in here. I doubt you ever will. But I appreciate your attitude and I believe it will get easier. Don't let the women like Sarah get to you. Stick close to Mary and Joy and a couple of the others. You'll learn which ones will help you and which are jealous or suspicious. And don't hesitate to come to me if you need help." She rose from the bench. "I teach a computer class, and it's about time to begin. Why don't you go up to your room and rest?"

Jeena mustered a smile. "Thanks, I think I will. What happens after lunch? Do I start at the thrift store?"

"We won't put you to work today. I realize this has been a stressful transition for you. I have to be careful to not show favoritism, but come to my office after lunch, and I'll explain your duties at the thrift store. Then if you'd like to go to your room before dinner, that's fine." Rachel turned and took a stride toward the door, then stopped. "And Jeena?"

Jeena raised her head, wondering what could possibly be coming now. "Yes?"

"I want you to know how thankful I am that you called. I truly believe God has a wonderful plan for your future, and He's so pleased that you were willing to listen. He loves you, you know." She smiled, and her face lit up as though something inside had ignited.

"Does He now? I wonder," Jeena said under her breath, then raised her voice. "Thanks, Rachel." She waved at the woman and watched her exit the room. *God brought me here? I'm not sure whether to yell at Him or thank Him. Guess I'll just have to wait and see.*

CHAPTER 29

Jeena awoke in the twilight hour before dawn to the gentle snore of one of her roommates. Mary? No, the sound rumbled from Carla's bunk. No matter, Jeena doubted she'd get back to sleep anyway. The street outside her window seemed uncannily quiet, but even dishonest people found little need to be out this time of the morning.

She sniffed, surprised that the odor that seemed disagreeable the first night didn't assault her senses now. Could she already be growing accustomed to this place? She had to admit that neither Carla's nor Mary's presence offended her.

A glimmer of light seeped around the edge of the drawn blind. Jeena slipped out of bed and padded to the window, then raised the shade. She sank into the old, overstuffed chair and gazed out at the world springing to life.

How long had it been since she'd watched a sunrise? Years. No—a lifetime ago. Life had raced at such a furious pace before "the crash" as she was coming to call it. Time didn't stand still, and she'd wanted to pack as much fun and self-indulgence into it as the hours would allow. Self-indulgence? Where had that thought come from? It must be her father speaking again. Somehow she had to remove that man's voice from her head.

Besides, what was wrong with having fun? Money existed to be spent, and careers were created to help one climb the ladder to wealth. At least, that's what she'd always told herself.

Grammie didn't believe that, though. She could almost hear her grandmother's voice, full of laughter and teasing most of the time, but serious when she knew Jeena needed to listen. *Money won't buy happiness, child, and your friends will desert you if your money is ever snatched from you. Jobs come and go, people walk*

away, but God never fails. Remember that if times get rough, my
dear. He'll never fail you.

But it felt like He had. Jeena was living in a shelter instead of
her new townhouse, and her friends had headed south as soon as
a hint of suspicion pointed its finger her way. Except Tammy, and
Jeena's own pride was keeping her from letting Tammy know
what she'd sunk to.

And then there was Charles. He had the reputation of being vindictive toward anyone who crossed him. Sure, she'd only repeated
what she'd overheard him say, but it was one more nail in his cof-
fin and could be the reason he'd slipped into hiding. Chances were
he'd never find her here, and hopefully he had enough trouble to
keep him occupied without thinking of her. But she'd start watching her back.

A soft pink glow suffused the edges of the wispy clouds
hanging midway in the sky, turning the dingy gray fluff into a
magnificent work of art, worthy to have come from the brush
of a master. She sat chained to her chair, barely able to breathe.
Gorgeous! Did this sight appear every morning while she slept
through it? Maybe God *did* leave small gifts strewn along the
path of life, after all.

When the pink finally subsided, chased away by the bright-
ness of the new day, Jeena roused from her thoughts and pushed
to her feet. A glance at her watch showed almost an hour before
breakfast. Snuggling under the covers for a little longer sounded
inviting. She felt sure this day would hold enough stress, and
she'd better face it with all the strength she could muster.

✻

Jeena rushed through breakfast, barely tasting her food.
She'd overslept after crawling back in bed and barely made it to
the dining room in time to get served. Mary must have decided
Jeena needed to take care of herself today, as she hadn't hung
around to walk her to breakfast. Maybe the older woman's chari-
table feelings didn't run as deep as she'd acted yesterday. No

surprise. So often people put on an act when they first met you, then lost interest and slid back into their true persona.

A hand touched Jeena's shoulder, making her jump. "Sorry, dearie. Didn't mean to startle you. Mind if I sit down and join you?" Mary's voice sounded weary, not like the cheery tone she'd heard yesterday.

Jeena watched the woman slide into a chair across the table from her and carefully place her tray on the Formica surface. The normally bright eyes looked dull and puffy, and her hand shook as she picked up her fork.

"Are you all right?" Consternation flooded Jeena's heart as she thought about the unkind thoughts she'd had only moments before.

A wan smile pulled at Mary's mouth, and she toyed with her fork, idly pushing the eggs around her plate. "I'll be fine. Don't ya worry. Jest had me a bellyache and a bit of a sore throat in the night, so's I went to see the nurse this morning. I felt bad not being here to walk ya to breakfast."

Jeena felt her face pale as the twist of guilt and shame dug their talons in deeper. "I'm sorry," she whispered.

"Nothin' for you to be sorry about. Weren't nothin' you did that made me sick. Guess I picked up a bug or somethin'. Nurse says I'm to take it easy and not do chores today, but I'm signed up to scrub our bathroom, besides my usual dustin'. Can't see my way clear to not keepin' my word."

"I'll do it." Jeena had no idea where the words sprang from, but as soon as they were said, she felt the shame slide away. "You do what the nurse says and go to bed. I've always done my own housework, and I'm sure I can handle your chores and whatever they assign me."

Mary shook her head, but it didn't have much strength behind the assertion. "I can't let you do that. It's too much, you bein' new and all."

Jeena reached across the table and touched the work-roughened hand. "It's not too much, and I'll be fine. Go to bed. I'll let Rachel know that I'm covering for you. I'm sure she'll approve."

Mary squeezed Jeena's fingers and nodded. "All right, then, maybe I will. A short rest might not be a bad idea."

"Can you eat, or do you want to head right up?"

"Food don't sound good right now. Guess I'm still not feelin' real pert. Think I'll go on up and lay down for a spell. And I thank ya." She wobbled to her feet and gripped the back of the chair, then straightened when Jeena began to rise. "I'll be fine gettin' up there on my own. You're doin' enough. Sit and finish yer breakfast. Ya need your strength." She turned to smile, then disappeared out the door.

⚘

A few minutes later Jeena headed upstairs to tackle cleaning the bathroom, unsure of what she'd find.

Women scurried along the hallway, carrying cleaning supplies—each one apparently heading toward her assigned task. Jeena searched for the area Rachel had mentioned and found it—*Utility Room* emblazoned on the door. It stood ajar, and she gingerly pushed it open and stepped inside. The bare bulb in the ceiling fixture illuminated a neat and tidy cubicle, with shelves and cupboards lining three of the four walls from floor to ceiling. Each door was labeled, making the needed supplies easy to locate. Jeena released a pent-up breath—so far, so good—pulled open doors until she found the required tools, then headed toward the bathroom she'd been assigned.

She shoved open the door and stuck the broom and mop handles in ahead of her while juggling the bottles of cleaning supplies under her arm.

"Ouch! Watch where you're going!" An irritated voice caused Jeena to jump back a step, and her bottle of scrubbing granules hit the floor, scattering small grains in its wake.

The looming figure of Sarah stood rubbing her cheek where a red spot sprouted. "It's you, is it? I should've known. What ya think yer doing, blasting in here? You could-a put my eye out with that thing." She glowered at Jeena, her brows scrunched over irritated eyes.

Jeena's mortification at her mistake subsided at the sharpness of Sarah's accusation. "Well, I'm sorry! It's not like I did it on purpose. You apparently weren't watching where you were going, either."

She knew the words were unfair as soon as they left her mouth, but the woman set her teeth on edge. No matter what she did, Sarah saw it in the opposite light from what Jeena intended. First accusing her of trying to harm Kirsten, then jumping on her in the chapel, and now thinking Jeena had hurt her intentionally. Enough was enough.

"I didn't say you done it on purpose, just that you oughtta try to slow down and watch where yer going, that's all. I gotta get to work." She pointed at the granules of powder scattered across the floor and smirked. "Looks like you'd better hustle it up, too, or you won't get done on time." She jerked open the door and stalked from the room, whistling a jaunty tune as she disappeared.

"The witch!" Jeena fumed. She slapped the rest of the supplies on the counter and glowered at the floor. "I'll show *her* who can get her work done first."

For the next twenty minutes, Jeena flew from toilet to sink to floor, scrubbing, sweeping, and mopping as though racing for the prize of a lifetime. She stripped off her rubber gloves and stared at the shining bathroom. Where normally she'd be repulsed at cleaning a bathroom after several strange women, now her only feelings were grim determination and satisfaction at a job well done.

She snatched the supplies from their resting place, then dashed for the door. Oops. No sense in knocking into someone else. She slowed down, eased open the door, and walked down the hall, exchanging her tools for dust rags and spray, and heading to the common room. Ten minutes later, she stood back and surveyed the area with grim satisfaction. She'd finished Mary's chores with time to spare. Rachel had excused Jeena from her own regularly scheduled chores, only requesting that she check on Mary when finished.

Jeena stopped outside the door to their room and drew in a deep breath, uncertain what she'd find. Visions of her grandmother's stomach pain her last day on earth assaulted her, sending fresh trickles of fear through her mind. Was Mary dying under the care of a nurse who didn't know enough to diagnose her properly? Jeena knew she was overreacting but hated the thought of seeing the kind, older woman in pain.

She pushed open the door and tiptoed inside, noting the drawn blinds dimming the room. "Mary?" she whispered.

A quavering voice sounded from the far side of the room. "I'm here, dearie. Ya didn't disturb me." She coughed and cleared her throat. "How're ya doin'? Did the extra cleaning cause ya trouble?"

Jeena released a large sigh and walked across the softly lit room to the side of Mary's bed. "No trouble at all. I got it done in plenty of time." No need worrying Mary over the episode with Sarah.

Mary patted the edge of her bed, and Jeena hesitated, unsure of the wisdom of disturbing the sick woman. "Sit down, dearie. I don't bite."

Jeena smiled and sank down on the edge of the bed. "How are you feeling?"

Mary's smile lit up her face. "I'm doing better, I am. The pain in my stomach seems to be leavin', and I'm thinking I should get up. My throat's a little raspy, but it don't hurt no more." She tried to push to a sitting position.

Jeena gently touched Mary's shoulder. "No. You stay put. Rachel asked me to make sure you stayed in bed till lunchtime. If you feel up to it, you can get up then, but not before." She mustered all the firmness she could and hoped Mary would listen. To her relief, the older woman lay back against her pillow with a weary sigh.

"All righty then. Maybe I'll take a wee nap before lunch, but I do hate missin' that nice Pastor Grant at chapel. He's such a kind man."

Jeena looked at her watch and stood. "I didn't realize it was so late. Are you all right if I leave you alone, or would you like me to stay?"

Mary pulled the sheet up under her chin. "You go along, now. I'll be right as rain by lunch. Hurry up, so's ya won't get in trouble for being late." One eye peeked open, and she smiled, then turned on her side.

CHAPTER 30

Late the next morning, Jeena kicked off her shoes and sank down on the bed. "Ohhh . . . this feels so good." Mary was up and around again and able to do her own chores, but floor duty fell to Jeena today, and her muscles felt the strain of pushing the broom and mop over what must be hundreds of feet of linoleum. She had thirty minutes to rest before heading to lunch and planned on taking a short nap while she had the chance. She rolled over on her side and snuggled deeper into the pillow.

Sometime later a tapping at the door jerked her eyelids open. "Jeena?" A familiar voice sounded outside.

"Joy?" Jeena struggled to a sitting position and groaned. She'd completely forgotten lunch duty. "Come in, the door isn't locked." She pushed her fingers through her hair and searched for her shoes.

Joy poked her head in the door. "Did I wake you?"

Jeena sighed. "No. I wasn't down long enough to get to sleep. Sorry. I totally forgot about serving today."

"No problem, but we'd better get going. I got Kirsten settled with her aunty, and I'm running a little late, too."

Jeena ran a brush through her hair and grimaced at the mirror as she walked past. No time for more than a touch of mascara when her day had started this morning, and not a minute to spare since.

The two women hurried along the quiet hallway, their quick steps accelerating as the dining room came into view. Women were trickling in, and workers scurried behind the serving bar, readying the meal.

"Joy? You're late." A grim-faced woman stood in the doorway to the kitchen, beads of perspiration dotting her forehead.

She mopped the area with the back of her sleeve and frowned. "You're supposed to be here before anyone arrives. I had to pull one of the other women out of the dining room to help."

"I'm sorry, Martha. I had trouble getting Kirsten settled with her aunty, then I stopped by Jeena's room. This is her first time serving. It's my fault. I'm sure Jeena would've been on time if she hadn't waited for me." A red flush crept up Joy's neck and stained her cheeks, and she ducked her head.

Martha glanced from Joy to Jeena and back again, then managed a tight smile. "It's all right this time, I suppose. You did right to get your friend and bring her along. New people don't always know the rules." She looked pointedly at Jeena, who returned her stare. "Come along then, and grab an apron."

Jeena followed directions with only half her mind taking in what she was told and the other half immersed in questions. Why had Joy covered for her? She knew Jeena was almost asleep when she stopped by. Joy could've used Jeena's not being ready as an excuse for her own tardiness and swung the woman's ire away from herself. She didn't get it. People in her world were more apt to stab someone in the back than try to protect them

The woman commissioned to take Jeena's place had already whipped the potatoes. She handed over the bowl and the large serving spoon and removed her apron with a grunt. "You might try coming on time so we don't have to do your work."

With thoughts of Joy still tumbling through her mind, Jeena stifled a retort and allowed the woman to walk away.

"Hey, I'm waitin' for my potatoes. You gonna stand there or serve them?" A gruff voice jerked her back to attention, and she grabbed the large serving spoon.

The next fifteen minutes rushed by as a steady parade of women held out empty plates. The dining room filled, and the line dwindled. Jeena took a moment to peek at Joy, who worked alongside her serving salad to the passing women. Joy's gentle smile met her gaze; then Jeena turned her attention back to the next person in line. Sarah.

She shoved her tray under Jeena's nose and smirked. "Well, lookee who's in the gutter with the rest of us sinners, gettin' her hands dirty—Miss High and Mighty, herself."

Jeena clamped her lips shut and glared. She wouldn't allow this woman to get under her skin.

"Cat got your tongue?" Sarah laughed at her own weak humor. "Well, look at that, will ya?" She set the tray on the metal bars in front of her and pointed at Jeena's hand. "I can't believe you got the nerve to wear that ring. I'd imagine you'd want to hide that beauty for fear one of us worthless pieces of trash would steal it. Why don't ya just sell it and get outta here?"

Jeena withdrew her hand and stuck it behind her back, as several heads turned at Sarah's loud voice. "It was a gift from my grandmother, and it's precious to me."

"Ha! See! I told ya so. You're afraid it's gonna be stole. You'd best be hurrying back to yer room and lockin' it up." Sarah moved on down the line, her rough laugh floating behind her.

Joy leaned close and whispered. "Just ignore her. She's not usually mean to people. Sarah has a good heart, but she's had a bad life and doesn't trust people who appear to have money." Joy blushed. "I'm sorry," she apologized. "I didn't mean to imply . . ."

Jeena shrugged. "Don't worry about it. Besides, I haven't had a chance to thank you for covering for me."

"You saved Kirsten that day from getting hit by a car or possibly worse. I'd do more than lie for you if I had to." Joy lifted her chin and squared her shoulders. "I'm sure you would've remembered and made it to the dining room."

"Not likely." Jeena made a face, then fell silent as another line of stragglers came along. She didn't know what to make of Joy. The head-server's anger caused Joy to shrink like someone who'd been abused. Then she took the blame for Jeena and made it clear she had the nerve and willingness to do more. Mary, Joy, Sarah . . . so different, and all stuck here for various reasons. This place didn't make sense to her, not at all.

Jeena slipped up to her room after lunch, intent on hiding her ring. She felt foolish giving in to Sarah's ridiculous assertion, but the amethyst and diamonds were valuable and might be a temptation to someone. Besides, the last thing she wanted was to stand out in this place. Sarah's comments proved her decision to wear it was foolish, no matter how much it reminded her of Grammie.

Where had she put the key to the locker? She tore through her suitcase and hunted around her bed with no success, then glanced at her watch and groaned. Rachel was waiting to take her to work at the thrift store. Jeena yanked the ring from her finger and looked around, hunting for a spot to hide it. No one would look in one of her shoes. It might not be safer there, but better than flashing it around and drawing attention—at least until she returned and found the key.

Hastily she stuffed it into the toe of a loafer, slipped the pair under the edge of her bed, and dashed for the door. Now she wouldn't have to worry about some indigent attacking her on the way back to the shelter. She slammed the door of the room and rushed down the hall. Being late one time today was enough.

Jeena followed Rachel into the thrift store, wrinkling her nose as she entered. It appeared clean enough, but she remembered the smell of donated clothing and cast-off items people brought to these places. The management didn't have the time or manpower to wash everything that came in, and most items that appeared in decent condition were hung as they were—and the smell lingered in the air.

What she'd give to be back in her townhouse, sitting with a friend over a cup of tea. She missed her cell phone, her car, her job, and having someone to chat with—but having a bed at the shelter and a place to eat, however humble, bathed her mind in gratitude. At least this was a job, even if it wasn't what she'd planned. Thankfully, none of her old crowd would ever stumble

in here. She suppressed a shudder, the mere thought sending a
shaft of horror through her mind.

"Hi, Tara." Rachel's voice broke into Jeena's thoughts, effec-
tively silencing the memories.

A young woman with bleached hair, a nose ring, and multiple tattoos on her neck and arms lay aside a magazine and
grimaced. "Rachel, am I glad to see you. It's been some kind of
crazy morning. This loony woman and her four screaming brats
came in and practically tore the place apart. I spent an hour
after she left putting clothes back on hangers and picking up
toys they'd scattered across the floor."

She stood and stretched, her hands on her lower back. "I
didn't sit down but five minutes ago." She raised her penciled
brows. "This the newbie I'm breaking in?"

Rachel nodded toward Jeena. "Tara, this is Jeena Gregory. I'll
be leaving her in your capable hands until closing at five. Take
her through the steps for opening and closing, as well as how we
deal with donations. Tara, you can count the till and bring the
deposit by the office after you've locked up for the night."

Jeena looked from one woman to the other and frowned.
"You allow the employees to handle the money?"

Tara emitted a snorting laugh, a curious cross between a
bark and a bray. "Yeah, but we always count it in pairs, and at
least one of us has to have worked here for six months with
no black marks on our record. That would be me. Otherwise,
Rachel or one of the staff comes to the store at closing time and
picks it up."

She stepped out around the high counter. Jeena gawked at
her clothing. Tara wore an ensemble that could've easily come
from several different departments, none of them related to
the other. What looked like men's army boots hugged her long
feet, and baggy pants with huge pockets and multiple patches
sewn on the legs hung low on her hips. She'd made an attempt at
decency by slinging a multicolored scarf around her bare waist.

"Like my outfit?" Tara grinned and tugged at the three layers
of assorted tank tops and a crocheted vest riding just above her

navel. "The shelter people won't let me show bare skin, so I wear this scarf. I like to be unique—know what I mean?"

Jeena knew, even if she didn't care for the look—but she kept silent and turned toward Rachel. "She's training me?"

Rachel smiled and nodded. "Tara's the general manager. She's a whiz at math and great with the customers. She'll teach you the ropes faster than anyone else." She turned toward the door with a wave. "I need to run. Have fun, girls!" The heavy, glass door swung shut, leaving behind a heavy silence.

CHAPTER 31

Two hours later, Jeena sat down for the first time, wondering where in the world Tara got her energy. The young woman moved like a whirlwind through the store, straightening racks, organizing shelves, and dragging Jeena along in her wake. Seeing Tara sitting behind the counter when they'd entered, Jeena had assumed the girl might be lazy, but never was anything farther from the truth. Right now, a little laziness would be refreshing.

"Tired?" Tara grinned like an imp. "Go ahead and sit for ten minutes; you've earned it. Didn't think you'd be able to keep up with me, but you've done pretty good," she stated grudgingly. "You don't look the type to be working in a place like this, know what I mean?" She glanced at Jeena, her gaze lingering on the designer jeans and name-brand sneakers.

"Yeah, you're right, I'm not. But I'm here." Jeena regretted her words as soon as they left her mouth. Tara had given her the first compliment she'd had since arriving, and she should treasure it, not throw it back in the girl's face. "I'm sorry. I shouldn't have snapped at you." It took an effort to get the words out, but a sense of relief enveloped her afterward.

"Kinda touchy, are ya?" Tara hitched herself up on the counter and perched on the edge, swinging her leather boots. "Can't say I blame you. I remember my first few days in this place. Man, I hated it. Wanted nothin' more than to escape."

Jeena leaned forward, her interest held. "Why didn't you?"

Tara shrugged, and her mouth twisted in a cross between a grin and a frown. "Not sure. Guess I'd run out of options, know what I mean?"

"Yeah, I think I do." Jeena wanted to ask more. This girl wasn't her type, and typically she wouldn't give her a second look, but now . . . well, life wasn't normal anymore. Besides, Tara seemed genuine and down to earth, something Jeena didn't encounter often among her old crowd. The last two hours, Tara had crammed in lessons about life as well as knowledge of the retail industry—along with an awareness of new fashion trends. Jeena had come to this job with no expectations other than boredom and found herself surprised at her change of attitude.

"So, what gives?" Tara's heels clunked against the wood doors under the counter, making Jeena jump.

"Excuse me?"

"Why are you here? Not that there's anything wrong with the shelter. There's some good people there. But most of the women that come through are druggies, or alkies, or running from something . . . or someone. You one of them?" She titled her head to the side.

Jeena bit her lower lip and stifled the desire to give vent to a hysterical laugh. Down to earth was putting it mildly; this girl was blunt. "No. I'm not a druggie, or an alcoholic, and no one is after me. I found myself in some unusual circumstances and lost my job, then my home. Rachel's helping me out for a week or two, that's all."

Tara shrugged and hopped off the counter, her heavy bracelets clinking together as her feet clunked on the hard linoleum floor. "I get it. It's not my business. Like I said, most of the women here are running from something, and everyone has secrets." She glanced at the clock behind the counter. "We'd better get to work. The store doesn't close for another couple of hours."

No way was she confiding her life story to this woman. "Thanks for the break." Jeena pushed herself out of the chair with a sigh. "So, what's next?"

Tara stood with her fists planted on her slim hips and tapped her toe. "Hmm. It's not often I get a stretch of time without customers. We'll get stuff out of the back and onto hangers and shelves. The door has a bell on it, so we'll know if anyone comes in. Hope you don't mind getting your hands dirty, 'cause some of the boxes that come in aren't too clean."

"I love to garden, so I'm no stranger to dirt. If a customer comes, do you want me to help them?"

"No way," Tara snorted. "Donations are piling up. You'll stay in the back with the boxes unless I need extra help up front. Sorry, but you're the gofer today."

Jeena nodded and spun on her heel. She'd already stained her shirt and broken a nail. But at least she had a job, even if it paid only minimum wage. Since she didn't have a house payment or other expenses, maybe she could save enough to get back on her own.

An hour later, the buzzer sounded, signaling a customer. "Just stay on that row of boxes where we left off. I'll be back as soon as I can. You're doing great," Tara called over her shoulder, then hurried to the front.

Jeena placed her hands on her back and stretched, then reached with renewed determination for the next box in her path. She pulled it open and stared. It couldn't be. No way. A sick feeling hit her stomach, and she groaned. This box contained the clothing she'd donated early this summer. A teal green sweater lay on top, and a black skirt peeked out from underneath. At the time, she'd considered both garments old and outdated.

With shaking hands, Jeena lifted the sweater and draped it across her lap, then reached for the skirt. The box brought back memories of her life as it had been and all she'd lost. Why had she cast these aside so easily? Was she such a shallow person back then that she didn't see the value in good quality clothing that didn't have a bit of wear?

The sound of footsteps signaled Tara's approach, and she looked up. "Tara?"

"Hmm?"

"Would it be okay if I buy a couple of things out of this box? Are we allowed to do that before they go on the rack?"

"Sure." Tara peered over her shoulder at the clothes on her lap. "Find something you think would fit? Maybe you should try them on first."

Jeena dropped the items back in the box. "I don't need to. Can I buy all of them?"

Tara frowned but didn't push. "Sure. We get a good discount for working here. I'll figure it out. The bookkeeper will take it out of your check."

"Thanks." Jeena stood and hoisted the box to her hip. "I'll put these in the office for now."

"Jeena?"

She swiveled around. "Yeah?"

"You okay?"

"I think I will be." She strode to the office, a gamut of emotions flooding her. This was freaky, finding her own clothes that should've been on the shelves and sold months ago. Just plain freaky and weird.

CHAPTER 32

Jeena sank onto her bed with a tired sigh. She'd dragged herself through dinner, barely tasting her food. The remaining time before closing had flown by, the two women emptying boxes as though racing against an unseen foe. Closing procedure had been simple, but the unusual activity of the day had left Jeena feeling drained.

"Long day, dearie?" Mary's slightly raspy voice spoke from the doorway as the bedroom door drifted shut behind her.

"Hmm."

"That bad, was it?" Mary's worn face creased in a sympathetic smile.

Jeena rolled over and pushed herself up on an elbow. "I guess I'm not used to that type of work. Not that it was hard, just nonstop. I always thought I was a high-energy person, but I pushed myself to keep up with Tara."

Mary's cackling laugh reminded Jeena of the older woman's earlier sore throat. "Tara was a wonder even when she lived here. My old bones ached just watching her whirl through this place."

"Used to live here? I assumed since she works at the thrift store . . ."

"Nope. Not a rule you have to live here to work there. But she use'ta."

"So why'd she leave?"

"Worked her way through the program here, and now she's the manager at the store. Got her own apartment and all. One of the shelter's success stories, guess you'd say."

"Interesting." Jeena swung herself to a sitting position and started to rise. "Is your throat bothering you again? You'd better lie down and get off your feet."

"Now you sit down, you hear me?" Mary wagged a finger at Jeena and frowned. "I'm just fine. No need to worry about this old woman, no sir. Just had me a frog in my throat is all. Hasn't hurt a bit."

"Are you sure?" Jeena sank back on the bed and stared at the wrinkled countenance, trying to see beneath the surface.

"For sure and certain. I'll kick my shoes off and set a spell, so's you won't be worryin' about me. Kind'a nice though." One shoe followed the other across the floor, and a grin lit up Mary's face.

Jeena cocked her head to the side. "What is?"

"Havin' someone what worries about-cha. Ain't had no one do that 'cept Miss Rachel for more years than I care to remember." She sank down into the easy chair with a contented sigh.

Jeena blushed and dropped her eyes.

"Aw, now I've gone and embarrassed you. I'm sorry, dearie. I didn't mean nothin' by it."

"No. I'm glad you told me. I was just thinking that you remind me a little of someone . . ."

Mary's voice dropped to a gentle whisper. "Someone you cared about, I reckon?"

"Yes." Jeena's voice trembled. "For a minute, you sounded like my grandmother."

"Ah." Mary nodded. "And where would she be, now?"

Jeena drew a deep breath. "Grammie would say she's in heaven."

Mary narrowed her eyes. "You think she's not?"

Jeena punched her pillow and avoided Mary's probing stare. "No . . . it's not that I don't believe she'd go there—if anyone could get there, she would." She shrugged. "I guess I'm not sure what I believe anymore."

"I'm sorry yer gramma's gone," Mary's soft reply pulled Jeena's gaze back to the older woman's face. "But I'm guessin' she's in heaven, and I declare—livin' in this shelter surely has convinced me heaven must be real. I never met such carin', givin' people before comin' here."

Jeena nodded slowly. "I understand what you're saying, but there's good people everywhere."

"I don't know how it all works, but from what Preacher says in chapel, you have to know God yer own self, not just be good. But Preacher would be the one to ask, I reckon," Mary said. "Yer gramma was a religious woman? How 'bout you? Looks like at least one of yer parents would'a been religious with a mama like her."

"She was my mother's mother, and yes, Grammie passed along her faith." Jeena paused, wanting to keep the harsh note out of her voice. "But my father did a good job of nearly killing my mother's sweet spirit, and he beat any desire for religion out of me."

Mary leaned forward, clasping her hands in front of her. "Yer father beat you? I'm sorry, honey. I jest assumed you'd had a good upbringin'. Why didn't yer mama leave him and take you with her?"

Jeena shrugged and struggled to sit up on the bed, then leaned her back against the wall. "I think he made her feel guilty. Told her she'd go to hell if she left him and threatened to come after her and drag her back. Mama was too ashamed to let anyone know, even her mother. I think Grammie suspected, but my father didn't allow us to see her much. He needed to be in control of his family and wouldn't tolerate interference." She sighed and twisted a strand of hair between her fingers. "Maybe Mama was afraid he'd try to keep me if she left him. He'd probably have done it to teach her a lesson."

"Ah, I've known men like that. Cruel, they can be. Little thought for any but themselves, and always thinkin' they're right. Our Joy might be married to one like that." Mary plunked back in her chair with a sigh, shaking her head so her gray curls bobbed.

Jeena started at the sudden change of direction, struggling to keep up. "Joy? Kirsten's mother? You think she's been abused?"

"I don't know for sure, mind you. Prob'ly shouldn't be repeatin' gossip, either. But that's the word, and the shelter grapevine is pretty reliable." She clucked her tongue. "A shame it is, her havin' that sweet little girl and all. Not easy takin' a child and runnin' from a man what's determined to find you."

"What makes you think he's trying to find her?"

"I'd just come around the corner one day, down a ways from the bulletin board. Joy didn't see me—she was too busy readin' some notice—but I seen her. She turned pasty white and fled down the hall. I waited a minute, then went down to see what spooked her." Mary crossed her arms.

Jeena felt her pulse quicken. "So . . . what did you find?"

"A notice. Some man tryin' to find his runaway wife and little girl. Course, the names were different, but that don't surprise me none. Most runaways change their names. From the look I saw on her face, I'd say she's the wife of a no-account husband. Mind you, I could be wrong." She wagged her head. "But I don't believe I am. She's a sweet girl, and I'm bettin' the gossip is true . . . her man beat her, same as yer daddy did you, and she up and run."

"You could be right. If so, I hope he doesn't find her. She's got a lot of courage, trying to start a new life. It's not easy breaking free of a man like that." Jeena propped her knees up and hugged them close to her chest. She felt an affinity for Joy, or whatever her name might be, and the old ache resurfaced in her chest. A picture of a dark-haired little girl popped into her mind—Kirsten's age, clinging to her mother's dress and trying to hide from the big paddle wielded by an enraged father. Shouting voices, mama's tears, and slaps that even now made her head ring.

He'd pushed her sobbing mother aside and jerked little Jeena's arm, causing her to cry out in fear and pain. "Don't pull away from me. Stand still and take your medicine. The Bible says it's a father's duty to drive evil from the hearts of his children with the rod, and I'm taking that serious."

"But Henry, I don't think the Bible meant it that way . . . not that you hit her so hard you leave welts." Mama's shaking voice sounded behind her. "Doesn't it also say to teach your children to respect you? You're scaring her, Henry."

Even now, the memory of her mother's challenge shocked Jeena. She didn't remember it ever happening prior to that episode, and it certainly never happened again.

Henry spun on his heel and drove his palms against his wife's shoulders, slamming her against the wall. "You will not question my authority, woman," he growled. "Not if you know what's good for you. Leave the room. Now." He pointed at the open door and glared. "And shut the door behind you."

Jeena's memory faded with the sound of her mother's footsteps leaving the room, her quiet sobs echoing back along the hall. Stark fear blocked the images from her mind, and darkness swam in their place.

"Jeena honey?" A timid hand touched Jeena's knee. "You okay? You're shiverin'. You gettin' sick now, too?"

Mary's worried voice broke into Jeena's thoughts and propelled her back to the small room. Thank God she was here, and not in that dark bedroom of her childhood. At least she felt safe here—and for some reason she didn't understand, no nightmares had plagued her since arriving.

CHAPTER 33

Jeena rolled over and stared upward, struggling to remember. The ceiling wasn't familiar, but the soft, whiffling snore from a nearby bed brought a flood of realization. The shelter. She heaved a sigh and looked at her watch, hoping for a few more minutes of rest. *Six o'clock; good.* She snuggled back into the pillow, but the images roused by last night's talk with Mary roiled to the surface, refusing to be silenced.

An image of Joy and her small daughter rushed to Jeena's mind. Maybe helping someone besides herself might be a way of putting her own demons to rest.

She pushed aside the blanket and struggled to rise, then stopped. Joy wouldn't appreciate being woken earlier than necessary. Sure, Kirsten might be awake and bouncing around, but Jeena didn't care to push boundaries she had no business breaching.

Maybe later today she'd find an opportunity to talk to Joy— but what could she say? *I'm sorry you've been abused, and I know what it feels like?* No, that wouldn't work. Or would it? When had she ever been that honest and open with anyone other than her mother and Grammie? Never, that she could remember.

What if Joy denied it, or worse, laughed? Jeena had been ridiculed before, but rarely as an adult, and never since moving up the financial and business ladder. *Until recently, that is.* Memories of the women gossiping about her in the ladies' room and of her image splashed across newspapers and on TV stations rushed back, demanding to be considered.

No need to concern herself over Joy's reaction now; the day had yet to begin, and all sorts of possibilities abounded. Funny thought, that there could be possibilities in this place. She ran back over yesterday's events, dissecting each one and turning it over in her mind.

Tara made an interesting study, with more than a little potential in her makeup. As much as Jeena hated to admit it, the younger woman had taught her a thing or two during the course of the day. Sticking with a distasteful job wasn't a new concept, but the energy and drive that Tara brought to her less-than-glamorous work certainly was. What drove the girl?

For that matter, what kept someone like Rachel here? Jeena's mind skipped ahead at laser speed, and the image of Pastor Paul leapt into place. The man was handsome, obviously educated, an eloquent speaker with a church of his own, yet he chose to volunteer at a shelter. Why? What motivation could each of them have? It was doubtful they made much money, and there certainly was little to no praise for this type of work. She couldn't see any advancement looming, so what made them stay?

She knew what they'd say if asked—God. But that was rubbish—wasn't it? She doubted that God cared about individuals. She didn't doubt He existed, but why would He love imperfect people?

Deep inside, she had to acknowledge that someone bigger than herself must exist. If this was all there was to life—if people like her were in control of the world, with no one wiser watching over them—she shuddered to think of the outcome.

If that were true, how could the inconsistencies she'd seen in her father's life line up with what they preached here? Jeena's mother had tried to protect her, but she wasn't strong enough to do so—and until recent years, Jeena's grandmother had lived too far away to make much difference. Both women had loved her, and they must be an example of God's love. But her father's influence so overshadowed that love, it nearly choked her to remember.

The soft buzzer on her alarm sounded, and none too soon. Too much thinking was leading down another painful path.

Jeena swung her legs over the edge of the bed and onto the cold linoleum floor. The longing for an emotional escape, if not a physical one, surged. The past few days had been so busy, she hadn't thought about finding a drink, but now, the desire nearly overwhelmed her with its power.

No. The shelter did periodic drug and alcohol testing without advance warning, and she'd better wait till after the next time that happened. No sense in taking chances. Maybe today would bring more promise. Maybe today she'd find a real job and—if an opportunity arose—see what she could do for Joy.

❦

Jeena clamped her teeth tight, wishing to be anywhere but in this small chapel. She'd managed to come in late the day she'd cared for Mary, but no excuse presented itself today. She sighed and glanced around the room, doing her best to tune out the pastor's words.

A number of children were present, but only young ones, as the older kids were in school. A blond little boy who couldn't be much past four sat two rows in front of Jeena, wriggling and whispering to his mother. The woman glared at the boy and smacked the top of his head. He hunched his shoulders and sank against her side. Jeena felt a twinge of empathy for the youngster.

She turned her attention to other rows of women, hoping to spot Joy and Kirsten. A number of new faces dotted the room, but not the ones she wanted. Rachel didn't appear to be present, either. Strange. Chapel was a requirement for residents and staff, the exception being sickness or a staff member working the reception desk. Rachel took a turn there occasionally, but what about Joy?

Pastor Paul's normally quiet voice intensified, drawing Jeena's attention away from scanning the room and back to the pulpit. His message must be coming to a close.

"I'd like you to remember the most important aspect of prayer I've talked about today. We can't look at God as a glorified Santa Claus, ready to dole out gifts whenever we ask. Rather, prayer has a deeper purpose. God desires that prayer would bring us into a personal relationship with Him. Is it all right to ask for things? Of course. Should that be our primary goal in praying? Absolutely not."

The pastor leaned over the small podium, his face earnest, and made eye contact with several of the women, letting his words soak in. "What have your prayers been? Or do you even pray? Are they mostly centered around your wants and needs?"

Jeena tried to suppress a frown. She had no desire to pray, as God never listened when she'd tried. Prayer hadn't saved her from a beating when she hid from her father in the closet, and prayer certainly didn't keep Sean from leaving. It didn't seem to matter whether a child or adult uttered the petition, God appeared to either be deaf or uncaring. Either way, she was finished with trying. Disappointment hurt too much.

Paul's voice dropped, and the intensity eased. "Have you ever felt as though God didn't care, that your prayers bounced back at you and fell lifeless to the floor?"

Jeena stared. Was the man a mind reader? Or did most people feel this way and she hadn't realized it? The pastor's words captured her attention, and she leaned forward.

"I understand. I felt the same way a few years ago. My life was spent on drugs and alcohol, and nothing I did mattered. I made all the wrong choices, and God didn't appear to care. I figured He'd forgotten I existed and life was a joke. Then He sent a man into my life who offered a challenge, and I'd like to tell you what he told me. Don't ask for anything material. Instead, pray a simple prayer that goes like this: 'God, if You're real, show Yourself to me. Help me to understand what a relationship with You means. I'm not asking for anything other than to prove that You care.'

"Keep it simple, ladies, and I promise God will answer that prayer."

His face softened, and he stepped to the edge of the platform. "I'd like you to bow your heads and let me pray for you." A hush fell over the women and children. "But first, I'd like to ask a question, with your heads bowed and eyes closed. If you'd like to try that experiment, would you slip your hand up?"

Jeena gripped her hands together in her lap. The idea of asking God to prove Himself real, the concept of praying only for relationship rather than for tangible things stunned her. Her father had never discussed knowing God and rarely mentioned God's love.

The pastor's voice moved into prayer as Jeena continued to wrestle with the idea. What could it hurt? Sure, it might not work—probably wouldn't, in fact—but what if it did? What would it be like, having a relationship with God? She'd think about it before taking the risk of yet another rejection. Maybe, just maybe, she'd see if it could work.

Jeena hurried away from chapel, intent on finding Joy. After Mary's recent illness, she had a sinking fear that Joy or Kirsten might be next. The little girl had burrowed her way into Jeena's heart, and the thought of the child lying ill worried her.

Jeena strode around the corner and into the foyer to find Rachel sitting at the desk. "Rachel? Do you have a minute?" Jeena slowed her pace.

Rachel stood and smiled. "Gladly. I've been sitting too long. What's on your mind?"

Jeena stepped over beside the desk. "Um . . . it's not a big deal. I just wondered if Joy or Kirsten are sick, or if anything's wrong? I didn't see them in chapel . . ." It sounded foolish. Other people missed chapel, and here she was, running to Rachel and checking up on someone she barely knew.

Rachel smiled and patted Jeena's arm. "And you were worried? That's understandable—Kirsten has that effect on a lot of the women. She's a sweetie. She had the sniffles this morning, and Joy wanted to stay with her while she slept. Pop up there for a minute if you'd like."

The surge of relief startled Jeena and left her feeling rattled. "Oh. Good. I mean, thank you." She took a step back, working to gather her composure. "I believe I will. Thank you, Rachel."

"You're welcome." Rachel gave a small wave and settled back into her chair with a sigh.

CHAPTER 34

ive minutes later, Jeena tapped on Joy's door. Would she
wake Kirsten and make matters worse?

The door opened a crack, and Joy's somber eyes
peeked out. Her face lit with a soft smile. "Hi, Jeena," she
whispered. "Just a second . . ." She pulled back the door
and slipped into the hall, leaving the door open a bit. "Kirsten's
been asleep for almost an hour, and I don't want to wake her."

Jeena nodded and stepped away from the room. "I missed you
at chapel. Rachel told me Kirsten's sick. Is she feeling any better?"

Joy reached out and gave her a quick hug. "How sweet, thank
you. I'm probably just overprotective. It's only a sniffle. But she
seemed tired and wanted to stay in bed, so I let her."

Jeena touched her shoulder where Joy's arm had rested, surprised at her reaction to the woman's hug. Other than Tammy, it
had been a while since someone had shown her the kind of love
that asked nothing in return. Sean hadn't understood that type
of love, and she'd only just begun to see that.

One other person had touched her heart this way right after
Grammie's death—Irene. She'd hugged her at the memorial service, and Jeena had promised to go back and visit but hadn't
followed through. What she'd give now to sit and chat with the
older woman. Tears stung her eyes, and she turned away, hoping
Joy wouldn't notice.

"Jeena?" Joy's fingertips touched her arm. "You okay?"

"Yeah." She forced a smile and tried to laugh. "Sure, I'm fine."

Joy studied Jeena's face, then gripped her hand. "Come on.
Let's sit here in the hall. I can hear Kirsten if she wakes and calls
me." She led Jeena toward a bay window tucked into a small
alcove with a bench that had a padded back. "Now what's wrong?

Did I upset you?" She sank onto the bench and drew Jeena down beside her.

"No. I guess I miss my grandmother," Jeena blurted. "Your hug made me think of her and her best friend where she used to live."

Joy leaned toward Jeena. "Used to live? She's gone?"

Jeena nodded and bit her lip. "Yeah. She passed away late this summer."

"I'm sorry."

"Thanks." The silence stretched out a few moments, and Jeena searched for a way to turn the conversation. She'd come to help Joy and somehow ended up with Joy helping her. "Actually, I came up to talk, but I'm not sure how to begin."

Joy smiled. "I guess just talk. I don't bite, you know."

Jeena chuckled and relaxed in her seat. "I know. Since you asked about my grandmother, maybe I'll start there." She felt like she was rambling but pushed on, desperate to get this over. "My mother and dad both died a few years ago, and Grammie was my only close relative. Her death left a huge hole in my life, the same as my mother's death did."

"How about your dad? Were the two of you close?"

"Not at all. I think I hated him." Jeena twisted a strand of hair around her finger and sighed. "I'm sorry, I didn't come up to talk about my problems, but about you."

"Me? I'm afraid I don't follow."

"Mary told me you seemed shook up over a sign posted on the bulletin board. Some guy that listed his wife and little girl as missing."

Joy's face paled a shade. "And that has to do with you hating your dad . . . how?"

Jeena shook her head. "I'm making a mess of this, but I understand what it means to be abused and live in fear. My dad beat me when I was a kid, and nobody helped me. Mary said there's talk that you're running from someone. There may not be any truth to it, and if not, then I owe you an apology. But if there is . . . well . . . I want to help, if I can." Jeena halted, unsure what to say next. Joy's pale face and compressed lips didn't encourage any more words.

Jeena pushed to her feet. "I'm sorry. I can see I was wrong, and I've made you angry." She turned and started down the hall.

"Wait." Joy's soft voice barely reached her. "You weren't wrong, and I'm not angry."

Jeena spun on her heel and faced Joy. "Then why don't you tell Rachel or go to the police?"

Joy's hand went to her throat, and she stood. "No. I can't let anyone know. If I do, he'll find me. I can't take the chance that he'll get Kirsten back. If I file a police report, he might track me down. I know it probably doesn't make sense to you, but I tried to get help before, and it didn't work."

Jeena nodded. "I tried to tell someone about my father when I was a kid, and they didn't listen. He appeared to be such an upstanding man in the community and a pillar in the church that they didn't believe me."

"That's how Kevin is. He swept me off my feet, and we married ten weeks after we met, against my parents' wishes. The first five months were great; then he lost his job. After Kirsten was born, the expense of a baby put an added strain on our marriage."

Jeena led the way back to the bench and patted the seat beside her. "So he started hitting you?"

Joy sank down. "He'd never done anything before, but as the money got tight and the stress grew, that changed. He loved Kirsten, but her wails would send him up the wall when he was trying to sleep, and if I couldn't make her stop, he'd yell at me. One time, he totally lost it and shoved me against a wall on his way out of the room. I know he hated what was happening as much as I did, but we seemed to keep spiraling downward."

"So you think it was mostly stress that caused it, rather than him having a mean streak?"

Joy sighed. "Yeah. Kevin was basically a sweet guy. He started having worse spells where he'd lose his temper. He'd finally found a job, but the hours were long, and the pay wasn't great. His boss didn't treat him well, and he started changing."

"What made you finally leave? It sounds like you still care."

Joy nodded and wiped away a slow tear that trickled from the corner of one eye. "That's just it, I did. One day, he lost it and slapped me—hard. And not long after Kirsten's third birthday, I caught him shaking her. That scared me. Plus, his mood swings made Kirsten withdraw, and that seemed to push him into a deeper depression, if that's what you'd call it."

Jeena sucked in a breath. "Depression can do strange things to a person."

"Yeah. He never hit me again, but he threatened to. I couldn't take a chance that Kirsten would be next. I begged him to get help—go to counseling—but he refused. Said men should take care of their own problems."

Jeena gave a dry laugh. "I've heard that one before. Unfortunately, they rarely do."

Joy nodded and twisted her hands in her lap. "I didn't deal well with the stress, either. Near the end, I got so furious at his mood swings that I flipped. I threw a glass against a wall near his head. The glass shattered, and pieces flew everywhere. One cut his face."

Jeena winced. "Uh-oh. What'd he do?"

"I thought he'd be furious, but he turned cold. He went to the hospital without a word and got stitches. Came back and said if I ever tried to leave him, he'd take Kirsten and claim I was an unfit mother. He promised to use the hospital visit as proof that I'm violent."

"So . . ." Jeena leaned back and folded her arms. "Is that when you decided to leave?"

"Yeah. No way would I put Kirsten in danger. I saw the signs, and I didn't have the money to fight him. I knew I had to take her and run."

Jeena touched Joy's clenched hand and smiled. "I don't blame you for running. Do you think he could've changed?"

Joy shrugged. "I'm not willing to find out. I loved him, but he changed so much between when we met and when I left that I didn't feel I even knew him anymore. Besides, if he's still the same, I'd be trapped. Maybe if I hadn't had a child, I might have tried to put my marriage back together, but I couldn't put Kirsten in that situation."

Jeena suppressed a shudder. "I agree. So you ended up here?"

Joy nodded and leaned back in her seat. "Yeah. After a number of other stops along the way."

"How about your parents?"

"We drifted apart when I married Kevin. My dad's a stubborn man and tends to hold a grudge, and I was too proud to let them know they were right. We stopped talking, and I didn't even let them know when I became pregnant or when Kirsten was born."

"Maybe it's not too late. You should contact them. Let them know they've got a granddaughter."

Joy rubbed her hands over her arms and nodded. "I've thought about it, but Kevin calling here has me spooked. He knows where my folks live, and he'll be watching there, too. I'm not sure what to do. But if he gets any closer, I'll have to run again, and I hate the thought."

Jeena lightly touched Joy's arm. "Don't run without telling someone. Tell Rachel or the pastor . . . let someone help you."

Joy got to her feet. "I can't promise, but I'll think about it. I'd better check on Kirsten. Thank you for caring, Jeena. Really."

Jeena stood, suddenly feeling helpless. "Tell me if you decide to go? Don't just disappear."

Joy squeezed her shoulder and stepped away. "I'll see. Maybe it won't happen. Maybe Kevin will give up and decide I'm not worth the bother, and I can start a new life."

Jeena nodded and tried to smile. "Maybe. I guess we can hope."

Joy tipped her head to the side and smiled. "Or as Rachel and the pastor say, we could pray. Who knows? It might even do some good."

Jeena walked down the hall and slipped into her room. She stood staring at the wooden door, her heart pounding and her thoughts whirling. Praying for someone to save her when she was a kid hadn't helped. She'd considered praying in the way the pastor suggested to see if God might care but hadn't yet taken that step. Joy might be right. Prayer might be an option in this case, since there didn't seem to be many other avenues open.

A picture of an angry man grabbing tiny Kirsten and dragging her out the door left her shaking. *God, I'm asking You to take care of that girl and her mother. Please. I don't know if You listen to anything I say, but I'm hoping this once You'll make an exception. Amen.*

CHAPTER 35

Jeena rushed through dressing and brushing her hair. How did she oversleep and not hear Mary or Carla getting ready? She reached under her bed and felt for her shoes. Nope. Wrong ones. She'd discovered comfortable loafers were more suited for her shift at the store.

An alarm sounded in her mind and stilled the motion of her hand. Something bothered her about these shoes. Ah . . . her ring. She'd tucked it into this toe. Better find a more secure hiding place even if it made her late for breakfast.

Her fingers explored the toe of one shoe, then the other, with no result. She turned them upside down and shook, but no ring bounced off the hard linoleum floor. A cold feeling washed over her skin, and she fell to her knees in front of the bed. It had to be here. She couldn't lose Grammie's ring—the last gift she'd received and her last connection to Grammie.

She lay on her stomach and swept her fingers across the floor under the bed, but only small dust balls rewarded her efforts. A sneeze blew more dust into her face, and she pulled back with a frown. No one knew she'd hidden the ring in her shoe, and it should've been safe. Besides, she'd only worn it a short time prior to the day she'd hidden it.

Sarah. Jeena felt a tingle at the base of her neck as she remembered the words the woman had spoken. *"You're afraid it's gonna be stole. You'd best be hurryin' back to yer room and lockin' it up."* Had she made the suggestion hoping Jeena would indeed hide it in her room? That had to be it. No one else had commented on her ring.

She slid her feet into her shoes, stalked out her bedroom door, and headed for the dining room, determined to find the thief.

Sarah would return her ring now, or she'd call the cops. The woman had harassed her enough to last a lifetime, and Jeena didn't intend to let her add theft to the list.

Sarah's loud laugh led Jeena right to her table. She slid to a stop beside the chortling woman and drew a deep breath, then stuck her palm under Sarah's nose. "Give it back, Sarah, or I'm calling the police." A hush fell over the table and spread to the others nearby. Out of the corner of her eye, Jeena saw a woman elbow another woman and snicker.

Sarah's chuckle died, and her cold blue eyes swung to meet Jeena's. "What are you talking about? Give what back? I got nothin' of yours." She crossed her arms over her striped T-shirt.

Jeena didn't flinch. "My amethyst ring. You told me I should hide it in my room, and that's exactly what I did. Well guess what? It disappeared, and I think you're the thief."

Sarah jumped to her feet, slamming her chair back. It hit the floor with a loud metallic clang, making the women at the table jump. Whispers and snickers filled the air.

"You can take her, Sarah," a voice hooted.

Jeena took a slight step back, realizing the physical damage the big woman could do, then stopped. No way would she back down without getting her grandmother's ring, even if she had to fight for it.

"I ain't no thief, and you can't call me one." Sarah spat the words and shoved her face forward.

"I'll call you what I like. I think you've got it—if you haven't pawned it by now." Jeena threw back her shoulders and stood firm.

"What's going on?" Rachel covered the space to where the two women stood. "I'd like an explanation. Now."

Sarah dropped a loud expletive, then took a step back. "She said I stole her ring and threatened to turn the cops on me. I won't stand for that, Miss Rachel. Nobody calls me a thief. I've done some wrong things in my life, but I ain't never stole."

Rachel placed a gentle hand on Sarah's arm. "We'll get to the bottom of this, but why don't you pick up your chair and calm down? And everyone else," she raised her voice, "if you're finished eating, please go take care of your chores. If you know anything about Jeena's ring, see me in my office."

Jeena started to speak but Rachel held up her hand. "Not here. I want you both in my office. Never mind chores." She waited while Sarah picked up her chair, then motioned the two women in front of her.

The silent trio made their way to Rachel's office. Jeena's mind flew to the words Sarah said, replaying the strong emotion in the woman's voice declaring she'd never stolen from anyone. Could that be true? Was it possible she'd wrongly accused Sarah? If so, then who took her ring? She'd been stupid when she'd almost sold it, but she'd been desperate for food and a place to live. This was different—and it scared her that she might not see her ring again.

She shot up a quick prayer, hoping God might have time to listen but doubting He'd care. Didn't the pastor say that relationship was more important to God than material things? Well, not to her. If God didn't care about something this close to her heart, then she didn't need a relationship with Him. She felt confused by her own thinking. The last thing she wanted was to make Him angry, but trying to discard the childhood impressions of a distant God seemed almost impossible.

Rachel stopped outside her door and reached for the knob, then ushered the two women in. She waited until they sat before sinking into the chair behind her desk. "Jeena, tell me what's going on, since it appears you've made some type of accusation against Sarah."

Jeena leaned back in her chair and folded her arms. "I think she stole my grandmother's amethyst and diamond ring. She's the one who suggested I hide it in my room before someone stole it. I did, right after the meal. I put it in a place I didn't think anyone would look, and it's gone."

Rachel propped her elbows on the desk and cupped her chin in her hand. "Did you put it in your lockbox?"

"No. I couldn't find the key and planned on coming right back, but forgot."

"Is there any possibility you moved it?"

"None. Today is the first time I've thought about it."

Sarah pushed back her chair and started to rise. "That's not my problem. Ya got two roommates, don't ya? I know Mary wouldn't touch nothin' that ain't hers, but how about Carla?"

Rachel motioned toward the chair. "Please sit down, Sarah. Accusing someone else won't help. Jeena and I need to check her room again."

Sarah grunted and scowled at Jeena. "About time someone used some sense." She swung her gaze back to Rachel. "I'm sorry I said that about Carla. Guess I'm upset. I'm tellin' you, I didn't take that ring. Besides, other women heard me tell her she oughta hide it."

Rachel pushed up from her seat. "I understand. Jeena"—she nodded toward the door—"would you mind if we take another look in your room?"

Jeena stood and stepped around Sarah. "Sure, but I don't think it'll do much good. I checked under the bed and emptied my shoes."

Rachel turned toward Sarah. "I'll catch up with you later. You might ask around."

Sarah nodded and shoved to her feet, then stalked out the door.

Rachel and Jeena headed upstairs and spent several minutes searching the room, scanning the area under the bed with a flashlight. Rachel snapped off the light. "I'm sorry, Jeena. I'd hoped we'd find it."

Jeena sank onto the end of the bed and frowned. "So what comes next?"

"I'll need to take it before the shelter committee."

"What's that?"

"It's a small group of staff mixed with a selection of our women. They've been voted into their position and have earned the trust of the other residents. Any time we have an issue where possible discipline is needed, the committee meets and makes a recommendation."

"Will they question me?" Jeena asked.

"Yes, you and Sarah both, as well as Carla and Mary."

Jeena groaned. "But I don't believe Carla or Mary had anything to do with it. I'd hate to have them think I'm accusing them."

Rachel brushed dust off her knees before replying. "There's one other option. We can pray about it and not move forward with the committee. I'm fairly sure Sarah won't change her story. Since we didn't find anything here, there's little the committee can do. They might suggest searching the three women's belongings, but they could also remind you that personal items are your responsibility."

Jeena sat without moving for a full minute, trying to think. "I'd hate it if Mary's and Carla's things were searched. Can I think about it?"

Rachel nodded and stood. "I'll pray about it, and I suggest you consider the same. God cares about the little things in our lives, and it sounds as though your grandmother's ring is more than that to you."

"It is, but I don't think He cares."

Rachel gave Jeena a quick hug, then stepped away. "That's where you're wrong. He cared enough to send His Son to die for you, and His Word says He wants us to have an abundant life."

Jeena frowned. "Abundant life? That's what you think He's given me? I've lost everything. My home, career, my car, even my good name, and I'm living in a shelter. That's not my idea of abundance."

"There's more to life than things. We all make poor choices, or things happen in life that don't seem fair. Knowing Jesus brings more joy than anything money can buy. I hope someday you'll believe that."

Jeena felt a sting in her eyes. "That's what Grammie used to tell me, but it doesn't line up with how my father lived."

"How about your grandmother?"

"Yes . . ." Jeena said, then drew a deep breath. "But she's one of the rare people I saw who did. If you'd known my father"—she tried to suppress a shiver—"you'd understand."

"Maybe you need to understand that your father wasn't God's representative and may have gotten things wrong."

"He thought he was." Jeena glanced at her watch and frowned. "We've missed most of chapel service. You want me to head to the thrift store?"

Rachel tried to smile, but a shadow of worry remained. "Sure. Thanks for talking, Jeena . . . and for waiting before taking any action. I'll be asking the Lord to return it to you."

Jeena reached for the door. "Thanks. See you later." She headed down the hall, her heart in turmoil. If only she could remove the picture of her father's angry face from her mind. He'd be the first to dispute the suggestion that he wasn't God's representative. The thought of God caring about the little details of her life brought a longing she'd not known since childhood. Today it was harder to brush that longing aside—maybe this time she wouldn't try quite so hard to silence it.

CHAPTER 36

"J eena, wait up." Joy's voice floated down the sidewalk and turned Jeena around. "I'd like to walk with you to the store, if you don't mind."

Jeena waited, watching the passing cars with interest, wondering where the people rushed to. Did they appreciate their homes and families? Did they know how fortunate they were not to live at a shelter, or did it even occur to them that homelessness might be just one mistake away?

Joy arrived at her side, breathless from jogging the last half block. "Hi," she managed, then drew a deep breath. "I got permission to do some shopping for Kirsten at the store, and Rachel gave me a credit voucher."

A truck roared by, spewing diesel fumes and blaring its horn at a car nearing the intersection. Jeena waved her hand in front of her nose and grimaced. "Let's hurry—diesel gives me a headache."

They walked in silence until they reached a crosswalk and paused for the light. Jeena punched the walk button and glared at the signal. "I don't know why they put these things here; it sure doesn't make much difference."

Joy chuckled and nodded. "Yeah. Kirsten thinks if she pushes the button we should be able to run across the street. Are you liking your job at the store?"

Jeena shrugged and shifted her weight from one foot to the other. "It's a job." The light changed, and they stepped off the curb. "Tara's decent to work with and I have something to occupy my time. Till things turn around, I mean."

They stepped out of the crosswalk, and Joy nodded. "Yeah. So what exactly did you do . . . uh . . . before? Sorry. If it's something you'd rather not talk about . . ."

Jeena slowed her pace. "No big deal. I worked as an independent design contractor for building firms. I did the landscaping layout, as well as a lot of the interior design and decorating. I didn't draw up the blueprints, but I worked alongside the engineers, suggesting what might be aesthetically pleasing or more cost effective for the company."

"Ah, sounds like a challenge, but I imagine one you enjoyed." Joy sucked in a breath, then drew to a halt.

Jeena stopped a stride past the frozen woman and turned back. "Joy?" She touched her arm. "Joy. What's the matter?"

Joy pushed a lock of hair from her face with a trembling hand. "I'm not sure. I think . . . no, never mind. It's nothing. Let's go."

Jeena shrugged and swung back into a ground-covering walk. "If you say so."

The women covered the next block in silence, but Joy peered over her shoulder repeatedly. At one point, she stumbled, almost losing her balance.

"You sure everything's all right?" Jeena pressed. "Are you worried about Kevin?"

"Yeah. Let's get to the store." Joy picked up the pace but looked over her shoulder again.

A dark-clad form stepped around the corner, and Jeena barely saw him out of the corner of her eye.

The man's shoulder struck Joy square on her chest. She let out a shriek and turned as if to run.

The man reached to steady her. "I'm sorry. I wasn't paying attention."

Joy shrank at his touch, and the eyes she turned toward Jeena were haunted and fearful. "No. My mistake. I was looking behind me." She stepped around the confused man and almost sprinted away.

Jeena smiled and shrugged at the man, then trotted to catch up. "Joy, wait." She pulled alongside the ashen-faced woman and drew her to a halt. "That's enough. I don't care if I *am* late for work. Spill it. And don't say it's nothing 'cause I don't buy it. You look like someone told you that your best friend just died. What gives?"

Joy drew Jeena up against the wall of a nearby brick building. "I thought I saw Kevin," she whispered. "Back there." She waved in the direction they'd come. "When that man bumped into me, I thought he'd caught me." She shuddered and covered her face with her hands. "What am I going to do? What if Kevin finds me?" She looked up, her face set. "I'll run. He's not going to get Kirsten."

Jeena grabbed Joy's arm and shook it. "Stop it. You don't even know it was Kevin. Did you get a good look at him?"

Joy's face lost some of its rigidity. "No . . . not a good look. But he had the same dark hair and build as Kevin."

Jeena released her hold and took a step back. "That's it? Just the same hair color and build? You didn't see his face?"

"No. But I thought, I mean, it seemed like . . ." She stared at Jeena. "You think I'm losing it, don't you? That I'm imagining things?"

"No. I know you're frightened, but you aren't sure you saw him, and even if you did . . ." She gripped Joy's arm again when the other woman started to bolt. "I'm sorry. But he doesn't know where you are, and the man, whoever he was, didn't see you, right?"

Joy released her breath, and her shoulders slumped. "You're right. But I've seen him a couple of times since we left the shelter and didn't think anything of it until now. I guess I've got the jitters since Kevin called the shelter and asked them to post about his missing family. But he probably called every shelter within five hundred miles of our home."

Jeena patted her arm. "I agree. I can't believe he'd be lucky enough to land in the right town when there are so many to choose from. Come on. Let's get you to the store."

Joy picked up her pace till Jeena almost trotted to keep up. "Right. I'm not leaving Kirsten alone any longer than I have to."

"Joy?" Jeena touched the woman's arm. "There's something that might help."

Joy slowed again. "The store is a couple of doors down. Let's talk there?"

Jeena looked around, wondering if the man Joy thought she'd seen might be following. "Sure." They walked the last few steps and pushed open the glass doors.

Tara waved from her place behind the register. "Hey, Jeena. How goes it? Get a late start?" She tipped her head toward the clock behind the counter.

Jeena groaned. "I'm sorry. I'll punch in and be right back."

Tara stretched her arms above her head, making the tattoos move and bend along her skin. "No worries. Hi-ya, Joy. Doin' some shopping?"

"Yeah, for Kirsten. Would you mind if I talk to Jeena for just another minute?"

"Sure. No customers here now anyway. Go for it." Tara flipped her hair over her shoulder and picked up a magazine lying on the counter. "Take your time." She propped her boots up on the desk and waved them away.

Jeena dropped her voice. "I don't think it was Kevin." She looked back over her shoulder at the big, glass windows. "Someone could be following me."

Joy ground to a stop and gripped Jeena's arm. "Following you?" she repeated. "Whatever for?"

Jeena motioned her into the small cubicle that served as an office and drew the door shut behind them. "I may have to testify against my old boss, and that testimony could help put him away if they're able to find him. It wouldn't surprise me if he paid someone to keep an eye on me."

"You need to go to the police."

Jeena reached for her time card. "I don't think so. Since he's on the run, I'm not a threat."

Joy frowned. "Promise me you'll report it if it happens again?"

"I will if you promise to tell me if you do see Kevin, instead of running." She raised her brows and waited.

Joy rolled her eyes. "All right. Deal. Now you'd better get to work. I'll find some clothes and get back to Kirsten."

Jeena strode to the front to see what work Tara had lined up. One thing was for sure: she'd be watching her back and keeping an eye on Joy's as well.

※

Later that day, the bell on the door tinkled again. Tara was on break in the back, and Jeena sat on a stool behind the counter, thankful only an hour remained till closing. A woman backed through the door with a stack of boxes in her arms. Something about her looked familiar. Jeena felt the blood drain from her face. Connie. She flew off the stool and headed around the end of the counter, intent on getting away before being spotted.

"Hello? Can someone *please* take these?" The petulant voice spoke from behind the stack. "Hurry up, won't you? My arms are tired."

Jeena glanced from Connie to the back of the store, willing Tara to appear, and wishing she could disappear. No such luck— she'd have to deal with her one-time friend and all-time biggest gossip on her own.

She stepped forward and slid the top two boxes into her arms, then turned and set them on the floor out of the way. "You can put the other one on top." She waved at the small stack and walked behind the counter, her back stiff and her shoulders erect.

Connie dropped the box with a thud and stood, not yet facing Jeena. "I need a tax receipt. Give me the largest donation amount you can." She swung around and stared straight into Jeena's steady gaze. "Jeena?" She gaped at the counter separating them. A small smile tugged at her lips, then quickly grew into a smirk. "You work here?"

Jeena nodded. "Connie." She reached under the counter, pulled out the receipt book, flipped it open, and poised her pen above the pad. "What did you bring in? Clothing? Housewares? Collectibles? What's the approximate value?"

Connie placed her hands on her hips and laughed outright. "No way! The high and mighty Jeena Gregory working at a thrift store. This is rich." She nearly hooted with laughter.

Jeena felt the slow crawl of blood creep from her neck up to her cheeks. She couldn't remember a time when she'd wanted to slap someone as badly as she did now. On second thought, slapping was too gentle. She sighed. It would only get her fired;

Connie would see to that. "Snap out of it, Connie. You wanted a receipt—what type of items and what value?"

Connie made a show of pulling a tissue from her bag and dabbing at her eyes. "Honestly, Jeena, is this some kind of game? I mean, nobody who is anybody works at a place like this." She narrowed her eyes. "So the rumors were true—no one hired you after Browning got nailed. I thought you left town." She glanced around the store and back at the silent woman behind the counter. "You live near here?"

Jeena didn't reply. What could she say? *I live at the women's shelter because I couldn't find work and got kicked out of my house?* She remembered when she'd dropped off the boxes of clothing at the shelter, what seemed a lifetime ago. She'd believed that only lazy people would end up there—people with no dreams or vision and no motivation to succeed. Connie's expression proved that she felt the same.

And if she believed that, nothing would change her mind—unless life threw her a hardball that forced her to reevaluate. Connie wouldn't care what brought Jeena here—she'd believe whatever she chose.

Connie leaned her forearm on the counter and put her face inches from Jeena's. "Cat got your tongue?" The smirk reappeared.

"I used to be just like you." Jeena drew a deep breath, then rushed on. "Judging anyone who didn't share my standard of living, thinking I was above the people struggling to make ends meet. And the ones who ended up in welfare lines or at a homeless shelter—or worse yet, sleeping on the streets? I made a point to walk as far away as possible."

Connie straightened and crossed her arms over her chest. "Your point?"

"You don't have a clue what you're talking about. You've never had to stand in that line, see the disdain on the face of a clerk when they realize you're using food stamps, or had to stomp on your pride to accept a tray of food from a shelter. You have no idea what it does to someone's spirit when they endure those looks after they've done all they could to escape. If you cared to understand, you could. But you're like I used to be—you only care about yourself and about what money and relationships can bring. If the rest of the world goes up in flames, it's no skin off your nose as long as you're not burned."

Connie's face contorted into a deep scowl, and her chin rose. "And you're different? You've walked on a lot of people, and it didn't seem to bother you."

Jeena placed her palms on the counter and leaned forward. "That's what I'm talking about. I've been there, done that. And believe me, it doesn't bring any joy. I've also been on the losing end where my pride's been dragged in the dirt." She stopped, hating the thought of revealing more.

Connie shrugged. "Yeah . . . so? From what I heard, you brought this mess on yourself. Trust me, I'll never end up working for a living or going hungry."

"Life is strange, Connie, and I've learned to never say never anymore." Jeena made a notation on the receipt book and signed the bottom, then ripped it out and handed it across the counter. "Here. Fill in the dollar amount for whatever you think it's worth. I need to get back to work."

Connie stuffed the paper in her purse and spun on her heel. "I'm sure I won't see you again, darling." She waved and tittered before waltzing out the door.

Jeena sank onto the stool. The encounter had been difficult but not as bad as she'd expected. For some reason, Connie's biting remarks didn't seem to have the same power to sting as they'd once had. One thing she knew: she'd never again judge someone by their appearance. She'd learned her lesson on that score. Living in a shelter or buying groceries for a few months with food stamps didn't make you a worthless person. Sure, many people abused the system, but many others didn't. Maybe she'd grown up a little since losing her house and arriving at the shelter.

CHAPTER 37

Tara and Jeena headed to the office to clock out. Jeena's back ached, and her shoulders felt like someone had smashed her across the back with a crowbar. She'd been moving heavy boxes from the drop-off bay to the sorting area for the past hour and wasn't sure she had the energy to drag herself home. *Home?* Funny thought.

Tara eyed her. "Thinking about your missing ring?"

Jeena stifled a gasp. "You know about my ring?"

Tara shrugged a shoulder and sank into a chair. "Sure, it's been the talk of the shelter for days. Even if I don't live there anymore, I hear the gossip."

Jeena gaped, not caring that surprise must be blazoned across her face. "What do you mean, the talk of the shelter?"

"Aw, you know—whispers about you and Sarah gettin' into it the other day and you accusing her of stealing your ring, know what I mean?" She leaned back in her chair and crossed her arms over her multicolored vest.

"How'd they find out about it?" As soon as she asked, Jeena wanted to bite her tongue—she saw all over again the confrontation in the cafeteria and Sarah's loud denial.

"I see you remember." Tara's boot toe tapped the floor in a rhythmic pattern.

"Yeah, I guess I do." Jeena ducked her head for a moment, trying to think. The issue hadn't been resolved, and she'd shelved the idea of an inquiry. Her ring would be sold by now and probably turned into a snort of cocaine or a bottle of whiskey, stashed somewhere in the shelter or hidden outside. She wasn't stupid. Some of these women still found ways of using and hoped not to get caught. The thought of her grandmother's ring providing payment for someone's habit turned her stomach and made her angry at the same time.

Jeena met Tara's eyes. "I might not be here much longer."

"Whad'ya mean? Where you goin'?" Tara's toe ceased its dance across the floor. "Because of your ring, or because the women are talking behind your back? It digs at you, doesn't it?"

Jeena started to shake her head, but the denial froze on her lips when she saw the look in Tara's eyes. The young woman had never been anything but straightforward with her. "Yes. I don't care to be the brunt of gossip, especially by a bunch of . . ." Her voice trailed off.

"By a bunch of homeless women? That's what you almost said, right?" Tara gazed steadily at Jeena. "Let me tell you a secret. You're homeless, too, in case you've forgotten. And there isn't any shame in it. Sure, sometimes it's caused by bad choices, and sometimes it's what life throws at you. But we're all people, we've all got feelings, and none of us want to be hurt—me included."

Jeena stretched her fingers toward Tara's arm, then let her hand fall to her side. "I'm sorry. I didn't mean it that way."

Tara pursed her lips and stared.

Jeena sighed and closed her eyes for a brief moment. "Okay, maybe I did. I don't know much of anything anymore. Why I'm here or what keeps me at the shelter. There's something—I don't know—different about it, that I can't put my finger on."

Tara nodded and smiled. "Rachel and Pastor Paul would say it's God. I'm not so sure but I think they're right. I'm not very old, but I've seen a lot, and most of it I wish I hadn't. I used to think God couldn't exist in such a stink hole as this world, but now? After the people at the shelter gave me a chance, I'm thinking there must be a loving God."

Jeena sat motionless while a small shiver crept up her back. The words rang true.

Tara pushed herself out of the chair and reached for her jacket. "So you're leaving. I'll talk to Rachel about finding somebody else to work."

Jeena rose slowly and picked up her sweater. "No. Not yet. Who knows, if God really does care, maybe He'll work a miracle and bring my ring back—and you never know, maybe I'll land a good-paying job in the bargain." She laughed at her own half-hearted joke and turned away.

Tara touched her shoulder. "Hey. It doesn't hurt to hope."

⚘

Almost dusk. Jeena couldn't believe October was nearing an end and November loomed ahead. What she'd give to have her car to drive to the shelter at this time of night. Too bad Tara had paperwork to finish. She'd feel safer with someone beside her as she walked through this seedy part of town.

Streetlights glowed and headlights flashed as the sky darkened. Jeena glanced at her watch and pushed the small button illuminating the face. Six o'clock? No wonder—she'd talked to Tara longer than she'd realized. She picked up her pace and skirted around a dark form lying up against a building. Never in a million years would she have believed she'd live in a place like this. Not Jeena Gregory. She pushed on, determined to get back as fast as possible.

Light steps sounded behind her and she turned in relief. "Tara? That you?" Jeena waited, but no one replied and the footsteps stopped. "Tara?" She stared into the growing darkness. Nothing. The hair on the back of her neck prickled. Time to get moving.

A half block passed with no sound, then she heard it again. Footsteps, and this time she was sure they were closer. She spun on her heel and stared. A shadowy form ducked around the corner behind her and disappeared. Her hand came to her mouth, and she stifled a cry.

She remembered what she'd told Joy. Panic gripped her stomach, and bile rose in her throat. Would Charles really see her as a threat? No way was she waiting to find out. She bolted down the street, thankful she wore sneakers. No sound of footsteps pursued her, but she wasn't sure she'd hear them over the pounding of her own feet hitting the pavement and her blood hammering in her ears.

Twice she slowed and peered over her shoulder, knowing the streetlight would illuminate her as well as the person who followed but determined to spot her pursuer. Maybe he'd taken off—maybe he wasn't still following and didn't know where she lived. Maybe. At this point, all she could do was get to her room and hope.

⚘

"Mama, can the pretty lady read me a story?" Kirsten's plaintive voice reached Jeena, who sat curled up in a chair in the common room. She'd come hoping to sort out her thoughts. So much had transpired in such a short space of time, and most of it still didn't make sense. The loss of her ring bothered her more than she wanted to admit, and every time she saw Sarah, her anger increased. The advent of Kirsten and Joy in the room offered a respite from her turbulent thoughts, and she turned their direction with a smile.

The little girl had on an emerald green, one-piece corduroy jumper with a white blouse underneath. Jeena guessed the outfit to be one Joy had procured at the thrift store. "Is your dress new, honey?"

Kirsten stopped, and a shy smile tugged at her small mouth; then she pirouetted where she stood and giggled. "My mama bought it for me. Do you think I'm pretty?"

Joy rolled her eyes and smiled. "Kirsten, that's not something you ask people."

Jeena chuckled. "Yes, I think you're very pretty today, and your mama did a good job picking out your new clothes. You brought a book you want me to read? Or did you mean someone else?" She surveyed the common area but found her corner empty for a change. Some of the women were out for the evening on visitor's passes, and others were grouped in front of the TV on the far side of the large room. Thankfully, the volume wasn't cranked to its normal obnoxious level.

Joy sank into a nearby chair and drew her small daughter close. "Please don't feel that you've got to read to her, Jeena. I can do it."

Kirsten turned an entreating face to her mother, her mouth pleading. "Oh please, Mama. You read to me all the time. I want her to do it."

Jeena laughed outright, and it brought a pleasant sensation. "I don't mind. In fact, I'd enjoy it. I haven't read to a child in . . . why, I'm not sure how long it's been. Probably clear back in my middle-school, babysitting days." She beckoned to Kirsten, then patted her lap. "Do you want to sit on my lap or on the couch beside me?"

Kirsten's head dropped, and her two middle fingers popped in her mouth. One foot shuffled against the carpet, and the book she clutched came up against her chest.

Jeena leaned forward and softened her voice. "It's all right, honey. You don't have to sit on my lap, and your mama can read to you, if you'd rather."

Kirsten peered up through her bangs. "Uh-uh. I want you," she mumbled around her fingers, then crept closer.

Jeena waited, unmoving, not wanting to cause another retreat. Her patience paid off as Kirsten walked two steps closer and held out the book.

"What's the name of your book?"

That seemed to break the child's reserve. "*David and Goliath.* God saved the little boy from the big, mean giant. But first God saved his sheep from a bear and a lion."

Jeena cocked her head and looked at the book. She'd been asked to read a Bible story? Oh well, a child's book couldn't take too long, could it? She patted the couch again. "Want to sit by me?"

Kirsten marched forward, placed the book in Jeena's out-stretched hand, and promptly climbed up in her lap. Two little arms wrapped themselves around Jeena's waist and worked their way right into her heart. "Thank you, Jeena."

She patted the child's back, then smoothed her hair as the little arms continued to hug. "You're welcome, sweetie," she whispered, then cleared her throat. "Now, before we read, why don't you tell me how old you are? And when is your birthday?"

She worked to smooth out her voice, hoping Joy didn't notice the break.

Kirsten pulled back and peered up into Jeena's face, her eyes lit with shining joy. "I had a birthday"—she turned to her mother—"how many days ago, Mama?"

"One month ago, sweetie."

The little girl nodded. "I'm four. I'm a big girl now." She sat up straight and smiled up at Jeena. "How old are you, and when is *your* birthday?" she asked.

Joy sputtered and covered her mouth. "Kirsten," she choked, "we don't ask adults how old they are."

"Oh. I forgot. When is your birthday?"

Jeena stopped and thought for a moment. "Hmm . . . why, I think it's just a few days from now. I'd forgotten how close we are to November. And I don't mind answering your first question, although your mama is right about not asking. I'll be thirty on Sunday." A sense of sadness washed over her heart. Thirty. Such a momentous day to spend here. No one but these two homeless wanderers would even know, and she doubted they'd remember. "Let's see what your book has to say, okay?"

"Okay." Kirsten snuggled against Jeena's chest and gazed at the book. "One day, long, long ago . . ." Jeena's words were echoed by the little girl on her lap, and she couldn't help but wonder what her life would've been like if she'd married and been blessed by a child like this one.

She cast the thought aside. She doubted it would ever happen with Sean gone from her life. Not that she'd marry him now if he begged her to—she'd misjudged his character and imagined traits in him that hadn't existed. The best thing to do was forget, and she tightened her grip on the child.

A longing for a drink swept over her, but she pushed it aside. She wouldn't desecrate this time with those thoughts. The present joy of this girl cuddled on her lap was enough.

CHAPTER 38

The following day, Jeena arrived at the chapel service out of breath and out of sorts. She'd rushed through breakfast and barely completed her chores before slipping through the chapel doors as the attendant drew them shut behind her. A glance at the room showed only a smattering of chairs vacant. No way would she announce her presence by sauntering up the aisle to the front. She'd stand against the back wall before that happened.

A second look revealed a lone chair tucked into the corner in the back row. Jeena tiptoed behind the standing worshippers, edged the chair out of its place, then slipped into the seat as the small band of congregants quieted and settled into their chairs.

Why did she keep putting herself through this misery? Not that Pastor Paul wasn't easy to look at and occasionally something he shared stirred her interest. But this wasn't her lifestyle, and no amount of hanging around this shelter would change that fact. She longed—no—needed to return to her career and get back on her feet. Living here was better than she'd expected, and some of the people she'd met had changed her opinions of the homeless. But she couldn't stay forever.

She'd prayed about her ring, and it hadn't gotten her anywhere except further down the road toward yet another disappointment. She'd been Portland's rising star not so long ago, and now she lived in a homeless shelter with thieves and drug addicts. She slumped deeper in her seat, jarring the elbow of the woman alongside her.

A pair of irritated eyes glared her way, the corners of the permanently drawn lips positioned at a more pronounced downward tilt. "What?" the woman hissed.

Jeena pulled away, clasping her hands in her lap and making herself as small as possible. "Sorry," she whispered.

"Humph." Her mouth retained its position in spite of the snort, and her head swiveled on the bulky neck and once again faced the front.

Jeena directed her attention to the pastor. He'd stepped away from the wooden podium and down the single step, placing himself on the same level as the chairs that stood in rows across the room. A wistful smile touched the corners of his mouth. Jeena wondered at the quiet hush that held each woman in her place. Not even the children fidgeted.

Pastor Paul slowly scanned his audience before speaking again. "I can't begin to stress the importance of this time in history. Right now. Today. Your history.

"You aren't here by accident. You're here by God's design. Did He force you to come? No. Did He tell you to make the choices that brought you to this point? Of course not. Did He design this time and this hour just for you? Yes. He most certainly did." He paused his pacing and smiled.

"God didn't make your choices for you, but He did make a way of escape from those choices. He's been with you through all the horrible things you've done and all the terrible things that have been done to you. He loves you in spite of yourself and longs to shower that love into your life. More than anything, He wants to reveal Himself to you—show you who He is at a deep, heart level. He wants to be your father, your brother, and your best friend all rolled into one."

Jeena saw a variety of responses cross the women's faces. Disbelief. Ridicule. Desire. Still, no one stirred. Her gaze was drawn to the man who suddenly seemed larger than life. The thought of God wanting to reveal Himself pricked at her heart and touched her at a level she hadn't known existed. But the thought of God being a father repulsed her, and she steeled her heart against the longing rising inside. One father had been enough. She could only imagine the tyrant God would be if she fell short of His impossible expectations the way she'd continually done with her human father.

Pastor Paul stretched out his palm toward them, and a look of longing crossed his face. "It's not too late, you know. You're writing your own history with God this very minute. Nothing you've done is too big for God to forgive. Nothing is too great for Him to undo. He gave His Son that you might have life, and that more abundantly. He said that now is the time of salvation. Don't let another hour go by without taking Him at His word and putting Him to the test. Make the decision today that will change the rest of your tomorrows, forever."

He stepped back behind the narrow podium. "I'd normally ask you to bow your head, but I'm not going to do that. Each of you has walked a hard path, and most of you have done harder things than what I'm going to ask next. Making a change isn't easy, especially in front of your peers. But if it's important, that won't matter. Right now, with all your friends as witnesses, I want you to stand and walk down here beside me if you desire to meet God and let Him change your life."

No one stirred, and it seemed as though no one in the room breathed. A few curious women glanced around, then turned their faces back to the front.

Pastor Paul waited another moment, then spoke in a soft, gentle voice. "This may be one of the hardest things you'll ever do, but I guarantee you, it'll be the best. Making Jesus your friend will be the first step toward a new life."

A rustling movement caught Jeena's attention, and a woman across the room rose. A small gasp swept over the crowd as Sarah stepped into the aisle. Tears coursed down her cheeks, and she let them fall unchecked. She strode with a determined step to the front and stopped in front of the pastor.

He held out his hand, and Sarah's large, rough fingers grasped his. "Sarah." His strong voice reached to the far corners of the room. "Welcome home." He turned to the gaping women sitting nearby and smiled. "Sarah's made a choice concerning the direction her life will take. I'll wait just a moment more. If anyone else wants to join us, we'd love to have you."

Another moment passed before someone rose from her seat

and headed toward the front. Mary. Jeena swiped at her eyes. Why in the world was she crying?

Jeena sniffed and settled deeper into her seat. Mary, she could understand and even believe. The older woman needed something to lean on after the rough life she'd lived.

But Sarah? Could her decision be real? The woman constantly snapped and snarled at those around her and made life miserable for Jeena. The only person she appeared to care about was Kirsten, and maybe Joy.

Jeena crossed her arms and closed her eyes for the preacher's prayer but shut her ears to the words, too confused to listen. Sarah's tears had stirred a feeling of pity and compassion she hadn't expected. What kind of life had Sarah encountered before coming here? For that matter, what troubles had brought the majority of the women to this point? A wave of shame swept through her. She'd been so fixated on her own loss that she'd never considered the personal struggles of the women around her.

⚘

Later that night, Jeena lay in her bed, staring at the ceiling in the dim light of moonbeams casting their soft glow across her bed. Carla's soft, rhythmic snore no longer irritated Jeena; instead, the light rumble brought a sense of home and belonging. Strange. She'd never believed this place could feel like home. She turned over in bed and sighed, then plumped up her pillow and burrowed her head in its softness.

"Jeena? You awake?" Mary's quiet voice came from the nearby bed.

"Yeah. Sorry if I woke you."

"Naw, I couldn't get to sleep, either. Just thinkin', I guess." Mary's smile sounded in her words.

Jeena rolled over and propped herself on her elbow, looking through the dim light toward the form in Mary's bed. "What about? Something good?"

"Yeah. You seen me go forward at chapel service this morning?"

"Yes." Jeena stopped, unsure what to say. She'd grown to care for the older woman and didn't want to hurt her.

"It's okay, dearie. I know you got your own demons to deal with where God is concerned, and I don't expect you to understand. But He did something wonderful in my heart today, and I can't get to sleep 'cause of the joy that's been hammerin' at me."

Jeena nodded, then realized Mary wouldn't see. "I'm glad. You deserve some joy in your life."

Mary chuckled. "Naw. I don't think anyone deserves what God did for 'em, leastwise not me. I've lived a rough life since losing my family, and I've made some bad choices. But somehow God seems to care in spite of all I've done." A tone of awe crept into her voice. "Can't understand why, but He loves me. Sarah seen it too, I think. She didn't lollygag around and wait for the preacher to beg. No, sir. But she don't care what people think. She's a strong one."

Silence hung in the room for several moments before Jeena replied. "I don't get it. Sarah's a hard person, but she walked up that aisle in tears. Part of me wants to believe she's honest, but part of me doubts it will last."

Mary rolled over and switched on the lamp, then turned it down to its dimmest setting. The light revealed worried eyes. "Ah, I don't think she's lyin' about what she did, dearie. Sure, she's a tough woman and hardheaded at times, but that's what'll help keep her on the right path, don't ya think?"

Jeena shrugged and worked to keep the frown inside from showing on her face. "I suppose. But even if she does make some type of change, that won't bring back my ring. She's probably already sold it, and I doubt she'll ever admit it."

"You never can tell, dearie. If she did take it—and I'm not saying she did, mind you—but if she did, God might jist tell her to bring it back."

Jeena rolled her eyes and smiled. "Now that would be a miracle." Her voice softened. "I'm happy for you, Mary. I suppose we'd better get to sleep, or I'll never get up in the morning."

Mary snapped off the light, and Jeena could hear the springs in the bed squeak as the woman settled into her covers. "Not sure how much sleep I'll get tonight, but I'm restin' just the same. Restin' in God's love. Remember, dearie—God does the changing. We just come to Him the way we are, and it's up to Him to change our hearts."

CHAPTER 39

Jeena arrived at the door of the thrift store with her mind chasing an idea. She wanted to call the detective who'd given her his card. What was his name? *Stan. Lieutenant Stan*, she revised with a smile. The only man who'd helped her before she came to the shelter. But what could she tell him? Joy thought her husband might be on her trail? But what if he wasn't—and what could the lieutenant do, anyway, if Kevin didn't threaten to harm his wife? She shook off the thought and went in search of Tara.

"Hey, Jeena. Glad you made it." Tara's disembodied voice floated out from behind a rack of men's jeans. Her head poked around the end of the display, revealing disheveled hair and a frazzled expression. "I got sick of the mess and tackled the men's section. Can you stay near the front and find something to do in case a customer comes in?"

"Sure." Jeena walked to the middle of the store, stepped around the rack, and looked at the pile of jeans on the floor. "But wouldn't you rather I stay and help?"

"Naw." Tara shook her head, sending the wild colors flying. "It doesn't look like it, but there is a method to my madness. I'll do better alone—know what I mean?" She waved her hand and disappeared.

Thirty minutes later, Jeena finished organizing the DVD display case near the front door and looked around for another job. The bell on the door tinkled as a nicely built man entered the store.

Not bad looking, maybe late twenties or early thirties at most, with dark blond hair and hazel eyes. If he'd turn that glower into a smile, he'd be one hot-looking guy. His perfectly pressed Dockers and designer shirt certainly weren't purchased from a thrift store, so she doubted he'd come here to shop. And from his determined, bulldog look and the flyer clutched in his fist, she'd bet his business wouldn't be pleasant.

"May I help you?" She used her most professional voice coated with just a hint of honey.

"I hope so," he snapped. "I'm about fed up with people in this town, and you're my last stop." He thrust the color flyer into her hands. "Take a look, would you? Tell me if you know these people."

Jeena stared at the determined face of the man, then down at the paper. She tried not to gasp. Blazoned across the top were the faces of Joy and Kirsten. Kirsten looked at least a year younger, and the name below the image of Joy was Nikki Sullivan. She glanced up at the man, sure that she stared into the unyielding face of Kevin Sullivan, Joy's husband.

She mustered a smile. "No, I'm afraid I don't know a Nikki Sullivan. Are they relatives?"

He crossed his arms. "My wife and child. They've been missing for months. You're sure you haven't seen them? I'd have sworn you recognized them."

Jeena's mind scrambled for an answer while she stared steadily into the man's eyes, refusing to drop her gaze. "The little girl reminded me of someone, that's all. A child I saw at someone's home."

Kevin took a step closer and leaned in. "Whose home? Where does she live?" He snapped out the words with a brisk staccato.

Jeena held up her hand, palm out. "Wait a minute. I said she *reminded* me of a child, not that she *was* the child. My friend adopted a girl when she was three months old." Jeena was reaching, but somehow she had to convince this man she didn't know Joy. "At first glance, they look a lot alike." She held the flyer out.

Kevin dropped his arms and clenched his fingers into fists, then reached out and snatched the flyer. "Yeah. Sounds like a nice coincidence."

Jeena studied his face, unsure whether his words contained the sarcasm she feared they hid or if he'd bought her story. She shot up a silent prayer for help, hoping this time God might be listening.

He stepped around her and gazed down the aisle nearby. "Anyone else around? Maybe she's been in here when you weren't working."

"No. I mean I'm the only one working the front today, and I'm sorry, but if you don't need anything else, I have to get back to work." She headed toward the register.

He grunted and turned away, then swung back. "Here's my card and the flyer. I'd appreciate knowing if she comes in."

"You said she's missing?" Jeena locked eyes with Kevin, who'd come to a halt midway toward the counter.

"That's what I said."

"Missing usually implies something's happened to them, but you seem to think she could be in town. She'd surely know how to get in touch with you, wouldn't she?"

He tossed the card and flyer on the counter and took a step back. "Your point?"

Jeena drew a deep breath, wondering if she'd stepped into deep waters. "That if your wife hasn't contacted you, maybe she'd rather not be found. That is, unless this is a kidnapping—then I assume you've brought the police into the matter."

He glared at her, his eyes saying things she'd probably not want to hear. "Good day, miss." He took two long strides to the door and propelled himself through it.

"Whew," Jeena released a pent up breath. "That was close."

"Jeena?" Tara came up the aisle from the back of the store, dusting her hands on her coveralls. "Anything wrong? I heard the door bang. You have to deal with an irate customer? You should've called me."

"No worries," Jeena smiled. "I took care of him just fine."

※

Three hours later, Jeena glanced at the clock behind the counter. Break time and none too soon. Her feet hurt, and she needed to use the phone. The stream of customers had been almost non-stop since Kevin left, with more than the usual number of loud children and inattentive mothers. Why couldn't more mothers be like Joy—lots of love mixed with firm correction instead of ignoring their kids or screeching when they wandered away?

She sighed and sank into the chair, then kicked off her shoes and massaged her tired feet. "Tara?"

Tara looked up from sorting the nearby rack. "Hmm?"

"Mind if I use the phone in the back? It's not long distance."

The girl waved. "Sure, go for it. And take your time."

"Thanks." Jeena trotted to the office and shut the door behind her, then dug her wallet out of her jacket pocket and riffled through its contents. "Come on, where are you . . . ah, I knew I didn't throw you away." She smiled and sank into the chair in front of the desk, then reached for the phone and dialed.

"Lieutenant Evans speaking, may I help you?"

Jeena slumped in relief at the sound of the deep, rumbling voice. "Lieutenant, I'm so glad I caught you. This is Jeena Gregory. I'm sure you don't remember me. I came to your office over a month ago when—"

"You lost your bag. Yes, I remember." His tone warmed, and she could almost hear the smile it encased.

She hesitated, hating the thought of telling him where she lived, but she plowed forward. "You said if I ever needed anything I should call."

"How can I help you, Jeena?"

She loosened her grip on the phone, then shifted it to her other hand and flexed her stiff fingers. "A friend of mine needs help." The silence on the other end wasn't lost on her. She knew the impression she'd made the day she'd stopped at the station might not have led the lieutenant to believe she had an abundance of friends. She cleared her throat and started again. "There's this woman who has a four-year-old little girl, and they're in trouble."

His voice turned serious. "What kind of trouble?"

She heard paper rustling and smiled, envisioning the detective pawing through his mile-high desk for a pen and paper. "They're people I met where I'm living." She hesitated, then forged on. "At the women's shelter. You know, the one you mentioned when you gave me their card?"

"Ah-ha." He paused a moment. "I'm listening."

Jeena peeked out the door and saw Tara at the front helping a customer, then settled back in her chair. "She ran away from her abusive husband. A few days ago, she walked me to the thrift store where I'm working." Jeena paused, realizing the image she'd just given, then raced on. "She thought she spotted Kevin. I told her I doubted he'd found her, as he lived over five hundred miles away, but she was spooked. I thought it might be someone following me, since Charles is probably having me watched."

"Slow down. You're being followed? Who is Charles, and what's he got on you?"

"Nothing. Nobody. I mean, he used to be my boss. He's under indictment for larceny, but I want to talk about Joy, not me."

"Fine, we'll talk about Joy. But why do you think this character, your boss, might have someone following you?"

She heard something tapping in the background. He must have retrieved a pen from the pile. "I testified against him at his preliminary hearing. The IRS froze my accounts, as well as everyone else's in the firm. That's why I'm in this position. He jumped bail and is in hiding in South America, but I'm guessing he's keeping an eye on me, just in case."

"Humph. What's his last name?"

"Browning. But please, can we get back to Joy and her daughter?"

"Yeah. But I'll do a little investigating about this other matter, as well."

Jeena took a paper clip from the small bin on the desk and pried it apart with her thumb. "Kevin came in the store today, asking about his wife and child. I know she's afraid of him and what he'll do if he finds her."

"What did you tell him?"

"He showed me a poster, and I told him I'd never seen anyone named Nikki Sullivan before."

"He believe you?"

"I'm not sure." She fiddled with the clip, then tossed it back into the bin. "I had a hard time not gasping when I saw the picture, but I told him the little girl resembled a friend's daughter. His wife's real name is Nikki, so I didn't lie when I told him I don't know anyone by that name. Lieutenant, I'm terrified for Joy and Kirsten. This guy means business, and he's got a ton of anger sitting on his shoulders just waiting to be dumped in someone's lap."

"Yeah. I've seen that type too many times."

"So . . . is there anything you can do?"

He sighed, and Jeena knew what was coming. "I hate this part of my job. It stinks. So far, the man hasn't done anything. He hasn't assaulted her—"

"But he has," she cut in. "He hit her in the past and got rough with Kirsten. That's why she left him."

"In the past. Not now. If she filed a police report at the time, they'd have followed through." He muttered something under his breath that Jeena couldn't catch, then continued. "I'm sorry. We can't pick him up and hold him without cause."

"So you have to wait for him to hurt her before you can act?" She heard the panic in her voice but couldn't seem to stop. "I thought you'd at least try to help."

"Look—I'll send a cruiser by in the evenings and have them keep an eye out for anyone skulking around, but that's all I can do unless he tries something. I wish I could offer more."

Jeena slumped in her chair and frowned. "Yeah, so do I. But I appreciate the patrol car. Really . . . and I'm sorry for snapping."

"No problem." His tone turned brisk. "Anything else?"

Jeena shot through her memories of the encounter with Kevin and began to shake her head, then sat upright. "He left his business card on the counter. Would that help?"

"It might. I'll have an officer pick it up. We'll check for any outstanding warrants. And call me if you have any other concerns. Especially if you think you see someone following you or your friend again. Understood?"

"Sure. Thanks, Lieutenant." She hung up the phone and leaned back, gazing at the ceiling. Why couldn't life be simple? Just when things looked like they'd hit bottom, the bottom seemed to retreat farther south.

CHAPTER 40

Sunday evening, Jeena plunked into an overstuffed chair in the common room, putting her feet up on a nearby stool. No chores this morning, and a chance to sleep a little later on Sunday, but there'd been no escaping chapel. Sarah showered them all with smiles in her newfound life, but Jeena still had a hard time buying it. The store never opened on Sundays, no classes were offered, and the day had dragged.

She'd picked up something at the thrift store she thought Kirsten might like and brought it to the common room, hoping the little girl and Joy might stop by. If they didn't show up soon, maybe she'd swing by their room on her way to bed. The brown paper sack nestled next to her side gave her an unusual feeling of comfort. She hadn't realized that giving a gift without any expectation of return could evoke so much tenderness. But it could have something to do with the sweetness of the little girl who would receive it.

She noted the small group of women and children grouped around the TV in the far corner of the room. No hope there. The noise level from the kids would drown out anything they chose to watch. No current magazines were among those littering the tables and chairs.

The challenge of climbing the corporate and social ladders had been part of her lifeblood, but now it felt as though all her creative energy had drained from her body and puddled on the floor of this shelter. No way around it: boredom had sunk its fangs into her mind. Tomorrow, she had a half day at the thrift store. Time to hit the streets again and see what she could stir up for work. Not that she wasn't thankful for the bed, job, and food the shelter offered, but it was time for a change.

She swung her feet to the floor, placed her hands on the arms of her chair, and stood. At least she'd find quiet in her room—an attribute that didn't exist in here tonight.

A sweet voice floated into the room, followed by a bouncing Kirsten. The little girl held her mother's hand and hop-skipped on one foot across the threshold while humming a tune.

Kirsten spied Jeena standing near the door and squealed. "Mama, there she is!" She raced to Jeena's side, her face glowing. "I've got a se . . . cret." Her sing-song voice chanted.

Jeena grinned and tickled Kirsten's tummy, sending the child giggling to her mother's side. Joy sank onto the worn couch and kicked off her shoes, then pulled Kirsten down beside her. "How's your day been, Jeena?"

"It's getting better now that you're here." Jeena smiled, then reached across the small open space and tweaked Kirsten's nose. "So you have a secret, huh? So do I."

"You do?" She turned wide eyes to Jeena. "Is it about me?"

Jeena chuckled. "Maybe. Can you tell me yours?"

"I can't tell you yet." The child chirped. "Well, maybe I can if Mommy says so." She peeked up at her mother. "Can I, Mommy, please?"

"Okay, sugar." Joy turned to Jeena and winked. "Kirsten had been pestering me all evening to find you. She remembered that it's your birthday, and she has something for you."

Jeena sank back into her chair. "You remembered." She tried to clear the choked feeling from her throat. "Thank you, Kirsten." She turned to Joy. "You didn't have to buy me anything."

Joy smiled at the glowing face of her daughter. "I didn't. This is Kirsten's surprise—I don't even know what she has. She found some scraps of wrapping paper and asked Rachel for tape. I gave her a box, and she wrapped it herself."

"I made you a card, too. See?" Kirsten handed over a colorful paper folded in half. The front sported a balloon in a rainbow of crayon colors, and the inside had Kirsten's name penciled in large letters, with a smiley face tilted on its side. *Thank you for reading to me—I love you* was printed in an adult's handwriting, and *Kirsten* was scrawled across the bottom in slanted crayon. Jeena raised her brows at Joy, who nodded and smiled.

Real tears welled up in Jeena's eyes, and she brushed them away before they obscured the image on the card. *I love you.* What simple but profound words. Words that meant nothing unless poured from a person's heart. Words she'd forgotten could touch her so deeply—and to think, they'd come from a child.

"Open it!" The childish excitement in Kirsten's voice sent an answering tingle through Jeena. "I want to see if you like it."

Jeena grinned and held the box in the air. "It feels very light. Are you sure there's something in here?"

Kirsten's curls bounced around her face as her little head nodded. "Yes. There's lots of paper. But something's in there. I promise."

Jeena and Joy laughed aloud; then Jeena unwrapped the package, being careful not to tear the paper. She lifted the lid on the box and drew out a large handful of crumpled newspaper. Then she reached in and pulled out a small wad liberally covered with tape. "Is this the present?" She held up the walnut-sized lump.

Kirsten nodded eagerly. "Yes. Hurry!" She jumped from the couch and danced to Jeena's side, peeking over the arm of the chair.

Jeena plucked at the tape and tore the paper apart to reach the center of the tight mass. A glint of color shone from the center, and Jeena pushed back the remaining scrap of paper. She gasped, nearly dropping the sparkling object onto her lap. "My ring." She turned toward Kirsten. "Honey, where did you find my ring?" Her voice came out sharper than she'd planned.

The small face crumpled, and Kirsten took a step back. "Don't you like my present?"

Joy pushed to her feet with an exclamation of dismay. "Kirsten! You need to answer Jeena."

Jeena leaned forward and gently grasped Kirsten's hand. "Did you take it from Sarah's room?"

Kirsten jerked away and flew to her mother's side. "You don't like my present," she sobbed, then flung her arms around her mother's knees and buried her face in Joy's skirt.

Joy smoothed the blond curls and looked at Jeena. "I'm sorry. I don't know what to say."

Jeena struggled with her emotions, but her muddled thoughts couldn't seem to piece together the unfolding events. How did Kirsten get her grandmother's ring? Did Sarah hide it and the child found it? Kirsten's sobs pulled Jeena back to the child.

"Come here, Kirsten." Jeena held out her hand. "Please? I want to talk to you about your present."

Kirsten didn't stir, and Jeena tried again. "I love the ring, honey, I really do. Would you come tell me about it?"

The little girl loosened her grip on her mother and rubbed at her wet eyes. "You like it?" she whispered. "You're not mad at me?"

Jeena smiled and continued to extend her hand. "No. I'm not mad, and I love it. Thank you for wrapping it so nicely. The card is beautiful, too. Would you sit on my lap and talk to me?"

Kirsten nodded, popped her fingers in her mouth, and inched over to Jeena's knees.

She scooped the girl up, cuddling her against her chest, and smoothing back the damp hair from the flushed face. "I'm sorry I made you feel bad, honey." She tipped up Kirsten's face and placed a kiss on her cheek. "Can you tell me where you found the pretty ring? Did someone give it to you?" She worked to keep a light tone as Kirsten looked up.

"I finded it." She reverted to the childish words Jeena had heard her use when upset. "A can got stuck in the door. It was open, but nobody was home." The clear blue eyes held Jeena's gaze. "Somebody throwed it away, and I finded it."

Jeena nodded without smiling. "Do you remember when, honey?"

"Long, long time ago. Days and days and days."

Joy leaned forward and touched Kirsten's arm. "Kirsten, why did you go into someone else's room? What were you doing alone?"

Kirsten pulled her fingers from her mouth and sat up straight.

"I . . . hmm. Oh—I remember. You was working, Mama. And Aunty put me down for a nap." She nodded with a serious look. "Aunty goed to the bathroom down the hall. I was trying to sleep. Bang! Something made me jump. But nobody comed. So I finded an open door and peeked in." She looked from one expectant face to another.

Jeena hugged the little body against her chest and peered over the rumpled curls into Joy's worried eyes. "Go ahead. You went in the room?"

Kirsten bobbed her head. "Ah-huh. Nobody was home. I saw some bee-ootiful shoes under the bed." She turned to her mother. "I love bee-ootiful shoes, Mommy."

"I know you do, honey. Now go on."

"I just weared them for a minute. But something hurted my foot. I finded the pretty ring that somebody throwed away. I took it home with me!" She ended on a triumphant note and smiled at each woman in turn.

Jeena leveled a look at Joy and gave a slight shake of her head. "Thank you for telling us, sweetie. And thank you for the won-derful present." She slipped it onto her finger and gave Kirsten a gentle hug. "Now for my secret. I have a surprise for you."

Kirsten raised a beaming face to Jeena. "Can you tell me?"

"Uh-huh. Better yet, how about I show you?" Jeena drew the paper bag from beside her and placed it gently into the little girl's hands.

Kirsten peered at the sack and pulled open the crumpled paper. She reached inside and slowly drew out the contents. "Mama," she squealed. "Lookee! It's my dolly." Kirsten's beaming smile returned. She gave Jeena a loud kiss on her cheek. "I love you, Jeena. I prayed for a dolly, and you gived me one. I gonna call her Miss Jeena." She slipped from Jeena's lap and stopped in front of her mother. "I ready to go to bed now, Mama. I'm tired."

Joy gathered the little girl into her arms and rested her cheek on the tousled hair. "Sounds good, honey." She met Jeena's eyes and mouthed two words. "Thank you." She rose and headed for the door, Kirsten secure in her arms.

"'Night." Kirsten turned at the door and lifted the doll's arm, waving it at Jeena.

"'Night, sweetie." Jeena leaned back in her chair and groaned. What a mess. She stared at the ring and felt moisture gather in her eyes, remembering her harsh words. She hadn't asked questions, hadn't listened to Sarah's explanation. She'd simply assumed Sarah must be guilty and judged her from that point forward. A picture of Grammie hovered in Jeena's mind—never quick to accuse and always ready to listen and forgive. She'd be so disappointed at the way Jeena had handled this.

Rocking her head back against the chair, Jeena closed her eyes. What now? Apologize and try to make it right with Sarah. A small shiver shot through her body, and she groaned. From past experience, she knew what Sarah's reaction would be. Vindictive anger and cursing would spew from Sarah's mouth as soon as word reached her ears.

No matter. Jeena had learned the other women didn't respect someone who slacked off on their work or who bad-mouthed another woman who didn't deserve it. She'd never shirked her work, but she'd sure done a great job sticking her foot in it with Sarah. She'd make it right even if Sarah didn't accept it. And hopefully, she wouldn't get decked for her effort.

CHAPTER 41

At breakfast the next morning, Jeena stood on the outskirts of the cafeteria and scanned the room's occupants. She'd been rehearsing her words to Sarah. Part of her wanted the security of a public place, assuming Sarah wouldn't cause a scene. But the memory of their past two clashes in this room remained strong—and there'd been an audience both times.

Mary stood on the far side of the room, motioning for Jeena to come over. Jeena waved and then pointed across the room toward Sarah. Mary nodded and placed her hands together as though praying.

Jeena drew a deep breath and squared her shoulders. Time to face Goliath and see if she survived. She marched between the tables, her eyes locked on Sarah's back. Heads turned as she wove her way between the chairs, and whispers flew. By the time Jeena arrived at Sarah's side, the entire table had quieted, and each face was turned her direction. All but one. Sarah remained facing away.

Jeena kept her gaze trained on Sarah. No turning back. Accusing Sarah hadn't been fair, even if the woman had harassed her from the start.

She stopped two feet from the table. "Sarah?"

The big-boned woman slowly turned and stared.

Jeena drew in a breath and blew it out between pursed lips. "I know you're angry—you have every right to be. I accused you of stealing and didn't listen when you denied it." She stopped for breath and waited, but Sarah sat motionless. "I found my ring, and I realize now that you didn't take it. I hope you'll for-give me."

Sarah's eyes narrowed, and her lips drew down in a scowl. "You're right I'm mad. Wouldn't you be?"

Jeena froze. It hadn't occurred to her how she'd feel if the tables were turned. "Yeah. I guess so."

"But you still think I should forgive you?" Sarah's glare deepened. "You have a lot of nerve."

"I don't blame you." Jeena shrugged and took a step back. "Forget I asked?" She hadn't expected anything more. "But for what it's worth, I'm sorry." No tirade had slammed into her—that in itself felt good. Time to get out of here. She swung around and took two steps.

"Jeena." Sarah's voice halted Jeena's retreat. "Wait."

She turned and waited.

Sarah's eyes met Jeena's and didn't flinch. "This ain't easy for me, but I accept your apology. If you want the truth, I'd rather shove it down your throat."

She winced. "Thanks. I'd better go."

"Hey." Sarah heaved up from her seat and towered above her. "I'm sorry, too." She drew in a deep breath and released a loud sigh.

"For what?" Jeena blurted. "I'm the one who called you a thief."

"Yeah. But I've jerked you around since you came. No surprise you thought I stole it." Her earnest eyes gripped Jeena's and didn't let go. "This forgiveness stuff is freaky—but God says we're supposed to treat people the way we want to be treated. Guess I got a lot to learn in that department." She grunted and turned away.

Jeena took a small step forward and touched Sarah's shoulder. "Thank you." She spun and headed across the room, all thought of breakfast forgotten.

Mary reached out as she passed, but Jeena smiled and kept moving. This didn't make sense. It wasn't supposed to happen like this. Sarah was supposed to get ugly or refuse to forgive her and continue the feud. But she'd not only forgiven her; she'd offered an apology of her own.

Sarah offered her new relationship with God as the reason. Jeena had never seen Christianity change someone's life. She'd only known people who played church with little truth in their lives—except for Grammie and Tammy, but they'd been Christians for years, with no rough past to redeem.

This new insight intrigued and confused her. Could it be that simple? Could turning your life over to God bring transformation? Sarah's actions seemed to indicate it could. Maybe time would pass, and the old Sarah would emerge. This could be a honeymoon period where everything seemed wonderful until real life set in again.

But Jeena's ring had been returned, albeit in a rather unconventional manner. She could pretend God had nothing to do with it, but again, fairness prevailed. She'd asked God to intervene, and it seemed that He had. Sure, it could be a coincidence. But just a few days ago she'd railed that He hadn't answered her prayers. Could she now ignore Him when He might have answered?

Not sure her mind could take in much more, she headed to her room. Keeping an eye on Sarah and seeing what transpired—that seemed her best option. Time would tell if the transformation were genuine, and Jeena would watch. She still needed a good job and a place of her own, but maybe she didn't need to leave too soon. For now, she had the shelter and her job at the thrift store to fall back on.

Jeena picked up her pace, anxious to get home before dark settled too deeply over the city. The less-than-savory neighborhood didn't encourage sauntering this time of night. Some of the women at the shelter had lived in this area most of their lives and didn't mind the walk, but Jeena dreaded the five blocks between the thrift store and the shelter.

Dinner started at six thirty, leaving barely enough time to get to her room, clean up, and change. After the day she'd had, skipping the meal sounded heavenly, although her stomach argued against such action.

The lights of the shelter drew her forward, casting a homey glow on the final block. She peeked into the depths of the alley off the side of the building. It wasn't often a car passed through this alley, but it paid to check. A dark form leaned against the brick wall of the adjoining building, and a spark dropped from the tip of a smoldering cigarette.

A homeless man or someone resting on his way home from work? She shrugged and kept moving. Shuffling sounded from the alley, and she slowed, peering over her shoulder. The man stood illuminated in the light from the street lamp, but she couldn't see his face. Something about his stance seemed familiar. "You need to watch your step, lady."

A light shiver coursed down her back, and she drew her coat closer around her and picked up her pace. The sound of footsteps behind her increased. "You hear me, lady? Stay out of what doesn't concern you."

She rushed up the sidewalk and yanked open the door, chancing another look over her shoulder. The dark shadow slipped deeper into the darkness. Rapid footfalls hitting the asphalt heralded his retreat. Kevin? Or possibly the person who might be watching her? But Charles hadn't turned up, and the publicity about his disappearance had long since died down. Would the man care what happened to his one-time employee while he was safely ensconced in some far-off location?

Her imagination must be in overdrive. So many of the people in this area were hooked on alcohol or drugs, and nothing suggested either Kevin or Charles was behind this. More than likely, someone mistook her for another one of the residents. She shook off her apprehension and slipped in the front door.

CHAPTER 42

J oy troubled Jeena's thoughts all the next day. Her friend seemed to be avoiding her. Kirsten's involvement with the missing ring must have embarrassed the young mother. It had been a day and a half since Jeena's apology to Sarah, and already the word had spread that the two combatants had called a truce.

She rubbed her sore feet and picked up her shoes, tucking them under her arm. Nothing to do and no one to talk to in the common room, so maybe she'd find Joy and put her mind at ease.

She padded down the hall and laughed at herself. A few weeks ago, she'd never have considered walking sock-footed down this floor. She'd thought it full of germs and probably nasty to the touch. Little had she known the hard work and constant scrubbing this place endured. These floors were easily as clean as the ones in her old home.

Home. The thought no longer pained her like it used to do, but a swift longing still held her in its grip from time to time—especially when something reminded her of Grammie. Would she ever have a home again, or was she caught in perpetual limbo? She smiled. She'd only been here a few weeks—it wasn't like she'd been sent to prison and couldn't escape. One of her job applications would pay off soon. She'd made a determined effort to use the office phone and called each business she'd applied to, letting them know she was available and willing to work.

Jeena turned a corner. Joy's door lay just ahead. She slowed. Would Joy want to see her, or had she kept away for some other reason? She pressed on, determined to clear up any misunderstanding.

She started to knock on the door and hesitated. Would Kirsten be in bed? After tapping gently, she heard footsteps. Joy opened the door and peeked out through the crack.

"Oh, hi, Jeena. Just a sec, okay?"

"Sure." Jeena waited while the door closed, then opened again, and Joy stepped out into the hall.

"I wanted to make sure Kirsten was asleep. I'd hate to have a repeat of her last little adventure when her aunty left her." The tone of her voice left nothing to the imagination, and the look on her face said even more.

Jeena touched Joy's hand and smiled. "Can you sit on the bench and talk?"

Joy nodded and followed Jeena's lead. They perched on opposite ends of the cozy, padded bench. Silence settled over the pair like a soft woolen blanket. Joy's face lost its harried look, and her shoulders relaxed. "It's good to see you again. I'm sorry if it seems like I've avoided you."

"Have you been?"

Joy grimaced. "A little, I guess. At first I was embarrassed at what Kirsten had done. Then when I heard about you talking to Sarah—"

"What? Why would that stop you?" Jeena sat back and pulled her feet up under her.

"I don't know. I guess I felt a little awed."

"Huh?"

"Sarah's always been kind to Kirsten and me, but I've seen the way she's treated you and some of the other women she doesn't like. She can be frightening if you get on her bad side."

"Yeah. But I was a jerk when I accused her of stealing my ring."

"Maybe. But I don't think I'd have had the nerve to tackle Sarah the way you did. It took guts to apologize in front of the others. I think she needed to apologize to you, too." Joy rested her elbow on her knees and propped her chin on her cupped hand.

"She did."

"I didn't hear that."

"Yeah. She told me she was wrong, and that since God had forgiven her, she should do the same. I guess she needed someone to practice on." Jeena tried to chuckle but it came out more like a grunt.

"Wow. I guess her decision that day in chapel must have been real, huh?"

"Yeah. I guess."

Joy smiled and the corners of her eyes crinkled. "Are we okay, too?"

"You mean about my ring and Kirsten?"

"Yeah. I'm sorry about that."

Jeena shook her head. "You are not to be sorry about anything. Kirsten didn't know she was taking something of mine—she thought someone didn't want it."

"I know, but she shouldn't have gone into another room. I talked to her about it, and she understands."

"Then it's fine. I'm ecstatic to have my grandmother's ring back, and it was awesome Kirsten remembered my birthday."

Joy grinned and held out her hand. "Friends?"

Jeena scooted over and hugged Joy instead, feeling a newfound peace course through her. "Friends." She gave Joy an extra squeeze, then released her and settled back in her corner.

They sat silent for a moment. How amazing, finding such a strong, caring person in such an unexpected place. Other than Tammy, Jeena didn't remember anyone she could call a true friend during her growing-up years, and she hadn't discovered Tammy until late in high school. As an adult, she'd had only surface acquaintances who cared about the parties she threw or the rungs they could climb. Joy's friendship had nothing to gain.

Susanne had been different, too. The sorrow over the loss of that friendship cut, but Jeena understood now why Susanne had pulled away. More than once, she'd bullied her friend and tried to control her life. There was so much she still needed to understand, but for the first time, she felt a small shaft of light penetrate the darkness. Both Tammy and Susanne had loved and accepted her. Susanne's decision to put a barrier between Jeena and her own family had probably been wise.

Would Joy be ready for what Jeena needed to share? As much as she hated to alarm her, the timing wouldn't improve. "Do you need to check on Kirsten? I'd like to talk longer, if you don't mind."

Joy's eyes widened. "I'll be right back."

Jeena watched her friend disappear into her room. Never had she wished more for the ability to pray than she did now. She'd hate to scare Joy, but leaving her in the dark about Kevin's visit could be just as damaging.

Joy slipped back to the nook where Jeena waited. "Kirsten's still asleep." She plumped up a pillow and tucked it behind her back. "What's up?"

"I'm not sure." Jeena hesitated.

"It can't be much worse than Kirsten taking your ring." Joy's smile seemed to light up the small corner of the hall.

"Kevin came to the store, asking about you and Kirsten."

Horror flashed across Joy's face, and time seemed to halt. Then she bolted from the chair, sending the pillow flying across the worn floor. "Kevin? When?" Her voice rose. "What did he want?"

Jeena tugged at Joy's hand. "Please, Joy. Sit. Calm down, okay?"

"I'll never be calm as long as Kevin's following me." She sank onto the bench but didn't lean back. "What happened?"

"He showed me a flyer with a picture of you and Kirsten, but it identified you as Nikki Sullivan."

Joy nodded. "My real name."

"Yeah, I figured. He asked if I'd seen you."

"You didn't tell him I'm here?" Joy's voice rose.

Jeena winced. "Of course not. I told him I'd never met Nikki Sullivan."

"I'm sorry. I shouldn't have asked that. I'm so scared!"

"I know, and it's okay. I called a friend after Kevin left—a lieutenant at the police station—and he agreed to help."

Joy plucked at a lock of her hair and twisted it. "Thanks, but no one can help. I'll pack Kirsten up and get out of this town, fast. I'd hoped I wouldn't have to, but I've done it before, and it's time to do it again."

"You can't keep running. The lieutenant is sending a patrol car by the shelter a couple of times each night. Maybe you should stay in one spot, get a restraining order, and make Kevin stay away from you."

"It won't matter. I've got to leave, and the sooner the better." Joy pushed to her feet and started for her room, but Jeena jumped from the couch and grabbed her wrist.

"Wait! You can't run. You don't have a place to go, and you probably don't have any money. Right? Let's talk to Rachel or the pastor, if you won't go to the police."

Joy's shoulders slumped. "Nobody can help me. I don't think even God can help where Kevin's concerned. Maybe I need to give up and just go back to him, instead of running the rest of my life. Maybe it would be different this time. He may have changed." She raised bleak eyes.

Jeena wrapped her arms around Joy's shaking shoulders and held her close. "I wish I had the answers, but I don't know how to fix this. You can't run, and you can't go back to Kevin. Promise me you won't run? Please?"

Joy drew a harsh breath. "No promises, but I'll think about it." Her eyes darted toward the door of her room, then back to Jeena. "I don't want to leave Kirsten alone any longer." She took the last few steps to her room, then turned back. "I appreciate all you've done. No matter what, you're one of my dearest friends." She opened her door and slipped inside.

⚘

Jeena stepped out of the bathroom and headed for her room, bone weary and sick of trying to figure out her life, much less anyone else's. The talk with Joy had drained the last of her energy.

She cracked open the door of her room and peeked in. Darkness and soft snores. Mary and Carla had decided on an early night. She glanced at her watch in the dim light of the hall. Nine o'clock and time to be in her room—early for sleep, but maybe she'd curl up in bed and think of a solution for Joy. There was a time when she'd been good at finding solutions, and she hated this feeling of helplessness.

She lay down on her bed, not ready to undress and slip under the covers. Why was life such a mess? Joy and Kirsten deserved some happiness. She'd ruined her own life by getting into debt and making poor choices, but Joy's abusive husband had created this situation. Where was God in all this tragedy?

Memories of the past weeks at the shelter surfaced, and one in particular stood out. Riding here in that old beater with Rachel. What had she said when Jeena questioned her about God allowing evil?

Rachel's words returned full force. "He gave people free will. He didn't want robots. He created us able to choose—so if we decide to love and follow Him, we do it because we want to, not because He forces us . . . Evil is real and has its own ruler who is constantly working to force his will on others, unlike God who wants us to come to Him out of our own free will."

Was that the problem? There was an evil counterpart to God running around, stirring up trouble and luring people onto a path of destruction? When she was a child, Jeena's father had ranted about hellfire and destruction, and she'd tuned him out. She knew the Bible claimed Satan was real, and according to Rachel, she had to choose whose camp she wanted to live in—his or God's.

Tammy had said the same thing, but in a different way. She'd suggested that God's love was strong enough to overpower any evil if she'd allow it to take control of her heart. Jeena's problem had been that she didn't want anyone else in control of her life.

But what if Tammy and Rachel were right—what did she do with this knowledge? Ask God to keep evil away from Joy and Kirsten? That might work, but would He listen if she kept Him at arm's length? She struggled to an upright position. No rest for her now, and no answers, either. Maybe a short walk to clear her head was in order.

Could she slip down the hall and out the back door without anyone seeing her? Curfew had passed, but the courtyard area was a safe zone for anyone wanting to stand outside. The problem lay in getting back in. She'd have to use the buzzer for the door to be unlocked, and the supervisor would want an explanation.

She pushed to her feet and groped for her shoes. She couldn't stay in this room another minute without screaming. Maybe the cool night air would clear her head and help her find some answers. She'd live with the consequences.

CHAPTER 43

Jeena pushed open the back door of the shelter and winced at the high-pitched squeak. She paused before stepping outside. No heads popped out of doors, and no angry shouts yelled to be quiet. Of course, it sounded louder to her overwrought nerves than it would to anyone in their room.

She slipped out to the small courtyard and drew a deep breath of the night air. Very little traffic cluttered the street this time of night, and the pollution levels were low. A floral scent reached its gentle fragrance toward her, but that could be her imagination again, concocting an image of a real home.

Home. The word had never possessed the power to stir her as it did now. In her childhood years, the word conveyed a sense of fear that brought a physical response akin to sickness. In her adult years, it stirred a longing for marriage and family. But as time progressed, *home* began to lose its meaning, since Grammie's health hadn't allowed her to live with Jeena.

The longing mystified Jeena. What did home mean to her now? A second chance at a good life, and maybe someday at love? She'd learned so much more here than she'd thought possible. Lessons about love, friendship, and forgiveness. Lessons about unselfishness and caring. Lessons she'd never have learned if she'd continued on her career path. Did God play a part in bringing her here, as Rachel had stated?

She leaned against the wall and stared up at the sky, amazed at the stars penetrating the black reaches of the heavens and sending out tiny shafts of light. Could this awesome panorama exist without an intelligent designer?

How could anyone buy into the idea of life having come

into being randomly? That would be like tossing random bricks, boards, nails, and glass into the air and expecting it to land in the formation of a finished housing development. It might be a lame comparison, but her old philosophy of life hadn't been much stronger.

So why had she balked at the concept of a personal God for so long? Her father, pure and simple. Her memory of him had turned her away from the belief that God could be anything but cruel. Better to believe God didn't exist than try to equate Him with her earthly father.

Maybe it was time for a change. Maybe she needed to look deeper and begin to let go of the past. Maybe Sarah's decision to give God a chance hadn't been a sham. Sarah *had* changed; she'd proven it more than once these past few days. The deep-seated anger in Sarah seemed to have faded, and a new peace had taken its place—a peace that only an all-powerful God could orchestrate. The longing swelled in Jeena's heart. She wanted that peace—no, she *needed* it in a way she'd never imagined before.

"God . . ." She looked up at the stars and whispered, "if You're really there, and if You care, please show me. Help me to believe, and help me to find the peace that I've seen in some of the lives here. I'm so tired of being alone—so tired of fighting and running."

She couldn't hold it in. The words tumbled over themselves, rushing to find their way to God's ears. "Please, please forgive me. I've made such a mess of my life. I've made so many stupid choices. I haven't believed in You, and I've pushed you away for so long. I need You, God."

She waited, not sure what she hoped for, but nothing magical materialized. No shooting star or bright lights from heaven. Just silence. Then . . . a slow stirring deep inside. A simple knowing—no, not simple, but profound—bubbled up like a clean, refreshing spring from a place she'd never imagined existed. It washed over her, first lapping like a gentle tide, then nearly swamping her emotions with the reality of its presence. Peace. Forgiveness. Love.

She leaned back against the brick wall, the feeling so strong her knees started to shake. Why hadn't she known it would be this way? Why hadn't she listened to Grammie and Tammy when they'd tried to explain?

She gazed up into the heavens, immersed in the wonder of the moment. "God, You love me? You really love me?" She cleared her throat and wiped her eyes. "Awesome. It's too much to take in. I had no idea." She wanted to sob, to laugh, to whirl around in circles and skip on one foot the way Kirsten did when she was happy. She felt like a child—clean and forgiven. New. Several minutes passed as the soothing peace continued to blanket her.

Something niggled at her mind. Had she heard something in the nearby alley? She drew a deep breath and listened. More than likely it was her own thumping heart pulsing the blood in her ears and nothing more. Time to head in. She'd share this new relationship with Mary. She'd understand.

A movement registered in the corner of Jeena's vision. She tried to discern what lurked in the shadows. Nothing. No sound broke the silence in the small corner of her world.

A scraping noise, then a bump and a small cry. A child out here in the dark? Determination drove Jeena forward while concern kept her from dashing into the unknown. She'd seen a man lurking in the alley earlier—could this be a ploy to lure a lone woman away from the safety of the shelter?

"Mama, I want my bed," wailed a small voice. Shivers chased their way up Jeena's spine. Kirsten? Why would Joy have her out at this time of night, unless—

Jeena dashed forward, all thought of her own safety discarded. Realization doused her like a cold wave. Joy had decided to run.

She darted around the corner of the building in time to see a woman's form dragging a suitcase in one hand and a child with the other, headed toward the mouth of the nearby alley. "Wait! Joy, wait!" Her voice hurled ahead, and Joy swung around. She paused for a heartbeat, then lunged forward, picking up speed.

Another shadow seemed to merge with that of the two fleeing

figures. What in the world? A streetlight washed over the eerie scene with a flickering glow, bringing with it dread and a sense of unreality.

A dark-clad man reached out and clutched Kirsten's small arm. In an instant, he wrenched the child out of her mother's grasp and into his own. "Mama! Mama!" Kirsten's wail pierced Jeena's heart and renewed her sense of purpose. That man, whoever he was, couldn't be allowed to harm Kirsten.

"No! Let her go!" Joy's scream rent the air. The man shoved Joy and pulled the child closer.

"Nikki, I want you home," he panted. Kirsten struggled, her sobs and cries shaking the small form.

"Kevin." Joy stumbled against the wall, then righted herself. "For the love of heaven, please don't hurt her."

Jeena slowed to a halt, unsure if Kevin had noted her approach from behind. Retreat to the shelter for help, or try to pry the girl out of his hold? How long before the half-crazed man hurt Kirsten, or worse yet, disappeared with her into the shadows?

She flattened herself against the brick wall and willed her breathing to quiet. Slowly, she slid toward Kevin, praying his attention would remain on Joy.

Kevin pulled a large flashlight from his jacket and shone it on Joy's face, making her shield her eyes. "You think I'd hurt my own daughter? You took her from me, Nikki. You took her and ran and didn't give me a chance." The light cast a glow on his profile, and Jeena saw anger and frustration warring there.

Joy reached a little farther toward the girl and dropped her voice. "I'm sorry I hurt you, Kevin, but you changed so much. You scared and hurt me. You didn't have any patience with Kirsten. I couldn't take a chance with our daughter." She took a small step toward him. "Please. Give her to me?"

He pulled the child closer. "No. I hate scaring her, but I want you back. If you won't come, I'll keep Kirsten."

His eyes seemed to bore into Joy's, and Jeena knew she might not have another chance. She lunged for Kevin and slammed her shoulder into his back, barely catching herself against the wall before hitting the pavement. He fell sideways and lost his grip on Kirsten.

"Grab her, Joy. Run!" Jeena righted herself and flew at the stumbling man again, gripping his arm as he reached for the child. Joy snatched the sobbing child into her arms and raced down the alley, screaming for help.

Kevin spun and threw off Jeena's hands. He gripped her shoulders and shook her so hard her eyes felt like they'd fly from their sockets. "You made me lose my wife and little girl again. I wasn't going to hurt her!"

"Let her go!" Screeching filled the night air. A large body slammed into Kevin and Jeena, sending Jeena reeling to the side. Her head banged into a metal door, and she leaned against it for a moment, trying to get her bearings.

"You can't hurt my friends and get away with it." Sarah vaulted onto Kevin's back and wrapped her arms around his shoulders.

"Get off me! I've got to find my wife!" Kevin fell with a thud against the building, then spun in a circle. Sarah held on. He grabbed her wrists and jerked her arms apart, then shoved her back. A loud grunt escaped her lips when the force of his shove landed her on the ground.

Jeena braced her hands on her knees, mind racing. Where had Sarah come from? Had she heard Joy's cries as she fled down the alley? Was Joy back at the shelter, or had she run again?

"Lord, please help us all!" Jeena ran toward the two combatants, not sure how to help Sarah subdue Kevin but determined to try. She slowed for a second, trying to still the swimming sensation in her head.

Sarah rolled and lunged to her feet. She barreled forward. Her tight fists pummeled the man on his back and shoulders, pushing him toward the middle of the alley. Kevin spun to face her, but Sarah locked her arms around his waist and squeezed.

Jeena's prayer turned from a silent plea to a scream as a flash of metal whipped through the air above Sarah. Jeena froze as Kevin swung his arm and the heavy flashlight he wielded bounced off Sarah's shoulder. Sarah grunted but somehow maintained her grip.

The two stood fixed under the direct glare of the streetlight. Kevin stared into Sarah's eyes for a moment, and Jeena saw a look that gave her pause. Agony flashed across Kevin's face, quickly replaced with fear. He frantically pried at the arm grasping his waist and pushed, then jumped back. The jolt of his sudden release threw Sarah against the wall. Crack! Sarah's head connected with the brick, and she fell to the ground with a groan.

Jeena screamed again and lunged for the man. Sirens split the air, and flashing lights lit the interior of the alley. "Oh, thank You, God. Thank You, thank You!" She changed direction and raced to Sarah. The police could deal with Kevin.

He stumbled over a box and fell against the wall, then pushed away and ran, disappearing into the darkness at the far end of the alley.

Jeena sank to her knees beside the injured woman, fearful of what she'd find. "Sarah? Oh God, You've got to save her!" Jeena lifted her face to the sky, not caring about the stream of tears coursing down her cheeks. "I need to tell her that I'm sorry. I need her to be okay. Please, please God."

She bent over Sarah's still form, afraid to touch her. She placed shaking fingers against Sarah's neck, fumbling for a pulse. A surge of relief hit her when a strong throbbing met her fingers.

A uniformed officer raced into the dimly lit area and shone his light on Jeena's face, then swung it to Sarah. "What's going on?" He dropped to one knee beside Sarah and felt for a pulse, then looked up at Jeena. "Who did this?"

The door of the shelter slammed open and Rachel raced out with several of the residents close on her heels.

Another squad car pulled up and shone its lights into the alley, illuminating the growing crowd.

Jeena jumped to her feet and addressed the officer. "She attacked a man who was trying to hurt someone else. She hit her head and needs an ambulance."

He waved toward the second squad car. "Radio for an ambulance. We've got an injury." The officer stepped toward the murmuring crowd and held up his hand. "Stay back." He turned to Jeena and motioned. "I'll need to ask you a few questions."

More lights illuminated the crowded space, and two medics hurried toward the fallen woman. Jeena reluctantly relinquished her place beside Sarah.

"Hold on, Sarah, honey. We're praying for you." Mary's sweet voice came from the edge of the crowd.

Rachel stepped from the cluster of women and approached the officer. "I work here, and these are two of our women."

A car door slammed at the end of the alley and heavy steps hurried toward them. "Jeena? Is that you?" A familiar voice reached Jeena's ears, and she turned to see Lieutenant Stan stop alongside the patrolman.

"Lieutenant!" She controlled the urge to throw herself at his muscular form but couldn't resist the impulse to grasp his arm and squeeze. "Kevin Sullivan just got away. He ran out of the alley after he tried to grab Kirsten. Sarah attacked him."

"You know this woman, Lieutenant?" The patrolman looked from one to the other.

Stan nodded his neatly cropped head. "I do. I'll take it from here. Send men out and find this character. Here's his card." He pulled the business card out and handed it to the man. "We've already checked, and he's not in the system, but if he manages to elude us here, he may show up closer to his home." He turned to Jeena. "Can you give us a description?"

"Tall. Dark blond hair, hazel eyes, square jaw, probably late twenties."

The patrolman snapped a quick salute and turned to his partner. "You heard the lieutenant. Let's get an APB out on Kevin Sullivan." His strides lengthened as he headed toward his car.

Stan fixed his eyes on Jeena's face. "You got that good of a look at him in the dark?"

"No. Remember? I told you he'd come to the store before."

Stan nodded. "That's the guy? He attacked your friend?"

"Yes." She spun back to the silent medics. "Is she all right? How badly is she hurt?" Stepping closer, she tried to get a glimpse of the fallen woman.

Someone touched her shoulder, and she turned to see Rachel. "We're praying, Jeena."

"I'm not dead yet, if that's what you're wondering," a rasping voice sang out.

"Sarah!" Rachel and Jeena's voices blended together and the two women dropped to the ground beside their friend.

"You're alive." Jeena choked out the first coherent thing she could grasp. "I'm so sorry you got hurt trying to help me."

"Couldn't have you dying and going to hell, now could I?" The hoarse voice gathered strength. "I couldn't let that scumbag kill you or grab Kirsten, so I figured I'd give him another target."

Jeena rocked back on her heels, completely speechless and shaken to her core. This woman whom she'd hated for weeks had tried to save her life, to the point of giving her own. How did one answer that kind of sacrifice? She put the back of her hand against her mouth and stifled a sob.

"Aw, knock it off. Don't get all watery on me. Just get your life together, ya hear?"

Jeena attempted a smile, but her face contorted, and she gave way to tears again. "I will, Sarah. I promise. I'd already given it a start before Kevin showed up."

"It's about time," Sarah slapped at the medic kneeling on her other side who tried to hush her. "I'll be quiet when I'm ready. I'm not hurt bad, anyway. Just banged my hard head when I fell, and knocked me cold."

The medic smiled at the brusque tone and sat back on his haunches. "You've cut your arm, and we're concerned about a mild concussion. We're taking you to the hospital." He waved at his partner, who brought a stretcher and placed it on the ground beside her. They shifted her onto it and then to the gurney close by.

"Fine," Sarah grumbled. "Check me out. Then I'm coming home to my family." She looked up into Jeena's eyes and winked. "Ain't that right?"

Jeena gasped and tried to smother a laugh. "Why, yes, if you say so."

Sarah nodded and crossed her arms over her chest. "I say so."

Stan stepped toward the stretcher. "Wait just a minute, boys. If the lady feels like talking, I have a couple of questions." He bent over Sarah and smiled.

She snorted, but a smile broke her solemn features. "Lady, huh? Guess I can talk to you, although you look like a cop to me, even in those fancy duds." She peered at the suit and tie.

Stan's face turned crimson. "Just got back from a concert when the call came over the radio." He cleared his throat. "Tell me what happened, Sarah."

She hesitated a moment, closed her eyes, then opened and fixed them on Stan. "First, Kevin tried to grab Kirsten away from her momma. Then when Jeena jumped him, Joy and Kirsten got away. I came in to help Jeena and tried to keep Kevin from running. But he didn't hurt me, if that's what you're askin'."

Jeena stifled a small gasp. "Didn't hurt you? I saw him swing his flashlight!"

"Yeah, I know. But I seen the look in his eyes. He didn't want to do it. I think I startled him, jumping him that way and punchin' him."

"You saw which way he went?" Stan leaned close.

Sarah shook her head, then winced. "Not really. Guess I just figured he ran. After he looked at me, he spun away. I stumbled and knocked my noggin on the wall. Don't remember nothin' else."

"Thanks, Sarah. You're a hero in the truest sense of the word." The lieutenant waved at the medics. "I'm finished."

Sarah turned her head. "Get to pushin', boys, we ain't got all night."

Grins split the faces of the two young men, and they hustled to do her bidding. The next few minutes passed quickly as they loaded Sarah into the waiting ambulance and slammed the doors.

"The doctor will probably keep her overnight for observation at Memorial General. You can check on her in the morning, ma'am." The older of the two nodded toward Jeena and turned back to the waiting vehicle.

Rachel put her arm around Jeena and looked up at the lieutenant. "Would you like to come inside and finish up, or do you need us to stay out here?"

"Wait!" Jeena struggled against Rachel's arm and turned toward the detective. "Where are Joy and Kirsten? Did Kevin get them?" She swung back to Rachel. "Did they make it back inside the shelter?"

CHAPTER 44

The blank look on Rachel's face answered the question, and Jeena sagged against the woman. "No . . ." She covered her face with her hands, then looked up at Stan. "You've got to find her before Kevin does. She's running with nowhere to go."

Rachel grabbed Jeena's hand. "We're going to pray, right now."

"Count me in," Stan's large hand gripped Jeena's free one.

Jeena stared at the man. A cop offering to pray in public?

"Lord Jesus." Rachel's words pulled Jeena back. "Protect Joy and Kirsten. Keep Your angels around them, and don't allow harm to come to either of them. Thank You for keeping Jeena and Sarah safe, and we're trusting You to bring good from what the Enemy planned for evil. Amen."

"Amen." Stan echoed the word. He squeezed Jeena's hand, then released his grip.

"I just thought of something." Jeena dashed for the door of the shelter and stopped. "I need my wallet. Don't leave yet, Lieutenant." She grabbed the door handle and yanked it open, then raced up the stairs to her room. A few minutes later, she arrived downstairs to find Rachel and Stan inside the entry.

Rachel motioned the two of them toward her office. "The pastor is here. He's gathering the women in the dining room to answer questions; then he'll join us. Until then, let's step into my office."

Stan nodded and fell in beside Jeena. "I'm interested to see what you've found."

Jeena waved a paper in the air, then thrust it into his hands. She plopped into a nearby chair. "This might help find Joy and Kirsten. Kevin left it on the counter at the thrift store, and I didn't want anyone seeing it, so I stuffed it in my purse. The picture isn't current of Kirsten, but it's a good likeness of Joy. Maybe it'll help some of your men spot her."

"It can't hurt. I'll make copies and get them into the hands of our patrol officers."

"One question for you, Lieutenant." Rachel turned toward Stan.

"Yes?"

"Did someone call in a report? How did the officers get here so quickly?"

Stan shot a glance at Jeena, then returned his gaze to Rachel. "They've driven past a couple of times each evening. Jeena called me a few days ago. She was concerned about Kevin following Joy. We got lucky that someone screamed as one of the cars drove by."

Jeena drew a deep breath and released it slowly. "I don't think it was luck. I'd just prayed and asked God to show me if He cared. I'd say He answered me, but I'm still worried sick about Joy and Kirsten."

Stan nodded, his smile softening the chiseled planes of his face. "You couldn't be in a better place to get your answers." He looked at his watch and headed for the door. "Keep trusting God. We'll keep you posted, and if you think of anything else, you have my number." They heard his footsteps slap the floor as he trotted toward the outer door.

Rachel sank into the chair behind her desk. "You have his number? And he's been patrolling because you called him? I assume he's a personal friend."

Jeena rolled her eyes. One more thing to explain. "You remember when you picked me up at the phone booth?"

"Yes."

"The night before, I slept in the park and someone stole one of my bags. Stan took my statement and gave me his card, so I ended up with one from both of you. I guess God was trying to get my attention."

"I agree." Rachel leaned back in her chair and smiled. "Stan seems like a nice man."

"Yeah. He's a Christian, and the kind way he treated me . . ." Jeena's voice trailed off. "He tried to tell me about God, but I didn't want to hear it."

Rachel's eyes lit with a soft glow, and the softness transferred to her entire face. "But you're ready now?"

Jeena nodded. "Yes. I'd just finished praying before Sarah . . ." She choked and tried again. "Before Sarah risked her life saving me. I had such an amazing experience after I prayed—like a blanket of peace and love settled down over me."

A tap at the door drew their attention. "May I come in?"

Rachel rose and smiled. "Paul." A soft flush rose to her cheeks. "*Pastor* Paul. We were hoping you'd join us. You don't mind, Jeena?"

"No. I could use your insight. I have some things to deal with. I doubt I'll get to sleep with Joy and Kirsten still out there, so maybe we could talk for a while?"

Pastor Paul smiled at both women, but his gaze lingered a moment longer on Rachel. "Glad to help."

Jeena fiddled with a string on the arm of her chair, then looked up. "I asked Jesus to take control of my life tonight, but I've still got some anger toward my dad, and I'm not sure how God fits into all of that."

Rachel settled back and nodded toward Paul. "Why don't you take over? I'll offer my thoughts, but I think you have unique insights on this issue."

Paul nodded. He slipped into the straight-backed chair and crossed one leg over his knee. "Is your father still living?"

Jeena shook her head. "A part of me is glad he's not, but another part wishes he were. Maybe I'd find it easier to forgive him if he weren't dead. But then he'd probably still be hurting me."

"How did he hurt you?" Paul's voice softened.

"Physically, mentally, emotionally, spiritually . . . I think that covers it. He was an abusive, controlling man who had no idea how to show love. I'm not sure an ounce of it even existed in his body."

Paul let out a breath. "You've got a lot to forgive. How about your mom?"

Jeena smiled and relaxed. "Mom loved me and showed it in every way she knew how, except she never had the strength to leave my dad."

Paul pursed his lips and took a moment to reply. "So . . . you've equated your dad with God?"

"Yeah. He attended church religiously, and everyone thought him a saint. He served as an usher and taught a Sunday school class. You can't believe the sermons I heard at home about being a good girl or God would send me to hell."

Rachel winced. "I'm so sorry," she whispered, then spoke louder. "God isn't that way, you know. He loves you and wants to show you what a real father can be like."

Paul leaned forward, his face intense. "Rachel's right. Your father had what the Bible calls 'a religious spirit.' He was like the Pharisees. Pretending to be righteous and holy, spouting all the right words, but casting judgment on anyone around who didn't agree with their rules and regulations."

Jeena nodded and tried not to scowl. "I'd say that about sums him up. But people bought into his lies, and no one held him accountable."

Paul nodded, and his eyes held Jeena's. "Some people are good at fooling others, and often it's the family who suffers the most. Do you think you can forgive him? God doesn't want you to stay bitter toward anyone—especially your dad."

Jeena shrugged and dropped her eyes. "I'm not sure."

Rachel looked into Jeena's eyes. "You only need to be willing. God will do the rest."

"I hated him, you know. At one time, I hated him so much I could have killed him." She stared at Paul. "Does that shock you?"

He didn't flinch. "No. Believe me, I've not only heard worse, I've felt worse."

"You?" She sat back and crossed her arms. "But you're a preacher."

He emitted a low laugh. "I wasn't always a preacher. My dad abandoned us when I was ten, and my mom struggled to keep the family together and provide a living. When I was a teen, I ran with a gang. Mom worked long hours and pretty much left me on my own after school—so getting hooked into a gang was easy."

Rachel's smile appeared sad. "Sounds similar to my life. I didn't get pulled into gangs, but I ran with a bad crowd. That's one of the reasons I chose to work here—to make a difference in other people's lives. I could be in your place, Jeena, but for God's grace."

Jeena stared at first one, then the other. "But I thought . . ."

Paul smiled. "You thought we'd both been perfect Christians all our lives?"

"Something like that. Although I did notice your tattoo one time . . ." She looked at Paul and blushed. "Before I lost my home I saw you playing racquetball at the club and wondered . . ."

"That's a gang tattoo. I'm not proud of it, but I keep it to remind myself of what God delivered me from. The thoughts you had toward your father are mild compared to some of the things I did."

Jeena wrapped her arms around herself. "But I've been struggling with alcohol, too. I've been craving it so bad lately that I nearly stopped a man on the street on the way home and asked him to buy me a bottle. The only thing that stopped me was fear of being kicked out of the shelter. But you have no idea how tempting it's been."

"Yeah, I do." Paul locked his gaze with hers. "Remember, God delivered me from that, as well as from drugs and more. I'm not the same man I used to be because I gave it all to God. The ugliness and bitterness, the anger at my dad for leaving us, and all the self-loathing for what I'd become. He changed me, Jeena, and He can change you, too, if you'll let Him."

Jeena felt a tear roll down her cheek. "I'd like that. God gave me such an amazing peace when I prayed earlier tonight, and I want Him to have all of my life. I don't know what God has for me, but whatever it is, it's got to be better than what I've done with my life."

Rachel slipped out of her chair and came to kneel beside Jeena, placing her arm across Jeena's back. "I'm proud of you, sweetie. You're never going to be sorry."

Jeena leaned her head against Rachel's and sighed. "Grammie told me that God would never fail me, if I'd only trust Him. I think you were right when you said He brought me here, Rachel. I'm so ready to get rid of this anger and try to forgive." She let

Rachel and Paul's warm prayers wash over her like healing oil penetrating her wounded heart. All the time when she'd believed God had failed her, He'd really been sheltering her. Sheltered. What an amazing thought. Sheltered through all the past shadows of her life.

꒜

Jeena flew out of bed the next morning, shocked at the time. Why hadn't Mary or Carla wakened her? She threw on her clothes and raced down the stairs to the dining hall, then skidded to a halt. "Joy?"

Joy turned at the sound of her name, and a sob flew from her parted lips. "Jeena!" She raced forward and flung her arms around Jeena, then began to cry. "I'm so sorry I ran. I shouldn't have left you there alone. You could've been killed."

Jeena held Joy as she cried. She stroked her hair and hugged her, glancing above Joy's head to the sea of faces in the dining room. This time, no one stared or frowned. They simply cast compassionate looks before turning back to their meals.

Jeena patted Joy's back. "It's okay. Sarah's all right, and so am I. I'm thankful you're safe."

Joy gave Jeena a quick hug and pulled away. "I heard about Sarah. I'm sorry I worried everyone."

Jeena led Joy to an empty table on the edge of the room. "Is Kirsten okay? Where were you? When did you come back?" The words rushed from her lips.

"Kirsten's fine." Joy went to the heart of the most important question, then tackled the rest. "Your friend Lieutenant Stan stayed up all night patrolling the streets and found us this morning. He convinced me we'd be safer here than on the run. Since Kevin tried to grab Kirsten, they can make charges stick and keep him away from us."

Jeena patted Joy's hand and smiled. "Stan's a great guy—and you need to listen to him. Where's Kirsten?" She looked around the room for the little girl.

"Sleeping. We stayed at an emergency shelter across town, but the noise kept us awake. Kirsten wanted her own bed and her doll. I didn't grab the suitcase when we ran."

Jeena nodded. "We found it and hoped that might keep you from going too far."

Joy sighed and rubbed her forehead. "I'm not sure what kept me from jumping on a bus and leaving, but something stopped me."

"We prayed you'd be safe and come back," Jeena whispered.

Joy's eyes grew wide. "*You* prayed?" She gave a rueful smile. "I'm sorry. I didn't mean that the way it sounded."

Jeena grinned. "It's okay, I wouldn't have believed it a week ago, either. But yeah. Rachel, Lieutenant Stan, and I joined hands out on the street and prayed."

Joy gasped, then giggled. "That must have given people something to talk about. Imagine a cop praying in front of people."

Jeena stifled a chuckle, then sobered. "He's a pretty cool guy. What about Kevin? Have they caught him?"

"I don't think so. He's probably halfway across the state by now."

"Sarah said she could tell he was scared." Jeena looked at her friend and waited. "Do you think he's capable of seriously hurting someone?"

"I wouldn't have thought so before. I just don't know anymore."

"So do we call you Nikki or Joy?"

Joy thought for a moment before answering. "I'd prefer Joy, at least for now. It's my mother's middle name, and it's what everyone here knows me as—and it's what I want in my life, more than anything. Maybe Nikki can come back soon, but not today."

Jeena nodded and stood. "That makes sense. Want to get some breakfast? I'm starved."

Joy grinned. "Me, too. That other shelter doesn't have a clue what real food is."

CHAPTER 45

Rachel tapped Jeena on the shoulder. "There's a call for you. You can take it in my office."

Jeena wiped her mouth with a napkin and reached for her breakfast tray. "How's Sarah this morning? Has the hospital called?"

"Sarah's being discharged just before noon. I think she's too feisty for the hospital staff and they're ready to send her home." Rachel grinned.

Jeena and Joy exchanged a smile, then all three women broke into a laugh. "Sounds like Sarah." Jeena paused. "Did they say who's on the phone?"

Rachel shrugged. "No, he just asked for you. Better scoot."

Joy reached for Jeena's tray. "Get going. I'll take care of that."

"Thanks." Jeena waved and hurried to Rachel's office. She couldn't think of anyone who knew where she lived besides Lieutenant Stan and her banker. Of course, she did have this number listed on her recent job applications. Maybe one of them was paying off. The office door was closed, but she pushed it open and picked up the phone lying on the desk. "This is Jeena Gregory."

"Jeena, this is Cecil Edmonds at First National." His genial voice reflected the sound of a smile.

Jeena sank into a nearby chair and tried to still her pounding heart. "What's going on, Cecil? More problems?"

"No, no, nothing like that. I've got good news for you, my dear. Good news." His voice hesitated, then continued. "I'm sorry you've had to stay at the shelter. Your grandmother would've been sad to see you there."

Jeena straightened in her chair and gripped the phone tighter. "Thank you, sir, but I think she'd be proud."

He cleared his throat. "Ahh. Well . . ." She heard the rustle of papers over the line; then he continued. "The reason I'm calling is this: Charles Browning returned to the States and got picked up. He's in custody, as well as his secretary Pat, and your name has been cleared. The IRS released your accounts. I need you to sign a couple of papers, and you can access your funds."

Jeena sat frozen, unsure she'd heard correctly. "Released my accounts? Charles is in custody? I've been cleared? You're sure?" Relief and thanksgiving washed through her soul.

She could envision the iron gray head bobbing up and down and the smile lighting his face. "Oh yes, my dear. Very sure." He drew a deep breath. "I almost forgot. There's one other thing."

"Yes?" She sank back in her chair, wondering what could possibly come next.

"Your grandmother's attorney called, unsure where to find you. Apparently, he's probated her will and needs to see you."

"Grammie left a will? But she lived at an assisted-living center and didn't own anything."

"I wouldn't know about that. He asked me to have you call when I spoke with you."

"Thank you, Cecil. I'll see if I can get a ride to your office to sign those papers." She ended the call and sat staring at the wall.

A tap on the doorframe startled her, and she swung around as Rachel entered the room. "Is everything all right?"

Jeena tried to smile, but her emotions were so confused she wasn't sure her mouth got the correct signal. "I think so. That was my banker. My accounts have been released by the IRS, and my grandmother's attorney wants to see me about her will." She sank back in her chair. "I'm blown away."

Rachel leaned over and hugged her, then slipped into a nearby chair. "I'm happy for you. Maybe you can get your life back in order."

Why didn't those words have the power to stir her as they would have a few weeks ago? Get her life back in order? What life? No friends but Tammy remained, there was no home to go to, and the old Jeena had died in the alley last night. She had no wish to resurrect that person or go back to that life. Besides, she'd found new friends and a better life since coming here. "I guess I'll catch a bus to the attorney's office and find out what's up."

"I can take you to your bank and the attorney's office." Rachel reached for the phone book and slid it across her desk. "Think you should call the attorney first?"

"Yeah, I'd better."

A few minutes later, Jeena covered the receiver with her hand and whispered to Rachel, "Can you take me around two?"

Rachel nodded. "Sure."

"That would be fine. I'll see you then." She hung up and looked at Rachel. "You're sure it's not a problem?"

"Nope. I'm off at noon, and we can go anytime after that. I just need to pick Sarah up before lunch and get her settled."

Jeena nodded. "Thanks. I'm not sure what I'm feeling right now. Even if I can use my money again, I don't have a job. I suppose I can rent a small apartment. I have some money in a mutual fund and a CD, but that's not much to start over on." She looked up and met Rachel's warm eyes.

Rachel reached across the desk and touched Jeena's arm. "Worry about that later. You need to see what the attorney has to say first, right?"

"Yeah. I guess. Want to go with me?"

"If you want me to. I can wait in the car."

Jeena suddenly knew she'd appreciate Rachel's support. "No. I'd love for you to come with me when I talk to him."

The two women made a quick stop at the bank, then headed to the attorney's office. Curiosity had been poking at Jeena the past twenty-four hours. "Rachel?"

"Hmm?"

"Can I ask you a personal question?"

"Sure." Rachel pulled up to the curb in front of the three-story, wood-sided attorney's office and switched off the engine.

"What do you think of Pastor Paul?"

A startled look crossed Rachel's face, and she paused. "He's
. . . very nice. Why? Are you interested in him?"

"Me?" Jeena almost choked. "No way. If I were interested in
anyone, and I'm not, mind you . . ."

Rachel turned knowing eyes on Jeena. "Lieutenant Stan?"

"Hey, I started this conversation, remember?" Jeena laughed.
"I think the pastor is perfect for you."

Rachel's face clouded. "He'd never notice me."

Jeena crossed her arms and snorted. "Are you kidding? I think
he has already. You're sweet, smart, and pretty. Any man would
be lucky to have you."

"Thanks, but I'm not getting my hopes up."

"I'm going to pray about it."

Rachel's eyebrows rose and she stared.

"Yep. It's going to be my very first real prayer project." Jeena
grinned. "Guess we'd better go in and find out what's up, huh?"

Rachel patted Jeena's arm. "Yeah. And remember, God is in
charge."

Jeena smiled. "That's still hard for me to take in. But since I've
made a mess of my life, it's a good thing, huh?" She reached for
the handle and pushed open the door.

Rachel stepped out onto the curb. "Trust me. We all still try
to take back control occasionally."

Jeena nodded toward the building. "Let's find out what comes
next."

They walked in silence till they found the correct office and
stopped beside the receptionist's desk. "I'm Jeena Gregory. I have
an appointment with Mr. Robertson."

The young, red-headed woman smiled. "He's expecting you.
Go on in." She pointed to the door standing open a crack.

Jeena tapped on the door and entered the room, Rachel on
her heels.

An older gentleman with silver hair and wire-rimmed glasses
got to his feet. "Miss Gregory?"

"Yes." She shook his hand, surprised at the strength in the
older man's grip. "And this is my friend Rachel Stevens."

He nodded and settled back as the women sank into the plush leather chairs across from his desk. "I'll get right to the point. Your grandmother didn't have much, but she retained the deed to an older home on the far side of the city. I believe it belonged to her daughter—your mother." He peered over the rim of his glasses at Jeena and cleared his throat. "Apparently, your mother and father lived there in the early years of their marriage. Your mother left the house in trust with your grandmother, to be willed to you on your thirtieth birthday."

"Why in the world didn't Grammie tell me? I had no idea my mother owned a house or left me anything."

"I can't say, Miss Gregory. It's not been lived in for a number of years. Our firm has a caretaker looking after the grounds and keeping an eye on the house. Your grandmother left you a letter along with the deed." He withdrew an envelope from his desk drawer. "She also left this box, with instructions to give it to you at the same time."

Jeena stared at the older man, trying to take in yet one more surprise. "I don't know what to say."

"Maybe the letter will explain. The deed is in order, and the keys and paperwork are in this envelope. After you sign these documents, you're free to take possession."

Jeena dashed her signature on the papers the attorney thrust in front of her, barely registering their meaning as he rattled off the details of each document. When they'd finished, she pushed up from her chair. "Thank you, Mr. Robertson. I hope you'll forgive me for rushing. I'd like to see the house before dark."

He rose to his feet and gave a courtly bow. "Certainly. Best wishes to you, young lady. Your grandmother was an amazing woman and a friend."

Jeena and Rachel exited the room and returned to the car. Rachel reached for the ignition, then turned to Jeena. "You want to read the letter first?"

Jeena held up the envelope and stared at it. "If you don't mind heading over there, I'll read it on the way."

"Sure. I shouldn't have any trouble finding it." Rachel started the car and pulled out into traffic.

Jeena tore open the envelope and drew out a sheet of paper covered with her grandmother's elegant script:

Jeena, my dear,

I'm so sorry to surprise you this way. I meant to tell you about your mother's house but couldn't muster the courage. I didn't think you'd want to live there, knowing your taste in houses. I guess I worried that if you knew you'd try to talk me into letting you sell it after your birthday. I couldn't stand to part with that last link to my daughter.

That was selfish of me, as she was your mother as well. I should have shared the house with you. I'm writing this as my health is beginning to fail, and I find I don't have the strength to deal with it.

She and your father lived there before you were born when times were happier between them. When you were three, they left this area for a new job and never returned. Your mother knew your father would sell it, so she put the deed in my name and left it in trust for you.

I kept it up as best I could over the years, and no one has lived there since their deaths. I disposed of most of the old furniture, but some of their personal items remain in plastic boxes in the kitchen. I hope by the time you read this you'll want to keep the old house. At least, take the time to walk through the rooms, and see if you can connect with your mother's memory.

There's a key to my safety deposit box at my bank in the box that Mr. Robertson has given you. I hope what's there will be a help to you. Know that I love you, and I'm sorry for not sharing your mother's house with you sooner.

Grammie

Jeena read the letter a second time. Some of her mother's belongings were stored in the kitchen. Her heart beat faster, and she sat forward in her seat, suddenly anxious to see the house.

Rachel's car slowed, then turned down a quiet residential street where large maple trees lined the sidewalks. The quaint area must have been part of the original town. Some of the homes looked to be over a hundred years old. Victorian and Craftsman two-and three-story houses sat back from the street, giving a turn-of-the-century feel to the neighborhood, and manicured lawns suggested caring owners resided within.

Rachel drew her car to a stop in front of a two-story, tan and cream Victorian with deep red trim. "It looks like this is the one." She peered across the short lawn toward the house. "See the numbers on the porch post? The house is charming, isn't it?"

Jeena peered through the windshield and swallowed a lump in her throat. Oh, to have been raised in this house and neighborhood. Why did her parents move? The house drew her out of the car and across the lawn with its old-world charm.

"It needs a fresh coat of paint, and a couple of boards on the steps should be repaired, but overall, the exterior is in good shape." She stood on the freshly trimmed lawn and stared. No life stirred behind the shuttered windows, but Jeena could imagine a family sipping cool drinks and sitting in comfortable chairs on the wrap-around, covered porch on a summer's evening. "Let's go inside."

An old-fashioned foyer embraced them with the grace of an almost forgotten era. The next few minutes were spent throwing open the shutters and raising the shades to allow the soft November light to filter into the rooms. Jeena ran her fingers over the dark wood banister leading up the solid mahogany stairs, absently noting the light coating of dust. The wide moldings accenting the top of the high ceilings added charm to the interior, and she could imagine a cozy fire burning in the living-room fireplace. Earlier this year, she wouldn't have seen the value or character this house exuded. Only an upscale condo or townhouse had suited her then.

After peeking into several rooms, she turned her attention to the kitchen. Four plastic boxes with snap-on lids sat on an old-fashioned, oval, cherry-wood table with chairs, the only pieces of furniture remaining downstairs.

She snapped off the lid of one box and found several small, cloth-bound books, with a note penned neatly in her mother's handwriting lying on top: *Gene's boyhood diaries.* Nothing more.

Jeena picked one up, wonder and fear wrestling for dominance. Gene. Her father. She'd never pictured him as a boy. Would these diaries help her make peace with her father?

Rachel popped back into the kitchen from exploring the downstairs living area. "I'm going upstairs to look around. There could be an attic, too. Want to come?"

Jeena sank into a wooden chair with a brocade seat. "You go ahead. I'd like to stay here for a while."

A soft light filled Rachel's eyes as she focused on the book in Jeena's hand. "Sure. You call me when you're ready, okay?"

Jeena nodded and tried to smile. She waited till Rachel disappeared, then opened the small book. The next thirty minutes slipped by on quiet feet while Jeena turned page after page of the childish scrawl, trying to equate the voice of the boy with her father. Shock, disbelief, and finally pity gripped her heart as she took in the import of the boy's words. The room started to dim, and the page grew harder to read. The electricity wasn't on, and twilight would soon darken the room. Jeena pulled her jacket collar up around her neck, suddenly aware of the chill.

She stepped into the living room and walked to the base of the stairs. "Rachel? I'm ready to go."

Rachel appeared at the top of the staircase and made her way to the bottom. "You okay?"

"Yeah. I'm sorry I took so long." She ran her fingers over the finely crafted handrail. "I found my father's diaries he kept when he was young."

Rachel squeezed Jeena's shoulder in a light hug. "I thought it might be something like that. I'm glad you took your time. Ready to head back now, or you want to stay longer?"

"I'm ready. I'd love to see the rest of the house, but it's getting dark. I'll come back tomorrow. I'd like to take that small stack of boxes back so I can go through Mother's things."

"Sure."

They loaded the boxes and shut the blinds and shutters, then locked the house and headed back to the shelter.

They rode in silence for several minutes; then Jeena spoke. "My grandfather abused my father."

"Your grandfather? Your grammie's husband?" Rachel glanced away from the road for a second and looked at Jeena.

"No." Jeena leaned back against the seat. "Grammie was my mother's mom. I don't remember either of my grandfathers. According to my dad's diaries, his father terrified him."

"That would account for your father's treatment of you."

Jeena thought for a moment. "My father said his dad beat him a lot. He told him children were born with the Devil in them, and it had to be beaten out. That must have made a deep, horrible impression. Some of the things he wrote made me want to cry. The loneliness he felt, the longing for a safe place to hide. So much that I felt as a child. Why couldn't he have learned from what he experienced and treated me differently?"

Rachel pursed her lips. "I wish I knew. Many abused kids follow in the footsteps of the abusive parent. Not all, of course. They don't know how to parent or relate to a child. They're so damaged inside, so full of self-hatred or fear, that the cycle continues even if they don't want it to."

Jeena closed her eyes and sighed. "There's so much I don't understand. But I got a glimpse of my father I've never seen before. I'm going to keep reading, and maybe it'll help put my own childhood into perspective."

"It might even help you forgive him. Remember, forgiveness is a choice, not an emotion." Rachel glanced sideways at Jeena and smiled. "And it has a way of setting the forgiver free. Even if the person is dead, the power of forgiveness is life changing."

"I believe that." Jeena looked down at the diary clutched in her hand. "I really do—and I'm ready for that freedom."

CHAPTER 46

The following Sunday morning, Jeena stepped off the porch of her mother's house and looked back with a deep sense of satisfaction. Home. She'd finally found a place where she could put down roots—and with her newfound life, she'd find peace here as well.

Nothing could convince her to part with her mother's old home, and she planned to move in next week. She'd purchased a few pieces of decent furniture from the thrift store, and Rachel had donated some dishes and basic utensils. Nothing fancy, but it would help her get by till she got a good job. The last thing she wanted to do was burn through her savings buying new furnishings.

She stepped back inside and glanced up the stairs. The four-bedroom house would seem quiet after the noise and activity at the shelter, but she'd adjust. Maybe Joy and Rachel would visit after she settled in.

A renewed sense of love washed over her heart as she thought of the sacrifice her mother had made to keep this home for her when times were tough and selling it would've helped. Maybe someday Jeena would have a family of her own, but until then, her new friends and at least one of her old would help fill that empty spot in her life.

She'd invited Tammy over to see the house and to catch her up on everything that had happened in the past couple of months. Her friend had invited her to church—to Jeena's surprise she'd discovered it to be the same one where Pastor Paul ministered. After the service, Tammy would take Jeena to lunch and then stop by the house.

Jeena looked around at the familiar pictures already mounted on the walls and the small pieces of furniture she'd been able to keep. Thankfully, the storage company hadn't sold her things, and they allowed her to catch up on the three months back rent. What a blessing to have more of her clothing and the keepsakes she'd cherished over the years. With what she'd gotten from the thrift store and the items she'd kept, her house was nearly complete.

The safety deposit box contained another note from her grandmother. It had been short but tender, once again affirming her love and asking Jeena to trust in God as her source and supply. Over the years, Grammie had saved a large number of silver dollars in mint condition, and two dozen ounces of gold. In her note, she urged Jeena to use them or save them as she saw fit. Jeena hesitated to part with anything of Grammie's but knew she'd understand. The small nest egg combined with the remainder of Jeena's savings would help her survive until a job opened up.

She continued to attend the daily chapel services at the shelter, wanting to learn as much about her Savior as possible. It had only been a couple of weeks since she'd made her decision to trust God with her life, but a hunger to know more had grown, nearly consuming her. There was so much she still didn't understand. One of the treasures she'd found among her mother's things was a well-worn, much-underlined Bible. The margins were full of notes, and she found her own baby dedication certificate tucked in the back. Beside it in her mother's hand was a small card with Jeena's date of birth, the date of her dedication, and a Bible passage: Isaiah 43:1–3—"But now, this is what the Lord says—he who created you, O Jacob, he who formed you, O Israel: 'Fear not, for I have redeemed you; I have summoned you by name; you are mine. When you pass through the waters, I will be with you; and when you pass through the rivers, they will not sweep over you. When you walk through the fire, you will not be burned; the flames will not set you ablaze. For I am the Lord, your God, the Holy One of Israel, your Savior.'"

Jeena was amazed at her mother's choice of a life verse for

her daughter. How could she have known that someday Jeena would need this passage? She found herself drawn to it more each day, and each reading raised more questions that caused her to search for nuggets of truth.

Yesterday, Pastor Paul had seconded Tammy's suggestion to visit his church. She'd agreed but wondered if she'd made the right decision. Her old friend Susanne attended there with her family. Would they welcome her, be thankful that she'd changed, or be irritated she'd found her way to their church? Jeena desperately wanted to apologize but knew she had no right to expect a restoration of their old friendship. She couldn't see Susanne refusing to forgive, knowing her friend had recently developed a relationship with Jesus herself, but Susanne might want to keep her distance. Jeena wouldn't blame her, but the thought of permanently losing Susanne stung, when they'd both made such life-changing choices.

Either way, Jeena had promised the pastor and Tammy that she'd come. She climbed into the older model Honda she'd purchased, backed out of her short drive, and headed down the road.

The minutes passed, and Jeena's agony mounted. She called Tammy and blurted out her fear. Her friend understood and urged Jeena to sit with her, then promised to pray for her. Knowing she'd have Tammy's support boosted Jeena's courage, but she still dreaded the meeting. She shivered, remembering her attempted apology to Sarah. It had been too public, and this could well be the same.

The last time she'd spent an evening with Susanne, they'd gone to the bar and grill and had a few drinks. Susanne shared the story of the girl who'd appeared on their doorstep, claiming to be David's daughter. Jeena cringed at the suggestions she'd pushed on her friend: hand the girl off to social services, ditch David, find someone else . . .

Her hands gripped the steering wheel, and she fought to continue on rather than turn the car around and race back to the house. How easy it would be to run and hide. She didn't blame Susanne for cutting her off. After seeing what real friendship could be, it amazed her that Susanne had tolerated her interference for as long as she had.

The memory of her behavior on the courthouse steps back in August almost brought her car to a halt. What a brat she'd been. She'd never realized how self-centered and materialistic she'd become.

Jeena pulled into the church parking lot. None of the cars appeared occupied, and no stragglers entered the church. She released a long breath and pushed open the door, thankful for the reprieve God seemed to offer. Slipping in the back door unnoticed didn't seem such a stretch. Maybe she'd make it through the morning without meeting Susanne; then she'd find a different church to attend. Her apology could come later, in a more private setting.

She opened the front door of the church noiselessly and slipped into the foyer. A table laden with flowers, candles, and a small stack of church bulletins graced the area to her right, and a set of double doors stood straight ahead. As she hesitated, wondering whether she had the nerve to step through those doors, they swung open from the inside and a woman came through.

Jeena looked up and gasped. "Susanne?"

"Jeena?" Susanne stood as though riveted to the floor, then moved forward, the sanctuary door swinging shut behind her.

Jeena took a small step back and glanced at the outer door, but Susanne seemed to notice. Her face lit with a brilliant smile. In one long stride she reached Jeena and threw her arms around her. "It's wonderful to see you!"

Jeena stood still, not sure how to respond. She looked down at Susanne's petite form, feeling the warmth and acceptance in the arms around her, and slowly returned her friend's hug. "I'm so, so sorry, Susanne," she whispered. "I hope you can forgive me. I wouldn't blame you if you hated me for how I acted."

Susanne pulled back and looked up with a frown. "Hate you? Whatever for?"

"For pushing you to leave David and being so vindictive. And for urging you to get rid of his daughter when she came to your house." Jeena avoided Susanne's eyes.

Susanne drew Jeena to a set of chairs on the opposite side of the foyer. "I forgave you a long time ago. I tried to tell you at the courthouse that I'd made a lot of changes in the past couple of months. I understand now that you were trying to protect me, not hurt me."

Jeena nodded. "I remember. I've made some changes, too. I . . ." She took a deep breath, then continued. "I lost my job, my house, my car . . . pretty much everything, and ended up at a women's shelter."

Susanne touched Jeena's shoulder. "I'm sorry. If I'd known, I'd have offered you a room at our house."

Jeena shook her head and smiled. "I wouldn't have accepted. I was too proud, not willing to see what I'd become. Besides, I had a serious issue with Christian men because of my dad, and I couldn't accept David as a result. God allowed me to hit bottom so He could show me the way back up. He taught me lessons living at the shelter that I needed to learn."

A wide smile broke the serious planes of Susanne's face, and she clapped her hands. "I'm so happy for you! Oh, I'm thankful God brought us back together!"

Susanne stood and pulled Jeena to her feet. "Come on. You can sit with us during the service. Then we'll tell David what's happened. He'll be thrilled—and I want you to meet our new daughter, Brianna. God has worked miracles in our lives recently." She hugged Jeena again and laughed. "I don't remember why I came out here, but I'm sure David and the kids are wondering what happened to me. You ready to go in?"

"Yeah. Very ready. Hey, you know Tammy, don't you?"

Susanne nodded, her face still bright with her lingering smile.

"She asked me to sit with her family, and I'd hate to disappoint her. Maybe the three of us can get together later—I'd love to catch you both up on what's happened these past few months. If the two of you aren't friends already, I know you will be."

"I'd love that."

The two women locked arms and walked toward the sanctuary, their hearts and minds at peace and at home—at last.

DISCUSSION QUESTIONS

1. Before life starts unraveling for Jeena, how would she have described herself? Does her view of herself align with her words and actions?

2. Jeena's love for her grandmother seems to be the only thing that takes priority over her drive to be successful. Why do you think this relationship is special for Jeena?

3. Memories from Jeena's past haunt her night and day, and color how she looks at Christianity. How do our life experiences influence our view of God?

4. Jeena decided to donate clothing to the shelter but felt a strong sense of revulsion while there. Why? Have you ever had similar feelings when a homeless man or woman approached you on the street?

5. When Grammie dies, Jeena's world is shaken more deeply than ever before in her life. She feels adrift and alone, and believes God has abandoned her. Have you ever been shaken in a similar way? What helped you through the difficult time?

6. Hints of trouble at work make Jeena suspicious something is wrong, but she's hesitant to dig too deep. Do you agree with Jeena that it's not her business to judge others for what they are doing? If you were in Jeena's shoes, what would you have done?

7. Jeena hates the thought that her friends or co-workers might discover she's destitute and in need. What keeps Jeena from asking for help?

8. Time at the shelter begins to turn Jeena's attitude toward homeless people from judgmental to accepting, but it doesn't happen overnight. What are some important steps Jeena takes to adjust her mind-set?

9. Grammie's gifts to Jeena and the inheritance from Jeena's mother give her a new start. Do you think she will slip back into the habits of her old life, or is she a changed person?

10. Jeena wants to run from her old friend Susanne rather than take the chance of being rejected by her again. Is Jeena's hesitation and fear normal? Is it healthy?

AUTHOR'S NOTE

J eena appeared in my first book, *The Other Daughter*, as a secondary character, but one who stirred a lot of interest among readers. Jeena was bossy and materialistic, but she really cared about her friend Susanne. The only character who received more comments was David and Susanne's daughter Megan.

Jeena Gregory turned out to be a very demanding character. She insisted that she have a book of her own, and she continued to demand until I agreed. You see, Jeena didn't want people to think she was a snob—she needed to be understood, to have readers see underneath the hard layer to the real Jeena. Of course, she also tried to cover up the soft side, and it took some digging on my part to discover it.

During my journey into Jeena's life, I first had to look at some of my own prejudices. I thought about the people who stand on street corners begging for money and always seem to be at the same corner with the same sign saying they're stranded and traveling. I thought about those who sit on bus benches holding an empty wine bottle. I thought about nicely dressed women in the checkout line who pay using food stamps. It's often easy to judge. But we have no idea what has put these people in the position they're in.

The economy is in a tough spot right now. People are losing their jobs, their homes, and everything they've worked for, often through no fault of their own. As Christians, we're called to help the widows, the orphans, the needy. Do we walk across the street and continue on down the block when we see a homeless person, or do we offer (at the very least) a prayer on his or her behalf? I'm not suggesting we empty our wallets to every person begging on the corner. But why not allow the Holy Spirit to show us who He might want us to minister to in some way? Perhaps the Holy Spirit will lead us to show someone a simple kindness, like Lieutenant Stan did for Jeena when she hit bottom.

I interviewed a woman who had been a normal housewife and mom but got hooked on drugs and lost it all—her marriage, her home, her job, her family—and ended up in a shelter. The other women didn't accept her because she didn't fit the typical "street person" profile. While there, she came to know the Lord and eventually got her life back together, even going on to volunteer at that same shelter. (Unfortunately, she slipped in her struggle to stay clean. I'm praying that the Lord brings her full circle again, if He hasn't already. I've lost touch with her as she slid back into her old life, but thankfully, God hasn't.) Talking to her, and digging deep within myself to write about Jeena's struggles, helped uncover some of my own prejudices that I didn't realize I had. The Lord convicted me more than once, and made me realize that the Jeenas of this world are the "least of these" that Jesus spoke of remembering (Matt. 25:40).

Now that you've finished the book, I hope you will take time to examine your own prejudices—to dig deep into the fabric of your soul and allow the Lord to soften your heart. Not everything is as it seems on the surface. As Rachel says, "I could be in your place, Jeena, but for God's grace."

THE OTHER
DAUGHTER

Miralee Ferrell

EXCERPT FROM
THE OTHER DAUGHTER

Dark clouds mushroomed, and thunder rattled the windows of the Carson home on Mountain Brook Road, disrupting the peaceful May afternoon. Above the diminishing rumble, a motor roared, and the sharp ping of flying gravel sprayed the side of the house. Susanne ran from the laundry room and peered out the front window in time to see a battered old pickup tear down the lane away from her home, sounding like a steam boiler ready to explode. *What in the world? Some teenagers out playing a prank?*

They must have turned down the wrong lane, an easy thing to do this far out of town. She headed across the living room and stopped in the kitchen doorway, stifling a groan. The kids had tracked in mud before they'd left for school, and dirty breakfast dishes still littered the kitchen counters. She'd been busy changing beds and catching up on laundry all morning and had forgotten about the kitchen. She leaned against the wall, feeling about as energetic as the loser of a ten-mile race, her enthusiasm drained by the recent phone call from her husband, setting back their plans for her birthday.

The doorbell rang. The truck had disappeared down the road, and she hadn't heard anyone else arrive. Great. The last thing she needed was company. The house certainly wasn't in its usual neat state. She sighed and smoothed back her rumpled curls. She should have stayed in bed this morning.

The doorbell rang again, its insistence pulling her forward.

"I'm coming, I'm coming!" she muttered.

A glass of wine and an hour to relax would help put her back in the mood for tonight, if David kept his word and made it in time for their reservation. She'd get rid of whoever was at the door and try to pull herself together. This needed to be a special evening. They'd had so few of those lately.

Susanne swung open the door. "May I help you?"

A bedraggled young girl who appeared to be about twelve stood on the step, clutching a well-worn suitcase. Small boned and not very tall, she might have been pretty but for her greasy dark hair and dirt-streaked face. Staring up at Susanne was a set of strangely familiar eyes that gazed at her shyly before darting away in apparent fear.

A prickle of apprehension ran through her as she looked in those eyes, but she brushed it away. Her imagination must be working over-time today.

"Is Mr. David Carson here, ma'am?" The waif shifted her weight from one foot to the other, glancing over her hunched shoulder to the base of the driveway.

What was someone thinking, dumping a child off and driving away? If she was selling something or needed directions, the driver could have stayed nearby, not headed down the road.

"I'm afraid he's at work right now. Is there something I can help you with?" Susanne pushed open the screen door, both curiosity and sympathy drawing her forward. "Are you selling something? Do you need help?"

The youngster's gaze returned to Susanne's face, a worried pucker showing around the corners of her mouth. "I've come to live with him." Her barely audible voice hit Susanne like a clap of thunder. Confusion raced through her mind. Was this someone's idea of a joke?

"Live with him? What do you mean?" She pushed the door open a bit wider. Had David offered to take this poor girl in without discuss-ing it with her? They hadn't taken foster kids for more than a year now. Of all the times for him to drop a strange child in her lap.

The girl took a deep breath, pulling her suitcase a little closer to her trembling legs. "My mama's dead. He's my daddy."